BY JANET EVANOVICH

ONE FOR THE MONEY	TO THE NINES
TWO FOR THE DOUGH	TEN BIG ONES
THREE TO GET DEADLY	ELEVEN ON TOP
FOUR TO SCORE	TWELVE SHARP
HIGH FIVE	LEAN MEAN THIRTEEN
HOT SIX	FEARLESS FOURTEEN
SEVEN UP	FINGER LICKIN' FIFTEEN
HARD EIGHT	SIZZLING SIXTEEN

VISIONS OF SUGAR PLUMS
PLUM LOVIN'
PLUM LUCKY
PLUM SPOOKY

WICKED APPETITE

FULL HOUSE

WITH DORIEN KELLY

LOVE IN A NUTSHELL   THE HUSBAND LIST

WITH CHARLOTTE HUGHES

FULL TILT	FULL BLOOM
FULL SPEED	FULL SCOOP
FULL BLAST	

WITH LEANNE BANKS
HOT STUFF

WITH INA YALOF
HOW I WRITE

AVAILABLE FROM HARPERCOLLINS
HERO AT LARGE
MOTOR MOUTH
METRO GIRL

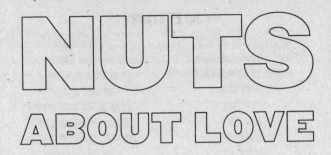

NUTS
ABOUT LOVE

TWO BOOKS IN ONE

THE HUSBAND LIST

and

LOVE IN A NUTSHELL

JANET
EVANOVICH
& DORIEN KELLY

St. Martin's Paperbacks

NUTS ABOUT LOVE: THE HUSBAND LIST copyright © 2012 by The Gus Group, LLC and LOVE IN A NUTSHELL copyright © 2011 by The Gus Group, LLC.

All rights reserved.

For information address St. Martin's Press, 175 Fifth Avenue, New York, NY 10010.

ISBN: 978-1-250-29484-5

Our books may be purchased in bulk for promotional, educational, or business use. Please contact your local bookseller or the Macmillan Corporate and Premium Sales Department at 1-800-221-7945, ext. 5442, or by e-mail at MacmillanSpecialMarkets@macmillan.com.

Printed in the United States of America

St. Martin's Paperbacks edition / December 2018

St. Martin's Paperbacks are published by St. Martin's Press, 175 Fifth Avenue, New York, NY 10010.

10 9 8 7 6 5 4 3 2 1

THE HUSBAND
List

ONE

Close your eyes and think of chocolate cake, Caroline Maxwell told herself. It was the only way she could get through this tedious dress fitting. Even in the advanced year of 1894, an American heiress had certain rules to follow, and allowing herself to be a pincushion for the House of Worth seemed to be one of them. What Caroline really wanted was adventure, independence and to see the world. But she doubted her parents would ever come to their senses enough to set her free.

The seamstress, who accompanied Caroline's new wardrobe from Worth's Paris dress shop across the Atlantic to the Maxwell family's Fifth Avenue residence, wielded another pin. Caroline winced in anticipation.

The angry-looking woman had already caught skin twice. Maybe her aim was off due to the lingering seasickness that delayed yesterday's fitting. Or perhaps she was intimidated by the dozens of china figurines Mama had positioned about Caroline's enormous sitting room. The sense that one was being watched by countless beady little eyes could be unsettling. Not to mention the house itself . . . With sixty rooms, it, too, could rattle a soul.

"Your measurements have changed," the Frenchwoman accused.

And then there was that.

"Impossible," Caroline fibbed.

She glanced at her mother, who kept an eye on affairs from her regal perch atop the massive red velvet and gold-gilt settee that she'd also insisted must be part of Caroline's quarters. Normally, her mother wouldn't tolerate such talk from a servant, but Agnes was secretly intimidated by the French, which was why they'd left Paris before the dresses were done. Mama brushed away an imaginary crumb from the fabric of her conservative, high-necked dove gray morning dress and then fussed with the tiny bit of lace at each cuff. Caroline knew she was on her own in the battle of the pins.

The seamstress stepped back on the thick carpet to assess her work. Caroline caught her own reflection in the cheval mirror that was positioned so that Mama could see Caroline in profile. Mr. Worth's style sense was clearly incomparable.

The low-cut—almost risqué—ivory silk ball gown Caroline wore had been embellished with what felt like pounds of pearls and dark green crystals. Assuming she could bear up under the weight, it would complement her clear complexion and hair as dark as her mother's. Rumor had it that Mama's maternal great-grandmother had been a Cherokee princess, which Mama would not confirm.

Worth's skills had also made Caroline's slight surplus of curves an asset rather than a detriment. Come the season, she was doomed. She had no idea what she could do to top last year's anti-marriage efforts. All the same, she intended to escape this year's marriage market as she had 1893's: unwed, unpromised, and as independent as she could be. Which, in her opinion, was not saying much.

Caroline released her breath and unclenched clammy palms as another pin met only fabric. And in other sunny news, her mother's insecurity meant that at least Caroline would not be facing French *ducs* on top of the English dukes Mama kept pushing her to marry.

"*Absolument,* you have gained since your last fitting," the seamstress said. "And more than a little."

Caroline answered with a vague smile. It would never do to confess that she'd begun midnight kitchen forays to ease her tight nerves.

"Caroline, have you varied from our agreed-upon menu?" her mother asked. Alarm had made her dark brows arch closer to her perfectly coiffed hair with its beginning threads of silver.

There had been no agreement. There hadn't even been negotiations, just no outright objection from Caroline. She'd decided long ago that working around her mother was more diplomatic than upsetting her. Easier, too. And since her mother's eating edict had made Caroline fifty percent a spectator at family meals, she felt she deserved a fat slice of chocolate cake whenever she wished. It wasn't noon yet, and her mouth watered at the thought of tonight's pilfered treat. Actually, not so very pilfered, since Cook had caught on to the scheme and now left cake waiting for her.

Mama pursed her lips and scrutinized Caroline more closely. "You must have been straying. You're looking plumper in the face when Amelia and Helen are still as slim as can be."

At sixteen, her twin sisters didn't yet have the avoidance skills Caroline possessed at twenty-one. Or the same ability to hold their tongues under their mother's inquisition techniques. They *always* confessed.

Caroline kept her silence.

Mama narrowed her eyes.

Caroline widened hers.

Mama cleared her throat, giving warning of a lecture to come.

Caroline did her best to exude an aura of innocence as strong as her mother's favored gardenia perfume. It must have worked, because Mama heaved a resigned sigh.

"Stand taller," she ordered. "Shoulders back and chin up."

Caroline complied, though the gown would be no looser around her waist for the effort. Tonight's cake would have to be her last for a while. It wasn't as though she could eat her way to freedom. American heiresses were as popular with unmarried and underfunded English noblemen as chocolate cake was with Caroline.

"If you are to wear a coronet, you must look as though you were born to it," Mama said. That and "you are this family's crown jewel" were two of her mother's favorite things to say. Caroline found both statements as uncomfortable as the corset currently mashing her innards.

Mama had been about to issue another proclamation—probably about crown jewels—but was distracted by a one-person stampede down the mahogany parquet hallway.

Annie, Caroline's new personal maid, appeared. Breathless, she took an instant to compose herself. It was hopeless. During her dash, her red curls had sprung free from their tight bun and were now nearly at right angles from the white cap atop her head.

"Mrs. Maxwell, ma'am, O'Brien has asked me to tell you that Mrs. Longhorne is calling," Annie said.

She thrust out a calling card. She did not, however, have the silver tray that the butler used, so Caroline's mother pretended not to see it.

Annie waited for a response, then plowed on, either unaware or uncaring of her breach of decorum. "Ma'am, she's on her way up here now."

"Really, here?" Agnes asked, rising.

Annie was saved. Mrs. Longhorne venturing to private quarters without invitation was an even greater violation of Mama's rules than Annie's slipup.

Mildred Longhorne rushed in, her hands fluttering on either side of her face like two of the finches that Mama kept caged in the conservatory. Her pointy nose was red at the tip and her usually nondescript gray eyes sparkled with excitement. She hadn't even changed out of the black riding habit she wore for a morning turn about the park, and the knot of early June pansies at one buttonhole looked ready to jump ship.

"Agnes, I have the most exciting news! Lord Bremerton is visiting with friends at Newport this season."

Caroline's mother gasped. "Bremerton, the son of Viscount Bellingham, grandson of the Duke of Endsleigh?"

"Yes."

"He's married," Mama said in a dismissive tone.

While Caroline was hardly in love with her mother's determination to marry her into English nobility, she had to give her credit for an impressive level of study.

"No, no . . . not that one. He's dead. There's a new Bremerton!"

"Dead?" Caroline's mother repeated. She'd sounded a little gleeful, too.

"Yes, a riding accident, I heard. The younger son has taken the title, and his father is rumored to be in poor health. You know what that means, don't you?"

Mama walked a circle around Caroline and the seamstress. Apparently content with what she saw, she returned her attention to Mrs. Longhorne.

"He'll be a duke," she replied.

"Yes!" her friend cried. "And Caroline will be a duchess!"

Where was a slice of chocolate cake when a girl needed one?

At ten minutes until eight that evening, most of the family sat in the Oriental drawing room awaiting the call to dinner. All they lacked was Caroline's brother, Edward, who at almost twenty-seven lived down Fifth Avenue in the lesser mansion the family had left behind when this one had been completed.

"Any time Edward isn't where he's promised to be, he's off with that Jack Culhane," Mama complained to Caroline's father.

Caroline hid the smile that seemed to work its way across her face whenever she thought of her brother's best friend. She could guarantee that wherever they were, Eddie and Jack were having more fun than she was. For as long as she could remember, she'd tried to tag after them with little success. When she'd walk in on their tale-telling, she'd catch just enough to make her more determined to be part of their adventures.

They were all grown now, with Eddie working at Papa's side, and Jack buying up businesses almost as quickly as his father did. But Caroline's greatest adventure had been frightening off a handful of dukes last year, and that was before Mama had taken away most of her freedom. She hated to sound ungrateful, because she knew how lucky she was. All the same, she'd trade a steamer trunk packed with Maxwell money for just a few days of living like Jack and Eddie.

"Edward said he'll be here at eight, and he will be," Papa replied. "He's a Maxwell man, which means he's a man of his word."

He turned his attention to Caroline, who had been doing her best to blend into the bold orange and green chrysanthemum-patterned brocade of her chair—not an easy job when one was wearing a peacock blue dress.

"Maxwell women, too. Am I right, Pumpkin?" he asked. Pride shone from his craggy features, and from under his thick gray moustache—so startling in contrast to his fading auburn hair—as it moved upward with his smile.

Caroline hesitated. His question was simple enough on the surface, but since just minutes ago her parents had been discussing Lord Bremerton's visit, she knew what Papa really meant. She searched for a comment positive enough to make her father happy, yet still not an outright promise to lure and marry some Englishman she'd never met. Not when she had someone oh-so-much better in mind.

"Really, Bernard, you must stop calling her that," Mama said, saving Caroline another diplomatic dance. "It was bad enough that it slipped out at the Astors' ball last year. Imagine if you said it in front of Bremerton?"

"There's no mistaking her for a gourd, Agnes," Papa said. "And you'll always be my Pumpkin, won't you, Caroline?"

"Of course I will." Even from across the sea.

Deep male talk and laughter sounded from outside the room. Jack was here with Eddie. This time Caroline couldn't stop her smile from appearing. They walked in together with Jack standing inches taller than Eddie, who was of average height. And where Eddie was on the wiry side, Jack looked as though he could take on Calcutta street thieves and win.

Jack's black frock coat sat well across his broad shoulders, and the white of his starched shirt and collar set off the sun-darkened color of his skin and deep brown hair. She liked that he was clean-shaven, too. Eddie's attempt at a moustache seemed a little scant, though she'd never say so to her brother.

"Six minutes to spare," Eddie said before kissing Mama on the cheek. "You were counting, weren't you?"

"I was doing no such thing," she said, but bright flags of pink on her face let Eddie know he had caught her.

Mama's gaze drifted past Eddie and on to Jack. While she didn't permit her disapproval to show in her expression, she still managed to convey it by stiffening her posture. Even Pomeroy, the little mop of a lapdog Mama had acquired so she could feel a bit like Queen Victoria, seemed to tighten up.

"Good evening, Mrs. Maxwell," Jack said, giving a slight bow.

"We were late getting back from Jack's new business concern. I hope you don't mind if he joins us for dinner," Eddie added.

"No, really, I need to be on my way," Jack said. "I just wanted to say hello to the family."

His smile briefly settled on Amelia and Helen, who wore matching yellow satin dresses in appropriately girlish styles. And because Mama believed in playing the asset of their twinhood to the fullest, their wavy auburn hair had been upswept in identical fashions, too. They smiled prettily and inclined their heads to Jack, but never met his eyes.

His attention moved on to Caroline, who had no qualms about meeting Jack Culhane head-on.

"Hello, Caroline. Are the social rounds treating you well?" he asked, a devilish light shining in his blue eyes.

How her girlfriends could not find him handsome was beyond Caroline. They used phrases like "too earthy" when they spoke of him. She thought the men they found attractive looked half-starved.

Jack was perfect.

Her heart beat faster at the sight of the two dimples that always appeared when he teased her. He knew how she felt about the endless gatherings that Mama insisted she attend. And Jack felt the same way, too. He might slip into a party, but he was always quickly gone.

"Very well," she said. "I've been having a wonderful time."

"Really, wonderful?"

"Bordering on delirious."

His smile became a full-out grin. "I'll bet."

"Stay for dinner," Eddie said to Jack. "Tell my father about the new brewery and your plans for expansion."

Caroline waited for his answer. She'd make a devil's bargain of her own and trade away tonight's final slice of cake if he would stay.

"Another brewery?" her father asked Jack in a tone that was disapproving and yet curious, too.

"Yes, sir," Jack replied.

"Don't you already have one in Pennsylvania?"

"And one in Boston, as well."

Papa frowned. "Then why buy any more?"

"For the same reasons your grandfather bought those regional railroads, sir. Consolidation of power and resources."

Papa flicked his hand as though shooing away a gnat. "Breweries aren't the same thing at all."

Caroline settled in to eavesdrop. She felt sheer joy at hearing a conversation of more import than whether it was appropriate to have the lettering on one's calling card embossed.

"With all due respect, sir, you're wrong," Jack said.

Papa rose from the ornate carved chair Mama claimed was Imperial Chinese. He joined Jack and Eddie in front of the cavernous fireplace, stepping on one of the two tiger skins on the floor while on his way. Caroline tried to avoid looking at the tigers. She'd been thirteen when Papa had brought them home from a hunting trip, and she'd cried well into the night upon seeing them.

Caroline focused on the gentlemen. They looked so civilized in their black evening suits, though Papa's was cut to accommodate his girth. He ate with the same robust passion he gave the rest of life.

"I'm wrong, am I?" he asked Jack, clearly warming to the debate.

Caroline's mother must have known that her window of opportunity for a dinner without Jack Culhane had closed.

"O'Brien, see that there's room at the table for Mister Culhane," she said.

The butler, who was an expert at appearing and disappearing with ghostly skill, left only to appear an impossibly short time later and announce that dinner was served.

They entered the dining room, which had been known to seat three hundred when Mama was having one of her larger parties. Their footsteps echoed all the way to the ceiling, with its frescoes of fat little cherubs, platters of fruit, and women who'd always looked to Caroline to be in some form of distress.

Jack was ushered to a spot just to Caroline's right. She glanced at her mother to see if a mistake had been made. Jack should have been seated far closer to Papa so that they could continue to converse. Apparently not, since her mother wore a content smile, probably at the thought of having quashed business talk. O'Brien looked pleased with himself, too. Caroline would never understand how the butler managed to read Mama's mind, but he was a master at it.

The family settled in, and wine was poured. Mama and the twins talked of the tea they'd attended in the

afternoon while most everyone else attempted to appear
interested. Caroline, however, was too occupied by trying not to be so conscious of Jack.

Warmth seemed to roll from him. She caught a hint
of wood smoke that must have traveled with him from
his afternoon's adventures. She glanced his way and
found that he'd been looking at her, so she pretended
great interest in the silver of her place setting.

The first course was served: a little quail that had been
stuffed with something or another. After a tiny bite, Caroline set her fork on the plate's edge. Good thing, too,
because she was under extra scrutiny after this morning's
fitting.

"We must improve Rosemeade's grounds and refur-
nish it immediately. It's entirely lacking in elegance. If
we didn't need to be in residence no later than July first,
I'd say to raze the whole thing and start over. But with
both Bremerton and the season upon us, I shouldn't get
carried away," Mama said to Papa after being sure Caroline had left her quail to languish.

"Do whatever you wish," Caroline's father replied.
That was his stock answer for anything regarding the
family's residences, which he left wholly to his wife.

Caroline wasn't feeling quite so calm. Their Newport
summer cottage was her favorite. While it was hardly
small at forty rooms, its Tudor-style stone-and-timber exterior gave it a sense of simplicity that this house lacked.
Rosemeade also held memories of the many summer
days when she'd chased after Eddie and Jack. Her heart
would break if those were wiped away.

"Why would Rosemeade need improvement? It's perfect just as it is," she said.

"Perfect? Perfect to entertain a duke?" Mama asked.

Caroline could feel her hard-fought control evapo-
rating.

"What duke?" she asked. "Bremerton's not a duke unless both his father and grandfather conveniently die."

Her mother couldn't have looked more shocked if frogs had sprung from Caroline's mouth.

"Caroline, really!"

"It's true, Mama. That's the one fact you have. What you don't know is what sort of man he is . . . if he's kind or smart or has a good smile," she said, thinking of Jack's smile. "And—"

"Caroline, be quiet!" her mother commanded.

But Caroline's words might as well have been those frogs because she couldn't stop them. "And for once, could we have something that isn't made to look like something other than what it is?"

She waved her hand at the room's rosewood moldings that her mother had ordered covered in gold leaf. "Could we have wood and not make it look like gold?"

She pointed a finger at the marble fireplace that had been detailed to look like burled oak. "And stone that isn't painted like wood?"

She settled one hand against the half-high bodice of her silk-and-chiffon dinner dress, which, as far as she was concerned, was too fussy to be tolerated.

"And me? What about me, Mama? Couldn't we just agree that my hair is as straight as a pin and stop torturing it into curls? Couldn't we stop dressing me as though I'm royalty when I'm just me . . . plain, unremarkable me?"

Caroline's words caught up with her, and her anger passed as quickly as it had come. She'd never been able to hang on to it, which she supposed was a decent trait. A handier one would have been keeping her frustration to herself.

Her mother and father were staring at her, aghast. Amelia and Helen looked as though they were about to burst into tears. And poor Eddie was gazing raptly into his wine goblet as though the secrets to life rested there.

Caroline didn't dare look at Jack. If she did, her humiliation would be complete. She pushed back her chair and rose.

"I . . . I think I'm feeling unwell," she said into the silence that hung over the table. "If you'll excuse me, I'll just . . ."

But because she had no idea what she planned to do, she simply turned and left. Her new shoes skidded on the hard floor, making her steps as wobbly as she felt inside.

She passed Annie in the hallway, but didn't stop to ask her what in heaven's name she was doing by the dining room. And instead of heading upstairs as she, too, should have done, Caroline rushed to the conservatory.

Once inside, she closed the glass and wrought-iron door that kept the room's warmth and humidity neatly trapped. She paused at the finch cage and shook her head.

"I know just how you feel," she said to the birds.

At least the birds couldn't see through the room's foliage to know that their kind flitted freely outside. Caroline had to watch Eddie being given full rein, while she and the twins were groomed to be Mama's idea of perfect wives.

But that was not going to change.

The best she could do was work well within the cage that surrounded her, too. Caroline touched the tip of one finger to the pinkish edge of a delicate orchid blossom and watched it quiver. At least it was a very pretty cage, if over-furnished.

"I knew I'd find you here," said a male voice.

TWO

CAROLINE LOOKED AWAY FROM THE FLOWER. JACK stood between the tall potted palms that framed the room's entry.

"It's just where I'd find you at Rosemeade, too. Would you mind some company?" he asked.

In his right hand was a plate bearing a thick slice of chocolate cake. Even though her appetite had fled with her outburst in the dining room, Caroline revised her prior assessment. Jack Culhane was not just perfect, he was gloriously so.

Caroline couldn't recall the last time she'd been alone with a male who wasn't a family member. Mama had deemed it unacceptable under any circumstance once Caroline had turned twelve. But here she was, alone with Jack. She couldn't think of a better man with whom to break a few rules.

"Of course I don't mind company, especially when it arrives with chocolate cake," Caroline said to him. "But why aren't you still in the dining room?"

"Amelia and Helen started sniffling, and I got the sense the dam was about to burst. Since I believe in self-preservation, I did what I had to do." He extended the cake. "Are you going to take this, or should I give it back to the red-headed maid who came running after me with it?"

So Annie was behind the miracle of the cake. She might prove to be a wonderful ally if she wasn't fired first. Caroline eyed the treat. Perhaps her appetite hadn't fled as far as she'd thought.

"I'd hate to send you out of your way over mere dessert," she said, reaching for the plate and fork. She speared a fat chunk of cake and sighed when its rich flavor met her mouth.

Jack grinned. "I take it the cake's more to your taste than quail?"

"That's me," Caroline said after she'd swallowed. "Plain, old me."

Jack followed her as she walked down the mossy green tile pathway between the benches of plants and on to a small wrought-iron table on which sat an open-mouthed blue-and-white jar holding a white water lily.

"Not plain, not old . . . and in no way unremarkable," he said.

She glanced over her shoulder at him. He appeared to be sincere.

Caroline sat, taking care not to snag her dress on the metal chair. She didn't usually believe compliments from gentlemen, because she had millions of reasons in the bank to doubt the giver's sincerity. Jack was rich, though.

"Thank you," she said.

"You're welcome." He was looking at her much as Eddie had been at that wine goblet. "You look different tonight."

"My temper must have brought some color to my face," she said.

He seemed to shake off the moment as he took the seat opposite her. "That's probably it." He paused and then added, "So, are you going to offer me some of that cake?"

Caroline froze. "From the same plate? And with the same fork?"

He laughed. "A lightning bolt won't strike us. I've been in parts of the world where everyone shares from the same pot, no utensils at all, and to the best of my knowledge, God hasn't turned on them yet."

Jack *had* brought her the cake and missed dinner, too. Caroline glanced toward the conservatory door. If her drama at dinner had stunned her mother, this would give her fits. But no one was watching, not even the ghostly O'Brien. She handed Jack the fork and felt a tingle of rebellious glee.

"Tell me about your almost duke," Jack said after he'd had a bite of cake. "From the stories I've heard about your visit to London last year, I'd have thought all Englishmen would be cowering on their side of the Atlantic."

"Exaggerations, mostly," she said.

"Mostly?" He leaned back in his chair and smiled at her. "Care to share?"

"I share cake, not tales," she said. "But as a point of information, the almost duke isn't mine. And I don't want him to be, either."

"That's not a very welcoming attitude. Almost un-American," Jack commented with a smile.

"I'm American enough that I don't see the benefit to the Maxwell name if I snare an English title."

"Point taken, again," he said. "But cheer up. You might even like the almost duke once you meet him."

Caroline couldn't sort out which part of Jack's statement she liked least: that he wanted her to welcome this latest marriage candidate or that he thought marriage must be orchestrated.

"Is that what you hope for with your future wife? That you'll *like* each other?" she finally asked.

He didn't look as though he appreciated having the conversation turned back on him.

"I don't have a future wife, and I don't plan on looking for one," he said. "But from my bachelor's point of view, liking one's spouse isn't all bad."

Caroline made a scoffing sound.

The corner of his mouth quirked in response.

"So what is it you want, then?" he asked.

Caroline rubbed her fingertip against the thin, silver-gilt edge of the cake's plate. She'd spent a lot of time thinking about what she wanted, and apparently could not have.

"I want passion," she said. "I want to adore my husband so much that the thought of life without him crushes me. I want love. True, forever, burning love."

He blinked. "You want *Romeo and Juliet*?"

The play happened to be one of her favorite Shakespearean works. She re-read it each summer by candlelight at Rosemeade. If that made her a romantic ninny, so be it.

"What's so horrible about Romeo and Juliet?" she asked.

"Other than that they died stupidly young?" he countered before tucking into the cake.

She glared at him. "Do you have a romantic bone in your body?"

"I've got practical bones," he replied. "Tough, Irish practical bones. And what do you know about burning love, anyway?"

Caroline knew about unrequited love. She knew how she felt nearly breathless—and not from a tight corset—when Jack entered a room. But she would never tell him that. He thought highly enough of himself already.

"I don't know as much as I plan to," she said aloud.

He laughed. "Your mother would keel over if she heard you say that."

She took the fork from him. "Which is why I watch my words in front of her."

"You're smart," he said. "And quick, too. If a little greedy with that cake."

"Ha! You try being starved nightly and let me know how it works for you," she said before taking more.

"Eat more in the afternoon," he suggested.

Caroline smiled, but also wished life were that uncomplicated.

"Is it so bad having your future mapped out?" Jack asked.

"Yes," she replied. "I want to do the mapping."

"We both know that's unlikely. You need to make the best of the situation. You'll be a lot happier if you do."

She had been thinking the same thing earlier, but that didn't mean she liked hearing it from Jack, of all men.

"That's easy for you to say, when your future's your own," she pointed out.

"Be practical," Jack urged. "You're lucky. You're a wealthy heiress who happens to be witty and attractive." He hesitated. "Some men might even find you beautiful."

But not you, she thought.

"Yes, I have money," she said. "And I can put words together, and I'm decent looking. But if you were in my shoes, would that and a spouse foisted upon you make *you* happy, Jack?"

He stared at her as though she were speaking in tongues.

"Well, that's different. I'm a man."

He couldn't have chosen a worse answer. Caroline stood.

"Which gives you a list of rights I don't have, but should," she said. "I can and will take care of myself.

And if you maintain this attitude about women, Jack, you're going to wind up eating your cake alone."

She picked up her plate and fork, and left. Jack Culhane was *not* gloriously perfect. He was another big, lumbering male who deserved no chocolate at all.

Later that night, Jack sat in one of the pair of timeworn gold brocade chairs in front of the drawing room fireplace, at the home he shared with his father.

Home?

It was a mansion, though not as serious in its pursuit of the title as the Maxwell family's near-palace. Less stuffed to the rafters, too. Having lived in a male household since his mother's death twenty years before, Jack didn't understand the apparent female need for clutter-gathering. And after dessert tonight with Caroline Maxwell, he was beginning to believe he didn't understand females, either.

The scrawny little girl trailing after him had grown up. He supposed he'd known that for a while, but somehow Caroline had become part of the landscape to him. Until tonight. When her face had lit up as she'd started speaking her mind, he'd realized she was beautiful.

Her black hair and those thick lashes fringing light brown eyes weren't what a man saw on the usual American Miss. Neither was her plump lower lip, which had riveted his attention. And her declaration of wanting to experience burning love wasn't the usual talk from a demure debutante, either.

Jack stretched out his legs and smiled. He'd enjoyed Caroline's opinions and independence, even when she'd turned on him. He'd bet that spark was going to be extinguished, though. Bernard and Agnes would marry her off to the highest title, and she'd end up in a damp ruin of a house with a man who would find her more odd than interesting. That was a shame, but it wasn't his business.

The pungent scent of the peat his father had shipped from Ireland wafted from the fireplace, drawing Jack from thoughts of Caroline Maxwell's circumstances. Others had struggled and won; she might, too.

Da had taken on America and ended up owning timber tracts and coal mines from here to the Mississippi. And he'd raised Jack to understand the benefits of hard work. One trip to Da's birthplace in hardscrabble County Donegal had driven that home.

And so Jack worked. Today's purchase had been six months in the making. After he picked up one more brewery he had his eye on in Rhode Island, his holdings would be complete. Da was proud, though he wished Jack had chosen whiskey over beer. But Jack had been keeping a close eye on the temperance groups. Hard spirits stood a greater risk of eventually being outlawed. And Jack liked beer, as wrong-headed as whiskey-loving Da might find that.

The fat, round-faced clock on the mantel had just chimed ten when Jack's father entered. Jack knew he was seeing what he'd look like in thirty years. They shared the same stubborn set of the jaw and the same dark Irish skin. And like his father, he'd probably still be dressed in his day clothes well into the night, with shirtsleeves rolled up and wrinkled after a hard day's work.

"You, again?" Da asked in a teasing voice as he settled into the chair next to Jack's. "Does it not bother you, livin' under my roof? When I was your age, I was long gone from home."

"I've seen the place. You had more incentive to leave."

Da gave a bark of laughter. "True enough. I should have made things rougher on you."

Jack grinned. "Are you kicking me to the curb?"

"I could have ten of you under this roof and our paths would still not cross more than once a day."

Jack noted the lack of a real answer. Da was crafty with his words.

"You are home early, though," his father said.

"Dinner was cut short. Domestic drama at the Maxwells'."

"No surprise there." Da gave Jack a sideways glance. "Are you not going to ask me why I'm home before midnight on a card night?"

"I'm not sure I want to know," Jack replied.

His father grinned. "Sure, you do. I won myself a Newport cottage off Harry Benton. The man doesn't know when to quit, and I do."

But Harry had also once won a tract of Michigan timber from Da. Jack had no doubt that winning the cottage had felt sweet.

"How large a cottage?" he asked.

"A house on Mill Street, looking over Touro Park. The place is small, I'm hearing. Less than twenty rooms, but more than a Culhane has owned there before."

"Great, but what are you going to do with it?"

"Why, sign it over to you, of course," Da said. "You can fix it up. It will make a grand gift for your bride."

"I don't have a bride."

"At your age, you should."

If today's warm spring air had spurred all the marriage talk, Jack hoped for a cold snap.

"Keep the house, Da. You might marry again."

"No other woman could be what your mam was to me. You, though . . . it's time you found a wife."

"I like being single."

"I'm meaning this, Jack. There comes a time when a

man needs to move on. This is yours. You've had your fun, and it's time to think of the future. Do you want to be alone?"

"I'm not. I've got you to bother the hell out of me."

Da snorted. "Only when you're being an arse. I've not given you many orders, and mostly you've done what you should. But now I'm telling you to get married and be sure there's an heir to grow what we've both built."

It looked as though Caroline's parents hadn't cornered the market on empire building. Now Jack had an inkling of how she felt. Of course, he had money of his own and could walk if he chose. But he respected his father and would hear him out.

"Is there any special sort of heiress you think I should be shopping for?" he asked, letting out some of his general annoyance.

"Don't be an eejit," Da replied. "The money doesn't matter. Marry for love."

Love. That, at least, should buy him some time.

Caroline's Saturday started with an early summons to her mother's sitting room. Mama let Caroline linger on the thick, floral Aubusson rug outside her door for a few minutes before she was allowed inside—just long enough for Caroline to begin to worry about the repercussions of last night's speech. She could take a lecture, but not another curtailment of her freedom. She'd had precious little of that since her last London season, when her methods for running off suitors hadn't impressed her mother.

"Good morning, Mama," Caroline said after her mother's maid had finally ushered her inside.

Caroline kept her gaze trained on her mother. Mama's quarters tended to distract her, and she needed to be focused.

"Good morning," her mother replied from her perch

at her ornate little Louis XV writing desk. Pomeroy, who looked quite imperial this morning, sat on a gold-embroidered pillow at her feet. "We need to consult about your schedule for the week."

"Yes, of course," Caroline said. Then, because she preferred to take consequences head on, she added, "But don't you want to address last night's dinner with me?"

"We're going to pretend it didn't happen," Mama replied as she paged though a sheaf of papers.

Caroline knew her mother was constitutionally incapable of holding back a lecture. And Caroline didn't want to pretend. After nearly a year of keeping her emotions bottled up, she felt ready to explode. It was wrong, though, to vent on Mama. She was only doing what she thought was right. Jack, though, had made an intriguing target. And she'd already forgiven him for thinking like a man. He could hardly help it.

"Are you *smiling*?" her mother asked.

Caroline started a bit. "I might have been."

She'd been thinking of Jack, after all.

"You were, and I can't see why, after last night."

"You were right to say we should let it go, Mama."

Her mother nodded firmly. "And so we shall. We're all under some pressure with the summer season about to start, and I can appreciate that your nerves might have gotten the better of you. But today is a new day, and we must begin to plan for Lord Bremerton's arrival."

And that was about the best one could hope for Mama letting something go.

"I will be occupied with the improvements to Rosemeade," her mother said. "I plan to leave for Newport this afternoon. If Mrs. Longhorne cannot accommodate me at Villa Blanca, I might have to stay at Rosemeade during the work," she said with a delicate shudder at the thought of such inconvenience.

"I'm sure Mrs. Longhorne will help out," Caroline said. Villa Blanca, which had been built six years prior for Esmé Longhorne's debut, had more than a dozen guest rooms.

"We shall see," Mama said. "I will expect you and the twins to follow your weekly schedules in my absence. No making a worry of yourself for your papa, and no extra eating."

"Of course, Mama," Caroline said. Her toes were twitching within her ankle boots at the very thought of getting out of the house and breathing free air.

Her mother held a piece of paper a distance from her eyes. "It says here . . ." She squinted, and Caroline bit down on the impulse to hand Mama her spectacles. "Ah, yes. It says that you have a luncheon with Harriet Vandermeulen, and later in the afternoon a group of you are scheduled for a bicycle ride in Central Park. Is that correct?"

"Yes, Mama."

That was the official activity, though Caroline had long had another destination planned. Because, of course, the best way of working with Mama was to work around her.

Her mother set the paper down. "Harriet wears knickerbockers when she cycles, does she not?"

"Yes, Mama."

"No matter what they say, knickerbocker outfits are unseemly," Mama said with a rueful shake of her head. "You must pedal away from Harriet."

That, Caroline was guaranteed to do.

THREE

BICYCLING WITH A PACK OF GIGGLING DEBUTANTES wasn't something Jack relished. Or even generally subjected himself to. But tomorrow he was heading to Newport to see the new cottage, and later in the week he planned to meet with the owner of the Providence brewery to negotiate a sale. That left him today to pretend to be wife-seeking. If he didn't go through the motions, Da would never let the idea rest.

This morning Jack had accepted a cycling invitation that Charles Vandermeulen had sent over a week ago. Whether it was a case of better late than never remained to be seen. The Vandermeulen family was anxious to see Charles's sister, Harriet, married off. And Charles seemed to have decided that he'd like Jack as a brother-in-law. Jack, however, found Harriet disinteresting, though well-mannered. In short, she was the total opposite of Caroline.

Jack approached the group gathered on the edge of Central Park where it met Fifth Avenue. A dozen future rulers of New York society stood by their bicycles under two broad and leafy sycamore trees, avoiding the bright afternoon sun. He wondered how the wool-clad group would avoid dropping of exhaustion on this unseasonably warm day. He worried about the women, especially, in their jackets with both blouses and vests beneath, not to mention their long skirts. Even those who wore shorter skirts with voluminous knickerbockers peeking from beneath would feel the heat. Because Jack chose not to roast, he'd grabbed a yachting blazer made of cotton. Functionality interested him, not fashion.

"There you are, old man," Charles cried as Jack coasted to a stop and dismounted.

Jack did feel old compared to this crew. Under one tree he'd already spotted the Maxwell twins, along with a handful of their little friends. They were all barely out of the nursery. Slightly older cyclists had gathered beneath the second tree. And he did mean slightly. At age twenty-three, Charles's sister appeared to be the eldest.

Charles approached and shook Jack's hand. Round of build, with wavy brownish hair and a usually serious demeanor, Charles looked as trustworthy as the heir to a banking fortune should. He'd entered Princeton the same year as Jack. Charles, along with classmate Eddie Maxwell, had made sure Jack received invitations into the best dining clubs, though he wasn't from a top-drawer family. Jack had appreciated the gesture, even if he hadn't cared one hell of a lot about making inroads with the worst of the snobs.

"So glad you could make it," Charles said to Jack.

"Happy to be here," Jack replied automatically.

Then he realized that might actually be true. He'd just spotted Caroline in the deep shade of the first tree. If her dark hair hadn't given her away, the seductive curve of her waist to her hips would have.

This outing might be tolerable, after all. Jack began to head in Caroline's direction, but Charles held him back.

"My sister Harriet is here," he said in a cheerful tone. "Have I ever introduced you to her?"

"Yes, you have," Jack said. When Charles's brown spaniel eyes drooped, he added, "But it's been some time."

"Then let's go over and renew the acquaintance," Charles said. "Bring your bicycle. We'll be heading off soon."

It was clear to Jack that he was expected to be Harriet's partner.

"Harriet," Charles called. "Look who's joining us at the last minute!"

Instead of just Harriet, the entire group looked their way. Jack lifted a hand in a casual wave and shot a smile specifically at Caroline. She smiled back. Maybe last night's storm had blown over.

Harriet hurried over to greet him. As she talked, Jack could see why any number of men might be pleased to have someone like her as a wife. Her blond hair was thick and beautiful, her teeth were straight, and her nose pert. She didn't require much participation in a conversation, either. Jack nodded and made polite responses as she chattered in her high-pitched tones.

All the while, Caroline kept looking over, aggravation growing more obvious on her face. Harriet and her brother were talking about Harriet's skill at archery when Caroline stalked over.

"Excuse me for interrupting, Charles, but do you think we could be on our way?"

Charles looked at her blankly.

She gave him a stunning smile.

"Oh, yes. Yes, of course," he stammered.

"Thank you," she said.

Charles trotted off to do Caroline's bidding.

"Good job," Jack said to her.

"I try to do my best," she replied.

"Caroline, Jack and I were just talking about archery," Harriet announced, moving a step closer to him.

Caroline must have noted the proprietary move because amusement began to sparkle in her eyes. "Were you?"

"Yes." Harriet tilted her head and assessed Caroline. "You know, I've never seen you engage in archery while at Newport. Why is that?"

Jack supposed Harriet was trying to showcase her superior assets.

Caroline grinned. "I guess I've never found the right target. Now, if you'll excuse me, I think it's time to ride."

Bull's-eye, Jack thought.

He glanced at Harriet. Even her little rosebud mouth had wilted. Because it was the gentlemanly thing to do, and because she deserved some consolation after venturing so far out of her league, Jack held out his elbow to her. "Shall we go?"

With Charles and Caroline at the front, the group pedaled the park's trails for more than an hour, finally ending up by the Lake, where a picnic site, complete with canvas spread on the ground to protect the ladies' skirts, awaited.

Jack managed to slip away from Harriet while she was being served lemonade. He took advantage of the time by catching up with various acquaintances. All the while, though, he kept an eye on Caroline. Before the food had even been set out, she'd moved on to linger on the path next to her bicycle. She kept glancing around as though looking for something . . . or someone.

Harriet caught up with him. Jack listened with half an ear to her description of the pearls her older sister had received when she'd married a French count. He didn't think Harriet would take well to the news that he had no pearls and didn't plan to offer marriage.

Caroline had beckoned her sisters over. Jack tried to catch what she was saying to them, but Harriet was coming through too clearly.

Caroline mounted her bike and took off.

Curiosity got the better of Jack.

"If you'll excuse me for a moment," he said to Harriet.

Jack joined Amelia and Helen, who stood at the path's edge, watching Caroline pedal away.

"Where's your sister off to?" he asked the girls.

"She's not feeling well and is going home," Helen—or was it Amelia?—said.

"It is a little warm today," the other twin chimed in.

"You might consider removing your jackets," he suggested since their faces had reached a crimson hue.

"We couldn't!" said one girl. The other piped in with, "Mama would be appalled."

But Mama was home, where Caroline soon would be. Except, Jack suddenly realized, she'd headed off in the wrong direction.

"Pardon me," he said to the girls before turning heel and heading to his bicycle.

It didn't take long to find Caroline. She had exited the park at West 77th Street. He watched as she walked her bicycle across Central Park West and started toward the Natural History Museum.

Was she having an assignation there with a secret beau? The idea left a bad taste in Jack's mouth. Caroline was sheltered and sweet . . . mostly. Who knew what sort of opportunist might be taking advantage of her?

Telling himself he was doing this for all the right reasons, Jack crossed the road, dodging carriages, wagons, and a few curses thrown his way. If any man was going to spend the afternoon with Caroline Maxwell, Jack was damned determined it would be he.

Another rivulet of perspiration worked its way between Caroline's breasts. As soon as she returned home, she would have money sent to the leaders of the rational dress movement to aid them in their cause. Why should a woman have to perish of heat or tangle in a bicycle chain when engaging in what was supposed to be healthful exercise?

The museum's meager bicycle rack was full. Caroline walked her bike to a cluster of shrubbery to the left of the front entrance and leaned it against a fat and tall yew. She still had to deal with the leather straps that were supposed to keep the skirts of her murderous bicycling costume closer to her ankles. She stepped between the bush and the building and bent down to free herself.

"The picnic is back in the park," announced a male voice right beside her.

Caroline yelped and worked hard not to tip over. She'd never give Jack the satisfaction.

"Yes, but there's a free lecture in the library right now," she said as she got the last of her straps undone.

She stood and smoothed her skirt.

He eyed her suspiciously. "A lecture?"

"Yes, on last year's Columbian Exposition. What did you think I was here for?"

He began to reply, but Caroline knew she'd find his explanation less compelling than the lecture.

"Never mind," she said. "I'm already late."

She was almost up the museum steps before she noticed that Jack was behind her.

"You'd better hurry back to the picnic. Harriet will be waiting," she half teased as he pulled even.

"She can keep," Jack replied. "I want to hear this lecture you find so important."

She smiled. "You don't think there's really a lecture, do you?"

His skeptical expression remained firmly in place. "I'll keep you company, if you don't mind."

"Suit yourself."

By the time they reached the library, the lecture had begun. All seats were taken. Caroline stood behind the last row and allowed herself only one smug smile at Jack for not having believed her.

The assistant curator giving the talk was so far away, and the lighting so poor, that Caroline knew she'd scarcely be able to see the photos. All the same, she'd stay. There was no telling when she'd be able to orchestrate a museum day again.

Jack stood by her side, arms crossed over his chest. About five minutes into the lecture, he leaned close and said in a low voice, "Let me see if I understand this. You're attending a lecture about an exhibition that's over and done with, which itself was just displays about how people in other lands live."

"Yes."

"That's life third-hand."

Didn't he think she knew that?

"I'm lucky to be here at all," she quietly said. "Mama thinks if I'm seen in a museum, I'll be labeled a blue-stocking. And certainly my parents didn't let me go to Chicago last year."

A silver-haired woman with spectacles who was seated in front of Caroline turned around and shushed her.

She whispered sorry and then glared at Jack.

"If you don't like it here, leave," she whispered.

Instead a large hand curled around her wrist.

She tried to tug free, but he mouthed, "Trust me."

Jack led her out the door and down the hallway.

"Where are we going?" she asked.

"To life once removed." He looked down at her and smiled. "That's an improvement, don't you think?"

"Yes," she agreed.

He released her wrist and ushered her down the main set of stairs. The heels of her boots tapped a quick rhythm on the marble as she worked to keep up with his longer stride.

They stopped outside a crowded exhibition hall that bore a sign reading ALASKA.

"I wish I could have had you here a few weeks ago," Jack said as they took their place at the end of the line.

She glanced up at him. "The exhibition opened only last week." This, too, had been one of the spots she'd hoped to visit today. "How did you get in?"

"I've met Lieutenant Emmons," he replied.

Some girls fancied stage actors or opera singers. Caroline dreamed of explorers. Emmons was both an officer in the navy and a renowned photographer and collector of Alaskan artifacts.

"You've met him? Where?" she asked. And, yes, she had sounded a little breathless.

"In Alaska," Jack replied casually. "Three summers ago."

"Really?"

He smiled. "Yes, really."

"And the wildest place I've seen is Central Park," she said, feeling a little glum. "What's it like in Alaska?"

"Savage," he said. "Beautiful. Wild. I've seen the blue ice of glaciers drop into the sea, and whales breach, and flocks of puffins work to get their fat bodies from the sea and into the air."

"Stop," Caroline said. "You're making me jealous."

"Then go there. See the world. You'd eat it up, Caroline."

"I can't. The only thing I'm allowed to see are flocks of nobles in need of a fortune."

He was silent for a moment. "Maybe later, then. After you've married your noble, you can travel."

Caroline did her best to work up a smile in response. Jack's words had been a valiant effort to give her hope, but they both knew he'd failed.

They approached a case holding photographs of Native Americans in their exotic ceremonial garb.

"Tlingit tribe," Jack said, and then told her of his experiences with them.

Life second-hand was better than nothing, Caroline supposed. And Jack did have a way of talking. She could almost see herself there, with him. And truly, she could think of no place she would rather be.

They toured the Alaska exhibit and moved on to the fossil hall. After that, as they walked into the mammalian area, Caroline happened to glance at a clock.

"Oh, no!" she cried.

"What?"

"Amelia and Helen will be home already. If they find I'm not there, they'll raise an alarm with our father."

Jack took her arm in his and turned them toward the exit. "Then let's get moving."

Caroline was breathless by the time he'd hurried them to the hidden spot where she'd left her bicycle, but she was calmer, too.

"It's not so bad," she said to Jack. "Mama is on her way to Newport, and she's the one who'd be most upset."

Jack laughed. "I can imagine."

Caroline smiled back. "Thank you."

"For what?"

"For today. The stories . . . touring the museum with

me. You're the first person who has had as much fun there as I do."

"It's not usually this good for me, either," he replied.

Caroline moved closer to him, close enough that they nearly touched.

Aha! she thought. *This* was how it was supposed to feel to be young.

Jack looked down at her, and she read a note of caution in his solemn expression. But she deserved this. She deserved to experience life first-hand.

Caroline set her hands on his broad shoulders and went up on tiptoe. With no grace at all, she landed her mouth on his.

He froze for a moment, and she thought he was going to push her away. Instead he settled his hands on her waist and adjusted the angle of their kiss. Dear heaven, it felt so good. His lips were firm and hot, and her heart pounded with wanting more.

They couldn't have been there long, not that Caroline retained a sense of time, when the sound of children laughing made them pull back. Two boys around age ten were watching. They made mocking kissing noises as they ran off, still laughing.

Jack took another step back and shook his head. "You shouldn't have done that. It wasn't a good idea."

"It wasn't, was it," she agreed, since it seemed that was what he wanted to hear.

He looked at her a moment longer. Embarrassment began to warm her face.

"I need to leave," she said.

She wrestled her bicycle from the yew, refusing Jack's help, then climbed on with no regard at all for her uncinched skirt, and headed home.

The ride was a blur. The possibility of having to deal

with Papa was less bleak than the sure knowledge she'd have to deal with Jack again. If she was going to be idiot enough to kiss him, could she have not at least done it in a private place and with some amount of skill?

Living life first-hand was a messy thing.

Once home, Caroline left her bicycle at the bottom of the steps to have a servant stow it away. Weary, she entered the house.

"Good evening, Miss Caroline," said O'Brien, who stood not three feet away.

Caroline jumped. "O'Brien, you startled me!"

"My apologies, Miss," he said.

She gave him a sketchy smile and headed upstairs. If she could make it to her room without crossing the twins' paths, she'd at least be safe from trouble here.

Caroline held her breath as she tiptoed past their doors and on to her end suite of rooms. She slipped inside. After her door was closed, she leaned against it, unpinned her hat, and breathed a sigh of pure relief.

"You needn't sound so content with yourself," her mother said.

Caroline jumped again.

"Hello, Mama," she said once she'd recovered. "I thought you were on your way to Newport."

"I was delayed. It appears that you were, as well. From wherever you were."

"I was on a bicycle ride," she said, thinking at least in this she could be honest.

"So were your sisters. They arrived home thirty minutes ago. They expected to find you in your room, recovering from the effects of the sun. Imagine their surprise . . . and mine . . . when we discovered you were not here.

"If you were not on a bicycle ride, where were you, Caroline?"

Caroline opted for another partial truth. "I went to the museum."

"Which one?"

"The Natural History Museum, right by the park."

Her mother sighed, "That sounds likely. But your sisters managed to stay with the group. Why couldn't you?"

"Because I find museums more interesting than bicycles. You know how much I love to learn. I wish I didn't have to sneak around you to do it."

"I let you take the admission examinations for both Oxford and Yale," Mama said as though that settled the matter.

"And I passed both. You should have let me go, even if it was just to Vassar. At least then I could have done one thing for myself before I gave up the rest of my life to some duke or viscount."

"It's an honor to marry nobility," her mother replied.

"Let Amelia or Helen have the honor."

"When their time comes, they will. But this is your year, Caroline, and Bremerton will be the man. I can just feel it! And this *is* for you . . . for your future and your children's future." She paused and then added, "And let's be clear about one thing. After today, there will be no more contact with other men."

Had someone other than those boys seen her kiss Jack?

Despite the sickly taste of panic on her tongue, Caroline calmly asked, "What are you talking about?"

"Jack Culhane," Mama replied. "The twins are good girls. They told me he left soon after you."

This time Caroline would go with a lie. Why bring Jack into the mess?

"He might have left after me, but he certainly wasn't with me," she said.

Her mother scrutinized her, but Caroline held steady.

"If you say so," Mama finally said. "But tomorrow afternoon, you and the twins will be with me on the Fall River boat to Newport. I won't risk a repeat of whatever might have happened today."

"Fine, Mama. I'll have Annie pack my trunks."

"It's already being done."

So, Newport it was. Caroline could think of worse fates. Among them would be seeing Jack Culhane before she could dim the memory of that kiss.

FOUR

Mama believed in schedules. If the steamer *Plymouth* was to disembark from Pier 28 of the North River at 5:00 p.m., all Maxwell females would be ensconced in their parlor rooms no later than 3:30. Caroline would have liked to believe that Mama's timeliness was out of consideration for their fellow passengers. She knew better, though. Mama did *not* believe in her daughters mixing with people whom she had not approved as socially acceptable. Thus Caroline and the twins had been whisked into solitude.

Only serendipitous timing had stopped Caroline's mother from using the family's private yacht, the *Conqueror,* for this Newport trip. Papa was having the ship's engines vetted to be certain he could vanquish even the Vanderbilts in a transatlantic voyage. Caroline could not have been happier. Public transport on the *Plymouth*, with its non-Mama-approved contingent, gave her hope for some adventure, even if it was simply seeing new faces and listening in on a conversation or two.

Caroline walked softly across the rose-patterned carpet and put her ear to the wall that separated her room from Mama's. Luckily, the walnut veneer did little to stop sound from traveling.

"I must fall asleep before supper or it will be another miserable voyage for me," Mama was saying to her maid, Berta.

Mama didn't get seasick so much as she got sea-worried. Thoughts of storms and sinking tended to work her into a state.

"Shall I have tea brought, ma'am?" Berta asked.

"Yes," Caroline's mother replied. "Actually, no. What if it arrives after I sleep and the commotion wakes me? Just sit, Berta, keep company with Pomeroy, and be ready to answer if anyone comes to the door."

Caroline smiled. That made two less pairs of eyes on her. It was unfortunate that Mama didn't take well to the water, but as Papa always said, "Seize the day."

And so Caroline would . . . or at least the time before dinner. Then Mama would emerge from her stateroom, pale and perspiring, and insist that she join—and guard—Caroline, Amelia, and Helen during dinner at the captain's table. Though Caroline's room was comfortable, boasting a double bed dressed in fresh white linens, as well as a sofa and a chaise, she wanted to see the rest of the ship.

It was now 5:30, and the steamer was well underway. Caroline took a quick look at herself in the small mirror above the room's three fitted drawers. Her dark blue hat with ostrich trim sat straight and true. Her color was a bit high, but if she kept her eyes downcast and worked to be unobtrusive, surely she'd blend in. She fluffed her blue jacket's fat leg-of-mutton sleeves and readied for adventure.

After opening the door and peeking out, she stepped onto the deck. All was good. No one was in front of Mama's room, or the twins', the next one down. She locked her stateroom door and slipped the flat brass key into her petit point purse.

Avoiding Mama's room, Caroline headed toward the ship's bow. A handful of her fellow passengers stood at the rail, watching the waves roll as the ship entered the mouth of Long Island Sound. The less brave stood back a conservative distance. Caroline slipped through a gap in the crowd and neared the rail. Above her, the Fall River Line's blue-and-white flag snapped in the breeze. Her heart felt lighter. For the first time since she'd returned home yesterday, she felt as though she could breathe.

The shore fell away to deeper blue-green water. If Caroline closed her eyes, she could imagine herself a thousand different places: in an Alaskan sound at the height of summer with those puffins Jack had spoken of taking flight around her, or perhaps Ireland, where a blue bay met rolling land so green that its beauty would capture her forever.

But actual life at the rail was growing chilly and damp as the humid air sank into the fabric of Caroline's dress. She went through the double doors amidships and made her way aft, toward the grand saloon. It seemed, though, that half the ship's passengers had the same destination in mind.

Instead of jostling in the hall, Caroline approached the main stairway. Its thick Turkish carpet seemed an odd mate to the Corinthian columns topped with wildly fanciful filigreed brass light fixtures that served as the stairs' newel posts. Mama would be envious at the sight of such busyness.

Caroline entered the gallery saloon, which looked down on the larger grand saloon. Ladies and gentlemen walked about below, watching as much as they were being watched. Some sat in chairs that lined the ornate plaster walls, whispering comments to one another as a woman in a particularly bright—and some would say unsuitable—dress strolled by.

Even Caroline couldn't stop herself from watching the canary amidst the quieter birds. The woman stopped and settled her hand on the arm of a broad-shouldered man who had his back to Caroline. His head dipped down as he listened to her, no doubt all ears. There was an intimacy between the two that Caroline envied.

She knew it was impolite to gawk, but having spent the years since her debut as the subject of much gawking, she allowed herself the pleasure. The woman was of indeterminate years and quite beautiful. Her lips were the shade of blood rubies, her hair the deep color of chestnuts, and her skin an unblemished ivory. She also seemed unruffled by the stares of others, almost as though she found them amusing.

She definitely sensed Caroline's rapt attention because she looked up to the gallery. This was no time to become reticent. Caroline nodded to her. The woman smiled slightly and nodded back. Caroline's hands tightened on the railing. She'd wanted adventure. Even a few words with a woman such as this would qualify. The woman murmured something to her partner. He turned and looked up.

Caroline froze. It was Jack Culhane.

His eyes were shaded by the brim of his hat. She wished for the same protection. Her shock had to be obvious, since her heart was leaping at a hare's pace. She wanted to know who this woman was to Jack, but at the same time she wanted to pretend she'd never witnessed them.

Caroline rounded the curved railing until she was in a spot where she could neither see him nor be seen. But Jack, too, had moved, and without his companion. He looked up at her. She'd never witnessed a pirate's cocky smile any more than she'd worn a bright yellow, low-cut gown in the early evening like his lady friend. Still, she'd wager a buccaneer had a grin no bolder than Jack's.

Caroline was irritated by his ease. She was the polished product of a lifetime of education in etiquette, decorum, and maintaining one's composure. But those lessons had fled. She wheeled around and nearly tripped over two little girls who'd been walking with their parents behind her.

"Oh, I'm so sorry," she said but didn't stop hurrying toward the stairway.

When she reached the stairs, Jack already stood at the bottom. Since there was only one way down for her, he looked quite pleased with his location. Caroline debated going back to the gallery, but the laughing glint of challenge she caught in his eyes stopped her. If she were still a reckless child, she'd bring him facedown on the carpet. Unfortunately, she was grown.

Caroline started down the stairs. She was two from the bottom when she spotted Annie quickly weaving through the other passengers. Her black coat was half-buttoned, and no hat sat atop her head.

"Annie?" Caroline called.

The maid halted. Relief washed over her features.

"There you are, Miss," she said as she shouldered her way in front of Jack. "Berta sent me to your cabin to dress your hair. Your mother's ready to dine. We must move quickly!"

Caroline brushed by Jack.

"Saved by the maid," he said as she passed.

Half an hour later, Caroline sat at the captain's table with her sisters and mother, an elderly couple from Boston, a scowling Philadelphia banker, and Captain Davis. All the room's white linen–covered tables were filled with diners. The long, narrow space buzzed with conversation, nearly drowning out the violinists who sat in the far corner playing to no one in particular. Waiters in black coats bustled about filling water goblets and whisking away empty plates.

Mama and Captain Davis were discussing the new ship currently being built for the line. Mama was giving advice regarding the décor, suggesting either Baroque or Louis XVI. Based on the mix of ornate woodwork and austere columns in this room, Caroline doubted the line's owners felt constrained to just one style. And since she didn't especially care, she let her attention drift.

Jack and the woman in yellow sat on the opposite side of the room at a table with one other couple. She was smiling at something Jack was saying to the gentleman across from him. The table broke into laughter. Caroline sighed. Clearly, their conversation didn't center on furnishings. Now the woman was speaking, and the couple opposite had seemed to move in closer. Jack looked as dark and handsome as ever, blast him. And if he sensed her watching, he wasn't letting on.

"Caroline, is that Jack Culhane over there?" Amelia asked.

Caroline lifted her fork as though she'd actually been eating the food on her plate. "Where?"

"Where you've been looking for the past five minutes," Amelia replied, her expression alight with excitement. "Right there, by the lady in the yellow dress."

Mama, who was sitting to Caroline's left, broke off her chat with the captain.

"Have you something you wish to add to my conversation with Captain Davis?" she asked Amelia.

"No, Mama. I was asking Caroline if that was Jack Culhane over there, right by—"

Caroline nudged her sister's ankle with the tip of her shoe. Amelia caught on and let her words drop.

But Mama scoured the room. Caroline could peg the exact moment her mother spotted Jack, and then Jack's lady friend. Mama's eyes narrowed and she looked as though she'd tasted something unpleasant.

Mama said nothing aloud. She returned her attention to the captain and apologized for Amelia speaking out of turn. But the damage had been done. Though Jack had never had a warm welcome from Mama, Caroline was sure it was bound to grow chillier, yet.

It was nearly midnight. Jack stood by the bow rail at the fore of the walkway that led to his room. The stars lit the sky almost as brightly as the small electric lights dotting the *Plymouth*'s outer passageway lit the ship's deck. Most of the passengers had retired to their cabins, but he was restless. Running into Flora Willoughby today hadn't done it. He'd always liked his father's ex-flame and had been pleased to see her again. Flora was genuine in a way that most women of his acquaintance were not.

Except Caroline. And she was his issue.

He'd seen her watching him tonight at dinner. His equally strong interest in her was robbing him of sleep in advance of the ship's ungodly 3 A.M. arrival at Newport Harbor.

Down to his right, a cabin door opened. A woman stepped out. All Jack could see was that she wore a coat and that her hair was down. She closed her room's door, erasing its shadow and giving him a clearer look. Jack smiled. It was Caroline.

His first impulse was to go ask her what mischief she planned to make tonight, but if mischief were her plan, she'd have put her hair up and been sure she was presentable in case of capture. She was still her mama's child, as hard as she seemed to be fighting against it.

Caroline stood at the rail and gazed into the night, much as he'd just been doing. Her hair was caught in a thick braid that reached nearly to her waist, and she held herself with an almost military posture he found oddly charming.

Jack kept his spot about thirty feet away. He'd give her some privacy, even if he did plan to keep an eye on her. After a minute or so, she turned in his direction, apparently planning to walk. She halted when she saw him.

Jack stepped away from the rail and closer to one of the lights. He raised a hand in greeting. He was sure she was going to turn back to the safety of her room, but she surprised him again.

"Why are you lurking about?" she asked once she'd joined him.

He laughed. "If I were lurking, I wouldn't have moved into the light so you could see who I was."

She fastened her coat's top button, but not before Jack had seen the telltale thin white fabric of her nightclothes. Her tapestry slippers would have tipped him off to her state of undress, in any case.

"Fine," she said. "I'll be polite and ignore the coincidence of finding you so near my cabin."

"And I'll do the same for you," he said.

She did a poor job of hiding her smile.

"I take it your mother was delayed in her trip to Newport?" Jack asked.

"Yes, and it seems my father isn't the only hunter in the family. She was laying in wait for me when I returned home yesterday."

He smiled. "And not surprisingly, you survived."

"I was trapped, all the same. I told her about the

museum trip, but nothing about you. As punishment
for straying, I'm now to be on display in Newport much
earlier than I had steeled myself to be."

He smiled at her analogy. "Newport has its share of
zoolike qualities."

"As does my life," she said, her tone light. Then she
sighed. "And while we might joke about this, I do have
to warn you to stay out of Mama's path . . . which means
you need to stay out of mine."

"Thanks for the advice, but I like being in your path.
It leads me to unexpected places."

"I'm going to start trying for more appropriate desti-
nations," she said.

"Impossible."

Caroline laughed. "You do know me, don't you?"

"I'd say I've gotten to know you a lot better over the
past twenty-four hours," he replied.

She stood silent. He knew they were both thinking of
that kiss.

"So why are you out here, Jack?" she eventually asked.

"I had things to think about, so I walked. And you?"

"I wanted to relish my last breaths of guaranteed freedom. We're staying with one of Mama's friends in Newport while Rosemeade is being improved. I don't have set
escape routes at Mrs. Longhorne's."

"You'll find them," he said. And make her mother mad
with worry once she did, too.

"I'll do my best," she agreed.

He inclined his head toward two deck chairs not under a direct spotlight. "Care to join me?"

"Why not?" she said. "Mama is sound asleep, and the
twins haven't yet learned to take advantage of those
times."

After they'd sat, Caroline asked, "Are you leaving
the ship in Newport, too?"

"Yes. My father seems to have landed a house there. I'm going to make it my base while I do some business in Providence."

"Ah! Is this part of your business expansion that Eddie mentioned the other night?"

He couldn't believe she recalled what had been no more than a passing reference, and that she sounded excited, too. "It is, but I won't bore you with the details."

"Talk of embroidery stitches bores me, not business." She edged around in her chair so she was facing him more directly. "You have no idea how difficult it is to induce a gentleman to speak to me about business."

She underestimated herself. For another of her haphazard kisses, he'd probably spill the ingredients to his Pennsylvania brewery's best-selling ale.

"I'm not surprised. Most of the men you meet don't actually set foot anyplace more taxing than their yachting clubs," he said aloud.

"Which explains why their conversation is limited to the weather." Caroline shook her head. "Why can't we all be more direct?"

Jack laughed. "I haven't seen you be indirect."

"Much to my mother's chagrin. But I am a bit of an oddity when compared to the other girls I know."

"You're not an oddity. How about we just say you're a rare bird?"

She fell silent for a moment, then said, "Speaking of which, who was the woman you were with today?"

Jack grinned. "That's direct, all right. Flora Willoughby is a friend."

"I see," Caroline said, sounding a little choked.

"There's no need to start tiptoeing now. I didn't say she's my mistress or lover, I said she's my friend."

He took a moment to decide how much he should share with Caroline. She craved direct conversation, but she remained a pampered heiress. "Flora's a retired actress. A number of years ago, she was also a flame of my father's. I liked her. She was raised as the only daughter in a privileged Chicago family, but disowned when she left to follow her own dreams of acting. She was an improbable mother figure, but she was the closest I'd had in a while."

"Your father introduced her to you?" Caroline asked, sounding as shocked as Jack expected.

"Da is even less concerned with etiquette than I am," he said. "But she never stayed under our roof, and he was never less than a gentleman toward her." Jack looked into the darkness, then added, "Da wasn't interested in marriage, though. Flora wasn't willing to be less than his wife and so she moved on. She and I corresponded for a few years, but we lost touch. When we happened on each other earlier this afternoon, she told me she was recently widowed."

"She wore an unusual choice of mourning garb this evening," Caroline said.

Jack shrugged. "She's always been colorful. Practical, too. It could be that she can't afford a long mourning period."

"I understand," Caroline eventually said.

Jack supposed she did, too. While her family might shelter her, Caroline was curious. He was sure she'd seen enough of those thinly veiled items about actresses and their patrons in the newspaper.

"I'm sure she's a very nice woman," Caroline said as she rose. "But I should get back to my room. I'd only intended to be out long enough to admire the stars."

Jack stood, too. He held out a hand to stop her. "Before you go, I want to make you an offer."

She tilted her head. "Really? Not of the marriage sort, I trust. You're not on Mama's list."

"Your mother has a *list*?" He shook his head. "Wait. Never mind. Of course she has a list." And it was no doubt chiseled in stone, too. "But I'm offering honesty, not marriage."

She laughed. "Heaven knows in our set those two seldom seem to go together."

"Another reason for bachelorhood," he said. "But I will promise to be your most honest friend. If you want to know something, ask. And I will not lie."

"Those are dangerous words, Jack Culhane."

Damn, but he liked this girl. "I know."

"It's a deal," she said.

She held out her hand, and he took it. Her shake was warm and firm. And even if he wanted to draw her closer, he wasn't going to.

She stepped back. "It's off to sleep for me." But she hadn't taken more than five steps before she turned back and added in a cheery voice, "And Jack, the next time I see you, be prepared to talk about kissing."

Jack was ready. Very ready.

FIVE

CAROLINE WOKE SLOWLY, HER DELICIOUS DREAM OF venturing through a rich tropical forest replaced by watery morning light nudging at her eyelids. She closed her eyes more tightly. Reality could wait.

"Miss, I know you're awake," said a voice indisputably that of Annie.

Caroline gave up the battle and opened her eyes. Annie's face hovered just above hers, wide blue-green eyes watching her intently.

"What are you doing?" Caroline asked.

The maid took a step back.

"I was making certain you weren't dead."

Caroline sat up. "Dead?"

"Well, I'm sorry, Miss," she said, sounding more amused than contrite. "But I knocked at the door as loudly as I dared without sending your mother into a temper, and then I got a key." She waved the shiny brass room key.

Caroline was going to ask Annie how she'd accomplished that feat, but the girl's laughing smile shone as a testament to the fact that she could likely wheedle more than a key, should the need arise. How could one not respect such resourcefulness?

"When I stepped in, I called your name and still you didn't stir," Annie said. "So I came close to check if you were still breathing. Good thing you were, too. It wouldn't be easy, even for me, to talk myself into another position if you die when this is my first time being a lady's maid."

She paused for an instant, another smile playing around her mouth. "I suppose yellow fever or a plague would be fine, but no mysterious dying, if you could please avoid it."

Caroline swung her feet to the floor, where her tapestry slippers awaited. "Thank you, but I'd prefer to avoid all three."

Now that she was fully awake, Caroline noted the actual daylight shining through the gap in the drapes covering the stateroom's sole window.

"Good heaven, where are we by now . . . Fall River?" she asked.

"Just about to Newport," Annie replied. "We stopped in the dead of night to help a six-man fishing dory that was sinking, so we're running late. Your mother and sisters have been up for some time, though."

"Of course," Caroline said as she quickly unwove her hair from its nighttime braid.

Annie handed her the heavy, silver-backed brush from Caroline's small travel case. Caroline whisked the brush though her hair. Mama was no doubt taking the ship's delay personally, as she would Caroline's being late.

"I let you sleep, Miss. I thought what with you out walking past midnight, some extra rest wouldn't hurt you."

Caroline stopped brushing. "You saw me?"

"Yes. I was taking a stroll with a gentleman friend and saw you talking to Mister Culhane," Annie said as she shook out the soft green morning dress she had brought for Caroline to wear. "It's no one's concern but yours . . .

though it would be easier to keep it just your concern if I knew when I needed to keep that harpy Berta occupied."

Caroline smiled at the eerie-but-accurate image of Mama's maid. Nothing made Berta happier than sinking her claws into a miscreant Maxwell daughter.

With some corset help from Annie, Caroline dressed as quickly as a female smothered in layers of fabric could. Annie pinned Caroline's hair haphazardly, but her broadbrimmed ivory-and-green hat would hide the mess. By the time Annie had packed the travel case and gone to join Berta to wait for the family's trunks, the *Plymouth* was passing the harbor's Long Wharf, where the shipbuilders worked. Its orderly row of clapboard buildings stood in sharp contrast to the wagons and men and supplies in a jumble in front of them.

With the sun full up and a crisp east wind blowing, fishermen had long ago left the harbor. Still, there was activity enough for Caroline to soak in as they docked, except she knew she shouldn't dally and annoy her mother.

She rapped twice on Mama's door before entering. Amelia and Helen were standing in front of Mama, who was inspecting them as though they were soldiers readying for war.

"Good morning," Caroline said.

Her mother peered at her. "You're looking pallid. As soon as we get to Mrs. Longhorne's, you are to take a rest. We need you at your peak for the season."

Clearly, Caroline had not passed muster.

"Now on we go," Mama said, scooping up Pomeroy, who sat in his wicker travel basket. "We mustn't keep Mildred waiting."

"What other engagements would Mrs. Longhorne have at six in the morning?" Helen asked.

"I'm sure I wouldn't know," their mother replied while shooing her flock out the door.

Passengers disembarking in Newport were hardly more than a handful. Most stayed aboard for Fall River and its connecting train to Boston. It was a simple matter to spot Jack about twenty yards away once they stood on the wharf. He was in his shirtsleeves and talking to a clutch of men bearing notebooks. One even held a camera. How curious, Caroline thought. Reporters chased after Vanderbilts and sometimes Maxwells, but never Culhanes.

She paused to take in the scene. Jack's hat was tipped at a rakish angle, and his smile made her want to smile, too. He glanced her way. Their gazes briefly met, and she did smile.

"Caroline, come along," Mama said. "Stop gawking at strangers."

"That's Jack Culhane, Mama," she replied. "He's no stranger to us."

The photographer was clearing a small cluster of spectators to take Jack's picture. He looked at ease, though not quite as happy with the situation as he had moments ago.

"He is a stranger to you, if not Eddie," Mama said. "You don't know him well at all, nor should you. He has no coat on *and* he keeps inappropriate friends."

His lack of a morning coat was a bit odd, but hardly worth Mama's censure. It was as Caroline had figured: Last night, her mother had not looked favorably upon Jack with Flora Willoughby.

"Eddie isn't all that horrible," Caroline said, trying to tease Mama out of her poor mood.

"Don't be impertinent," Caroline's mother replied. "You know I wasn't referring to Eddie."

Caroline's father would have laughed at Caroline's

silly comment. For that matter, only a few years ago Mama would have, too.

Just then, Jack approached. His good humor had returned.

"Good morning, Mrs. Maxwell," he said.

Mama made a harrumphing sound no one could interpret as a hello. Jack's smile did not fade. Instead it grew broader.

"Caroline, Amelia, and Helen, it's a pleasure to see you, too," he added.

The twins responded courteously, though Amelia was actually rather impolitely staring at Jack.

"Good morning, Mister Culhane," Caroline said. "Did you have a pleasant voyage?"

"It was an adventure," he said.

Caroline nodded absently. She had just noticed that his sleeves were rolled up almost to his elbows. She'd never seen even his forearms bare since they'd been youngsters. His arms were strong and the skin as tanned as his face, as though he'd spent time in the tropics she'd been dreaming of this morning. Her fingers twitched with the desire to feel the firm tautness of his skin. She clasped one hand over the other to stop herself.

"Did you truly help rescue those poor sailors last night?" Amelia asked Jack. "I heard a crewman talking of it as we lined up to leave the ship."

"I pitched in a hand," Jack replied. "And my spare clothes once we had the four we could find aboard."

"But I heard you did more than that. The man was saying that you spotted the men and saved their lives," Amelia said. "I think you might be a hero, Mr. Culhane."

"I'm nothing of the sort," he said, softening his words with a smile.

Caroline glanced at her mother to see how she might

take this self-deprecation. It seemed, however, that his good manners had bounced right off her.

Frowning, Mama said, "We must be moving along."

"Of course. I apologize for delaying you and look forward to seeing all of you again this season," Jack said.

"That is quite unlikely. We will *not* be entertaining," Mama proclaimed, as though a lie would settle the matter.

Jack grinned. "Really? I always find you entertaining, Mrs. Maxwell."

Caroline hid her laughter with a cough. And with a tip of his hat, Jack was gone.

Once they were settled in the Longhornes' carriage, Mama didn't speak again, choosing instead to scowl at Caroline from her perch opposite her. The twins ably filled the silence. On Bridge Street they speculated about the precise number of picnics and galas they would attend over the summer. Once the carriage turned south on Thames and into the shopping district, their talk moved to who sold the best chocolates in Newport and whether they might come back later in the day to sample some.

At Church Street they were on to who had the finer singing voice. Caroline looked out the window at Trinity Church, with its white spire pointing the way to heaven. Her concept of paradise was something more immediate: a book and a blanket beneath a tree, where she might read in peace. Or better yet, no book, but Jack at her side. Caroline sighed at the thought.

Mama's scowl turned into a glare. "Do not make the mistake of thinking I will tolerate another summer like last, Caroline. You must get control of yourself."

"I agree," Caroline replied. Of course she gave those words a different meaning from the one her mother had intended.

Once they had turned east off Belleville Avenue and onto Bath Road, the bustle of the commercial area gave way to quiet. Buildings no longer stood shoulder-to-shoulder. Rolling lawns, elaborate entry gates, and cottages that could house a hundred took over the landscape. In a matter of minutes, they had turned onto a private lane that led to the Longhorne family estate.

Villa Blanca might not be so large and grand as Mrs. William K. Vanderbilt's Marble House, just a handful of mansions away, but Mrs. Longhorne had hardly gone short on marble, either. Villa Blanca's three stories and two angled wings glowed ethereally white as the sun cut through the mist hovering above the house's smooth green lawns. It was perhaps the most lovely jail Caroline had ever seen. She would not bother pretending that it was intended to be otherwise for her.

Once they were up the broad—and, naturally, marble—steps, a footman in ornate livery opened the front door. Just inside, Mrs. Longhorne's Italian butler announced in charmingly accented English that Mrs. Longhorne would be found in the Blue Seaside Salon. Since there was also a Green Seaside Salon, the distinction was necessary.

With the butler ushering the way, Caroline and her sisters followed Mama and her little dog like silk-and-lace-garbed ducklings into the salon, in which someone— likely not Mrs. Longhorne—had shown an admirable restraint in the placement of decorations so that the view of the ocean was the room's focus.

Mildred greeted Mama with four excited words. "Agnes, a costume ball!"

"A costume ball?" Mama asked.

"Yes, you must have one," Mrs. Longhorne said. "It's early enough in the season that no one has said a word of holding one. If you let your plans be public, no one else will, for they'll know they cannot outdo you. What better way to show Bremerton what he will be gaining by marrying Caroline?"

Mama nodded excitedly. "Mildred, you're right! There is no better way!"

A desperate sort of humor overtook Caroline.

"We could always set out the three-hundred-piece gold dinner service," she suggested. "Or better yet, strap it to me with a diamond chain or two so the message is clear. I will clank and rattle behind him wherever he goes."

Mama, who was pulling off her gloves, turned to face her. "Did you not listen to me in the carriage? This is your future, Caroline, and it's one any healthy girl would embrace. I am becoming convinced that you are unwell."

"We will get you settled into your room in just a few minutes, dear," Mrs. Longhorne said to Caroline. "And until then, do sit." She made a shooing motion toward a fat, sapphire blue chair that was positioned to give an angled view of both the lawns and ocean and the room itself.

"Thank you, Mrs. Longhorne," Caroline replied.

She settled in, focused on the outdoors, and willed herself to be calm. There was no stopping Mama from having a ball and throwing her in front of Bremerton. Her smartest move would be to appear accepting so that she had some freedom left to maneuver. She pinned on a placid smile.

"Girls, you sit, too," Mrs. Longhorne said to Helen and Amelia.

The twins, who still stood where they'd stopped upon entering the room, took a sofa along the interior wall.

"Have you had any thoughts about a theme, Mildred?" Mama asked.

"I was going to suggest Independence. It seems to fit, as our national holiday is in July."

"Don't you find that somewhat ironic, Mama?" Amelia asked.

"Ironic? What do you mean?"

"You would be asking an Englishman to celebrate losing a colony."

Mama nodded. "Ah, I see. No, that wouldn't do at all."

Caroline breathed a sigh of relief. Celebrating independence at a fete meant to assure her captivity seemed too close to cruel.

"When is Bremerton to arrive?" Mama asked Mrs. Longhorne.

"I read in the *Mercury* that he will begin his stay with Mr. and Mrs. William Carstairs on Saturday the thirtieth."

"Of July?" Caroline's mother asked.

Mrs. Longhorne shook her head. "No. June."

"Too soon," Mama said. "I must have the ball almost immediately after his arrival."

"Definitely," her friend agreed.

"Which means that Rosemeade must be quickly finished."

"True."

Mama paced to the picture window and looked out for a moment, altering Caroline's placid view. When she turned back to rejoin her friend, her face was set in the same determined expression Caroline knew she wore when planning a secret foray. She and Mama were much alike in that, if not in their opinion of what best suited Caroline.

"With such a short time to prepare, I think it would be best to invite guests to attend as their favorite historical or mythological figure," Mama said to Mrs. Longhorne. "It's been done dozens of times, but we'll make up for the stale theme with the food, gifts, and music."

Mrs. Longhorne rubbed her hands together. "How wonderful! We'll have to shop!"

"That we will," Mama said before focusing on Caroline. "We'll need to start a costume for you immediately. You must shine the brightest of all. Who do you wish to be?"

"Joan of Arc," Caroline said. The Maid of Orleans had been a fierce warrior for her cause, as Caroline wanted to be. Though Joan hadn't fared too well, when all was said and done.

"Absolutely not. You must be alluring," Mama replied. "Perhaps Demeter, and you can wear a crown of jeweled flowers."

But Caroline had no desire to be the perfect and fertile Demeter.

"How about Queen Elizabeth?" she suggested. "She wore plenty of jewels."

Plus Elizabeth had known a thing or two about employing tactics to remain unwed.

"Athena," Mama decreed. "Elizabeth has been overdone."

"Artemis," Caroline countered.

Across the room, Helen giggled. She was student enough to know that strong and determined Artemis had vanquished all who wanted to see her captured, bedded, or wed. Mama, however, was not so well versed. And she already wore the dreamy expression of a woman envisioning an ivory silk gown, golden diadem, and a flowery quiver and bow.

"Yes, Artemis would be perfect," Mama said. "Just perfect."

Indeed she was, for Caroline had just begun her hunt for freedom.

SIX

HUNTING FREEDOM CERTAINLY LACKED IN THE THRILL of the chase. Instead, Caroline had spent the past three days doing her best to blend in with her surroundings so that she could gain the element of surprise. She had been obedient, patient, and subservient to Mama. And being all these saintly things had left Caroline feeling quite impatient.

Thursday morning, as she sat with her sisters in Mildred Longhorne's shiny black phaeton headed toward the Newport Casino, everything was annoying her. Even her hat. The wide-brimmed, pale yellow creation was adorned with a white ostrich plume that bobbed in relentless time to the matched bays' brisk trots. Caroline reached one hand to try to still the feather, but soon gave up.

Town remained relatively quiet. The real summer season would not begin until the first week of July. Still, Bellevue Avenue carried its share of social traffic. Caroline gave the obligatory small wave to the two Hadley sisters, who were also in an open carriage, as they passed each other. The Hadleys returned her greeting. Should they pass each other again, waves would be replaced by polite smiles. On a third passing, they needn't make eye contact.

Newport was built on rituals such as these. Daily, at no later than ten minutes past nine, one had to be on the way to the Casino to watch a tennis match or perhaps take a lesson. And so the Maxwell girls were, though only to observe. Mama might unbend enough to allow an occasional bicycle ride, but her girls would *never* play tennis. At least not that Mama knew about . . .

Across from Caroline, both Helen and Amelia were acting like dour little rain clouds, which was indirectly Caroline's fault. At breakfast, Mama had charged them with being at Caroline's side for the day. Mama and Mrs. Longhorne would be occupied until well into the afternoon planning the costume ball.

The twins were destined to fail in their supervisory duties. They knew it, too. It was not a matter of if Caroline would slip away today and breathe some freedom, but when.

Helen edged closer to her side of the carriage, moving her fluffy pearl pink skirts away from Amelia's.

"Would you please hold still?" Amelia snapped. "You know if we must face backward, I need to be on the left side of the seat. It's bad enough that you didn't give it to me. Do you need to bounce around, too?"

"I *never* bounce," Helen replied. "And if you hadn't dawdled, you'd have the seat you want, not that it would make any difference."

"What do you mean, no difference?"

"Backwards is backwards, whether on the left or right. You're acting like a spoiled child."

"*I* am?" Amelia gasped, kid-gloved hand to her heart. "You dare say that after telling Mama you want to be the goddess Minerva at the costume ball, when you know that being Minerva is all I've spoken of since Monday? You're the spoiled one of us."

"I'm the elder. I get first choice in costume, after

Caroline, and I'm better suited to be Minerva. I love books and wisdom. You just want to carry an owl."

"You get everything you want."

Caroline had heard enough.

"Markham, please pull over," she called to the Long-hornes' coachman.

The twins stopped bickering.

"Caro, what are you doing?" Helen asked.

"Out," Caroline said, reaching for the door's clasp before poor Markham could even get there.

Amelia—who actually was a tad dramatic—gasped again. "What do you mean, out?"

"I mean for you to get out of the carriage," Caroline directed. "You're being ridiculous. I'm moving to your seat, and the two of you are moving to mine. And the rest of the way to the Casino, we all are going to be Minerva and explore the wisdom found in silence."

Markham arrived. He took over his duties from Caroline, and readied to assist them from the carriage.

"Now, out," Caroline said firmly as her sisters gaped at her.

"We never stop the carriage like this. You're making a spectacle of us," Helen said.

"If I wanted to make a spectacle, I'd do far more than this," Caroline replied. "Move along so we can get to the Casino on time."

The girls were standing curbside and Caroline had just risen and was readying to change seats when a gold-gilt carriage that even Mama would deem overdone pulled beside them and stopped. In it sat Flora Willoughby, with Jack opposite her. Caroline tried not to stare as her sisters were.

"Are you having difficulties?" Mrs. Willoughby asked.

Caroline couldn't work up a response. Her silence wasn't due to the other woman's tennis attire, even though it was a wonderful near echo of what males were permitted to wear. Seeing Jack had scattered Caroline's thoughts. After three days without a glance of him, she'd managed to convince herself that he'd left Newport. Life would be duller, but more manageable.

Yet here he was. Jack, too, wore tennis whites, but where the color accented Mrs. Willoughby's exotic paleness, it made him look more vital than ever. An odd sensation danced through Caroline.

Hunger, maybe?

"No troubles," she managed to say after focusing solely on Mrs. Willoughby. "Just a slight rearrangement of contents."

"Good, then," Jack's friend replied.

Caroline wasn't sure what to say next. Rules required that she politely end the conversation. They were not formally acquainted, and Jack wasn't making the effort. But to his questionable credit, Mrs. Willoughby wasn't the sort of woman to whom Caroline should be introduced. Which, of course, made the introduction all the more appealing.

She frowned at Jack. The blasted man grinned in return. But if he thought he held the upper hand, he was sorely mistaken. She stood a little straighter.

"My name is Caroline Maxwell," she said to the other woman. "And I believe you are Mrs. Willoughby?"

Down on the curb, both twins gasped. This time she couldn't blame them. Caroline was indeed creating that dreaded spectacle, and it was being noted by Mama's friends in passing carriages.

"Please call me Flora."

Caroline nodded her assent. "Thank you."

"Jack and I were just on our way to the Casino. I have decided to take up tennis," Flora said.

"I'm sure you'll enjoy it," Caroline replied. Just as *she*

would enjoy the freedom of the other woman's clothing. While she didn't want to stare more than she had already, the outfit seemed to involve no corset at all.

"Do you play?"

"Yes, but not this morning," Caroline said and then laughed. "Which I'm sure you deduced from my morning dress. My sisters and I are going to watch, though."

"I'll give you plenty to watch." Flora paused an instant. "Perhaps you'd like to join me and give me a few words of advice before my lesson?"

She knew she shouldn't, but she so wanted to.

Jack gave a subtle negative shake of his head, which only cemented her resolve.

"I'd love to," Caroline said, relishing the look of shock on Jack's face.

"Lovely," Flora replied. "Jack, would you help Miss Maxwell in?"

His "of course" clashed with his grim expression.

Caroline turned her attention to her sisters as she took Markham's assistance and exited her carriage.

"I'll rejoin you at the Casino," she said to them.

"Caroline, you cannot do this," Helen cried as Amelia stammered, "But . . . But . . ."

"You'll be fine," Caroline said briskly. "Markham knows the way."

That, of course, had not been the genesis of the twins' objections, though the reassurance did neatly silence them. By the time she had reached Mrs. Willoughby's carriage, Jack had exited.

He offered her his hand. She took it and entered the fairytale carriage. Jack held on an instant longer than necessary, giving her fingers a squeeze in what could have been either a greeting or warning.

Caroline would wager it was a warning.

She seated herself opposite Flora. Up close, the woman

remained ageless in appearance. Jack sat next to Caroline, near enough that his leg nudged hers. She gave him a slight frown and moved over. The carriage pulled away, and Caroline took an instant to watch her sisters return to theirs.

"I wasn't quite sure you'd join me," Flora said as they rolled on.

"She shouldn't have," Jack said.

Flora's perfect eyebrows rose. "When did you become a slave to social dictates?"

"About two minutes ago," Jack replied.

The older woman laughed.

"You seem to have an odd effect on our Jack," she said to Caroline.

He was no more Flora's Jack than Bremerton was her almost duke, but Caroline let this reference slip by.

"Do you reside here in Newport, Mrs. Willoughby?" she asked.

"For a month or so, I am going to. I rented The Reefs from the Miss French. I was in need of a sea change from San Francisco, which was where my late husband and I spent much of our time."

"Jack told me of your husband's death. I'm sorry for your loss," Caroline said.

"And no doubt a little intrigued . . . or perhaps shocked . . . that I'm about to play tennis."

"Not at all," Caroline fibbed.

"You must learn to meet your opposition's eyes when dissembling," Flora said. "Looking down will give you away every time."

"Don't give her any help," Jack said. "She's dangerous enough already."

"Really? Dangerous?" Flora asked.

Caroline liked the idea of being seen as a woman with whom to be reckoned.

"Dangerous to herself," Jack replied.

If she'd had a parasol, Caroline would have stabbed his white leather shoe with its point. As it was, an ostrich plumed hat was of little help.

"So long as he believes that, you retain the upper hand," Flora said to Caroline. She regarded Jack a little more closely. "Though I think he has his doubts already."

"Jack is a stubborn man," Caroline said. "He's going to believe what he believes, evidence regarding my capabilities to the contrary."

"I can see why you like her," Flora said to Jack.

"She's my best friend's sister, nothing more," Jack replied.

"Of course, dear," Flora said, her blue eyes alight with laughter.

Caroline had to smile, too.

Flora returned her attention to Caroline. "And as for the tennis outing, my Clem made me promise to move on with my life. 'No widowing-up,' he said to me. He felt I'd wasted enough of my youth when I married him. He was older than I by a handful of years."

"Only if that hand has thirty fingers," Jack muttered.

"He was very youthful," Flora said sternly.

Caroline watched out of the corner of her eye as Jack shifted uncomfortably.

"My apologies," he said. "I'm sure he was."

"Better," Flora said. "That's our heroic Jack."

She looked at Caroline. "You did read about his exploits in the *Mercury* on Tuesday, didn't you?"

"I did," Caroline said. She wouldn't share that she'd also purloined the paper and hidden it in her room.

"I was so proud, but it was no less than I would expect," Flora said. "But back to my beloved Clem. I am doing as he wanted me to. No widow's black crepe. No year closed away. In his honor, I'm taking center stage."

And doing it with enviable flair, Caroline thought.

"So why no tennis for you today, Caroline?" Flora asked.

"My sisters would tell my mother, who does not want me to be perceived by potential husbands as the sporting type. Much as I enjoy tennis, these days I am choosing to save Mama's censure for better things."

"Such as?"

"Nothing so dire. Just solitary sunrise walks, museum trips, the occasional shooting practice with my brother, Eddie . . ."

"And kissing random men," Jack said. "Let's not forget that."

Flora smiled. "Ah, now we have the reason for Jack's displeasure."

Even though she could feel the rising heat of embarrassment, Caroline refused to give in to it. Nor would she back down.

"Not so random, Jack. I've kissed only you," she said.

Flora's laugh was light and musical, drawing disapproving looks from the occupants of the other carriages lined up for entry at the Casino.

"This gets better and better," she said. "I hope I see more of you here in Newport, Caroline."

Caroline hesitated. She could learn many things from Flora, but socializing with her was an impossibility.

"Oh, I know I won't," Flora said with a wave of her hand. "I'm aware I'm the sort that would make your mama grow all protective." She gave a slight shake of her head. "And apparently our Jack, too. But it has been a pleasure."

"Yes, it has," Caroline agreed as they rolled up in front of the brick building with its gaudily striped awnings. "Your home is at Bancroft Avenue, is it not?" Others might find that a rude question, but Caroline knew Flora would not.

"It is," she replied, smiling.

"Rosemeade is at Ruggles Avenue. Once my mother, sisters, and I are back in residence, we'll practically be neighbors."

"Then there's every chance that you might one day stroll by. Should you, please stop in. I'm finding the grounds quite inspiring."

Caroline returned the older woman's smile. "I would never turn down the opportunity for inspiration."

Beside her, Jack was growing restless. "You're going to be late for your lesson, Flora."

"I am certain my instructor will wait a heartbeat or two," she replied.

"No doubt." Nonetheless, he rose and exited the carriage.

He held out his hand. "Caroline?"

When she was back on solid ground, once again he kept her hand. He leaned close and said, "Let me know when you're feeling random again."

As she withdrew her hand, her knees wobbled. Perhaps the ground wasn't so solid, after all.

Charles Vandermeulen had never won a tennis match against Jack, though this morning he had come close. It wasn't that Charles had developed any level of skill on the grass court. Jack had simply lost his ability to concentrate. This lack hadn't come with the dawning realization that the Vandermeulens had followed him to Newport, but with Jack's acceptance that Flora was right. He had underestimated Caroline Maxwell, a mistake he would not make again.

While Helen and Amelia giggled with their girlfriends, Caroline sat at a small, round courtside table with Harriet.

Both had watched Jack, Harriet with maidenly yearning and Caroline as though she were planning her next great adventure. Jack hoped it involved more stolen kisses.

Match done, Charles and he now sat with Caroline and Harriet, all drinking tall glasses of water fancied up with slender lemon slices. Jack downed his and wished for a beer . . . or three. He remained thirsty and possibly in need of some numbing.

"Papa has promised to build me a home on Fifth Avenue as a wedding gift," Harriet said to him.

"How nice for you," Jack replied, hiding a smile at her lack of subtlety about as poorly as Caroline was concealing her restlessness.

She opened the small watch pinned to a bejeweled ribbon at her waist and awkwardly looked down at it. Her build wasn't nearly flat enough to make that an easy viewing.

"It's nearing eleven," he said to her.

She rose. "Then it's time for my sisters and I to be on our way."

She glanced where the twins had last been sitting, but the cluster of girls had moved on.

Caroline sighed. "And to think they're supposed to be watching me."

Harriet and Charles looked confused, but Jack laughed.

"I'd best go round them up," Caroline said before giving the Vandermeulens a cheery good-bye and moving on.

Seizing the opportunity, Jack rose, too. After he'd accepted a dinner engagement for tomorrow with Harriet's family, he jogged up to Caroline.

"Are you always going to bolt from Harriet like a spooked horse?" she asked as he pulled even with her.

"I prefer to think of it as a strategic retreat," he replied. "Harriet is a sweet girl, if relentless. I don't want to hurt her feelings, but even if I were entertaining thoughts of marriage, she's not my type."

"In what way? She's rich enough," Caroline said as they walked into a grove of sturdy elms to the far side of the Casino's tennis courts.

He'd promised to be honest with her, so honest he'd be. "I can't imagine her in my bed, night after night and year after year."

Caroline stopped. "She's the ideal of all that's beautiful. I'm not educated regarding lovemaking, but I'm sure you could bear up long enough to create an heir or two."

Jack shrugged. "It's not all about beauty. It's about wanting, too."

He looked at her more closely. His bluntness hadn't rattled her. She'd tipped up her head to watch him. Her gaze was level, as was her voice. Harriet would no doubt have collapsed in a heap of ruffles and lace at a conversation such as this.

"If you have that luxury, I suppose," Caroline said. "As you've pointed out to me, I don't."

"Luckily, I do," he replied.

"Am I your type, Jack?"

He hesitated. Honesty was only going to bring heartache.

"No," he said.

Caroline looked as though she were absorbing a blow.

"And yet you more or less offered to kiss me today," she pointed out.

"Better me than someone who will take advantage of you," he replied.

She laughed. "That's nearly noble of you."

"Isn't it?"

She moved a step closer, and he looked around to see if they were being watched. They weren't.

"But you made that dangerous promise, Jack. Be honest with me. Am I your type?"

"I have my rules," Jack replied, trying out some of his Da's sidestepping.

"And what do those rules include?"

"Not destroying my friendship with your brother."

"I don't plan to tell Eddie that I kissed you." She smiled again. "Or that you want to kiss me. And you do, even if you won't admit it. There's no other reason you would have said what you did in front of Flora."

She might be an innocent, but she was no fool.

The sea breeze pushed at the brim of her hat. "So kiss me, Jack."

The Casino grounds were a dangerous place for such things. Ironically, that made them safe, too. Here, he wouldn't forget himself. Here, she could have the ideal, chivalric sort of kiss she'd probably summoned in her maiden's imagination.

Without responding to her request, Jack drew her closer to the trunk of the nearest tree. He used both hands to bring her mouth to the perfect angle for exploration.

"Ready?" he asked.

Her brown eyes were alight and her lips were curved into a slight smile. "I was ready on Saturday at the museum."

He laughed. "Well, then . . ."

He brushed his mouth against hers once, then twice, and finally settled in with more intent than he had on Saturday.

Damn, but she felt good. But Jack knew he had to end it before he frightened her.

"More, Jack," she murmured when he drew back. "There has to be more."

There was, but her almost duke should be the man to awaken her to that.

"Please," she added.

Such a simple word, and one he couldn't fight against.

"Open your mouth for me," he said against her lips.

She did as asked, and he tasted her. She made a surprised little sound, but she didn't push him away. In fact, she clutched at him. She tasted so sweet that he could have stayed until sundown.

The longer he kissed her, the more she relaxed into him, and the more he wanted her. He could imagine Caroline in his bed, night after night, year after year. But that privilege was also destined for the almost duke.

Jack backed off, and Caroline steadied herself against the tree trunk they'd somehow ended up leaning against.

He drew a ragged breath and tried to will his heart to stop pounding with absolute hunger.

"Well, then," Caroline said after a drawn-out silence. She stepped away from the tree, straightened her hat, and brushed at her skirts. "Thank you very much for that. It was quite . . . pleasant."

Pleasant? That had been pleasant? What a damnably weak, obnoxious word.

And then Jack realized that not only was Caroline failing to meet his eyes, she couldn't look above his shoes.

Hah! She was as shaken as he.

"Now I'll go find the twins," she said. "I'm sure they're out front in one of the boutiques. They'd much sooner be there than here on the lawns. I'll see you around, Jack."

Jack watched as she walked away in a not-so-straight line.

He'd see her around, all right. And he would kiss her again when he did.

SEVEN

FRIDAY AT NOT QUITE ELEVEN ON A PURPORTEDLY sunny Providence morning, Jack squinted into bluish cigar smoke that hung like fog in Heinrich Krantz's massive brewery office. Somewhere at the far end of the room sat Krantz and his three sons. And no doubt all four of them had cigars clamped between their molars. No one man could produce this level of smoke so early on in the day. But not even this haze could block the smell of hops, barley, and yeast brewing. The sour scent was perfume to Jack.

Next to Jack stood Gustav Muller, Jack's brewmaster from Liberty Brewery, in Philadelphia. Wiry, temperamental Gus was also Jack's brewing mentor and the reason Jack had taken to the beer industry with such passion. Gus knew beer better than anyone else, and Jack knew business well enough that he hadn't been bested yet. He was sure that together they could wrap up the East Coast beer market as others were doing in the Midwest.

He'd asked Gus to join him this morning because the older man could speak the same language as Krantz in more ways than one. In exchange for Gus's help in closing the deal, Jack had promised him a small ownership percentage in Krantz and Sons. Apparently, he'd chosen the right incentive. The brewmaster was ready to spring.

"Steady," Jack said to Gus as they crossed the office's threshold.

Jack and Gus approached a mahogany table that easily seated twenty and was positioned next to broad windows overlooking the brewery's central courtyard. Krantz had built himself a redbrick castle of a business. He looked every inch the aging king in his crimson upholstered chair at the head of the table. His sons, in lesser thrones, were younger echoes of their portly, bearded father.

Jack and Gus reached the table. Jack waited for an invitation to sit.

And waited.

"What does an Irishman know about beer?" Krantz asked once he'd decided to set his cigar in the ashtray in front of him.

"I'm an American, sir," Jack said. "And a New Yorker. Manhattan drinks more beer than Erlich, Ruppert, and their competitors . . . including me . . . can produce. And I'm proud to be drinking and brewing my share."

"*Faugh!* Erlich!" Kranz spat. "*Verräter!* He cares more about his land and his mansions than his brew. He should be stripped of the title of brewery owner."

"One day I intend to do that," Jack said.

After a pause, Krantz laughed. The sound was rusty, probably from limited use.

"You think big," he said.

"Yes." Growing up with Da, it had never occurred to Jack that there was any other option.

"Sit down," Krantz commanded.

Jack and Gus took their seats opposite the Krantz sons.

"You see those boys?" Krantz asked Jack, who nodded even though the "boys" in question had to be in their forties.

"If even one of them put in a minute more than I had asked, you would not be sitting here. But that one," Krantz said, pointing at the son opposite Jack, "had to be a professor. And Friedrich in the middle, a poet." He shook his head with disgust. "A *poet*."

Krantz didn't even mention the third son, who apparently had done worse than a poet in his father's eyes. None of his sons looked to be disappointed with themselves, though.

Jack understood the need to move from beneath a parent's shadow. He could have stuck with Da, but then he'd have never had the knowledge he could make it on his own. Easy words from a millionaire's son, he supposed.

"The only thing they like that I do is cigars. And so I will sell this place, but only to someone who can prove they know *der arsch* from a drinkable lager," Krantz said.

Jack didn't need Gus to translate that.

"What will it take to prove it to you?" Jack asked.

The brewery owner pointed at Gus. "That is your brewmaster, yes?"

"Yes."

"Send him away."

This would be the easiest damn money Gus had ever made. He'd get his percentage for a trip from Philadelphia to Providence.

"Gus?" Jack asked.

To Gus's credit, he didn't hesitate. He simply rose and left. Gus trusted him, as he should. Jack would come through.

After Gus had departed, Jack asked, "And now that Gus is gone?"

"You will work for me," Krantz said. "You will shovel

der dünger in the delivery stables, build fires for the coopers, and then move on to the beer . . . when I decide you should."

"You understand that I own three breweries?"

"But not mine."

The man had a point.

"Until August, you will have my Mondays and Tuesdays," Jack said. "The rest of the week I need to make money."

Krantz laughed. "Good. Because if you succeed here, the price will be high."

"You have no idea how high," his son Friedrich added.

Jack suspected Friedrich wasn't referring to money.

"Report to the stables at four-thirty Monday morning," the elder Krantz said.

Four-thirty. Jack nearly winced. He'd forgotten how early the day started when delivering beer. Not that he'd ever done it, but he'd seen his brewery schedules often enough. He'd have to take the Sunday night boat to Providence instead of the Monday morning. But that, too, was a small inconvenience if it landed him this place.

"I'll be there," Jack said.

"Good luck," Friedrich Krantz replied.

But Jack didn't need luck. He had determination.

Caroline slogged her way through hip-deep seawater at Bailey's Beach. The sun shone down with a determined relentlessness and the pull of even the low, rolling ocean swells sucked the sand from beneath her slipper-shod feet. No matter how poised a young woman might be, no dignity could be maintained when wearing heavy navy blue wool while attempting to enjoy the waves.

She plucked her skirt away from the ankle-length white cotton drawers that covered black silk stockings encasing her legs. Clearly, the only swimming she was to enjoy was that of swimming in fabric. She almost wished she had used the headache excuse that Amelia and Helen had summoned. Mama didn't think it was odd that the twins had matching headaches. Caroline doubted Mama would give her the same latitude.

Caroline glanced ahead to Harriet Vandermeulen, who was reaching shore well ahead of her. Not only was lucky Harriet allowed to wear knickerbockers while bicycling, but her bathing costume was a non-heat-trapping pearl gray and shorter in length.

"Wait for me," Caroline called.

Harriet turned back and waved Caroline on. "No time! The noon flag is up, and the beach will soon be the gentlemen's. Hurry!"

Caroline had heard it whispered that sometimes the men swam *au naturel* on Fridays. She was probably doomed to perdition for being envious of their freedom, but that did not reduce her envy.

She picked up her pace, though. Caroline preferred the marble nudes she'd managed to catch glimpses of while in Paris at the Louvre Museum to the thought of seeing, say, Harriet's brother in the same state. There were certain things a girl simply did not need to know.

Harriet looked back once more, giving Caroline a clearly challenging smile. "Come on! Last one off the beach must dance with Gordy Bullard twice at the next dance!"

The other girls on the beach giggled and began to hurry toward the triangular pavilion that held the families' individual bathhouses. Clumsy Gordy had flattened more than a few toes already this summer.

Harriet shot across the sand. Her athletic gait suited her far better than the mincing steps she took when gentlemen were present. Right then, she was the rambunctious friend Caroline recalled—and missed—from childhood.

They had all changed. Even Caroline had not been immune.

Grabbing on to some of that long-lost joy, Caroline lifted her skirt to nearly her knees and began to run.

"Unfair! We should have all started in the water," she called.

But Harriet didn't reply. She had reached the building. Breathless and laughing, Caroline pulled up to the rear of the group of young ladies. Harriet was waiting for her.

"Don't leave without talking to me. We need a moment alone," Harriet said in a quiet voice.

Caroline nodded and then made her way to her family's bathhouse, so noted with Papa's initials painted on the door. Ten minutes later, Caroline was dry and pounds lighter in organdy as opposed to wool. Annie, who was already becoming more adept at clothing changes, was busy draping the wet swim costume over a wooden rack for transport home when Caroline exited the bathhouse. She headed toward the drive leading back to Bellevue Avenue, where the carriages and drivers awaited. As did Harriet.

Though she was too bright and sunny to lurk, Harriet was doing a fine imitation of it. While all the other young ladies were waiting for their carriages to pull up along the drive, Harriet stuck close to the shrubbery. Gone was any hint of the hoyden in her. She looked quite angelic in her petal pink dress and hat with a fat clutch of silken white roses pinned to the ribbon at its crown.

Caroline joined Harriet next to a dark green rhododendron bush.

"I have a secret to share," Harriet said. "Promise not to tell anyone."

Caroline didn't answer, hoping the conversation would stop there. She had secrets enough of her own to keep track of without adding in Harriet's.

Harriet, however, forged on.

"I'm going to get married before Christmas," she announced.

"That's wonderful," Caroline replied with what she hoped was an appropriate level of excitement. In public she tried to keep her current poor opinion of marriage to herself. "Who has proposed?"

"No one, yet. But I have decided on the date and I even know the man. I plan to marry Jack Culhane."

Caroline was certain she couldn't have heard that correctly. "Jack?"

"Yes."

"The Jack who is my brother's best friend?"

"Well, of course," Harriet replied while adjusting her white silk gloves.

From the time they'd been little, Caroline had felt as though Harriet had somehow been able to sense—and grab—what Caroline most wanted. When it had been the pinto hobbyhorse in Caroline's nursery, that had been one thing. Jack was another matter altogether. However, any reaction other than mild curiosity would only heighten Harriet's fervor. She had always been fiercely competitive. Right until this moment, Caroline had liked that about her.

"I don't believe Jack's the marrying kind," Caroline said with a slight shrug.

Harriet laughed. "*All* men are the marrying kind. Well, most. My Uncle Nathaniel is a confirmed bachelor, but Mother says he had his heart broken when quite young." Her blue eyes widened. "Has Jack had his heart broken? Has Eddie said something to you?"

"Jack's heart is intact," Caroline replied. "Possibly even untouched. The only thing I've seen him in love with is beer."

"Beer? Are you saying he overimbibes?"

"No, he owns breweries. He loves buying them and talking about them and plotting how to own more. You knew that, didn't you?"

Harriet looked somewhat confused. "No, I don't believe I did." Then she brightened and said, "But it's no matter. When he marries me, he won't have to work anymore."

"Harriet, he doesn't have to work now. He *likes* to work," Caroline replied.

Her friend laughed. "You've always had the oddest sense of humor."

Caroline didn't recall making a jest, but she had more pressing matters to pursue. "If you don't know how important business is to Jack, how do you know him well enough to be certain you want to marry him?"

"I can learn the details after we're married. I know he's a hero. My mother showed me the article in the newspaper on Tuesday. That made her quite happy. But all I really need to know is that he's the best candidate available for a winter wedding. And I will be married this year," she said with a scary amount of determination.

Caroline was speechless. When, exactly, had Harriet turned into a Mama-in-training?

"Besides, Jack needs me," Harriet said. "He has potential, but with his family roots, he'll never quite be one of us unless married to one of us. So, it's perfect. . . . He can benefit from my family's social connections, and I will get my winter wedding."

"This all sounds gloriously romantic," Caroline replied, unable to rein in her sarcasm.

Harriet didn't pick up on it, though. "Oh, it will be. I plan to reserve St. Thomas's for the fifteenth of December. I shall carry white roses with holly. The church will be filled with pine boughs bound in white ribbons, and the snow will be fresh outside."

"If there's no snow, will the wedding be called off?"

Harriet laughed, but again Caroline hadn't been joking.

"Of course there will be snow."

Thus spoke the girl who had always claimed the pinto hobbyhorse.

Caroline checked the carriages and was relieved to see Mrs. Longhorne's near the front.

"It's time for me to leave," she told Harriet.

"I'll see you at the polo field this afternoon, then?"

"Of course," Caroline replied. With luck, Jack would be there and at least she could share his holly-bedecked fate with him.

Caroline had just stepped though the front door of Villa Blanca when one of the Longhornes' liveried footmen ushered her to the Blue Seaside Salon. She gave the dining room a longing look as they passed it by. A small nibble would have been nice, and a real meal, even better.

But her food yearning left when she entered the Blue Seaside Salon. A storm of sorts must have blown through here while she'd been wading in the chilly water at Bailey's Beach. The room was bare of all decorations. The curio shelves and Chippendale secretary now held books and sheaves of papers instead of the porcelains and pretty glass pieces that had been there this morning. Mama and Mrs. Longhorne had set up a war room.

"You wished to see me?" Caroline asked the two women who stood shoulder-to-shoulder at a tall library table recently deposited square in the middle of the room. On the table's surface sat mounds of heavy velvet in various crimson hues.

"Yes. Sit, dear," Mama instructed with an absent flick of her hand.

Caroline opted for the sofa with the view of the lawn

and the ocean. Something more was out there today. Not far from the house, Amelia and Helen stood squinting up in Caroline's general direction. Neither girl looked as though she planned to come inside anytime soon. Their parasols and a small heap of books sat beside a blanket under a nearby elm, and Pomeroy was out there, farther from Mama than Caroline had ever seen him. This was odd. They would not linger outside unless a calamity was taking place indoors. The girls must know what was about to happen to Caroline.

Mama stopped scowling at the velvet and focused on Caroline. "As you know, I let your last governess go due to the unfortunate events in England last summer."

Miss Delbert's departure had also been unfortunate. She'd been fond of whiskey in her tea. After a few cups, she'd been very agreeable, which had made Caroline's various campaigns, over the years, not to wed a duke much easier to plan and execute.

"Yes, Mama."

"And then the winter season in New York left me too busy to properly choose a new governess for you, but the job is finally done. You will begin educational hours with Miss Peek-Jacobs immediately."

"Educational hours?" Caroline knew her mother could not be referring to more study of the classics. She could not possibly be that lucky.

"Your deportment is perfect, when you choose to let it be. You can converse on any topic a young lady should embrace, but Mrs. Longhorne and I agree that there are still certain lacks." Mama pushed aside the velvet and smacked her hand upon a fat book with a red leather cover. "Caroline, *this* is the book of your future."

Even from a distance away, she could recognize her fate. The book was *Debrett's Peerage*. She'd seen it before, and the sole thing in it that had amused her had been the advertisements.

"One day, you will be included in the pages of this book, but only if you impress Lord Bremerton with your depth of knowledge about those already here," Mama said. "Miss Peek-Jones—"

"I thought you said her name was Peek-Jacobs?" Caroline asked.

"Whatever," her mother replied. "What is important is that she joins us from the house of a marquess. She knows this book cover-to-cover, and the people who matter, too. By June thirtieth, you will be ready to meet Bremerton."

Caroline rose and joined her mother and Mrs. Longhorne. She planned to address the book, but in good time.

"What are the velvets for?" she asked first.

"To redo the draperies in Rosemeade's Grand Salon," Mama replied.

"Is the plan to match them to *Debrett's*?"

"And if it were?" Mama asked in response. "It is our goal to make all things conducive to a marriage proposal. Mrs. Longhorne did so in creating Villa Blanca, and Esmé is now a *contessa*. But as it happens, I have chosen the crimson to bring a royal aura to Rosemeade. Every element must convince Lord Bremerton that one day you will do honor to the title of Duchess of Endsleigh."

Mrs. Longhorne rubbed her hands together. "Imagine! Caroline, Duchess of Endsleigh. It sounds so very right!"

"It is what I raised her for," Mama said firmly.

"So where is this Miss Peek-Jacobs?" Caroline asked since she preferred not to contemplate how she had been trained in the manner of a prize show pony.

Riccardi, the Longhorne butler, who had been standing in the doorway, turned and left at Mrs. Longhorne's command.

"She will be here shortly," Mama replied.

Caroline said, "If you don't mind?" to her mother before flipping open *Debrett's*. "Oh dear," she murmured.

"What?" Mama asked.

"This is the 1890 edition. Can you imagine how many dukes, marquesses, and earls have gone to their eternal reward since then?"

"This is serious business, Caroline," her mother said sternly.

Caroline was working up an expression of contrition that might pass for heartfelt when Miss Peek-Jacobs arrived. At first sight, Caroline knew this woman was no Miss Delbert who might be plied with a few cups of extra-medicinal tea.

Miss Peek-Jacobs was tall and solid, with iron gray hair and a set to her jawline that was not just firm but quite aggressive. She wore a somber black uniform that added to her stern appearance. While Caroline could not be certain, she would guess that Miss Peek-Jacobs was past her thirties but not yet to Mama's age.

Mama was looking on her newest employee with great approval. "Miss Peek-Jacobs, this—"

"I prefer to be called simply Peek."

Mama's head rocked a bit, making the blue feathered ornament in her hair bounce. The shock of actually having been interrupted by a servant had to be great.

"—this is my daughter, Caroline," Mama said, neatly ignoring the interruption. Miss Peek might be intimidating, but in the battle for dominance, Mama always won.

"Hello, Miss Peek," Caroline said.

"Just Peek, if you please," the governess said in a brisk tone. "I see you are making yourself familiar with *De-*

brett's. Please tell me what you know of the Table of Precedence."

"That the queen trumps?"

Peek's thick brows nearly met above her nose as she frowned. "If by trumps you mean Her Royal Highness takes precedence over all, yes. But will a viscount's eldest son take precedence over a Privy Councillor?"

Caroline held even odds on getting the question right, but there was no point in guessing. She would be snagged up on the next question or the one after that.

"I have no idea," she replied.

"You will by the time the sun sets today. And you will also know how to seat Knights of the Garter, the Thistle, and the Star of India, *and* who takes precedence among the Bishops of Bath, London, and Durham. In short, you will see the Table of Precedence in your sleep." Peek turned her attention to Mama, who at least was not gaping, as Mrs. Longhorne was. "Your daughter has much work to do and little time in which to see it done. I hope she is bright enough."

"I passed the entrance examinations for Oxford and Yale," Caroline replied. "And I am also capable of speaking for myself without my mother's aid."

Peek's mouth twitched at the corners. Caroline opted to believe that had been a smile.

"I see," the governess said. "Have you had luncheon, or must you eat before you begin your work?"

"With some chocolate cake, I can begin now," Caroline replied.

"Good enough, then," Peek said. "Chocolate cake it is."

The governess looked to Mama, who was clearly trying to come up with a way to forbid chocolate cake and yet have Caroline start to work. But sometimes a girl could have her cake . . . even if it was washed down with a flood of peers, barons, and knights, too.

* * *

Jack had never seen the appeal of Newport. He'd visited often with Eddie and other friends, but the fierce competition to spend money that gripped this town had never interested him. He'd much rather earn it. Tonight, though, Jack's opinion regarding Newport was shifting.

As he walked the lawns of The Reefs with Flora under a waning moon, he had to admit that when he ignored all of the poor attitudes and excesses, the place was beautiful. It stood a world apart from the noise and elbow-to-elbow existence of city life. He supposed a few months spent here while wrapping up the Providence purchase wouldn't be too painful.

"I like having you here," Flora said as they stood looking out over the blackness of the ocean. "I lost the letter I received from you when you were still a young boy, talking about your studies and sporting events."

"I should have written back more," Jack said. "It's my fault."

"You were busy growing up and then busy being a man," Flora replied. "I didn't take the silence as an affront."

"And I'm here now," he said as he offered her his arm.

Laughing, she took it. "Yes, you are."

They strolled on. Music and laughter drifted to them, probably from the Forty Steps, north along the Cliff Walk, where the local servants gathered to socialize some evenings.

"You know, Jack, you could stay with me while you get the house on Touro Park put together," Flora said.

He glanced down at her, but he couldn't read the subtleties of her expression in the moonlight.

"That's a kind offer, but the house is more habitable

than a lot of places I've been," he said. "And in any case, I learned today that I'll need to spend a couple of days a week in Providence. I wouldn't want to disrupt you."

"I like disruptions. And I am really asking you to stay for my sake," she said.

"I'm saying no for the same reason," he replied. "People talk. Around here, they do little else. If you're in the market to marry again and you have me as a guest, you'll ruin your chances."

"First, I don't care what people say. I never have and never will. Second, I'll never marry again. Why should I?"

"The usual reasons?" Jack asked.

"Such as?"

The silkily dangerous tone to Flora's voice let him know he'd overstepped.

"You don't usually see this many stars when the sky is so hazy," he said, seeking a change of topic.

Flora gently squeezed his arm in warning.

"Such as?" she repeated.

"Security?" he ventured.

"Clem owned two gold mines, which I inherited, as well as a house on Nob Hill in San Francisco and a town house within a stone's throw of the Marlborough House in London. I must have failed to mention them to you."

Jack laughed. "You did."

They walked on until they reached the low fieldstone wall that separated The Reefs from its neighboring cottage. Jack decided to risk another question. "But what about children?"

"If I were going to have them, I would by now," Flora replied. "I am not childless from lack of effort."

"I believe that's enough information."

Her laughter joined the party noises. "I have embarrassed you. But you shouldn't have asked if you weren't prepared to hear the answer."

"True."

"So stay with me a few weeks. Let's play at being the family we could have been," Flora said.

"I can't."

"Can't . . . That's a word I have almost never heard you use. Why, can't?"

"It's difficult to explain," Jack said. All he knew was that if he could avoid it, he didn't plan to annoy Agnes Maxwell any more than necessary. Staying under Flora's roof would make him a pariah to Agnes. He couldn't let that happen.

"I have my guesses," Flora replied.

Jack had been about to ask what those guesses were when the sight of a silhouette moving toward them from across the neighboring lawn distracted him. The figure was female, but other than that, he couldn't distinguish details.

"I think we're about to meet your neighbor," he said to Flora.

"No one is in residence," Flora replied.

The woman halted about twenty yards away.

"Flora, is that you?" she called.

Jack knew that voice—slightly husky, as though just waking.

"Caroline, what are you doing?" he called in response.

She started in their direction. "Oh, Jack, it's just you. I thought perhaps Flora had a gentleman caller."

Caroline had reached the stone wall, which came about to her waist. "I was walking the Cliff Walk when it occurred to me I must be near your cottage, Flora. Since your neighbor's wall is so obligingly low, I decided to take advantage and see if I could get a peek of your grounds."

"Come on over," Flora said.

"I'd be happy to," Caroline replied.

Jack, however, wasn't ready for a repeat of the conversation on the way to the Casino. Flora and Caroline had the potential to be an unholy alliance, at least as it pertained to him.

"Shouldn't you be at a ball or something?" Jack asked Caroline.

"I pled exhaustion and stayed at Villa Blanca," she said before grasping her skirts in apparent preparation to hop the wall. "Mama and the girls won't be back for hours yet."

"Help her, Jack," Flora directed.

"I can do it myself," Caroline replied before he could even move.

Flora let go of his arm and nudged him forward. "A gentleman would help in any case."

"Take the help or we'll both be lectured," Jack said to Caroline.

"Fine."

Jack crossed the wall, which wasn't more than three feet. He scooped Caroline up in his arms. She smelled pretty, like flowers and sunshine. Some unthinking part of him wanted to hold her. But the thinking part quickly deposited her on the other side of the wall. She landed well, considering his haste.

"Thank you," she said as he hopped back over.

"I take it you're out and about without your mother's permission?" he asked.

"The matter wasn't discussed," she replied before turning her attention away. "Flora, how was your tennis lesson?"

"Very enjoyable, thank you," Flora replied. "I seem to

have some aptitude, not that I'm sure what I will do with it. One can play tennis only so much." She extended her arm to Caroline. "Come walk toward the house with me and tell me what you have been doing since yesterday morning."

Caroline linked arms with her.

"I have been doing almost everything a proper heiress should," she said, giving Jack a single glance over her shoulder before the two women started walking.

Jack followed after them, sure in the knowledge that this was to be like the ride to the Casino, when he'd been trapped in a feminine world he'd found as frustrating as he had intriguing.

"Yesterday, after the Casino, I stopped at Villa Blanca to change outfits," Caroline was saying to Flora. "Then I attended a tea at Miss Theresa Milburn's, followed by another clothing change and a concert at Fairview. From there, it was Villa Blanca to change yet again, and then on to supper at the Allen home. Then—"

"Villa Blanca to change?" Flora asked.

Caroline laughed. "Yes. And finally to a small dance in honor of Miss Courtney Johnston's eighteenth birthday."

"All that activity and a veritable mountain of clothing," Flora said. "Do you ever get time to yourself?"

"Only when I steal it," Caroline replied. "And today was breakfast with Mama and Mrs. Longhorne and then off to Bailey's Beach for some sea air. When I returned to Villa Blanca, Mama had a surprise for me . . . a new governess."

"A governess?" Flora asked. "Are you not too grown for a governess?"

"Yes, at twenty-one, I am. But this new governess is my fault, in a way. If I had been compliant last year and married as my mother had planned, I would now be governess-free, if unhappily wed. Instead, I have Peek. She'll be occupying my mornings. I am glad I learn quickly, because otherwise she'd take my full days."

"What are you learning?"

"Peek is to teach me all I need to know about the English peers' way of life. At this point, that seems to involve memorizing who may walk after whom in a procession, and how many strawberry leaves and pearls may be showing on a marquess's coronet. The answer to the last is three and two, respectively."

Flora laughed. "You might never know when that might come in handy."

"As soon as she marries her almost duke," Jack said.

Caroline stopped and looked back at him. "I'd be careful with that talk of marriage if I were you, Jack. You could be the first to fall."

"What are you talking about?" he asked.

"How do you feel about a winter wedding?"

"I feel that it has nothing to do with me."

"Maybe we should bet on who marries first," Caroline said.

"Heiresses do not gamble."

Caroline laughed. "Who told you that?"

Flora released Caroline's arm. "Well, here we are, almost back at the cottage." She feigned a yawn. "I've had a long day. Jack, may I trust you to see Caroline safely back to the Longhornes'?"

"Of course, but let me walk you to your door," he said.

"I doubt I'll be waylaid by thieves and brigands between here and there. I'll leave you two to do your arguing . . . or your courting . . . all on your own."

Courting? If this was courting, Jack would be a bachelor for life.

EIGHT

CAROLINE FLOATED ON A WAVE OF EXCITEMENT AS intoxicating as her favorite champagne. She had knocked tough Jack off-balance again, and she'd accomplished that only a few times in her life. She breathed in the sweet night air—and her happiness—as Jack watched Flora make her way to her summer cottage.

Caroline might not fully understand the friendship those two shared, but she appreciated Jack's loyalty toward Flora. And even his protectiveness, though Caroline had never met a woman more capable of guiding her own affairs—likely even literally—than Mrs. Willoughby.

Flora slipped inside The Reefs. Now it was just the two of them.

Caroline said the first thing that came to mind. "Have you missed me, Jack?"

He stood silent for a moment. "It's been less than two days since we last saw each other."

"True, but that doesn't answer the question I asked."

He held out his arm. "Let's get you back to Villa Blanca before you're caught wandering in the night by your hawk of a mother."

She took his arm and nearly shivered at the contact. Perhaps she'd been too hasty this morning when thinking she preferred chilly marble nudes over warm, flesh-and-sinew men. Or at least this particular man. But if she continued to think of Jack in such terms, she would knock herself off-balance.

"I was not wandering," she said firmly. "I was taking an invigorating walk. And you still have not answered my question. Have you missed me?"

He laughed. "You should be a lawyer. You're relentless."

"I will consider that a compliment."

"It was meant as one, though I'd rather see that relentlessness turned on someone other than me."

"But I can only share it with you. I would frighten others."

"You sound as though you enjoy that thought," he said.

The humor in his voice made her smile.

"I do. Very much," she replied as they headed back to the pathway that threaded along the coastline toward Villa Blanca. "You have no idea how wonderful it is to be myself . . . not to have to remember that a well-behaved heiress must not possess a contentious bone in her body. Or that a well-behaved heiress must always defer to the gentleman. His preferences must become hers."

"What are your preferences?"

Other than when it came to her choice of sugar or not at a tea, she couldn't recall having been asked that question. Caroline considered her list.

"French champagne, Greek philosophers, and American men. And I am not alone in the preference for American men," she added.

"Meaning?"

"I had a most informative morning with Harriet Vandermeulen. It seems she has you scheduled as the groom in a December wedding."

His pace did not falter. "Me?"

"Yes, you. And as you know, Harriet can be quite relentless, too."

"She'll have to be more than relentless. It will take a gun aimed at me to get me to the altar."

"I would not discount the possibility," she replied. "Harriet has made up her mind. She has already selected the flowers, the church, and the date. Being quite driven in her goal, perhaps she has selected a gun, as well."

Caroline had tried to keep her voice light, but she knew she'd failed.

Jack stopped. "I sense that Harriet's plans annoy you as much as they amuse me. Why is that, Caroline?"

She tensed. She could hardly admit the truth—that she was in love with him. Much as she preferred honesty, saying those words to Jack Culhane would have the same effect on her dreams of romance as flinging herself off the cliff upon which they now stood.

She urged him along in their walk. "Perhaps I find it wrong-headed that she should be fighting for marriage as strongly as I fight against it. She doesn't know you beyond the fact that you're a minor hero, and yet she wants to spend her life with you. It's madness."

He laughed. "Tangled up in there somewhere is a blow to my pride . . . and I'm not talking about the minor hero comment. I'm not in the mood to untangle, though. It's exercise enough to keep pace with you."

Caroline realized she'd begun to march at a very soldierly clip. She slowed, even if Jack had not been referring to her gait. Now that her frustration had been freed, she was in no hurry to return to Villa Blanca.

"There was no insult intended, just amazement at young women such as Harriet who are so fixed on marriage," she said.

"Why amazement? It is what she was raised to expect."

"Then it is time for Harriet to expand her expectations."

"Not all women have your talent for individuality, Caroline. And many men will find that good news."

He was smiling. She knew that without looking at him. And she would not look at him.

In the distance to her left stood the massive cottage being erected by Mr. Cornelius Vanderbilt II. It sat as dark and silent as the stones being used to create it. As she and Jack walked past, the music tumbling over the air from the Forty Steps became more distinct. The song was a merry jig, enviably far from the elegant Newport-style quadrille that Mama believed was the sole acceptable dance for Caroline.

"This music reminds me of my father," Jack said. "Were he to come to Newport, which he won't because he considers it a colossal waste of time, he'd be here, listening."

"I have never met your father," Caroline commented as they rounded the bend and the celebration came into view.

"Da has no use for society."

The fiddlers had just finished up the jig. Couples and groups of giggling females stood in the light cast by a dozen and more lanterns. In some ways, the scene was not so different from the parties she attended. But the atmosphere seemed happier . . . at least to Caroline.

She slowed even more as the music resumed. The musicians had chosen a sweeping and dreamy waltz.

"Let's watch," she said to Jack.

Jack stopped. Caroline could have released his arm and stepped away, but she didn't. She wanted to dance. However, while her advanced individuality would permit stealing the occasional kiss, it would not brook asking for a waltz. As wrong-headed as that might be, Jack would have to ask her. And as wrong-headed as *he* could be, the blasted man probably never would.

* * *

Jack should have known that Caroline was a romantic.
After all, in her parents' conservatory she had talked
about a burning, forever-type passion. Those had been
the words of a romantic, even if he'd chosen not to listen
too carefully.

"The music is lovely," Caroline said. Her voice, of
course, was romantically wistful as she swayed in time
to the melody.

Jack believed in maintaining a distance from romantics. They were dangerous. Male or female, romantics
committed rash acts in the name of whatever their particular passion might be. And he'd considered Caroline
dangerous enough already.

He gave her a slightly bored-sounding "it's decent"
that should have stopped her cold.

"If you think it's just decent, you need to develop your
ear," Caroline said. "Perhaps if you didn't bolt from ball-
rooms as though the house was about to come tumbling
down, you'd have a greater appreciation."

"I have appreciation enough."

"If you say so," she replied in the same slightly bored
tone he'd tried out on her.

When he stayed silent, she began humming along with
the tune. Jack tried to disregard her, but it was impossible. He apparently harbored a soft spot for this particular romantic.

"Would you like to dance?" he finally asked.

"Well, of course I would. What woman would not?"

"A practical one," he said.

"Practicality and a moonlit night do not mix," she said
as he took her in his arms. "And what is so impractical
about a dance?"

"Everything."

She hushed him. "Just dance. We'll be practical later."

Her idea had merit, and one dance would not make him into a romantic.

Then one waltz became two.

Jack liked the feel of her narrow waist beneath his hand and the way her warmth made him want to pull her closer. He assured himself that this did not make him a romantic. He was a man with a pulse.

The musicians stopped. Caroline drew a sharp breath.

"It's Peek," she said.

"Who?"

"Peek. My governess. Did you not listen when Flora and I were talking?"

"As little as humanly possible."

They had danced closer to the gathering, but not so close as to be part of it. He focused his attention on the women in the group. "Which one is she?"

"The tallest one on the fringes of the crowd," she said in a low voice.

"The one who just turned this way?" Jack asked.

"Yes," Caroline said before ducking behind him. When he tried to turn to face her, she whispered, "Stay where you are. Is she coming this way?"

"Yes."

Caroline held on to the back of his jacket. "We must leave. This is not the time or place to determine if she's my friend or foe."

He took a step toward the group, intending to bypass them and get back on the Cliff Walk.

"Not that way," Caroline said. "If she hasn't seen me yet, I don't want her to."

That left them a mad dash across the grounds of the Robert Goelet cottage. And if they were caught, Caroline would have greater problems than a nosy governess.

"Hel-loo?" called a crisp British voice. "Might I have a word with you, sir and madam?"

"Now!" Caroline whispered.

Jack doubted her sanity, but that was all the more reason to humor her. He took her hand and they began a dimly lit march across the lawn.

"Sir? Really, sir, you are quite exasperating me!" called the governess Peek, who had also opted for the overland route.

"Disregard," Caroline commanded Jack. "And more quickly, please."

He lengthened his stride, and she broke into a run.

"This is absurd!" Peek called. "Miss Maxwell, if that is you, I shall know the moment I return to Villa Blanca."

But Peek gave up the chase.

"This way," Jack said.

They cut around to the side of the house facing inland. No light shone from inside the brick-and-shingle structure. Newport's idle rich didn't tend to be all that idle. The Goelets were either at the same ball as Caroline's mother or abroad.

And Caroline was almost breathless.

"Are you feeling faint?" he asked.

"If I had the time to be, yes. Men should have to run in corsets, too," she replied between ragged breaths. But for all that, she seemed cheerful.

"Your only chance to avoid this Peek person is to go toward the carriage house," he said. "There has to be a gate leading onto Narragansett Avenue. Head to the Cliff Walk. You won't make it to Villa Blanca before Peek if you try to follow the streets. I'll keep her occupied."

"How?"

"With words."

Caroline gave him a hard-and-fast hug. "Thank you!" And then she was gone.

Jack quickly returned to the gathering at the top of the Forty Steps. Peek had cornered Caroline's maid. Jack wasn't worried. The little redhead had already struck him as independent enough to hold her own in any skirmish.

"Good evening," he said to Peek once he'd closed the gap between them. "Were you calling to me a few minutes ago?"

"I was," she replied in a disapproving tone.

"I am sorry I didn't acknowledge you immediately, but it was a matter of discretion, ma'am," he said. "I am sure you can appreciate that."

"I appreciate proper manners far more," Peek responded.

Jack aimed for a courtly bow. "And I indeed apologize. My name is Jack Culhane. May I have the honor of your acquaintance?"

"My name is Miss Peek. I am very recently in the employ of the Maxwell family of New York City and Newport."

"It is a pleasure to meet you, Miss Peek."

She didn't offer a return pleasantry, so Jack kept talking.

"The lady who was with me when you called out is a governess for young Beatrice Goelet. I needed to return my friend to the house before she was seen with me," he said.

"Really?" Peek asked. "And why would that be an issue?"

Caroline's maid coughed repeatedly. When he looked her way, she shook her head, but he couldn't decipher the warning she tried to offer.

"The Goelets do not approve of their servants mixing with their compatriots," he said to Miss Peek. "As a member of a number of the same clubs as the Goelets, I happen to be one. She would lose her position if we were discovered."

"As it should be," Miss Peek sniffed. "Such interactions are unacceptable in any civilized culture."

The iron Peek was not about charm or equality. But Jack had chosen his course and he'd stick to it long enough to give Caroline a running start.

"One cannot fight love, Miss Peek," he said.

"One most certainly can and should. And I highly doubt that a man of your professed social status could love a governess."

"Ah, but she is a very special governess," Jack replied before casting a glance toward the Cliff Walk. Caroline was darting north to Villa Blanca.

"How so, Mr. Culhane?"

He added a dash of status to his tale, since Peek seemed to be a bigger snob than most. "Her family is French nobility, though recently impoverished."

"The French. Feckless lot," Miss Peek said down her long nose. This was not an endearing trait.

Buying time, Jack looked to Caroline's maid. "How about you, miss? Do you believe a man should turn his back on love?"

"Oh, never, Mister Culhane," she said. "It's up to each of us to do everything possible to encourage true love. And if by chance you have a brother, I would be glad to make his acquaintance."

"No brothers, I'm afraid, Miss . . ."

She made a sketch of a curtsey. "Campbell. Annie Campbell. I am lady's maid to Miss Caroline Maxwell. And I know all about you, Mr. Culhane, from that article in the newspaper when you rescued the fishermen. Miss Peek just arrived today. She does not know she is talking to a genuine hero."

In this one instance, he'd happily use his so-called heroism. "Thank you, Miss Campbell."

Jack refocused on Caroline's governess. "Now, Miss Peek, was there some reason in particular you wished to speak to me?"

"I was under the impression that your companion to-night was the young lady under my charge."

"You think Mister Culhane was with Miss Maxwell?" Annie asked. "That's impossible, Miss Peek. Before I left for my evening off, she had me bring her a packet of headache powder and was in her room for the night. She said something about her mind spinning with knights and earls."

"Possibly true," Miss Peek said grudgingly.

"I have no reason to lie. If I did and lost my job, I'd land back home with my parents. That's reason enough for me to be honest. I love my mother and father, but—"

"That will be enough, Miss Campbell," Peek decreed. "I have no interest whatsoever in your familial circumstances. We are conversing solely because I believed I saw Miss Maxwell. But because Mr. Culhane is a gentleman . . ." She trailed off, clearly expressing her skepticism. ". . . I shall take his word that his companion was a governess."

Jack had stretched the conversation as far as he could. "That's generous of you, Miss Peek."

She nodded. "And now I shall commence my evening constitutional as I had planned."

Annie heaved a sigh of relief when Miss Peek headed south. "That was a close call. I think I'll be having a few more of those while working for Miss Maxwell."

Closer to one a night, Jack thought. And he was amused by the idea until an unsettling realization set in. Maybe he was a romantic, too.

On Saturday morning, Caroline's mother used her fork to flick her breakfast about her plate as though the food repelled her. Since Mrs. Longhorne's chef was among the very best, the airy cheese soufflé with accompanying fresh fruit was not the issue. Caroline glanced at Mrs.

Longhorne to see if she might shed some light on Mama's mood, but Mama's friend was doing her best to make no eye contact. Amelia and Helen seemed oblivious to the raincloud over the table, cheerily making short work of their breakfasts.

"We will be having a dinner party here at Villa Blanca on Tuesday," Mama said without showing any of her usual joy over a social event.

"A dinner party sounds quite nice," Caroline replied. Politeness seemed a wise choice.

"Nice?" Mama asked. "There is nothing nice about the situation. Last night at the Royces' ball, I talked with the Carstairs, who will be hosting Lord Bremerton in just a matter of days. Bremerton has asked them to identify Newport's gems of young womanhood, and Lurene Carstairs finds Katherine Royce to be the perfect example. She plans to have a small gathering upon Bremerton's arrival to showcase Katherine. Needless to say, the Royces are jubilant."

Mama picked up her fork and stabbed a strawberry. "I knew I should not have let you stay here last night, Caroline. I am sure that Emmett Royce is sitting down and fattening Katherine's dowry this morning."

"And I am sure Katherine will be very happy," Caroline said, engaging in some wishful thinking that this was to be the end of the Bremerton campaign.

"Katherine's happiness is not my objective," Mama said. "Yours is. In order to unwind this mess, I invited the Carstairs to a dinner party here on Tuesday night. They will meet you, and I expect you to show them that you are the correct choice for Lord Bremerton's wife."

"Of course," Caroline replied. She had always been very clear on Mama's expectations, even if Mama still didn't grasp Caroline's concept of happiness.

"Mildred and I have withdrawn ourselves from all en-

gagements between now and Tuesday," Mama said. "We
will need the time to properly execute this event. While
we are occupied, you three girls will follow your schedules with no deviation." She shot a stern glance across the
table to Caroline. "Especially you."

Since Caroline had already altered her schedule to include an afternoon lecture at the Redwoods Library and
Athenaeum regarding the early monarchs of the Kingdom of Hawaii, she was perfectly happy to comply.

"Yes, Mama," she replied.

"Fine, then," Mama said before finally tucking into
her soufflé, which had begun its downward descent. After
a few bites, she added, "Eddie will be here for the dinner, since your father will not leave the city until the
Conqueror is finished with its engine work. Any other
ship is too slow in your father's eyes. And since Mr.
Longhorne remains in Paris, I will need at least one more
single gentleman at the table."

Mrs. Longhorne looked deflated at the mention of her
husband. Apparently considering his family duty done,
Charles Longhorne had left for Paris on a vacation soon
after daughter Esmé's wedding, almost four years ago.
The vacation appeared to be of the permanent variety.

"I am sure Eddie would appreciate Jack Culhane's
presence," Helen suggested while giving Caroline an
arch look.

"That is out of the question," Mama said.

Mrs. Longhorne perked up. "Agnes, is he not the one
we heard this morning is conducting an affair with the
Goelet governess?"

So Jack had decided to distract dour Peek with a tale of
love? Caroline did her best to hold back a laugh. Still, a
choked sound escaped.

"I am sorry if I shocked you, dear," Mrs. Longhorne
said to her. "That was blunt language in front of three

young ladies, but it is the way of the world. One fancy French *oiseau* flits by, and a man is off to another nest."

"Not *all* men," Mama said. "Your father is quite exemplary, girls."

All three sisters nodded in agreement.

Papa was indeed faithful, unless one viewed his penchant for big game hunting as a substitute for a ladybird. But Mama tolerated tiger and zebra rugs far better than she would a mistress.

Mama took a sip of her tea and then proclaimed, "Jack Culhane, however, is not showing himself to be an exemplary man."

Caroline wanted desperately to argue that statement but knew she couldn't. The less she spoke of Jack, the better the chances of Mama warming to him. Or at least ignoring him.

"Mama, I have seen Miss Beatrice Goelet's governess, and she doesn't seem the type to interest a young man such as Jack Culhane," Helen said.

Caroline wasn't certain why Helen would choose to be helpful, but she was happy that was the case.

"What do you mean?" Mama asked.

"The governess is elderly," Helen said. "I think she must be at least forty . . . *much* older than you."

Everyone at the table was aware that forty had come and gone for Mama. And everyone—including Mama—knew that she turned as soft as butter with a little flattery.

"Yes, well . . ." Mama took another sip of tea before setting down her cup with a resigned sigh. "I suppose if I don't make a place for him, Eddie will just tow him along and upset the numbers. Jack Culhane will do."

Caroline hid a smile. He would do perfectly.

NINE

Tuesday evening, Jack exited the hired coach that had brought him from the harbor to Da's Touro Square house. The old brick villa bordered on bleak, and the sharply pointed wooden fence guarding it didn't help, either. But to Jack's tired eyes, the place looked like paradise. He paid his driver and made his way to the front door.

Wilton, one of the former owner's staff who Jack had kept on, greeted him once he'd stepped inside.

"Good evening, sir. Your father is in residence," the elderly butler/doorman/valet announced. "He is currently in the library."

Jack would have sooner believed that an impostor had wheedled his way into the house than that Da would be in Newport during the workweek. Either way, he headed toward the library. Wilton, who was remarkably spry given his bowed posture, followed Jack down the thread-bare Persian runner that covered an equally scarred floor. The butler somehow reached past Jack to open the door.

There, behind the heavy mahogany desk, was none other than Da. He had a cigar in one hand and tumbler of whiskey in the other. Jack looked away from the cigar.

Cigars now reminded him of Heinrich Krantz, and Krantz was the reason he currently required a two-hour bath and ten-hour sleep. It had been a hot, stinking two days spent shoveling manure, but Jack wasn't about to back down.

"Hello, Da. Having trouble finding something to read?" Jack asked.

Unlike the last time Jack had been in this room, random piles of books now dotted the floor and the shelves stood gap-toothed.

"I was having more trouble finding you," his father replied. "I came in before dawn Sunday and not a soul in this house knew where you were. It's time you hired a personal secretary, or better yet, a minder." His brows rose as he looked more closely at Jack. "I'm thinking you could use one."

Jack sat opposite Da in a deep leather chair. "No doubt. So why are you unshelving the books?"

"Curiosity," he said. "Harry Benton has no love for books, and he has even less love for banks. I'm looking to see if there's money hidden, because sure as I'm breathing, Benton didn't buy these to read."

"Any luck?" Jack asked.

"Not yet," Da replied. "And as long as we're asking questions, would you like to tell me why you reek of dung?"

Jack had cleaned up the best he could before boarding the late afternoon Newport-bound steamer, but he was numb to the scent of manure.

"I spent the past two days mucking out stalls," he said.

Da tipped back his head and laughed. "That's a fine one. Did you lose a bet?"

"No, I'm buying another brewery."

"You have a strange way of going about business, son."

Jack smiled. "I suppose I do."

Da nudged his whiskey glass in Jack's direction. "Drink up. You need it more than I do."

Jack shrugged. "Hard work never killed a man."

"True enough," his father said. "But that's not why you need it."

Taking Da at his word, Jack downed the rest of the whiskey. Its warmth as it made its way to his gut felt damn near life-giving.

"So you're here for a reason, right?" he asked his father.

"Aye," Da said. "Curiosity again. I decided I wanted to see this place, after all."

Jack shook his head. "You're going to have to spin a better tale than that. You might care about money, but you don't care about houses. If you did, you wouldn't be trying to fob this one off on me."

"As it turns out, you won't be needing it. Harriet Vandermeulen's father will be building you a grand place as part of her dowry."

In almost any other circumstance, Jack would have enjoyed his father's grin. But at the moment, he was bone-tired, blistered of hands, and short on a sense of humor. "You're saying that Harriet's father came to talk to you?"

"Aye," Da replied. "He's thinking you two would be a good match, and he wanted me to know that he'd be making it worth your while with houses both in the city and here." He hesitated before adding, "You're well off enough on your own, but falling in love with a rich girl isn't a sin, you know."

"Oh, for . . ." Jack said before trailing off. He rubbed his forehead. A headache was setting in, but more of his father's whiskey would evict it. He'd just have to find which stack of books was hiding the bottle.

Da drew in on his cigar, then exhaled the smoke in a long stream. "It's a rare thing, seeing you without words."

What could he say that Da didn't already know? Jack was a grown man. And he couldn't be bought.

"Where are you hiding the whiskey?" he asked.

Da laughed. "A fine start on talk." He pulled open a desk drawer, reached in, and drew out a bottle. "I'll bear up if there's no money from Benton, so long as I find another bottle or two of this left behind."

Jack stood, took the offered bottle, and poured himself another two fingers of Ireland's finest. He almost had the glass to his mouth when the library door groaned in protest as it swung open.

Jack turned.

"Mister Edward Maxwell," Wilton announced.

Eddie stepped into the room. He was dressed for a formal dinner and looking distinctly unhappy about it. Jack could sympathize.

"Where the hell have you been, Culhane?" Eddie asked.

"I'm assuming you're not speaking to me, boyo," Da said from his seat at the desk.

"Oh, no, sir." Eddie made a hasty bow and then came closer. "It's good to see you, Mister Culhane. I was speaking to . . ." His moustache twitched. "What is that smell?"

"Me," Jack replied.

"And you're not dressed for dinner, either. Get cleaned up or we'll be late," Eddie said.

It wasn't that Jack was averse to the idea of cleanliness, but he didn't need Eddie to tell him what to do. Da was covering that job just fine.

"Late for what?" Jack asked.

"Dinner. In an hour and a half. With my mother and sisters at Villa Blanca."

"I don't think so," Jack said before taking a swallow of whiskey.

"When my mother invites you to dine, you go," Eddie replied. "Otherwise, she has a way of making the punishment for declining to attend painfully worse than the dinner itself."

"Ah, but I wasn't invited."

Da began riffling through the papers on the desk.

"Not so true," he said, holding up an opened envelope. "'Tis right here."

Jack blinked. "You opened my correspondence?"

"I said you're needin' a personal secretary. If you had one of those, I wouldn't be reduced to digging through papers to find where you might be."

"Your father has a point," Eddie said. "Where were you?"

"Working," Jack replied. "And tonight I'm going to rest. I didn't respond to the invitation. Unless you did that, too, Da," he added while throwing a wry look his father's way.

"Of course I didn't," Da replied.

"But I did," Eddie said. "You're committed."

Jack sat. "I am unmoved."

He planned to stay home with whiskey, quiet, and the first food he'd eaten since last night.

"Be a friend, Jack," Eddie said. "They've got Caroline all primped up and are trotting her out to meet Lord Bremerton's hosts. Don't make me watch the boring show alone."

Caroline and boring never happened at the same time. Eddie should have known that. And Jack should have known better than to be tempted by the idea of more time with Caroline. But he was.

Jack swallowed the last of his whiskey and then rose.

"Keep Da company while he takes apart the library," he said to Eddie. "I'll be back downstairs soon."

Caroline loved her mother. She loved her enough to wear heavy, ice blue satin and what felt like pounds of pearls without a word of complaint. And on this hot and humid evening, that was a prodigious amount of love.

Even the open doors from Villa Blanca's Green Seaside Salon to the terrace beyond were providing little relief. A few miles offshore, angry clouds had gathered and a gray wash of rain was meeting the sea. Thunder rumbled. Caroline, who had always terrified her Mama with a love of storms, smiled at the thought of this one. Once it broke, the oppressive atmosphere would lighten.

"Perfection," Mama declared as she gave Caroline one final inspection five minutes before the guests arrived. Helen and Amelia had already passed muster and were whispering to each other on the far side of the room.

"Wonderful. Now may I have a glass of water?" Caroline asked. She felt as though she were cooking under her corset.

"Absolutely not," Mama replied. "What if you spill and mark the satin? You must be flawless."

"Alive and able to speak might be advisable, too," Caroline suggested.

Mama undoubtedly had been about to tell her to watch her words, but Mildred Longhorne entered the room.

Caroline had never seen a dress quite the shade of reddish purple that Mrs. Longhorne had chosen to wear. It reminded her of the grapes that grew wild along Rosemeade's fence line. She hoped they hadn't fallen victims to the recent renovations.

"Did you tell Caroline the news?" Mrs. Longhorne asked Mama.

"What news?" Caroline asked.

It had to be something amazing, for Mrs. Longhorne looked ready to spin in a giddy circle.

"Oh, it's nothing at all," Mama said in a cheerful voice. "Mrs. Longhorne is just pleased to have lobster salad on the menu, when her chef had said there would be none."

Mrs. Longhorne laughed. "Ha! Lobster salad!"

Caroline's mother shot her friend a quelling look. "Have another glass of champagne, Mildred. You seem overexcited."

Lobster salad was an odd passion, Caroline supposed, but she had heard of more peculiar.

A servant bearing a tray of champagne *coupes* stepped forward to oblige Mrs. Longhorne. Caroline's mouth watered. She glanced her mother's way, but Mama shook her head no.

"Do you think champagne does not spot?" her mother asked.

"I think it was created by fairies and will leave only gold dust should it spill," Caroline replied.

Mama's friend took a sip of hers. "Indeed! And it is the drink of a celebration such as this, too!"

"Have more, Mildred," Mama said. She sounded somewhat grim.

Caroline, however, was feeling too sticky to puzzle out why. If she could have no champagne, she demanded air.

"If you'll excuse me?" she asked Mama and Mrs. Longhorne, but did not wait for an answer.

Caroline walked outside and braced her hands on the stone balustrade that marked the terrace's edge. She tried to draw in a deep breath, but that was not an option with her corset pulled almost an inch tighter than usual. Instead, she focused on the horizon. Lightning flashed from cloud to cloud, followed by a sharp split of thunder. A welcome breeze ruffled her hair.

She wished she could escape from the dinner party, slip off her shoes, and walk barefoot across Mrs. Longhorne's impossibly green lawn to greet the storm as it made shore. Of course, Jack would be waiting at the water's edge. He would carry her to a small rowboat. They would slip offshore to his sloop, which he had naturally named the *Caroline*. He would show her the islands of the Caribbean before they explored South America. Once they'd seen their fill, they'd round Tierra del Fuego and head on to the Pacific. She would chronicle their adventures, and finally the newspapers would print something about her other than the supposed cost of the beadwork on her ball gowns.

Caroline sighed at her fantastical turn of mind. Of course, Jack had no sloop that she knew of and he could hardly lift her in this blasted dress, let alone wade into the surf with her. But he'd be at dinner tonight, and that would do. It had to.

"Caroline," Mama called a few minutes later. "You must come inside."

Caroline stepped back into the salon just as the butler announced, "Lord Bremerton and Mr. and Mrs. William and Lurene Carstairs."

Caroline thought she'd misheard, but three people were indeed entering the room. She looked to her mother. Mama refused to meet her eyes. The twins gave her sad faces of apology, and Mrs. Longhorne appeared pleased enough that one might have thought she'd conjured the Englishman from thin air.

Caroline approached the wine-bearing servant and accepted a glass. Her deep first swallow was decidedly unladylike, and her second just as large.

Lobster salad, indeed.

"Lord Bremerton, it's a pleasure to welcome you to Villa Blanca," Mrs. Longhorne was saying.

"Thank you," the Englishman replied in a deep voice. "It was kind of you to add me to your party at the last minute."

Caroline felt compelled to admit to herself that he had a pleasant voice. If she were to be fair, she'd also have to admit that he might be a perfectly pleasant acquaintance, even if she had no desire to marry him. It was entirely possible—and to be hoped—that he would not wish to marry her, either. Fortified by champagne and positive thoughts, she hazarded a look his way.

As it turned out, he was not unattractive. Her girl-friends would declare him sigh-worthy, even if she did not. He was tall, almost as tall as Jack, and certainly better dressed than she'd ever seen Jack. The Englishman's evening clothes fit with a precise elegance, as though he kept a tailor on call around the clock. But Caroline was fonder of Jack's more relaxed appearance.

Bremerton's hair was a sandy color and cut in a longer style than American men currently favored. He was pale, almost as though he never even walked in the sun. And his eyes were a startlingly pale shade, too. From her current distance, she couldn't decide if they were blue or gray.

His gaze settled on her.

Caroline shivered. While a proper heiress was not supposed to admit to having hair on her arms, she could feel hers rising. And not with excitement, either. She had always been a firm believer in instincts, and hers were sounding an alarm. Since running headlong into the downpour that had started would not sit well with her mother, she gave the Englishman a polite smile.

He did not return it. Perhaps that was because he was too occupied taking inventory of her, right down to the pearls sewn onto her dress's bodice. Whatever his opinion was, he kept it well hidden.

Thunder rumbled, but the storm had not yet broken in here. It would, though. Caroline quickly finished the last of her drink and accepted a replacement as Mama and Mrs. Longhorne said hello to Mr. and Mrs. Carstairs. Then Mama turned her attention to Lord Bremerton.

"Is there anything less formal than Lord Bremerton that we may call you?" she asked.

He stopped sizing up Caroline.

"You may call me sir," he said to her mother.

A brief silence fell, broken when the Carstairs began laughing. Mama and Mrs. Longhorne joined in, though they didn't look as though they had any idea what might be funny.

"Our guest has a deliciously dry sense of humor," Lurene Carstairs said.

Bremerton did not smile.

"My given name is Marcus," he said. "But I prefer to be addressed as Bremerton when I am among my friends."

Mama nodded happily, but Caroline had read his distant expression and heard his words for what they were. Other than the Carstairs, the Englishman did not count anyone in this room among his friends. Nor did he look interested in changing that situation, which was just fine. Caroline had made up her mind, too. Bremerton would not be in her life at all.

"Did you really have to give the butler your full name?" Eddie asked Jack as they stood just outside Villa Blanca's dining room. "We're late as it is."

"The only reason we're late is because you got caught up in the money search with my father," Jack pointed out.

"It was pouring. No point in leaving your house until it let up," Eddie replied. "And I now have a two hundred dollar finder's fee from your father. Not bad for an hour's work."

The money should have been Wilton's, who was going to have to put the library back in order now that the men had found the cache Da had suspected was there. Jack would make up for that in Wilton's next pay. Da, who could be tight-fisted, would not think of it.

"Mr. Edward Maxwell and Mr. John William Anthony Patrick Xavier Culhane," the butler announced to the other guests, who were readying to take their seats.

"He got it out in one breath," Jack said to Eddie as they stepped into the room. "Impressive."

"Better than most," Eddie replied.

They made their way to the long dining table, an over-fancy work of art that appeared to have been inlaid with alabaster and ebony. The south end of it had been laden with silver, crystal, and china for the small dinner party. Helen and Amelia, who hovered nervously near Bill and Lurene Carstairs, looked as though they wanted to disappear. Mildred Longhorne was as fidgety as usual, and Agnes Maxwell as commanding. But Caroline . . . she was breathtaking in a pale blue dress. Her dark hair was piled high, and around her throat was a pearl choker. Jack imagined himself removing it and tasting the skin beneath.

Eddie nudged him forward. Jack tried to refocus, but looking away from Caroline was no easy task. She was as electric as the storm that had just passed overhead. At the moment, she was speaking to a man Jack didn't recognize. The gentleman's back was to him, or Jack would have warned him off. Caroline appeared ready to hurl a thunderbolt his way.

Eddie and he moved on to greet Eddie's mother, who gave Jack the cross frown she seemed to save just for him. Mrs. Longhorne was far less annoyed by his presence.

"Come meet our guest of honor," she said, urging them in Caroline's direction.

"If you don't mind my interrupting, sir?" she said to the man with Caroline. "I would like to introduce you to Caroline's brother, Edward, and the Maxwells' family friend, Jack Culhane. Gentlemen, this is Lord Bremerton."

So the almost duke had arrived.

Jack kept his face empty of emotion, which was good work, considering the sudden surge of something close to anger rising in him. He didn't like the feeling or understand where the hell it had come from. And he refused to let it show, especially in front of an Englishman who looked cool enough to have arrived in Newport packed in ice.

Eddie held out his hand to shake Bremerton's, but the man inclined his head instead of accepting the handshake. Eddie's color rose.

"It's a pleasure to meet you," Jack said to the Englishman while keeping his hands at his sides.

"And you," Bremerton replied with an equal amount of insincerity.

Caroline was going to have to stay close to a heat source if married to this man. It was that or freeze. Jack gave her a quick glance. Then again, maybe he didn't need to be concerned on her behalf. Her color was brighter than Eddie's. She held out her champagne glass to a passing servant. When he replaced it with a full one, she tossed back half of that in a swallow. Jack smiled. It might turn out to be a long dinner, but it would not be a dull one. He signaled for a drink of his own and waited for the show to begin.

Perhaps a third glass of champagne so quickly had been excessive, Caroline thought. But a fuzzy sort of numbness had seemed a more diplomatic option than asking the Englishman to stop looking at her as though she were an unappetizing meal that he nonetheless planned to consume. She dared a glance at Jack as she took another sip of wine. He, too, was watching her, but amusement— and even possibly some sympathy—warmed his eyes. Small wonder she wanted him as much as she did, even though he didn't have a sloop waiting offshore.

As Caroline thought of a means of escape, the night marched forward. Royal blue–clad footmen entered the room single file and stood behind each of the massive dining chairs, waiting to move them for their occupants. Mrs. Longhorne told her guests where they would be sitting, though Caroline was sure all had read the seating cards, each of which rested on the back of a golden swan.

The Englishman offered his arm to escort her to her place.

"May I?" he asked.

"Of course."

Her first step was a bit off since all champagne and no food made for a wobbly heiress. Bremerton pretended not to notice, but Caroline could almost hear the scratch of pen against paper as he marked this point against her. This, however, was not grounds for optimism. It would take a great many points to remove the allure of her great many dollars.

Once everyone was at the table, Caroline noted Mama's careful control of the seating arrangements. Lord Bremerton had Amelia to his left. Given the way she stared fixedly at the silver charger plate in front of her, Mama had probably told her that she was not to speak, so that Caroline could occupy the guest of honor's attention. Helen must have taken a vow of silence, too. She was seated across from the Englishman, and gazed somewhere past his left shoulder. Eddie had engaged Mama and the Carstairs, who were raptly listening to a description of his newest polo pony. At the head of the table, Mrs. Longhorne had Jack occupied, asking him about his recent brave rescue at sea. Caroline was left nothing to do but talk to Bremerton.

"Lord Bremerton, have you been in America long?" she asked.

"Not very," he said, brushing at a lint speck on the edge of his shirt's white linen cuff.

She waited for him to elaborate, but he didn't seem to be inclined to do so.

"Other than Newport, where have you visited?"

"New York City," he replied in a clipped tone.

"And what did you think of the city?"

"It served its purposes."

All told, Caroline didn't want to know what those purposes might be.

"Are you fond of travel?" she ventured instead.

"Not particularly," he replied. "What could the rest of the world offer that England cannot?"

"An American heiress, apparently," she said, done with trying for polite conversation.

His mouth briefly bent in what could have been either his stingy version of a smile or a wince. He made no comment, though.

Waiters appeared with the first course—roasted oysters in sherry cream sauce, a dish that was her least favorite. Caroline didn't pick up her fork. Jack hadn't picked up his, either. Their eyes met. He gave a smiling shake of his head and mouthed two words: *chocolate cake*. For the first time since meeting Bremerton, Caroline felt completely in control.

When Bremerton was done with his oysters, he leaned closer to her and said, "After the meal, perhaps we could take a stroll?"

"I am sure Mrs. Longhorne has entertainment," Caroline said. "I doubt you'd want to miss it."

"And *I* am sure that they will forge on without us."

Caroline didn't need to look at her mother to know she was being watched. Mama's scrutiny made the air thick.

"A stroll would be lovely," Caroline said, and her mother dropped her gaze.

Control, it seemed, was as difficult to obtain as chocolate cake.

The antique gilt ormolu clock on the dining room fireplace's mantel had just chimed half-past ten when Mrs. Longhorne suggested that the guests retire to Green Seaside Salon. She had arranged for a local theatrical group to perform selections from Gilbert and Sullivan's works.

"Are you certain you wouldn't prefer some light opera to a walk?" Caroline asked Bremerton.

She knew *she* would, for she was tired of being subjected to his dramatic silences. He had a way of imposing his will on the room while saying nothing at all. And the more her champagne had worn off, the glummer she'd felt. Only Jack had seemed unaffected by Bremerton's brooding ways.

"I find Savoy Opera as unsatisfying as sugar," Bremerton said.

The Englishman had not touched his dessert, another reason Caroline found him suspect. But she was resigned to at least this small portion of her fate.

"Mrs. Longhorne, Lord Bremerton has asked to walk the grounds. I hope you don't mind if we do that rather than join you?" she asked their hostess.

Mama's friend was, of course, thrilled to be incubating the match of the year.

"Riccardi, please be sure that the electric lights on the back of the house are lit," she instructed her butler, who then murmured something to a footman.

Once Bremerton and she were outside, stars twinkled

overhead and the sound of the surf meeting the shore filled the uncomfortable silence that the Englishman seemed to prefer.

"Shall we walk?" Caroline asked.

"I find the view from the terrace sufficient," he replied.

In the spirit of equality, Caroline decided to indulge in some of his silence. She would not speak unless he directly solicited comment. He stood silent while she gazed out past the flood of light on the lawn and into the darkness beyond.

"I sense that you are not a woman who wishes for poetry and romance," Bremerton eventually said.

She nodded since it was true insofar as it pertained to him. She'd dearly love some romance from Jack, though she couldn't imagine him spouting a sonnet.

"We have that in common, then," Bremerton said. "And you are also aware that I am here for a wife, correct?"

"Yes," she said. "Though it seems a long way to travel."

"Virtually every time a debutante crosses the ocean, she has done so for the same reason," he replied. "You did last season, though without success."

She turned to look directly at him. "You know that I was in England?"

"I am a thorough man. I did not arrive unprepared. I even heard a tale about you giving a Wild West show, complete with a six-shooter. Apparently, you nearly missed hitting the Duke of Perryton."

Caroline felt compelled to defend her marksmanship. "One shot went slightly astray, but it never endangered the duke. He's skittish."

"And he is no friend of the Prince of Wales, either. I hear His Royal Highness declared you an 'American original and sweetly dangerous' after the incident."

"Unfortunately," Caroline said.

Bremerton nodded. "I understand your chagrin. Many

find the Marlborough House Set unseemly. But I find it is better to have no opinion at all."

"I should be clearer with my comments," Caroline said. "I don't care what the prince's group thinks of me, or the queen's more conservative friends, for that matter. My aim was and is to dissuade all gentlemen from courting me."

"That is a naïve and unattainable goal."

"I succeeded last year," she pointed out.

He shrugged. "You shot your way to a reprieve. You might not wish to marry, but you must do so to elevate your family's social stature."

"Hardly," Caroline replied, trying not to let his slight sting. "The Maxwells are now on their fourth generation in New York society."

"Exactly my point. I shall be the fourteenth Duke of Endsleigh when my time arrives. Your family can benefit from my name."

"And you can benefit from my dowry," she said flatly. "Why else would you be here?"

Caroline was certain she saw a muscle twitch in Bremerton's narrow jaw. His eyes went a shade more toward steel. "You sound disappointed," he said. "Perhaps you seek romance after all."

He placed his fingers beneath her chin and tipped her face upward. His skin was cold and his touch made her uncomfortable. His posture was meant to intimidate her, but she did not step away. If she didn't possess courage at the moment, she could at least pretend to.

"Lovely, and definitely quite naïve," he said before letting his hand drop.

"Is it so wrong to wish for happiness?" Caroline asked, still not allowing herself to take that step backward.

"Romantic happiness is a peculiarly American desire."

Caroline doubted that, but she would not argue the point. "Then I'm thankful that we Maxwells are American."

"Do you believe your family would accept it if you fell in love with a fishmonger? Or even with that rough-looking Irishman inside, the one with the absurd number of names for a commoner?"

If Caroline began to doubt about her parents' wishes for her true happiness, she would be lost. "Yes, they would accept it."

She'd kept up a bold front but knew he'd caught her hesitation.

"If that's the thought that comforts you, most definitely cling to it," he said. "But your reality will be what it is. You are the most suitable heiress for my needs. And I am the most suitable potential spouse for your family's wants. We both know that if I should ask for your hand, it will be given."

Caroline stepped back, but not in retreat. She squared her shoulders and readied to exercise another peculiarly American concept: Freedom. She might not have it long, but she would have it in abundance while she did.

"Lord Bremerton, I believe I will finish this walk alone."

TEN

AGNES MAXWELL WAS LOSING HER COMPOSURE IN front of her guests. That didn't happen any more frequently than Halley's Comet came around, so Jack had paid attention to the event. He'd noted the way she'd frantically waved her fussy silk-and-feather fan while the theatrical troop had sung the finale from *H.M.S. Pinafore*. The song's lyrics about joy and rapture didn't seem to have helped her outlook. The entertainment had since departed and talk was dying down, but her cheeks remained a fiery red. A truant daughter could do that to a mother.

"It has been a lovely evening, but we must be on our way," Lurene Carstairs said to Mrs. Longhorne.

"Perhaps just a moment longer?" Agnes asked. "I'm sure Caroline will be right back."

Jack knew better. When the almost duke had come inside and announced that Caroline wished for more air, Jack had known she was gone. He would have done the same.

"We're sorry to miss her, but this is Bremerton's first night in Newport. We must have him well rested for a victory on the polo field tomorrow," Lurene said. "He'll be playing with William's team while he is here."

"Of course," Mildred said while Agnes fanned herself again.

"This is not like Caroline at all," Agnes said to the guest of honor as he donned his hat.

Jack wanted to laugh. This was *exactly* like her.

The Englishman and his hosts departed. The twins then scurried out of the room after them like forest creatures fleeing a fire. It was a wise choice, considering their mother's mood. Jack stood to leave, but Eddie held out a hand, motioning for him to stay.

"Edward, you must go find your sister," Agnes ordered her son, who was busy filling two snifters with cognac. "Bring her here immediately."

"Don't worry, Mother. She'll return on her own. I'm sure she was just waiting for Lord Bremerton to leave," Eddie said in reassuring tones.

Agnes's color surged. "I am not worried. I am upset! How could she do this to me? My nerves cannot take any more of this rebellion from her. Go find her and make her come inside at once."

"Care to help me?" Eddie said as he handed Jack a snifter.

"Wouldn't have it any other way," Jack said as he rose.

"Hurry along, then," Eddie's mother said. "I shall be in my room, attempting to calm my heart. I am having horrible palpitations. Tell Caroline I will summon her when I am ready to speak to her."

She turned heel and left the room with a worried-looking Mildred Longhorne trailing behind her.

"Have a seat," Eddie said once the room was empty of drama. "We both know Caroline's out there lurking in the shrubbery, just as she did when she used to follow us around."

"She's probably improved her espionage tactics since

then," Jack replied as he took a chair opposite Eddie and relaxed.

A cool breeze rolled in off the ocean and through the open windows, smelling of salt and spent storm. All in all, the evening had proved more entertaining than sitting home with Da and a bottle of whiskey.

"So what did you think of the Englishman?" Eddie asked Jack.

Jack had no intention of sharing his true level of dislike. If he did, Eddie might believe that Jack had feelings for his sister. And while Jack did, they weren't the brotherly sort that gave him the right to opine on her future husband. They did, however, make Jack want to punch the Englishman. However, he'd keep that—and his fists—to himself.

"I've seen worse," Jack said.

"I'm going to give Bremerton the benefit of the doubt," Eddie said. "Maybe the standoffish behavior is because he's not accustomed to our ways."

"Maybe," Jack replied, sticking to his new policy of short, if not so honest, responses.

Eddie shrugged. "Or maybe not. But either way, there's no sense in angering my mother by objecting to the Englishman. I have no vote. Caroline is on her own when it comes to dealing with Mother." He took a swallow of his cognac and added, "But my sister's resourceful. No matter how this turns out, she'll make a workable life of it."

"Of course," Jack said, though the thought didn't sit as well with him as it had even a few weeks ago.

The Longhorne butler entered and held out a small silver tray. "Mr. Culhane, a message has arrived for you."

Jack stood and took the envelope. The script on the front was round and perfectly feminine . . . just what one would expect from a well-schooled heiress. He removed the note and read Caroline's request.

"Your sister is fine," he said to Eddie as he pocketed Caroline's message. "She's with a friend we have in common and has asked if I would bring her back to Villa Blanca."

It didn't escape Jack that Caroline could have asked her hostess to send her home in a carriage. The truth was, Caroline wanted to see him. Hell, she flat-out wanted him, even though she had only a vague idea what that wanting entailed.

"A friend? What sort of friend?" Eddie asked, frowning.

For Caroline's sake, Jack wanted to make Flora sound staid, wealthy, and respectably aged, even though she was only one of the three. "Mrs. Willoughby is recently widowed. She's renting The Reefs for the season and met Caroline at the Casino some days ago."

"That sounds harmless enough. You're fine with hauling her back here?"

"Of course."

"You're a good man," Eddie said, raising his snifter in a sketch of a toast.

Jack shook his head as he left Villa Blanca behind. He might be good, but he wasn't good enough to steer free of temptation when it summoned him.

Caroline sipped a cup of India tea as she sat in The Reefs' main salon. Being with Flora was both a literal and figurative step into the light. A small fire burned in the grate, and Flora had turned up all the gas fixtures so that the room, which was decorated in shades of gold and ruby, glowed. Flora, too, was colorful in her emerald-colored Empire-style satin dress—one better suited to playing the Empress Josephine on the stage than being used as at-home wear. All the same, Caroline envied her new friend and her lack of layers of petticoats.

"Are you sure I can't offer you something more substantial than tea? Some fruit, maybe?" Flora asked. "That was a long walk to make in such an elaborate gown."

Caroline returned the thin bone china cup to its matching ivory saucer and glanced down at her Worth dress. She'd taken care not to harm it during her escape, for it was very pretty. Unfortunately, now that it had been seen at dinner, Mama would never permit her to wear it again.

"The tea is perfect, and there's no need to fuss. You were kind to let me in after I arrived like a thief in the night," she said.

"Thieves generally aren't interested in the front door. And mine is always open to you," Flora said.

"Thank you," Caroline replied.

Flora took a sip of her tea. "A visit from a friend is just what I needed tonight, though I think this will be a short one. Jack will hurry you home now that you've let him know where you are. I believe he finds me a bad influence on you."

"And vice versa," Caroline replied.

Flora laughed. "True. Poor Jack is never going to quite grasp the bond among women. He's too . . ." She paused, considering her choice of words. "Well, he's just too *male.*"

"Very," Caroline said.

"But despite Jack's opinion, I think we are excellent influences on each other," Flora said. "You bring life whenever you arrive, and I can give you a more . . . shall we say . . . *mature* woman's perspective on your situation. Though I've already told you things from my life that would rattle Jack."

When Caroline had arrived, she'd given Flora a brief summary of her night. Sensing Caroline didn't wish to say more, Flora had let the conversation move on to stories of the places she'd visited while working as an actress.

"Jack could do with some rattling," Caroline said. "And I envy you your freedom. I wish I had seen a tenth of what you have."

"Ah, but as you know, freedom always has a price. I'm not going to share my early years with you." She paused as though pushing aside the memories and then gave Caroline a bright smile. "But I chose to move forward and make the best of this life."

"Choice . . ." The word felt foreign to Caroline, and sweeter than chocolate, too. "I wish I had choice. Oh, I know I could refuse the marriage demand, walk from my father's house, and try to get by on my wits. But for all my education, I'm not very skilled. I doubt I could even get a job as shop girl."

"I think that you are the sort who could do whatever she had to. But I'd never encourage you to make your way alone in the world unless it's your very last choice. I've been poor and I've been rich. Try to be rich."

Caroline smiled. "Very sound advice."

"So now tell me a little about this Englishman your mother has selected for you," Flora said. "Are you sure your real objection isn't that your mother did the choosing?"

"I'm very sure," she replied. "He is not a pleasant man. He's so cold and stiff that he might as well be stuffed and displayed in my father's trophy room. And his touch—"

"I take it you're talking about Bremerton," Jack said as he entered the room unannounced, cutting short Caroline's thoughts.

She didn't even try to hide her joy at seeing him. "None other."

"I hope you don't mind that I showed myself in," Jack said to Flora.

"Not at all," Flora replied. "Come join us. Would you like something to drink? There's a decanter of port on the far pedestal table."

"Thank you, but I'm afraid we're short on time," he said. "We need to be leaving."

He looked at Caroline again. His gaze held an intimate message. Her body responded to it even as her mind, with its years of schooling in propriety, rebelled. Something had changed between them. She didn't know how or why, but it had.

Caroline set down her teacup and saucer with a rattle. "Jack is right. I should be on my way home. Thank you for talking to me this evening, Flora," she said as she rose.

Smiling, Flora stood. "I understand."

That being the case, Caroline wished Flora would explain it all to her.

Jack's carriage waited out front. He helped her in and then paused to say something to the coachman before joining her. Instead of taking the opposite seat, he joined her on the black leather bench and carelessly tossed his hat on the other. Though she wasn't in physical contact with him, she could feel the warmth rolling off him. It made her shiver in a most delicious way.

"So he touched you?" Jack asked as they rolled down the drive to Bellevue Avenue.

"Who?" The urge to hold and be held was so strong that she could scarcely keep track of her own name, let alone a conversation.

"Bremerton. He touched you?"

"Yes."

"How?"

"The usual way," she said impatiently. "With his hand."

Jack leaned back against the seat and exhaled slowly. "I don't like it. I don't like the man touching you, and I don't like that I feel like this."

Though she'd never really paid attention to what impact she might have on a man, when it came to Jack, Caroline felt content in a very cat-with-the-cream sort of way that he cared enough to be territorial.

"I don't like the man touching me, either," she said.

Now that they were on the avenue, street lights glowed into the carriage as they passed them. The coachman was taking a leisurely pace, and the carriage swayed ever so slightly in time to the clip-clop of the horses' hooves.

"How did he touch you?" Jack asked.

"Just his fingers beneath my chin." The recollection rekindled her anger. "He held me there and scrutinized me as though he owned me. He said I'm a naïve child."

"Then he's a fool," Jack said. "And he sure as hell doesn't know how to touch you."

Jack had never before used rough language in front of her. Etiquette dictated that she should be offended, but she wasn't.

He drew her closer. "A man who knows you would touch you like this."

As Bremerton had done, he placed his fingers beneath her chin and tipped her face upward. But Jack's touch was warm and vital. She looked into his face. Even in the scant light, she could read his intent, and it matched her desire.

Jack's mouth settled against hers, and all thoughts of the Englishman evaporated. There was nothing but Jack. She opened to him, inviting him to kiss her more deeply. He did, and her heartbeat picked up. But far before Caroline was ready, Jack eased out of the kiss.

"And a man who wants you would do this," he said.

He angled on the bench so that he nearly faced her. She felt his hands at the back of her neck. In a few deft moves, he opened the clasp to her pearl choker, slipped it off her, and pocketed it.

"He would steal my pearls?"

His laugh was enticing. "No, he would taste your skin."

He braced one big hand on the bench's padded back so that she was captured. But Caroline didn't want to flee. He bent his head and kissed the curve where her neck met the top of her shoulder. She breathed her pleasure with a soft sigh. Then his mouth ventured upward, tasting the skin on her throat that he'd bared. She'd never felt anything so intensely thrilling. Her toes curled and she gasped.

He picked up his head. "More?"

"All," she said.

He made a sound of amusement, or perhaps regret. Caroline didn't care which one, so long as he kissed her throat again. And he did. Slowly, one caress at a time, he ventured his way back to her mouth.

He made a low, hungry sound and settled the palm of his free hand over her breast. Caroline knew she should be shocked, but she was more amused at the way he drew back and looked at the pearls and crystals his hand had encountered.

"I'd forgotten," he said. "A rich woman's armor."

Heiresses' mamas everywhere knew what they were doing, dressing their daughters like this.

"I'd prefer to be defenseless," she whispered.

Moving quickly, Jack scooped her up, swept his hat off the opposite bench, and settled her there. She was propped against the carriage's outer wall with her cloud of ice blue skirts spilling toward the floor. She reached for him and bumped her head on the rectangular calling card box just beneath the window, but she didn't care. All she wanted was more Jack.

He pulled down the window shades until little light entered. Caroline was more than willing to go by touch. He knelt on the carriage floor with his solid body holding her safely on the slippery leather seat.

"One day, we'll have to find a comfortable place to kiss," he said as he lightly ran two fingers over the contours of her lips, down her throat, and then traced the line of her collarbone.

Caroline let her eyes slip closed and didn't answer. Sight and speech were distractions when there was new pleasure to feel. His mouth took hers, and at the same time he placed his palm above her dress's square, low bodice. His warmth transferred to her, and his skin felt slightly rough. Strong hands, she thought. A true man's hands.

She reached up to touch his face as he kissed her. His beginnings of a beard were rough and foreign to her, too. But she trusted him, body and soul.

His fingers dipped down into the slight gap beneath dress, corset and chemise. She relaxed to give him more room, but ample curves and tight lacings left little space.

He kissed her again and let his hand slide over the fortress of clothing until it rested below her waist. His hand fisted in the heavy silk of her dress as their tongues touched.

The carriage slowed and then lurched. Jack picked up his head. "We're at Villa Blanca."

"Tell the coachman to go on," Caroline urged, but even as she spoke the words, she knew them for insanity.

He knelt upright and drew in an almost weary breath. "We can't."

She lay there, staring into the darkness. Why, of the

many off-kilter events she'd experienced tonight, did this one make her want to cry?

"Of course we can't," she said.

Jack's hands closed over hers. She took his offered help to get her feet beneath her, even if she was none too sure she could actually use them.

"I need a moment," she said, doing her best to put her coiffure back in order.

"Better now?" he asked after an interval.

She shook out her skirt. "I'm as reassembled as I can get."

"I'm sorry," he said.

"For what?" she asked, thinking that if he said for kissing her, she would be tempted to clout him.

"That Villa Blanca was so close to Flora's," he replied before giving her one last swift kiss. Then he signaled for the coachman to come round and open the door.

Jack stepped out first and helped Caroline from the carriage. She kept a decorous distance once she reached the ground. Mama had eyes and spies, after all.

"Good night, Mr. Culhane," she said. "Thank you for the escort home."

"My pleasure," he said.

But there had to be much more pleasure than what they had shared, and Caroline was determined to make it hers.

Flora was tired, the sort of tired that came from having too little to do. And yet she could not sleep. Jack and Caroline had rushed out a half hour earlier, and the staff had long ago gone off to sleep. Flora was jealous. She wished for just one night in which she would not wake, but knew tonight would not be it.

The house's front bell rang. Flora left the sofa, where she'd been curled up like a child seeking warmth. She would have ignored the summons, except it might be Caroline again. The girl was showing all the signs of perpetual wanderlust, which Flora could appreciate.

She peeked out of the door's sidelight, then blinked. She checked again to see if her eyes were being as faithless as her ability to sleep had become since Clem's death. No, her eyes remained true.

Jack's father stood in the doorway, looking little different from when she'd last seen him, fourteen years earlier. And the hurt she'd felt that night still lingered, too. But she'd never believed the old adage about time healing all wounds.

Cursing herself for being a fool, Flora opened the door.

"Hello, Patrick. This must be the night for Culhanes to roam," she said. "Jack left just a little while ago."

"Are you asking me in, then?" Patrick said.

He sounded as Irish as always, and apparently she was as soft as always for the music in his words.

"I suppose," she said curtly.

He smiled. "As kind as ever."

"Too kind," she said as she led him to the salon.

This time, she did not choose the sofa, but a tall chair that was quite regal. Better yet, the chair opposite it was squat. Of course, Culhane still managed to look commanding while sitting in the blasted thing. Now that she could see him in full light, she noted the deepening of the lines at the corners of his eyes and the added threads of silver in his dark hair. But like his son, he was one handsome devil.

"You're looking tired, Flora," he said.

"That's a fine compliment. Since I invited you in at this late hour, the least you could do is offer some hollow flattery."

He laughed. "Is there any other kind of flattery but hollow?"

She wanted to smile but didn't. "How did you know I was here?"

He looked down before answering. "I saw an article in the *Times* about who was summering in Newport."

"Really? I don't know whether to be more astounded that you were reading the social news or that I was mentioned."

"I was on a train," he said as though that explained everything.

She raised her brows in response.

He stretched his long legs in front of him, no doubt trying to find a way to be comfortable in the short chair. "I was sorry to hear about your husband's passing."

Flora ignored the sting of tears behind her eyes. When on stage, she'd always been able to cry at will. Now she could not seem to stop.

"I appreciated the note," she said.

"It was nothing. I know how deeply a loss like that can cut into a soul."

She nodded. "Yes. But I promised Clem I would pick up my life, and I will."

"I'm sure you will," he said. Coming from him, the words sounded a little sad.

Some people never fought free of the grief. Patrick had been one, though she hadn't understood at the time. All she'd known was that she'd loved him, but he hadn't been able to love her back. At least, not in the way she'd wanted him to, with vows and babies and forever together.

"In time, I'll be better," she replied. "It has been a year since I lost him, but sometimes it still feels like yesterday. Right now, I'm focusing on each day . . . each new adventure." Because, really, she had nothing else.

"Well, then, you have a plan, and that's half the battle."

"I suppose," she said.

They sat quietly for a moment. Then Patrick spoke again.

"I want you back in my life, Flora," he said in a rush. "Not as a lover, mind you, because I've no right to put a claim on your heart after all we've been through. But I miss you. I miss the laughter and the teasing and the knowing that if I'm being a bullheaded fool, you'll be the first to tell me. You can chase me out of here with that fire poker over there," he said, pointing to the fireplace set. "You likely should, but I knew that if I didn't ask now, I'd lose the courage to ask at all."

Never had he come to her hat in hand . . . well, actually hatless . . . like he was at this moment. Flora was touched.

"You, lose courage?" She shook her head. "Patrick Culhane, you are the boldest man I've ever met."

"Aye, and in some ways the thickest, too, or I wouldn't be here today trying to rebuild what I ruined."

She smiled. "I won't deny that."

"So then, will you do me the honor of being my friend?"

Flora knew the answer, even if she didn't feel completely comfortable letting him into her life again.

"I don't think either of us are so rich that we can afford to lose a friend," she said.

A smile slowly spread across his face. "You always were the smartest woman I knew."

And in some ways the thickest, too, Flora thought. But a life with both Culhanes far surpassed a life without them.

ELEVEN

DA MUST BE HAVING A REGULAR IRISH HOOLEY, JACK thought. The coachman had just pulled up in front of the Touro Park house, and all the lights on the ground floor were ablaze. Jack retrieved his top hat from beneath the bench where he'd sent it earlier, brushed it off, and set it back on his head. If there were guests, he couldn't enter the house looking as tired and frustrated as he felt.

Wilton opened the front door before Jack had even made it to the steps.

"I take it my father has company," Jack said as he entered.

"No, sir," the butler replied, closing the door after Jack. "Your father is not in residence."

"Then you have guests?"

"Hardly, sir. Mr. Edward Maxwell has guests. At the moment, they are in the billiards room."

Jack started to ask the unflappable Wilton another question but decided to go to the source. He handed the butler his hat and headed to Eddie.

"It's about time you made it home," his friend said when Jack came into the billiards room.

Eddie, who was in his shirtsleeves, looked to be losing a game to Charles Vandermeulen. Robert Conable and Harold VanAndel, two more of their customary New York set, were watching. Jack gave all four a hello but kept an eye on Eddie.

"I had Wilton set me up with a room," Eddie said without looking away from the shot he'd begun to line up. "I didn't think you'd mind."

Charles came over to shake Jack's hand. "I'd have had him stay with us when he arrived, but Harriet has the house packed with girls. Wedding plans or some such other female thing. The giggling is enough to kill a man. We all decamped for the night. If you don't mind putting the rest of us up here until her blasted picnic tomorrow, we'd be obliged."

Jack hoped it wasn't his wedding to Harriet being planned because that was a nonevent.

"You're welcome to stay," he told Charles.

"Grand, old man! You and I might as well get used to each other's company, if you know what I mean," Charles said.

Jack made a noncommittal noise in response.

"Which brings to mind, Harriet is worried that you haven't said whether you'll be at tomorrow's picnic. It will be the usual lot . . . Harriet, the Maxwell sisters, some of the Vanderbilt girls, and an Astor or two. . . . She asked me to inquire if I saw you."

Da's belief that Jack needed a secretary was beginning to ring true.

"I've been away on new business and have to spend tomorrow catching up on other matters," Jack said. "Please give your sister my apology for the late response and also my regrets."

Charles's demeanor drooped. "You're sure you can't appear for a short while? She has four girls to every man as it is. Take some pity on the rest of us and save us from being swarmed."

Jack smiled at the image of the men smothered in heaps of lace and parasols and ridiculously large-brimmed hats. "Tell you what, I'll try to drop in."

"You have my gratitude," Charles said.

"Vandermeulen, your shot," Eddie said from across the room.

Charles grinned just as a robber baron's son should at the scent of fresh money. "Time to finish him off."

Jack looked to Wilton, who had taken care of Jack's hat and now stood next to the doorway. "Wilton, three more rooms, please."

"Already done, sir. And I shall retire to my quarters, unless you have further need of me."

Jack thanked the butler and sent him on his way. Eddie joined Jack while the other men took bets on how long it would take Charles to empty Eddie's pockets.

"What happened at Villa Blanca?" Jack asked Eddie.

"My mother didn't stick to her vow to stay in her room. You were just out the door when she appeared. You'd think I'd told her I had sent Caroline off with the Devil when I said you'd be bringing her home. She filled my ears with lectures about young ladies going about unaccompanied with men." Eddie shook his head. "Unbelievable. There we were, talking about *you* . . . not the local Lothario. You've known Caroline since she was small enough to climb trees. You're practically her brother."

Or not, Jack thought.

"I pointed out to Mother how close to family you are, and she had one of her fits," Eddie said. "Once she was settled, I decided that Mildred Longhorne's house is no place for a man."

"What about Rosemeade? It's sitting vacant," Jack suggested. He didn't want to be inhospitable, but for a group of people with damn big houses, why did they have to be under each other's feet?

"That was my first stop," Eddie said. "Mother has guards posted. She has locked down the cottage until the big costume ball for the Englishman next Tuesday. Apparently, she wishes no one to see the improvements to the house or property before then . . . not even her own son. The guards are so cowed that I could have told them I was the Lord Almighty and they still wouldn't have let me in. So on I went to Charles's, and here we are."

"There's a ball for Bremerton?" Jack asked. He was surprised Caroline hadn't mentioned it to him. But then again, their most recent encounters had been brief and not taken up with talk.

"The invitation isn't that direct, but Mother's intent in having a party is clear. Check that stack of correspondence on the desk in the library. Your invitation has to be there. And I've already responded to my mother for you, of course."

"I should just hire you," Jack said.

Eddie looked a tad alarmed. "What?"

"Nothing. Just thinking aloud," Jack replied. "How long are you planning to stay here?"

"I don't know for certain. When Father gets here, I suppose I could always stay aboard the *Conqueror* if we're bumping elbows too much. But I'd much rather stay ashore." In a lower voice, he added, "I don't like it getting around, but I have no love for the sea. The thought of nights spent bobbing in that boat . . . well, let's just say I'd prefer the worst room at the seediest tourist hotel in town."

A ship the size of the *Conqueror* would barely sway in protected Newport Harbor, but Jack could appreciate a healthy dislike of something. He was feeling the same way about Harriet's picnic.

"I'm sure we'll work it out here," Jack said.

"I knew I could count on you," Eddie said while clapping him on the shoulder. "Are you ready for some billiards?"

"Sorry, but I'm ready for some sleep."

"What? The night is young. It's nowhere near dawn!"

Eddie took his professional life of leisure very seriously.

"And I'm the only one in this room who has spent the past two days shoveling manure," Jack said. "I'll thrash you at billiards another time."

"Don't be so sure. I'm just setting Charles and the rest of them up for the big kill," Eddie said.

"Enjoy," Jack replied.

He eyed the door, making ready to escape. Fate wasn't being kind, though. Da walked in, looking uncharacteristically dapper. And *dapper* wasn't a word Jack ever thought would come to mind about Da. His suit was brand-new and his shirt so white that it nearly blinded.

"To think I left an empty house not so long ago. What's afoot here?" Da asked the men.

He picked up Charles's cut crystal glass and sniffed the contents. "I need to be naming this place *Bhaile Uisce Bheatha*."

"Excuse me, sir?" Robert Conable asked.

"And here you're so proud of your fine college educations," Da said. "That means House of Whiskey in Irish. Contrary to my son's beer-loving ways, 'tis whiskey that's the water of life. Speaking of which, did you save any for me?"

"Of course, sir," Robert Conable said before speedily pouring Da a glass and bringing it over.

Da toasted Robert. *"Slainte."*

The party was in good hands. Jack made another break for freedom.

"Not so fast, son," Da said. "I'll be having a word with you. Come over this way, if you would."

Jack followed Da to the far corner of the walnut-paneled room. Eddie and the other guests were either too polite or too occupied with wagering to pay mind to them. Jack would guess it was the latter.

"Is there any reason you didn't think of telling me that Flora is back from San Francisco and staying in this very town?" Da asked.

"That's Flora's choice to make, and not mine," Jack replied. "She didn't contact me, either. I crossed paths with her on the trip from the city."

"Crossed paths or engraved announcements, it doesn't matter. You're my son, and you should have told me."

Da hadn't said that in a gruff-but-kindly sort of way; he was annoyed. Jack wasn't feeling too happy, either.

"How was I to know it mattered to you?" Jack asked.

"Of course it would matter! A man would have to be an *eejit* to think it wouldn't," Da said.

"Or he'd have to be your son," Jack replied. "I had barely reached my teen years when Flora was gone. And I've kept out of your private affairs since I've been grown. Up until a few weeks ago, you kept out of mine, too. I liked that arrangement."

"Well, I'm liking this new arrangement," Da replied. "At least until I have my questions answered. Flora said you were at her place tonight. You're not courting her, are you?"

"Hell, no." Jack was floored by the notion, even though Flora was closer to his age than Da's.

"She's a fine woman. No need to get your hackles up." Da took a sip of his whiskey. "If you weren't courting Flora, what were you doing there in the dead of the night?"

"Collecting Caroline Maxwell."

His father laughed. "Collecting her? Is the girl not collected enough already?"

"She has her moments," Jack said. Her greater talent lay, however, in leaving him uncollected. At the thought of what had taken place in the carriage tonight, his smile was both involuntary and completely obvious.

"Ah, now I see the way of it," Da said.

"I'm sure you think you do," Jack said. "But this evening's inquisition is at an end."

Da waved him off. "I'd rather play billiards and make myself some money, anyway."

Da was nearly unbeatable, so Jack escaped while he could. As he was trotting upstairs to the peace of his room, he noted an extra weight inside his coat pocket. He absently patted it and found the bulky shape of Caroline's pearls. He'd forgotten he had them. Jack shook his head at this slipup. Tomorrow's work would have to wait. Harriet's picnic had just risen to the top of his list.

By the crack of dawn on Wednesday morning, the Blue Seaside Salon had officially taken on every aspect of a war room. All the furniture had been pushed to the room's fringes, except for the library table anchoring the center of the room. A folding screen had been brought in for modest changes of clothing. Aides de camp—in this case, Annie, Berta, and a parade of other servants— bustled in and out, delivering notes and food. Pomeroy stood guard from his pillow. All that was missing was a cot on which to sleep, and Mama could move in for the duration.

Caroline stood at attention in her Artemis costume, while Helen and Amelia waited in line as Minerva, Goddess of Wisdom, and Demeter, Goddess of Harvest, respectively. And then there was Mama, who had a decidedly sharp edge this morning. She had not announced her costume, but Caroline felt that Bellona, Roman Goddess of War, would be a good fit. Though on second thought, Caroline did not want to see what sort of damage Mama could wreak with both a spear and a torch. Her weapon of choice at the moment was silence toward her eldest daughter, and Caroline was bearing up only tolerably well under that punishment.

"The vee at the bosom is not deep enough," Mama said to the harried seamstress making adjustments to the white silk of Caroline's dress. "Have I not told you that once already?"

Caroline drew in a calming breath. It was difficult to keep her tongue when it appeared that Mama was mistaking virgin huntress Artemis for a manhunter goddess, Tartemis. Caroline knew her comments would not be well received, so she gave Helen an imploring look.

Helen shook her head no.

Please, Caroline mouthed.

"Mama," Helen said with obvious hesitance.

"Lower!" Mama commanded the seamstress.

"Mama," Helen repeated more firmly.

"Ah, yes! Perfect," Mama said.

Except if Caroline looked down the costume's décolletage, she could see all the way to the floor.

"Mama!" Helen cried.

Her mother finally looked her way. "Oh, for heaven's sake, what, Helen?"

Caroline smiled her gratitude to her sister.

"Do you know how you speak of a young woman's honor and how it must be protected, for it is a gift greater than gold?" Helen asked Mama.

"Yes," their mother said as she walked a circle around Caroline, inspecting her much as Bremerton likely would.

"Well, Mama, I fear that dress exposes Caroline's honor to danger and her bosom to one and all."

Mrs. Longhorne, who was unrolling one of a dozen

velvet jewelry pouches on the war table, nodded her head. "I must agree, Agnes."

"After Caroline's reckless disappearance last night, we must regain Bremerton's attention and keep it," Mama replied to her friend.

Caroline couldn't stand silent another second. "And so you think to achieve that by having the top of my dress disappear?"

Mama wheeled on her. "If you are going to speak, make it a recitation of Bremerton's living relatives." She flicked her hand toward Caroline's governess. "Peek! *Debrett's!*"

Even Peek knew better than to argue. She pulled the red tome from the table and opened it to the Duke of Endsleigh's listing.

Caroline was not in the mood to cite chapter and verse, so she returned to silence, even when Mrs. Longhorne came close enough to peer down her dress.

"Oh, dear. We do have an issue here," Mama's friend said.

Mama stopped closer to investigate the view.

"You may bring the vee up an inch," she told the seamstress.

"Just an inch?" Mrs. Longhorne asked.

"She will be wearing a wide gold belt high on the waist," Mama replied. "That will cinch in the fabric and take care of the rest of the problem."

But it would also accentuate Caroline's ample curves up top. Among her friends, she was the only one she knew who didn't have need to add padding to her dresses in order to attain the current fashionable proportions. But without the proper restraint, she felt so . . . obvious. But that was Mama's strategy.

"And not too much bulk, either," Mama said. "Just one petticoat, I think."

"You're lucky!" Amelia exclaimed. Her wheat-embroidered Demeter costume was so petticoated up that she reminded Caroline of a hay pile.

Mama tapped her finger to her chin as she inspected Caroline's throat. "We want to keep the eye following the line of the dress. Perhaps the Russian pearl choker she wore last night," she said to Mrs. Longhorne, who had returned to the array of jewels.

Caroline's palms grew damp. She'd realized Jack still had the pearls as soon as she'd gotten into the house last night. She planned to find him today and reclaim them.

"No. Never mind," Mama said. "We can't have Lord Bremerton seeing her in the same jewels twice."

She turned away from Caroline, who surreptitiously wiped her palms on the dress, earning a gasp from the seamstress.

"She will wear the diamonds, I think," Mama said from her new spot next to Mrs. Longhorne. "When you slip details about the ball to the *Times* and the *Mercury,* be sure to say that Caroline's gems were once Marie Antoinette's."

"Were they?" Helen asked.

"No, but the newspapers won't know the difference."

"I'm glad they're not. I would hate for my sister to be wearing the jewels of someone who was beheaded. It seems like a bad omen, and Lord Bremerton seems like a walking bad omen as it is," Helen said.

"Don't be silly," Mama replied. "Lord Bremerton is a mannered, sophisticated gentleman."

She returned to stand nearly toe-to-toe with Caroline. "Last night was also your last hurrah, Caroline. We will not pretend that it did not happen, and we will place you under guard, if need be, between now and when Lord Bremerton begins to negotiate with your father regarding a marriage."

"Yes, Mama," Caroline said. What she thought was another matter entirely.

Caroline's mother waved Peek over. "You will accompany Caroline and the twins to Harriet Vandermeulen's picnic at noon today. You will oversee her activities and report back to me on her behavior."

"So I'm to be under guard already?" Caroline asked.

"Miss Peek is your governess."

Caroline took up the best compromise position she could think of. "No other girl there will have her governess as a shadow. Bremerton is sure to notice, and you don't want that."

"A good point," her mother conceded.

"Send Annie. Most of the girls will have their maids present."

"Annie?" She gave Caroline's maid a narrow-eyed look. "Absolutely not. Peek will go as your maid."

It was difficult to decide who was more affronted by this decree, Peek or Annie.

"But ma'am," Annie began, only to be cut off by Mama, who said, "Think carefully, young lady. Your next word could be your last as a Maxwell employee."

Annie nodded before joining the furniture on the edges of the room, and Peek glowered in silence.

"There!" Caroline's mother said in her first cheerful tones of the morning. "See how easily that was handled? Compromise is a fine thing."

And when practiced by Mama, an entirely one-sided affair.

TWELVE

"Do you think Lord Bremerton is here?" Amelia asked her sisters as they followed a pathway marked by potted daisies around the side of Thelmsford, the Vandermeulens' palatial cottage set on a rise overlooking Bailey's Beach.

"Of course he is," Helen said.

"He's going to be everywhere I don't want him to be," Caroline added. She had already shed Peek, sending her off with the other lady's maids inside the house. Bremerton wouldn't be so easily lost.

Caroline adjusted her grip on the beribboned lavender parasol that matched her equally beribboned lavender dress. Though she was not much for fluff and lace, she had a soft spot for this particular dress. The narrow bands of white trim at the bottom of the skirt and the puffy leg-of-mutton sleeves felt quite stylish. She'd had Annie pin her hair more loosely atop her head in the style of a drawing by Charles Dana Gibson. Caroline had decided that these small pleasures would have to tide her over until she was free of the Englishman.

"I don't know why the two of you think Lord Bremerton is so horrible," Amelia said. "I think he's quite romantic. It's as though he carries the weight of a tragic past and will not speak because of it."

"You've been reading too many Brontë novels," Helen replied. "There's nothing remotely tragic about him. He's bored silly by us and thinks himself a thousand times better."

"You have your opinion, and I have mine. But you'll both see. He simply needs to recover from a broken heart."

"Or the lack of one altogether," Helen suggested.

Caroline smiled. That, at least, would explain why he was so cold to the touch.

They'd just rounded to the rear lawn, and Caroline was about to remind her sisters that the time had come to watch their words. Instead, all three pulled up and fell silent. Harriet Vandermeulen had put the sort of planning into this picnic that Caroline wouldn't bother with for a wedding. Unless Jack was the groom, of course.

The Vandermeulens had borrowed a flock of sheep to lend a more rustic appearance to their perfectly groomed property. The poor, blank-eyed creatures were penned in an enclosure decorated with large white bows. Two sullen-looking teenaged boys tended them. Each was dressed in a romanticized version of a shepherd's garb, complete with a matching bow at the neck.

All the female servants had been dressed in colorful gingham frocks, and the linen-covered tables were adorned with low arrangements of wildflowers. Just past the picnic area, a fiddler sat playing high on a haystack while two cows chewed contentedly on his perch.

Harriet approached. She glowed with happiness in her rosy pink dress and wide brimmed hat decorated with fat bunches of cherries.

"Thank you for coming," she said to the girls. "It is a glorious day for a picnic, isn't it?"

Caroline quickly scanned the dark-coated men at the gathering, mentally charting a course that would keep her far from Lord Bremerton. Instead, she came up minus a Bremerton and plus a Jack. He looked her way and smiled.

"Absolutely perfect," she replied to Harriet.

Amelia and Helen went off to a group of their friends while Harriet led Caroline toward the cluster of guests that included Jack.

"It's going very well between Jack and me," Harriet said as they strolled.

"In what way?" Caroline asked.

"He's very charming and attentive."

"Jack is a nice man," Caroline said, attempting to keep at least the appearance of neutrality regarding Harriet's campaign.

"And my father has already talked to Jack's father. Since Jack is here, I have to believe he's agreeable to a marriage."

"Interesting," Caroline replied.

"And I have good news for you, as well," Harriet said. "Lord Bremerton is here. Everyone is quite taken with him. I think you will be, too. He's seeing the grounds with Alice Ames and should be back at any moment. I'll introduce you right away."

Caroline could work up no false enthusiasm. "There's no rush. I met Lord Bremerton yesterday evening."

Harriet's perfectly shaped mouth turned downward. "Oh. I was hoping to be the one to make the introduction. It would be a wonderful story to tell our grandchildren someday. But at least I have seated him at our table so I can tell him all the wonderful things I know about you. And you can do the same for me with Jack."

"Naturally," Caroline said.

They had reached Jack. He stood in the middle of a cluster of girls with Caroline's brother, Charles, and poor, graceless Gordy Bullard. Harriet cut her way through the throng with a charming yet relentless efficiency, telling the others that luncheon would soon be served and perhaps they'd like to find their tables.

Jack took a step toward Caroline and began to say hello. Harriet moved between them and edged close to Jack. Close enough that Caroline did not appreciate it.

"Jack, you will be sitting with me," Harriet said. "Caroline will be joining us with Lord Bremerton, and the table will be rounded out by Caroline's sister, Helen, and Alice Ames. Shall we?"

She tilted her head at an inquisitive angle, clearly waiting for Jack to act as her escort to the table. He held out his arm. Harriet latched on like a steel trap. Caroline followed behind and permitted herself one unladylike roll of her eyes. Jack chose that instant to look over his shoulder. He grinned and she smiled back.

The three of them hadn't been seated long when Bremerton and Alice Ames returned, and Helen made her way over. Jack rose. Bremerton's gaze flicked past him and Harriet, and settled on Caroline. Focus on the small pleasures, she reminded herself, preparing herself for his icy attitude.

But Bremerton beamed.

"Hello, again, Miss Maxwell," he said in a voice that oozed warmth and admiration. "You look radiant today. A true American beauty."

If Amelia's theory had been correct, Bremerton had just set a new world's record for recovery from a broken heart.

"Thank you," Caroline said, surprised that words had managed to work their way past her disbelief.

Jack, who had greeted Helen and Alice, acknowledged Bremerton after they had each held a chair for the girls. "Lord Bremerton."

"Mr. Culhane," Bremerton said collegially. "Jack, is it?"
Jack looked exactly as suspicious as Caroline felt.

"Yes, it is," he said as both Bremerton and he sat.

"I do recall those two names, though last night there seemed to be quite a few others packed between them," Bremerton said. "You must have an interesting tale behind that."

"Please share it, Jack. I feel so deprived, not having been there with you last night," Harriet said, and then shot a very pointed look Caroline's way.

Caroline understood the territorial statement. Jack was now the pinto hobbyhorse of their childhood, and Caroline was to keep her hands off. Jack gave Harriet a half smile, as though he couldn't see what all the fuss was about. He apparently hadn't believed Caroline's warning about the extent of Harriet's ardor.

"My late mother fell ill before my birth and was told by her doctors that recovery, let alone more children, wasn't likely," he said. "She had wanted a large family, so I was given all the names."

"That's very touching, don't you think, Lord Bremerton?" Harriet asked.

"Quite," he replied. Anyone who had not encountered him last night would think he was sincere. But the hairs on Caroline's arms still rose when he spoke, and she would put her faith in arm hair over the Englishman any day of the week.

Harriet forged on. "Do you want a large family, Jack?"

Seventeen-year-old Alice Ames gasped at Harriet's audacity. The query *had* been as blatant as Mama's idea of an Artemis costume.

"I haven't thought about it," Jack replied.

"But you would like a son to take on your name and inherit, wouldn't you?" Harriet asked.

"I don't know. . . . Having a son simply to be left my

belongings, goods, or carry on my name seems a pretty self-centered reason to bring a child into the world."

"What reason would you suggest for procreation, then?" Bremerton asked.

"Love," Jack said.

"Ah, of course," Bremerton said. "I believe that's a given for every human being. And while my future title demands that I marry in order to protect the line, I will do so only with the prospect of a deep and lifelong love." He fixed his gaze on Caroline. "It is what every woman deserves."

Young Alice sighed sweetly, while Helen made a choking sound. Caroline clenched her hands beneath the table, wishing she were a man and could punch Bremerton's long nose for this absurd deception. But she could try to push him until his shiny new veneer of caring cracked.

"Yes, it is," she said. "And every woman deserves to have a voice in her world, or we are little different from the sheep in that pen."

"I feel horrible for the sheep," Harriet said with a delicate shudder. "I begged my father to let them wander, but he wouldn't hear of it."

"I can guarantee they've been in less happy places than that pen," Jack said. "Though I can't necessarily say the same for the shepherds."

Caroline laughed.

Harriet looked up at Jack, which was no small feat since they were sitting down. "It's so kind of you to comfort me."

"Are you saying that ladies can be likened to sheep?" Alice asked Caroline. She sounded more intrigued than offended.

"I am saying that sometimes we are treated like livestock," Caroline replied. "We are given no more options than they are."

"We're certainly not sheep," Harriet said, clearly irritated that the conversation was veering away from her. "And I don't live in a pen."

"Caroline doesn't mean it literally, Harriet," Helen said.

"Then is this about not having the vote? Are you a suffragist with that Susan B. Anthony?"

"I am a member of her association," Caroline said. "And I have been lucky enough to hear Miss Anthony speak twice."

Jack smiled across the table at her. "That must have taken some maneuvering on your part."

"I'm becoming fairly adept at that sort of thing."

He laughed. "I'll bet you are."

Harriet took a quick sip of her ice water and put down her glass with more force than necessary. "I have no desire to follow politics or business."

"We all have different interests. But I was referring to a choice in love, actually," Caroline said to Harriet as a large luncheon platter was set down in front of her. She glanced at the slices of crusty French bread and the makings of a sandwich of one's choice. The meats and cheeses had been arranged like flowers. Caroline had a fundamental objection to flowers of meat, and she was growing to object to Harriet, too.

"We can all choose to love the man we wed," Harriet said, looking at Jack. "I think it would be very easy to do so."

"In some cases, yes," Caroline replied while she busied herself placing her napkin on her lap. If she even glanced Jack's way, the entire table would know how she felt about him. "But think how much better life would be if we could choose to love before we choose to marry."

Jack had another life-improving choice to add to Caroline's suggestion—escaping this table. Luckily, he'd already laid the groundwork for his departure. He needed to use it now, before he committed the apparent sin of making a direct comment. He pulled out his pocket watch, checked it, and closed it with a snap.

"I'm afraid it's time for me to leave," he said to Harriet.

"I know you said you had another engagement that you might have to attend to, but you haven't even eaten," she said, pouting. "Please stay a while longer."

Jack wasn't about to touch a plate that had been served to him by Caroline's governess, Peek. How Caroline had just missed her in that ill-fitting pink gingham dress and why she was acting as one of the Vandermeulens' staff were both beyond him.

"It's unavoidable," he said to Harriet, doing his best to sound disappointed.

"Let me walk you out," she offered.

"No . . . No, I'll be fine. Please stay with your other guests." He smiled at Caroline, who, without speaking, conveyed her irritation at his escape. But he had plans for her, too.

"If you insist," Harriet said. "I look forward to seeing you again, very soon."

Jack replied with a noncommittal thank you and said good-bye to everyone else. As he made his way past the sheep pen, he stopped near the so-called shepherd guarding the gate. He was a young man of stocky build, and not especially suited to wearing a big white bow.

"You don't look happy," Jack said. "Would you like a new job?"

The younger man cocked his head. "What would it be payin'?"

Ah, so the not-quite-real shepherd was Irish. "If it gets you out of that ridiculous costume, do you even care?"

"Not so much, sir," he said. "But I'd be a fool not to be askin'."

"Where are you from?"

"Dungloe, County Donegal, sir."

Jack grinned. That was a stone's throw from Da's old home.

"But how much are you payin'? You still haven't told me."

And he was persistent like Da, too. "Twenty-five dollars a month, and room and board, of course."

"That's twice what I'm makin' now." The pretend shepherd tugged the bow from his neck and threw it in with the sheep. "Done."

He fell in step beside Jack.

"What's your name?" Jack asked as they walked toward the front of the house.

"Fintan O'Toole," he said.

"How old are you, O'Toole?"

"Seventeen. Eighteen next month."

"No wife?"

"Ha! I can hardly support meself. Well, now I can, but I'm still wanting no wife."

"O'Toole, you're now my personal secretary." He glanced the younger man's way and thought he might be wise to cover a few of the job's requirements. "You can read, can't you?"

"Aye."

"And you like beer?"

"I'd never be drinking on the job, sir," O'Toole said.

"That's good, but do you like beer?"

"Aye, sir."

"Then you're going to be one very happy personal secretary."

O'Toole grinned. "I'm near thrilled already, just getting rid of that bow."

Once they were at the carriage, Jack dug into the carriage box. He'd tucked a telegram from Gustav Miller about the Philadelphia brewery in there. Jack handed it to O'Toole.

"Bring this to Miss Caroline Maxwell. She's the woman in lavender sitting at the same table as Miss Vandermeulen. Tell her it just arrived for her."

"Aye, sir," O'Toole said as he glanced at the paper. "Am I waiting for some sort of reply? Though I can't think what Miss Maxwell might be saying since this is addressed to you."

Jack smiled. "That's half the fun of Miss Maxwell, seeing what she might do next."

Caroline gazed diffidently at the French bread in front of her. She had no appetite. And for a man who'd recently made a rescue at sea, Jack had quickly forgotten the time-honored tradition of women and children first when abandoning a sinking ship. Heaven knew this meal was that and worse for Caroline.

"Do you enjoy watching polo, Miss Maxwell?" Lord Bremerton asked.

"When my brother is playing, I do," she replied.

"Perhaps you could extend that pleasure. I'll be playing at the Westchester Polo Club immediately after this. Would you do me the honor of watching?"

He seemed to be determined to play the chivalrous swain.

"I'm afraid I'm otherwise occupied today," she said.

"But Caroline, you know we were all to go to the polo field this afternoon," Harriet said.

"My mother has need of me at home," she fibbed.

"Ah, I see," Bremerton said. "And I fully understand. As we chatted about last night, we all must meet our families' expectations."

What a lovely threat disguised in sunshine, Caroline thought. She was about to reply when a young man who looked suspiciously like one of the shepherds approached the table.

"Miss Maxwell, begging your pardon, but this telegram was just delivered for you."

Caroline never received telegrams, especially from shepherds.

"Thank you," she said, accepting it. "Will you be nearby if I need to respond?"

"I'll be right by the house, miss." The young man executed a sketchy half bow and retreated.

Caroline unfolded the paper, read it, and put on a businesslike face.

"I'm afraid I need to step away from the table for a few minutes," she said.

"It's not anything to do with the family, is it?" Helen asked in an alarmed voice.

"No, nothing at all," Caroline said as she worked back her wooden folding chair and rose. "It's from an acquaintance I made in London last year. She has asked me to attend her wedding, which is taking place quickly, before her betrothed must go to India on government business."

Bremerton, who had risen with her, said, "Who is the bride? Perhaps I know her?"

Caroline mentally berated herself for committing the very amateur error of providing unneeded detail. Years with Mama had taught her to opt for short answers, but the lure of Jack without Harriet appended to him had distracted her. "I don't think you'd know her, Lord Bremerton. My friend is a very private person."

"And I am sure that if you wait until you return to Mrs. Longhorne's house to respond, the difference will never be known," Bremerton said.

"True, but the social whirl is so much these days that I might forget." She stepped away from the table. "Please eat without me. I would feel wrong holding you up."

Caroline was winding her way through the other tables when she saw Peek in a pink gingham dress heading her way. In point of fact, the governess was intently tracking her. Caroline wondered who inside the house now wore Peek's standard severe black dress. Whoever the woman was, she had a smaller stature than Peek's. The governess looked ready to explode out of her pink gingham. But she was nothing if not determined.

"Miss Maxwell," Peek called. "A moment, please!"

Caroline feinted right, but then went left around the last table. Peek was detained by one of the guests, who was holding out a fork and making some comment about its cleanliness.

Once Caroline had cleared Peek, she made her way across the grounds at as quick a pace as she could without actually running. The farther she got from the picnic, the more her smile grew. She reached the false shepherd, who waited for her at the top of the potted-daisy path.

"Where will I find Mr. Culhane?" she asked him.

"In his carriage, ma'am."

"Thank you," she said.

"'Tis my pleasure," he replied, this time with a sweeping bow.

Laughing, Caroline approached Jack's carriage. A few servants milled about, but no one who she felt concerned would gossip. Jack's coachman helped her into the carriage and then closed the door after her. She settled next to Jack.

"That was one tidy escape," she said.

"Jealous?"

"A little," she confessed. "I couldn't think of a way to leave for good without conjuring up a story that would alarm Helen."

"It sounds as though you need more practice with your maneuvering."

"With Lord Bremerton around, I'm destined to get it. And speaking of maneuvers . . ." She held out her hand. "I believe you have something of mine?"

Jack reached into his coat pocket and dangled her pearl choker from his fingertips. She reached for it, but he repocketed it.

"I had intended to exact a price for their return later this afternoon," he said.

She was optimistic it would involve more kissing. "Such as?"

"A walk."

"A *walk*?" That was not even close.

"Yes. A normal daytime excursion, such as two friends might take. Touro Park, maybe."

"Is that what we are, Jack? Friends?"

He smiled. "I hope we are."

"And I hope you don't kiss all your friends as you did me last night."

"Very few."

She wanted to ask if he'd ever kissed Harriet, but that was her own growing envy coming to the fore. Jack's behavior with Harriet was completely circumspect.

"Then we are more than friends," she said.

He sat silent for a moment. "We are what we are, Caroline."

She moved closer. "And what is that?"

"At the moment, on dangerous footing," he said, inclining his head toward the window. Peek paced outside, but she hadn't yet spotted Caroline. If she had, she'd be pounding at the carriage door. Caroline lowered the shades three quarters of the way, to cut Peek's view.

"Our footing might seem dangerous to you, but it's the most solid thing I have in my life right now," she said.

"At least the Englishman has decided to be civil."

"Which is all the worse. You see what Bremerton is

doing today, don't you? He's being all charm . . . the perfect suitor. And he'll continue that charade. My mother and father are going to be drawn in, just as everyone else has been. And if I don't marry him, I'll look like the most ungrateful daughter ever."

"You're getting ahead of yourself, aren't you?" Jack asked. "You didn't mention that he proposed last night."

"He has said he will. I am, in his words, 'the most suitable heiress.' And I will do what I must to become the least suitable."

Jack sat silent. He wore the impassive face she had thought was gone forever after last night. Her frustration was so hot that if she didn't release it, she would burn.

"You don't have any idea what I'm going through, do you? You're here and you're helpful and you certainly kiss very well, but you don't see things as I do," Caroline said. "I'm subjected to Harriet pursuing you. I watch her simper. I listen to her drop marriage hints. I'm sure it doesn't bother you at all to see Bremerton, but that's because you don't love me. I, on the other hand, love you, Jack Culhane, and that makes all the difference!"

Caroline's heart pounded as the realization of what she'd just said hit her. Then relief set in. The words were out, and she could breathe. It had grown very quiet inside the carriage, though. Her sense of relief thinned and quickly disappeared as Jack sat there, saying nothing at all. She'd never seen him this deadly serious.

He leaned across her and opened the window shades. Then he drew the choker from his pocket.

"Come closer," he said calmly.

She did, and he clasped the pearls around her neck.

"Now you're just as you were last night," he said.

Except she wasn't, and neither was he. They never would be again.

THIRTEEN

"I SHOULDN'T HAVE COME HERE," FLORA SAID TO Patrick Culhane.

"What? Touro Park is a public place," he replied. "And we're two old friends strolling on a Wednesday afternoon. There's no scandal in that."

Flora breathed in the fresh, clean air. The park was glorious, with its lush lawns, sweeping elms, broad pathways, and statuary. "It's not scandal that concerns me."

He smiled as he took in her dress, which, while cut appropriately for the hour of the day, was a bright crimson.

"I'm thinking not," he said.

"Color makes me feel as though I'm on stage. Sometimes I miss that excitement, the thrill of becoming someone other than who I am."

"I was always just fine with who you were." He took a seat on a park bench and patted its wooden slats. "Come sit by me."

Flora chose the opposite end. Patrick tipped back his head and let loose a full-hearted laugh she loved hearing. "You can do better than that."

Smiling, she moved closer, but still kept a circumspect amount of daylight between them.

"And that's as close as you'll come? I've been closer to a nun."

"Yes, in church," she said.

"True enough," he agreed.

They sat in companionable silence until Patrick asked, "So do you want to talk about it?"

"About what?"

"Don't be pretending I don't know you," he admonished. "What is it that has you so quiet?"

He was right. The years apart didn't seem to have changed a thing. "I don't even want to say it aloud."

"Well, now you've got me worried, so you have to."

"I'm lonely," she said, feeling better for even having made the confession. "And I don't want to be lonely anymore."

"You, lonely?"

"It is possible, you know."

He shook his head. "If you're lonely, it's because you choose to be. Look at you. You're a breathtaking woman who just so happens to have a bank balance that would stop most men's hearts. If you want a man, smile once, and a pack will come running."

"It's not a man I'm lonely for," she said.

Patrick gave her an odd look.

Laughing, she added, "It's not a woman, either. And while I'd be a liar to tell you that I don't miss the closeness of a man at night . . . or things as basic as sitting across the breakfast table from him, what I miss most right now is having connections. Clem didn't have family, and as you know, mine cut me off when I took to the stage. I have no interest in going to them now, but I wish I'd had children."

"It never happened for you?"

"No."

Patrick sighed. "I'm sorry for that. I wish I could have

wanted it when you did, but I had Jack to deal with, and he was a busy enough boy to earn all of his names."

Flora smiled. "I remember. You did well. He's a fine man."

"That he is." He nudged his top hat back a bit so that it no longer shadowed his face and then settled his arm across the back of the bench. "I know he's grown and I should be bootin' him out of my house . . . or houses," he said, gesturing at a somewhat tired-looking villa across the street, just past the old stone tower by which they sat, "but I can't bring myself to do it."

"I'd be the same way," she said. "It's not easy being alone, even with a houseful of servants."

He looked at her, humor evident in his blue eyes. "So what do you say? Will you move a little closer to me? I might be feeling lonely, too."

Flora laughed. "You're as bold as ever."

"Bolder, now that I've got no time left to waste."

"And that is why I'm keeping my distance," Flora replied.

He laughed.

"I'm quite serious, Patrick. You might talk me into coming too close. I can play at tennis and play at being a grand lady, but I can't end up playing at being your sweetheart again."

"You were my sweetheart," he said calmly. "It was no game. If you'll be remembering, you were my lover, too."

She nodded. "I know. But while I might make an astounding variety of mistakes, I try not to make the same one twice."

"And what made us a mistake?"

She'd spent a great deal of time lately thinking about past choices. "I expected you to be someone you're not. I tried to push you into changing, when you're as unmovable as that stone tower."

Patrick chuckled. "You'll note the tower's top is gone. It's done some moving in its years, whether it wanted to or not. I have, too. And neither of us is lookin' any better for the wear."

Flora had to laugh. "Don't mine for compliments."

"Then give them more freely," he said.

She'd been about to offer one when Jack rounded the old stone tower. He stood with his back to them, each hand gripping a spear of the sharp wrought-iron fence that circled the structure's arched base.

"Do you see who I do?" she asked Patrick.

"Aye," he said. "And I don't have to see my boy's face to know he's in a mood." Patrick stood.

"Maybe you should just let him be alone with his thoughts?" she suggested.

"You know as well as I that thoughts can be cold company," he said as he came to her and offered his hand.

Patrick had always been a smart man. Flora accepted his help and walked with him to see his son.

"So you're doing some sightseeing, are you?" asked a familiar voice to Jack's right.

Da had joined him, along with Flora. He said hello. Flora sounded somewhat hesitant as she returned the greeting. His dark mood must have worked its way to his face.

"I hired a personal secretary," Jack said to his father, trying to keep the conversation far away from what bothered him.

Da cocked his head. "Which has what to do with this Norseman's Tower?"

"It wasn't built by Norsemen." No matter what the name, even Jack's untrained eye could tell the structure was too new. And while it might amuse Newporters to think that Europeans had first landed here, why would one half-ruined tower sit as the only marker?

"I'm just readin' the sign," Da said. "That one, and a few others, actually."

Jack didn't care to engage. "My secretary's name is Fintan O'Toole and he's from Dungloe, County Donegal." Which should be enough to distract Da, he figured.

"And has he any experience?" Da asked, skipping right over the seed of home turf Jack had planted.

"None."

Da laughed. "Of course not."

"I've had Wilton give him a room."

"Grand. Now that we've got that out of the way, would you care to talk about why you're glaring at this heap of stones?"

"Patrick!" Flora said.

"I've told the boy I've got license to pry into his life, and so I'm prying," his father replied.

"And doing a thorough job of it, too." To Jack, she said, "Shall I step away and give you two your privacy?"

"No," he replied. "You're family. And you know what's going on."

"It's Caroline, isn't it?" she asked.

"I knew it," Da nearly crowed. "You *are* sweet on her, aren't you?"

"Caroline and sweet don't belong in the same sentence," Jack replied. Da should try Caroline and trouble. Or better yet, Caroline and disaster.

Flora settled her hand on Da's shoulder. "I think we should continue our walk and let Jack have some time to himself."

"Ha!" Jack shook his head. "Walks. Friends take walks all the damn time. Why not take a walk?"

"Have you been drinking, son?" Da asked after a silence.

"No."

"I'm almost sorry to hear it."

Jack let out a long, slow breath. "I'm sorry. I'm not making much sense. And I apologize for the rude language, Flora."

"It's quite all right," she said. "Believe it or not, I've heard worse from your very own father."

"I'm supposing there's a chance of that," Da admitted.

Jack gave a sketchy smile. "I'm taking leave of this place until my mood improves. I'll be on the evening steamer to Providence."

"So you're off to the brewery there?" Da asked.

Jack nodded. "Work will help me clear my head. Da, would you take some time to get O'Toole started? I feel wrong, hiring him and walking out."

"I'll take care of him," his father replied. "On the condition that you take care of yourself."

Caroline sat in Villa Blanca's small library, doing her best to lose herself in an account of Commodore Matthew C. Perry's skirmishes with Barbary pirates. She had thought that a little bloodshed might take her mind off love. She had been mistaken.

"I did not know that Percival Bremerton had died," Peek said from the library door.

Caroline looked up from her book. "Wasn't it in *Debrett's*?"

"I hardly have the tome memorized," the governess replied. "And your mother has not supplied me with the most recent year. Had she, I might have known by now."

Caroline closed her book and paid attention. Peek was not one for small talk.

"I take it Percival was Lord Bremerton's elder brother?" Caroline asked.

Peek came closer. "Yes. When everyone was in a lather about Lord Bremerton's arrival, I had assumed that it was Percival, and that his wife had passed away. Bremerton men tend to outlive their women."

"You knew Percival Bremerton, then?" Caroline asked after offering Peek a seat in the brocade-covered armchair opposite her, which the governess declined.

"I came to this house from employment with the Cavendishes, a West Sussex family who had moved to Belfast," Peek said. "*Their* daughter married at age eighteen."

"As a good girl should," Caroline replied, feeling slightly affronted by the comment. Her skin was a little thin after having had a declaration of love met with all the lightness of a funeral dirge.

Peek disregarded her comment. "At which point, my services were no longer required. My prior employers, the Fitzhughs, resided at Beame Manor, also in West Sussex. They were related to the Woolseys."

"This is beginning to sound frighteningly close to an entry in *Debrett's*. Am I about to hear what charities and garden clubs the Fitzhughs involved themselves in?"

But Peek continued. "Lord Percival Bremerton's home, Chesley House, was also in West Sussex."

"There is no stopping you, is there?"

"I believe we share that in common," Peek said. "Witness your running off at the Vandermeulen picnic today."

Caroline preferred not to think about that. "So, about Lord Percival Bremerton living in West Sussex, which is beginning to sound quite crowded, by the way?"

"Lord Bremerton was married to a Woolsey. They socialized often at Beame Manor, as did Lord Bremerton's family, though just from time to time."

"I'm sure it was very pleasant." Caroline was equally sure that Peek intended to torture her before reaching her point.

"For those who were there, yes. While both Viscount Bellingham and the Duke of Endsleigh would visit Lord and Lady Bremerton, it was well known that his only brother was *persona non grata*."

Ah, now they were getting somewhere. Caroline set the book aside. "They were estranged?"

"Yes," Peek replied. "Permanently, I heard. And the brother, this current Lord Bremerton, was estranged from his grandfather, the duke, as well."

Caroline smiled. "Really?"

"This is not a matter that should give rise to good spirits."

"Ah, but it is," Caroline said. "Thank you for the information."

"You are quite welcome," Peek replied. "Among my duties is to provide your family with any knowledge I might possess that could lead to a positive marital state for you. Unless the relationship between Lord Bremerton and his grandfather has mended, a definite shadow is cast upon Bremerton. The Duke of Endsleigh is a powerful man, and an advisor to Her Royal Highness."

Caroline rose. "I must tell my mother at once."

"That would be prudent," Peek agreed.

Caroline was at the library door when Peek spoke again. "Do not mistake my sharing of this information as any sort of approval of the dalliance I believe you are having with Mr. Culhane. When you returned to the picnic, I saw you hiding the pearls you'd been wearing the night before. If that odd shepherd hadn't detained me, I would have had you then. Once I have proof . . . and I *will* obtain it . . . I am honor bound to share it with your mother."

Proof of something that no longer existed? Caroline wished her luck with that.

* * *

Mama was in the war room, just where Caroline had expected to find her. Oddly, she still wore her blue silk afternoon dress, when it was well past the time to change into evening garb. Her mother had pulled up a chair—or more accurately, someone had pulled up a chair for her—to the library table. She was engrossed in whatever she was writing.

"Mama?"

Her mother looked up and briefly smiled. "I was just about to call for you. Come in, Caroline."

Caroline moved to the opposite side of the table from her mother.

"Lord Bremerton and the Carstairs paid a call on me, earlier," Mama said. "Bremerton asked when your father will be arriving in Newport. This is good news, indeed."

"Why?" Caroline asked.

"If he's asking for your father, I expect there's a marriage proposal in the offing."

"Simply because he asked when Papa will be here? That's as far-fetched as Harriet thinking Jack Culhane is going to marry her because her father had a conversation with his."

Mama took off her spectacles and focused on Caroline. "Harriet Vandermeulen thinks to marry Jack Culhane? Her father will never permit it. If he did any speaking, it was to tell Jack Culhane's father that his son should set his sights lower."

"You can't possibly mean that."

"They're in trade, Caroline. I'm not even sure Jack Culhane was born in America, and Patrick Culhane most certainly was not. The Culhane money needs to age for at least three generations before anyone in our circle will touch Jack."

But Caroline had touched Jack. She felt a sharp sting

of remorse that because of her confession, she never would again.

"But enough with the over-ambitious Culhanes," Mama said. "Let's talk about something endlessly more exciting . . . your future! I think a short engagement would be best. I am beginning plans for a fall wedding. New York City is beautiful that time of year."

"I've met the man twice, Mama! I'm not marrying him this autumn. That's hardly fair to Bremerton or me."

Caroline's mother sighed. "Yes, I suppose you're right. I'm just so excited that our years of work are finally coming to fruition. A winter wedding, then."

"This coming winter?"

"Of course."

It was Caroline's turn to sigh. "I would prefer the winter of 1995." Even if Jack didn't want her, it would take at least a century to adjust to the idea of marrying Bremerton.

"We don't always get what we prefer, dear," Mama said absently as she put her spectacles back on and picked up her pen.

"I had noticed that," Caroline replied.

Her mother muttered something about lilies, but did not look up from her list-making.

Caroline moved closer and pretended a casual interest in a copy of *Town Topics* that sat near her edge of the table. Mama always said it was wiser to read the gossip sheet than ignore it. Perhaps her mother would see the same wisdom in listening to Peek.

"I just had a conversation with Miss Peek," Caroline said as she turned a page.

"Mm-hmm."

"She was quite surprised when she saw Lord Bremerton at the Vandermeulens today. It seems she was unaware that Lord Bremerton's elder brother had died."

"She has lived away from England for a number of years."

"But when she did live in England, she had personal knowledge of the last Lord Bremerton. It seems that this one was estranged from both him and their grandfather, the duke."

Mama looked up. "As I said, your governess has been gone from England for years. If there was a rift, I'm sure it healed long ago. And even if it hasn't healed, did it occur to you that Lord Bremerton might not be the party at fault?"

"Peek says that the late Lord Bremerton was well liked."

"The current Lord Bremerton seems to be doing well for himself, too," Mama said. "He was very charming this afternoon."

"Of course he was," Caroline replied. She couldn't stop her bitterness from seeping into her voice. "And it's all an act."

She had her mother's full attention now. "Am I to understand that in this same two days you claim is far too short to get to know the man, you have already judged him?"

There was an uncomfortable measure of truth in Mama's words. But there was also truth in what Caroline felt. "I'm sorry, Mama, but he makes the hairs on my arms rise. And you saw how he was last night. He was not nice. Not at all."

"As I recall, neither were you."

"I'll agree my behavior was poor, but you were not outside with him, Mama. You didn't hear the way he spoke to me, as though I'm a child."

Mama gave a rueful shake of her head. "In many ways, you are. Marriage is to be accepted . . . even excitedly anticipated. Don't you want your own house? Your own staff?"

"No, I don't. I want to be young, first. I want to do the things I haven't been allowed to do . . . even something as simple as going target shooting with Eddie."

"Has it really been all that horrible?"

"I understand how lucky I am, which is what makes me feel so selfish. You've been attentive. I do appreciate that I've had more of your time than many of my friends have had from their mothers. But it feels as though every moment of my life with you has been focused on shaping me to be a bride. I want the time to do as I choose and be who I am."

"Marriage to Lord Bremerton will give you that. You see the freedom I have," Mama said, waving one beringed hand. "Your father and I have made our accommodations so that I can pursue my interests and he can pursue his."

Caroline was only too aware of that, since her mother's interests started and stopped with seeing her daughters married well. Sometimes she wondered what Mama would do with herself once that had been achieved.

"But I want to marry a man who shares my interests," Caroline said.

"I'm willing to guess that you don't even know what Lord Bremerton's are."

"Polo."

"And?"

"Not travel."

"And that is the sum total of your knowledge?"

"I also know there's something not right about him. I can feel it in here," she said, settling a hand over her heart.

Mama shook her head. "The heart is an imperfect thing, Caroline. Go by what you see and what you are told. Spend time with Bremerton. Engage him in conversation. Ask him about his family." She gave a brief laugh. "You're relentless enough that you will wear him down. And if he offended his late brother by putting a frog under his pillow as a child—"

"And his grandfather's pillow," Caroline added.

"Yes," Mama said impatiently. "*And* his grandfather's pillow, you'll know."

"What if it was more than a pair of frogs?"

"Sound the alarm, then," Mama said. "But not a moment sooner. And in the meantime, leave me be so I can write this list. We will be back to Rosemeade on Saturday, and I have much to do."

At least she'd made some small progress, Caroline thought as she left the room. And even small progress with Mama was a miracle.

FOURTEEN

AT FOUR ON THURSDAY MORNING, JACK WATCHED Heinrich Krantz's carriage roll up to the main gate at Krantz and Sons Brewery. He'd been told the owner prided himself on being the first one there each day. Knowing that, he had walked over from his nearby hotel around three this morning. Not that he'd been able to sleep, anyway. For the past hour, he'd talked with the guards and even joined in on a game of dice. The night had been better spent than if he'd stayed in Newport with Eddie underfoot and Da probably trying to give him romantic advice . . . as if Da had a clue.

Krantz exited his coach and marched down the sidewalk.

"Good morning, Mr. Krantz," Jack said as he neared.

"What are you doing here? It is not Monday," Krantz replied without stopping.

If Jack hadn't seen the look of surprise on the older man's face, he'd have thought his effort had failed.

He fell in step behind Krantz, and then drew even. "I'm here anyway."

Krantz glanced his way, but kept up a pace that was amazing for such a portly man. "Why do you think I would care?"

"Because now you know I'm the first buyer for this place who's done more than what you ask."

Krantz stopped. "So you shoveled for two days, and now you show up when you're not expected? If you think that's enough to impress me, leave."

They reached the door to the brewery's office block. As Krantz passed, the guard touched two fingers to the brim of his hat.

"Here's what I think, sir," Jack said as they started up the wide stairway to Krantz's office. "I think hard work is one thing I do consistently better than most people. I *like* hard work. I like going to sleep each night knowing I've achieved something, and I like getting up the next day and doing something even better."

"And what did you think to achieve today?" Krantz asked as he opened the mahogany door to his office's reception area.

"I want to come to terms on a sale." If there was one part of his life Jack could get right, business was it. "Not because I have a problem shoveling stables, or doing any other job that makes this business run efficiently, but because I have another pressing matter that will not allow me the pleasure of time spent away on an uncertainty."

Krantz walked on to his office. Jack followed. The older man turned on the electric lights, and the room began to glow. However, the bitter scent of cigar smoke still permeated every possible surface.

Krantz headed to his desk, where he settled into a chair that made his seat at the room's board table look like a pauper's stool. Ornate carvings that reached a good two feet above the older man's head depicted medieval King Gambrinus, the supposed patron saint of beer.

"Sit," the brewery owner commanded.

Jack did as ordered, his chair as squat as a toad. He had to appreciate the business ploy, if not the fact that his line of vision was not much higher than the top of Krantz's oversized desk.

"How old are you?" Krantz asked.

"Twenty-seven."

"And how many years do you have in the brewery business?"

"Four."

Krantz laughed. "*Faugh!* Four. When I was your age, I had spent fifteen years in breweries. But at least you don't lie." He reached for what appeared to be yesterday's half-finished cigar. "I have already talked to my contacts. I know all that is to be known about you."

With luck, that didn't include the recent development of being such a horse's ass he couldn't even recognize when someone was falling in love with him.

Or he with her . . .

Damn, he thought, as shock burned through him as strong as an electrical current. All the same, he tried to keep an impassive expression. He'd mucked up enough lately without letting this deal slip through his fingers.

Krantz pulled a match from the box on his desk and drew it across the striker. A sulfurous scent burned Jack's nostrils. While the brewery owner puffed his cigar back to life, he gazed levelly at Jack.

"My contacts tell me you have a passion for beer and a talent for business," the older man said once he was satisfied with his cigar. "But they also say you have just added a brewery in New York. I think you take on too much, too soon."

Jack smiled for the first time since yesterday afternoon. "That beats the hell out of too little, too late, don't you think, sir?"

Krantz gave him a tick of a smile. "Did you know you are not the first buyer I tried to send to my stables?"

"No, sir."

"But you are the first to go." He puffed on his cigar. "That makes you mad or a genius. I have decided you are mad. But I did like the two days of free labor."

Jack laughed.

"So what do you offer today?"

Jack thought quickly. "I offer you two more days of my time. If you let me see more than the stables, by the close of business tomorrow, I'll tell you what I would change about this place and what I have learned from you. I'll keep my nose out of your beer recipes and finances, but otherwise I need access from cellars to roof."

Krantz gave a slow shake of his head. "You *are* a madman. If you tell me anything I don't already know . . . which I say now is impossible . . . how will you stop me from using it? Just because you do this, I will not promise to sell the brewery to you."

"I don't want to stop you from using what I share," Jack said. "Even if you do sell this place out from under me, I'm ahead. The stronger my competitors are, the harder I work to be better. But by tomorrow night, you'll be ready to negotiate with me."

The brewery owner drew on his cigar and let loose a stream of smoke. "Then go to work, madman."

Jack smiled. Business, he knew. Love, not so much.

Lord Bremerton had come calling at three o'clock. According to Mrs. Longhorne's grandfather clock, it was now three-twenty-four. Time was creeping like a haggard crone, which was what Caroline expected to be before the Englishman departed. Caroline had picked up a few tidbits that Mama, who was chaperoning from the other side of the room, found enthralling. Caroline was not encouraged by them.

When Bremerton was not playing polo, he was fond of fencing. And when he was not fencing, he enjoyed passing time at one of his clubs. He did not read for pleasure. He did not wish to learn to golf or try deep-sea fishing or explore the world in any way at all. The sole common bond he and Caroline shared was breathing the same air. Caroline was tapped out. And bored.

"Miss Maxwell, perhaps we should walk the grounds. You're looking a bit sleepy," Bremerton suggested.

Caroline nearly rolled her eyes. *A walk*. What was it with men and their walks? Mama cleared her throat and made a *shoo*ing motion toward the terrace door. Caroline was trapped.

"A walk sounds delightful," she said to Bremerton. "I believe I owe you one in any case."

"We'll stay within view of the house," Bremerton said in an ingratiating tone to Mama as he ushered Caroline outside.

"Do you plan to run this time?" he asked once the door had closed behind them.

Deciding that he must have been trying to show humor with the question, Caroline smiled. "No. Do you wish to go farther than the terrace?"

"Yes." He offered her his arm in such a way that she knew refusing it was not an option. Caroline steeled herself but still couldn't hide her shiver when they touched.

"Are you feeling unwell?" Bremerton asked.

"I'm adjusting to the breeze."

They took the broad steps to the lawn. The lace on Caroline's pale-blue-and-white striped dress fluttered, and the scent of the roses that grew at the base of the terrace perfumed the air. It was an idyllic day with a thoroughly unsuitable man. Caroline supposed she had better become accustomed to that, since the only man who seemed to suit her was Jack.

"Please tell me about your family," she said as Bremerton led her toward a small Roman folly built close to the seaward edge of the property. "You've met my mother and my siblings, and you'll meet my father at the upcoming costume ball, but I don't know very much about the people in your life."

"My immediate family is small and scattered," he replied. "I have one sister who is married, and my brother passed away six months ago."

"I'm sorry," she said.

"We were not close."

"Really?"

"Percy was six years older than I," Bremerton said.

"My brother, Edward, is six years older than I, but we're still close."

"Percy was off to school before I was old enough to know him. We were distant."

"Always?"

"Yes, always."

Caroline tried again. "I know from being drilled on *Debrett's* that you have both a father and grandfather living. Do you see them on the holidays, at least?"

"Is there a purpose to this inquisition?" he asked in such a sharp tone that she looked up at him and stumbled a little at the anger on his face. He lengthened his stride and directed her into the middle of the temple-shaped folly. "I asked if there is a purpose, Miss Maxwell?"

She drew a breath and gathered herself. "Is there a purpose in trying to frighten me, Lord Bremerton?"

His expression grew bland. "I have no idea what you mean."

"I'm referring to your tone of voice and to the way you propelled me into here."

"I was merely helping you find your balance," he said smoothly. "And the folly seemed a suitable romantic spot to pause in our walk. You are seeking romance, Miss Maxwell, and I am endeavoring to provide it."

Caroline tried to slip her hand free from the crook of his elbow, but he pressed his arm closer to his body. She tried again. His face remained impassive.

"I would like my hand, please," she finally requested.

"All you ever need to do is ask," he said, letting her go. "There is no need for drama."

But there was a need for escape before she lost her temper. Because he stood in the doorway, she walked between two of the folly's columns and took a step toward the house.

"Please wait a moment, Miss Maxwell."

Mama stood on the terrace, pretending to be invisible. Caroline willed Mama to walk her way, but either Mama lacked the ability to read minds or Caroline lacked the ability to communicate telepathically.

"Do you enjoy the view better from there?" the Englishman asked.

"Yes," she said, with her back turned to him.

She heard the grit of his shoes against the pea gravel that surrounded the folly. He was directly behind her now.

"Your life could be very pleasant with me, Caroline," he said in a voice she would call seductive if he didn't unsettle her so. "I have few rules, though I am quite firm about those I have. I am a traditionalist. I lead. You follow. In exchange, all you need to do is ask. Whatever it is will be done for you."

He touched the back of her neck with one fingertip. She shivered.

"Do you have anything to ask, Caroline?"

"I would like to return to the house," she said.

He moved next to her and held out his arm. She took it. Up on the terrace, Mama smiled. Yes, to all outward appearances it was an idyllic day.

* * *

"Caroline, you are not eating your dessert," Amelia said at dinner that night.

But cake wasn't going to tempt Caroline, especially because she had the feeling that Mama had requested it as a special reward such as she'd give her dog, Pomeroy. Walk with a slightly scary Englishman and you get chocolate cake. That being the case, no thank you.

"If you want mine, you may have it," she said to Amelia.

Her younger sister excitedly nodded her head.

"Absolutely not," Mama said. "If Amelia wanted more—which she does *not*," she said with a glare at her youngest daughter, "she would simply ask for another piece. We do not pass around food like playing cards."

Amelia sighed her disappointment, Helen gazed into space, and Mrs. Longhorne had another hearty swallow of wine. Such was a ladies-only meal. They'd been jilted early on by Eddie, who was supposed to have brought a handful of his friends, including Jack. Instead, Eddie had dropped in around four and said that he and his friends would be dining with Mr. Culhane. Jack had left town indefinitely, and they didn't want to leave the poor man without enough people for a decent billiards match this evening.

Mama said that she understood entirely. Even if she was upset with Eddie, she would never show it to his face. He was the heir, after all. Eddie had departed whistling, and Caroline had fought hard not to cry. She would not be seeing Jack, even in passing.

Caroline was about to ask to be excused when Mrs. Longhorne's butler appeared.

"Mr. Bernard Maxwell," he announced, but not as quickly as Papa had entered the room.

"So *here's* my girls! I stopped at Rosemeade, and some blasted guards would not let me into my own house.

'Orders of Mrs. Maxwell,' one said. I questioned him some more and he finally admitted I might find you here. Those are some stubborn men you've hired, Agnes, not that I'd expect less."

Mama had risen. She went to Papa, who gave her a quick hug. Caroline smiled. Her parents might lead mostly separate lives, but they truly loved each other. Why Mama could not wish this for her made no sense at all.

"I didn't expect you until Saturday," Mama said. "Though I am quite happy to see you."

"The *Conqueror* was ready, my work was done, and so here I am." He glanced around the dining room. "But where is Edward?"

"He is staying at the Benton Villa, by Touro Park. According to *Town Topics*, Jack Culhane's father won it on a hand of cards," Mama sniffed.

Papa chuckled. "Good for him. Benton cheats."

"All the same, I do pine for Edward."

"Then maybe you shouldn't have put guards in front of our home. We'd all be there, then," Papa said as he took the empty chair next to Caroline and pulled it closer. "You're not eating your cake, Pumpkin. Do you need some help?"

"I'd love some," Caroline replied. She didn't bother to hide her smile as her father took over her cake and dessert fork. Mama turned her head in the other direction, as though an execution was taking place. She didn't say a word, of course.

"So what have you been doing with yourselves here in Newport, girls?" he asked between bites.

"All sorts of things. It's been wonderful, Papa," Amelia cried. "There have been parties and teas and beach bathing and more parties and—"

Papa laughed. "So, the usual array of ladies' events. How about you, Helen? Have you kept yourself busy?"

"Every moment, it seems," Helen replied.

"You don't sound very happy about that."

"I would love one single day in which I could do nothing at all."

"Nothing?" Papa asked.

"Well, only what I wish to do."

"Let's make tomorrow that day," Papa said. "Every member of this family will do only what they choose. Mildred," he said to Mrs. Longhorne, "are you free to join in?"

"I believe I shall," Mrs. Longhorne replied.

"A vacation from a vacation," Caroline said to her father. "What a decadent thought."

"Ah, but you are not on a vacation. It's your job to follow the busy social schedule your mother sets. And it's mine to give you a day off every handful of years."

"As is your right," Mama said briskly. "Unfortunately, I must keep to my schedule. We have a costume ball just days away. Bernard, if you will excuse me?" she asked, but rose before Papa could answer. "I need my rest. I am assuming you'll be on the *Conqueror* tonight, but I will see you tomorrow." Mama gave a perfunctory smile before she left. Mrs. Longhorne made her excuses and departed in Mama's wake.

"And that's why I generally keep to my business and let your mother keep the houses," Papa said good-naturedly. "She's not a woman to cross." He waved his dessert fork at Caroline. "Are you sure you don't want any of this?"

"No, thank you," she replied.

"Then I'll finish it," he said. Soon after the last bite had disappeared, he added, "So what do you plan to do with your decadent day, Pumpkin?"

Caroline smiled. "I believe I will visit a friend."

FIFTEEN

"ANY ILLUSION I HAD OF KEEPING UP WITH YOU IN A tennis match has disappeared," Flora said to Caroline, who had handily trounced her on the Casino's grass court twenty minutes earlier. "But I'll be kind to myself and admit I did well for a woman of my age."

Caroline tilted her head as though considering the matter. "You're ageless."

"Tell that to my legs," Flora replied. "They feel as rubbery as aspic. If this café table hadn't been open, you'd have been calling for the smelling salts."

Caroline laughed. "Really, smelling salts? I can't see that."

"Or maybe a fine Kentucky bourbon," Flora added with a smile.

"That sounds closer to the mark," Caroline said. "And I do apologize for playing so ferociously. I don't get to play often, so I wanted to take full advantage. The exercise let me get my mind off my problems, too."

"Would you care to share them?" Flora asked, suspecting she already knew what—or who—was behind them. "My advanced age makes me a good listener, so long as I haven't been into the bourbon."

"Have you ever made such a complete mess of things

that you didn't think you'd ever be able to straighten them out?" Caroline asked.

"Never," Flora said, and then quickly took a sip of her water to hide her smile. At Caroline's wide-eyed look, she added, "Try daily."

Yesterday evening, when she'd welcomed Patrick's parting kiss, was a prime example. After all her talk of strength, she'd melted for him. Though it was no real excuse, she had never forgotten how good they were together. And now that she'd kissed him again, that knowledge refused to leave her mind. But focusing on her friend did help.

Caroline looked around before speaking. "I did the most awful thing with Jack," she said in a lower voice. "Thinking about it mortifies me."

And the possibilities were suddenly terrifying Flora. She trusted Jack . . . mostly. But he was a Culhane, and Culhane men had a way of getting what they wanted, especially if what they wanted was a woman.

"What happened?" Flora asked.

"I . . . I told Jack that I loved him. I was so frustrated with him and with my entire situation in life that the words just flew out. Now I have absolutely no idea what to do."

Their waiter approached. Flora was glad to have gained some time. All she could think to say to Caroline was *thank heaven it was just that!* She doubted her young friend would appreciate the sentiment. With thoughts of sweetening the moment, Flora ordered two lemonades while Caroline sat there looking glum.

"I'm sure it was an uncomfortable moment," Flora said after the waiter had left.

"Yes, and it became absolutely painful when Jack tried to pretend the words had never been said. I wanted to disappear."

Flora's heart ached for Caroline. Once upon a time, she'd had that experience with a Culhane. "I'm sorry. Though there are exceptions, men aren't very talented at talking about love. And some can be complete clods."

"Oh, Flora, I was the fool, not Jack," Caroline said in a rush. "I knew he didn't love me. I amuse him, that's all. He finds me interesting, the way I do a specimen in the museum."

"I think it's safe to say he doesn't see you as a specimen."

"How do you know that?"

"Do you kiss museum specimens?" Flora asked.

"Of course not."

"I doubt Jack does, either."

Caroline smiled briefly, but then her eyes widened. "Oh, this *is* mortifying. I just realized that not only did I tell him I loved him first, but I kissed him first, too."

"And yet you have lived to tell the tale," Flora said, smiling.

"You're right," Caroline said, sounding a bit surprised. "It's really not so tragic. And unlike what Jack tried to do, I know I can't proceed through life pretending this never happened."

"Good for you!" Flora said. "That act never ends well."

The waiter arrived with the lemonade. It had been years since Flora had tasted any. She sipped it and smiled. It seemed that many of her old favorites remained true.

Caroline traced her finger down the moisture clinging to the outside of her glass. "Eddie said that Jack has left town."

"Yes, he has."

"Did he talk to you?"

Flora knew to choose her words carefully. Jack had honored her by calling her family. While she adored Caroline, he held her loyalty. "Yes, we spoke."

"Did he say where he was going?"

This, she could share. "He had some business to attend to at a brewery in Providence."

Caroline brightened again. "Well, that's a relief. I thought I had managed to drive him from Newport with my impetuous declaration."

And the truth, Flora would not share. Of course not.

Caroline sipped her lemonade and gazed at the passing scene. "We've agreed that I will live through the embarrassment, but what do I do about Jack now?"

Flora smiled. "Ah, the most difficult question of all. I think in this instance you wait and have faith that Jack is the man you think he is. Sooner or later, he'll come around and talk to you."

Caroline sighed. "I'm not very good at waiting."

"So it would seem. But sometimes it's the wisest thing a woman can do."

Now, if Flora could only take her own advice and not let her heart get ahead of her common sense when it came to Patrick Culhane.

Tuesday night, Caroline was a bundle of nerves. It was a blessing that her mother had managed to restrain herself and redecorate only the public areas of Rosemeade. As it was, Caroline kept rounding corners and jumping when confronted by unexpected pieces of lurking, life-sized statuary. But the conservatory, Caroline's favorite room in this house, remained blessedly as it had always been. She closed her eyes and savored the quiet. This sort of silence would soon be as rare as a statue-free stretch of hallway.

"Miss!"

Caroline yelped. Annie had appeared in front of her. "I'm sorry for startling you, but you have to hurry,

Miss. I've been looking all over for you. Your mother is after you. She has it in her head that you're trying to hide away and miss the ball."

Which, while a good idea, was unworkable. Even Rosemeade wasn't big enough to hide her from Mama, especially the day after Bremerton and Papa had met at a polo match. The introduction must have gone well. Mama was sure Bremerton was going to propose tonight. Thus, the heightened security on Caroline.

"I was just gathering my thoughts," Caroline said to her maid. "Where's my mother?"

"She and your father are in your sitting room."

The last time both of her parents had ventured into her quarters had been after the London six-shooter demonstration. It had not been a happy conversation. Caroline quickly made her way up the rosewood staircase, with its new scarlet-colored carpet, past a one-armed Grecian warrior, and to her sitting room.

Mama and Papa stood in the middle of the room on the worn floral needlepoint rug Caroline had loved since childhood. Judging by Mama's rather Byzantine golden headdress and Papa's jeweled crown and charcoal-colored silk ceremonial robe clasped at the shoulder of his evening coat, Caroline hazarded a guess that they were Empress Theodora and Emperor Justinian of the Roman Empire. She knew for certain that her mother had chosen the costumes to best display her jewel collection. Mama was practically her own light source.

"Your gown! You have altered it!" Mama cried as Caroline came closer.

Caroline loved her slender gold diadem and gilded bow and quiver of arrows. She had accepted the thin petticoat and had even come to enjoy the Empire style waist and minimal corset that were part of being Artemis. But when Annie's eyes had gone wide as Caroline had donned her costume this evening, she'd known she still had too much skin exposed up top.

"I want to survive the evening with some measure of dignity intact," she said to her mother. "The ecru lace Annie pieced in is hardly noticeable."

Mama sighed. "I suppose it's fine, particularly because there's no time to remove it. Guests will begin arriving at any moment."

Caroline's father looked relieved at Mama's capitulation.

"I've brought you something, Pumpkin." He reached beneath the opening to his long robe and into the coat pocket below. Out came a blue velvet box. "Your mother told me you would be dressing as Artemis, so I had our jeweler design a piece especially for tonight."

He handed her the box.

"That was so thoughtful of you," Caroline said, feeling both touched and regretful. If this was the night she had to say yes to Bremerton, she wanted nothing to remind her of it.

"A woman should have her jewels," Papa said. "They are insurance against a great many things in life."

Caroline opened the box. Inside sat an intricate necklace. Three narrow chains paved with diamonds met to hold a cameo of Artemis as the huntress, bow and arrow raised, set in gold with yet more diamonds surrounding it.

"The jeweler told me that diamonds symbolize Artemis," Papa said. "I've got no idea if that's true, but it was a profitable statement for him to make."

"It's beautiful, Papa. Thank you," she said and went up on tiptoe to kiss his cheek.

"It is quite tasteful," Mama said. She frowned at the

piece. "And I suppose it looks as though it could have belonged to Marie Antoinette."

"What does a dead French queen have to do with this?" Papa asked.

"I'm just making sure Caroline matches the details already given to the newspapers," Mama replied.

"You gave details regarding our own daughter?"

"Of course I did," Mama said cheerily.

Papa sighed. "Sometimes you worry me, Agnes."

"Annie, please help me with the necklace," Caroline asked her maid.

Once it was in place, Mama nodded her approval. "That will do quite well." She squared her shoulders. "Are we all ready for the most momentous night of Caroline's life?"

If it was up for a vote, Caroline was not in favor.

The only thing Jack hated more than costume balls was a bad batch of beer. Tonight, though, he'd almost take the bad beer. He adjusted the mask to his makeshift costume and then stepped out of his carriage. Rosemeade was lit up and festooned past the point of excess. But Jack knew that had been Agnes Maxwell's goal. Outdoing the neighbors in Newport was no easy job.

As he approached the house, he nodded greetings to those who looked remotely familiar, as well as to his fellow highwaymen. There was no better costume for a costume hater, and plenty of men matched that description.

O'Brien stood at Rosemeade's door, flanked by a squad of tall footmen in powdered wigs. Only those invited would be getting inside. The rest would be sent to the property gate to join the gawkers and reporters.

"Mr. Jack Culhane," Jack said.

O'Brien checked his list and nodded imperially. "Welcome, Mr. Culhane."

Jack nearly stopped dead when he made the entry hall.

"Unbelievable," he said to himself. The place looked like Agnes had lifted the Elgin marbles from the British Museum and had them shipped in. Knowing her level of determination, it was possible. He followed the flow of the crowd toward the ballroom, which he could have found by scent alone. Thousands of white roses and hundreds of people were squeezed into the space. He took a glass of champagne from a round table packed with them and began to hunt for Eddie, who was somewhere out there in the legion of highwaymen. Jack could eliminate a number of them by build, and more by voice. But then he saw Eddie.

"What the hell happened to you?" Jack asked his friend.

"This," Eddie said, gesturing at his white pantaloons and bright blue velvet jacket and cape embroidered with *fleurs de lis,* "is what happens when I am stuck under my mother's roof. No black mask and cape for me. I have to be Louis-stinking-XIV, the Sun King."

Jack grinned. Eddie's hair rose several inches above his head before it fell in twin waves of tortured curls. "Nice wig."

"And yet it's better than these damn pants," Eddie said with a long-suffering smile. "Where have you been? I kept your father company for as long as I could before Mother reeled me back here."

"I think you mean you kept my father and the whiskey company," Jack said.

He laughed. "It was tough duty, but someone had to take it. So where were you?"

"Picking up that Providence brewery. We finished negotiating at three this afternoon, and I'm out of the buying business until my cash reserves can catch up with my ambition again."

"It sounds to me as though it's time to marry Harriet," Eddie said. He inclined his head to Jack's right. "She's over there, done up like some princess or another. You could get her to the altar after our dawn breakfast without even waiting for her to change her dress."

"I'd rather do with less breweries," Jack said flatly. The moment he'd realized he was falling in love with Caroline, he'd also lost his sense of humor about Harriet's fervent pursuit.

"Good. You'd just be stealing Caroline's thunder," Eddie replied before handing his wineglass to a waiter and requesting whiskey instead.

Jack had a feeling he should be asking the waiter to make it two. "Caroline has news?"

Eddie nodded. "She should by the end of the night. Bremerton plans to propose."

Forget a glass. Jack wanted the bottle.

It was only an hour into the ball, and Caroline had already become very talented at both dancing with a bow and quiver on her back and dancing around Lord Bremerton. After one obligatory waltz and some cursory chat, she had made her excuses and headed off to dance with others. She now stood on the far side of the ballroom from the Englishman, taking a much-needed break. Caroline amused herself by counting the number of new gilded mirrors hung from the silk-covered walls beneath the equally new crystal-laden electric light fixtures. They numbered more than the male guests clad as highwaymen, but not by much.

Mama, who had been watching Caroline all night, sent her another disapproving look. She didn't need to bother. Caroline's freedom would end at midnight when

O'Brien rang the chimes announcing dinner. There was no escaping one's dinner partner. Naturally, hers was Bremerton. But until then, her time was her own.

Caroline was preparing to join a group of friends who stood not far away when a highwayman approached from her right.

"Hello," she said.

He nodded a greeting, but didn't speak. He must have decided to distinguish himself from the pack by being a mute robber, but his black cowboy hat in lieu of a top hat already did that for him.

His hand closed around her wrist with just enough firmness that she knew she was being instructed to follow. He turned back the way he'd come and led her from the ballroom. If anyone noticed them—and as wrapped up as they were in their own pleasures, Caroline doubted they had—they didn't say anything. He urged her out of the crush of the crowd and on to the south wing of the house. With his free hand, he pushed open the glass and wrought-iron door to the conservatory and drew her in.

Unlike the rest of Rosemeade, this room was lit only by gaslight. Its sole fixture, a filigreed, multiglobed bronze chandelier, was suspended from the conservatory's high center peak. It made for a romantic setting, if not too practical for nighttime botany. But her highwayman was no botanist.

"Hello, Jack," she said once the spring-hinged door had swung shut behind them.

He released her. Caroline could have stepped away, but she didn't want to.

"You knew it was me?" he asked.

"Of course." She'd known the instant he'd touched her. "Do you think I'd let just anyone abduct me?"

He laughed.

"It's good to see you," she said, then added, "Well, as much of you as I can see at the moment."

He took off his hat and set it next to a spindly fern. Then he reached behind his head, untied his black fabric mask, and let it drop to the hat. "Better?"

"Yes. Much." She tried to judge his mood by his face, but he wasn't giving anything away. And while she preferred to dance a circle around Bremerton, she wanted to be direct with Jack. "Now that you've gone to the effort of getting us alone, is there something you want to say?"

He reached out one black-gloved hand to touch her face. "You look beautiful tonight. You make the perfect Artemis."

She wanted to tell him that flattery wouldn't work, but it would. Too well.

"Thank you, though you didn't have to bring me here to say that," she replied before sidestepping him and walking farther into the large conservatory. When she'd been younger, this had been her jungle and each fern and flower an exotic new species to discover.

Jack pulled even with her. "I brought you here because it's your favorite place," he said, sounding slightly irritated.

"Well, thank you again. That was unusually considerate of you."

The corner of his mouth bent upward. "Unusually? You *are* upset with me, aren't you?"

She hadn't meant to send that arrow flying, but now that it had been shot, she felt better. "I have reason to be."

"I know." He looked down at the ground and then back at her. "I also brought you here because I'm not going to eat crow in front of six hundred people."

"But you will in here?" she asked, feeling pleased by the offer.

This time he full-out smiled. "Yes, if you want me to."

"A few bites might be nice."

"Okay," he said, and then drew a breath as though preparing himself for something strenuous. "I'm sorry for the way I acted the other day. You're important to me. You deserve better."

Which was exactly three bites, Caroline thought. "You're referring to the exchange in your carriage, correct?"

"Yes."

She could ask for more crow-eating, but Flora had been right. Impatience on Caroline's part had brought about this situation. More impatience wouldn't solve it.

"Thank you, then," she said.

Jack blew out a quick breath that Caroline figured was pure relief.

"I saw Bremerton all weighed down by gold chains," he said. "Which king is he supposed to be?"

"A young Henry the Eighth," she replied.

"Young, huh?"

"Those were his words, not mine," Caroline said, trying not to smile at Jack's skepticism. According to *Debrett's,* Bremerton was seven years older than Jack.

Jack shrugged. "He's got an old Henry's dissipated look."

Caroline laughed. "I've missed you."

He came closer. "Your brother says there's supposed to be an engagement announcement tonight."

"That's just Mama's talk. Bremerton hasn't asked me."

"Yet," Jack said.

She nodded. "Yes, yet." The thought hung over her like an executioner's blade.

Jack settled his hand on her arm. Caroline wished his gloves would go the way of his hat and his mask. She wanted the comfort of his touch, not leather.

"Since you're not yet engaged, it wouldn't exactly be a hanging offense if I did this. . . ." He brushed a kiss against her lips and then moved back.

"*That* was a highwayman's kiss?" she asked, pretending shock.

He laughed. "What, not dangerous enough?"

"Not even close," she replied.

Jack returned. His mouth hovered over hers. "Ready?"

"A highwayman just takes what he wants," she reminded him.

And so he did.

This time his kiss was all hot persuasion, quickly stealing what little sense of propriety Caroline had when it came to him. She wrapped her arms around his neck. The heavy satin of his black cape felt sleek against her bare skin. She held on as he teased her mouth, tempting her to give more, and then making a low sound of triumph when she did. If he was this good at stealing kisses, she'd happily give him whatever else he wanted to take.

Jack ran his hands from her ribs to her waist, jostling her bow and quiver. He broke the kiss to say, "Let's disarm you."

He helped her ease her costume pieces over her head, and she quickly set them on the floor. Then he drew her back into his arms. This time his hands ventured even lower, and he pulled her hard against his body.

"Now I'm *really* liking this costume," he said.

She smiled. "I'm growing fonder of it, too."

He kissed her again. His hands slid lower yet, past the curve of her lower back. She drew in a sharp breath, and he rather slowly retreated from the new territory.

"No. Stay. It was good," she assured Jack before kissing him again.

She had understated the feeling. This was *amazing*.

All she could think about was how much she wanted to feel him, skin to skin. She couldn't have that, but one wish could be granted tonight.

Caroline moved just far enough away to speak. "Take off your gloves."

Jack unwound her arms and set her away from him. He looked around the conservatory. For a heart-stopping instant, she thought he was going to call an end to their kissing.

"This way," he said.

He took her by the hand and led her to the outer wall of the hexagonally shaped room. He stood her with her back against a short stretch of solid wall where two angled expanses of glass met. Mama had not lit the lawns as she had the front. Nothing but darkness was on either side of Caroline.

"Put your hands on the glass," he said.

"But—"

"You heard me," he said in a mock stern voice.

Caroline did as he'd directed. The conservatory still held the day's heat, but the thick windows were cool beneath her palms. His gaze didn't leave her as he worked on the fingers to the first glove.

"Someday we'll have a bed," he said as he dropped the glove to the floor.

Caroline's heart pounded.

He started on the next glove. "A whole bed with just the two of us, and the rest of the world be damned." The second glove hit the ground.

Her breath was coming shallowly. She pressed more fully against the wall behind her. It was that or join the gloves.

Jack reached forward. He slipped her costume and the thin chemise strap beneath it off one shoulder. Both went without resistance. "When that day comes, I'll start here."

Caroline gasped as his mouth settled over the skin he'd just bared. He was hot. So hot. And now she burned, too. He kissed his way across her collarbone and down the slope of her breast. Caroline's fingers dug for purchase against the glass.

"Jack . . ." she said after a minute.

He looked up at her. Even in the flickering light, she could see how much he wanted her. "Yes?"

"The other side, too."

"You're full of commands tonight," he said. "So far, I like them."

This side of her costume did not cooperate as well. Hungry to feel his touch, she reached up and tugged at the silk. It gave, but not graciously.

Caroline returned her hand to the window. She felt safe with him. They could play at her surrender, but he would never really harm her. Jack ran the backs of his fingers across the slopes of each of her breasts.

"I'm one lucky highwayman," he said. And then he slipped his hand inside the fabric and cupped her breast. "Damn lucky."

Skin to skin. Caroline drew a ragged breath, tipped back her head, and closed her eyes as his fingers brought pleasure to parts she'd had no idea could be so sensitive.

He kissed her again, deeply. Caroline tried to concentrate, to capture every moment. She wanted to hold on to the newness and the excitement forever. But then something took her out of the moment. The sound was so small that she wanted to believe she'd imagined it. But she hadn't.

She turned her head, breaking off the kiss.

"I didn't say you could do that," Jack said in a teasing tone.

"Wait," Caroline whispered.

He slipped his hand from her skin and moved back a

half step. She looked toward the sound she thought she'd heard and listened intently, trying to pick it up again. "Did you hear that, a few seconds ago?"

"What?" he asked in a regular voice.

She held her finger to her lips. "Shh . . ."

"Yes, ma'am," he replied as though she were a librarian. He did use a lower tone, though. "What did you hear?"

"I thought I heard the door. The hinges have always squeaked," she said. "Didn't you notice it when we came in?"

"I wasn't thinking about the door," he replied, then dipped his head down to kiss the upper curve of her breast.

She couldn't fault him for that. Still, she braced her hands against his shoulders and held him off.

"Hello?" she called. "Is anyone there?"

Only silence answered.

"I'm sure I heard something that first time," she said to Jack. "We need to leave."

He didn't hesitate and he didn't ask questions. She loved him all the more for that.

He did give a shake of his head as he slipped her costume back onto her shoulders. "That bed, Caroline. It's necessary."

She nodded. "Maybe one day."

He gave her a quick kiss that was about comfort. "Absolutely one day."

Caroline was touched by his tenderness, but her sense of some sort of looming heaviness hadn't dissipated. She didn't want to worry Jack, so she worked up a smile. "Go on back to the ball. We shouldn't walk in together, anyway. I'll be right along."

He reached out a hand and brushed a loose tendril of hair from the side of her face. "You're okay?"

She nodded. "Fine."

Jack bent down to pick up his gloves and then stood and looked at her for a moment. "You're sure?"

"I'd feel better if we got out of here quickly," she admitted.

"I'm out the door," he said.

Caroline took a second to repin the few pieces of hair that had come down. Slight rustling sounds came from the front of the conservatory as Jack stopped to pick up his hat and mask.

"Don't forget your weaponry, Artemis," he said before leaving. "Not that you need it to vanquish men."

And then, as she'd expected, the conservatory door gave a tiny squeak on his way out.

Caroline walked to the front of the conservatory and gathered her costume parts. She'd just finished slinging the bow and quiver over her shoulder when the door opened.

Bremerton walked in. He looked unperturbed, unruffled . . . all things calm. For a moment, Caroline held on to hope that he hadn't been in here a few minutes earlier. But then she saw him glance at the spot on the bench where Jack's hat and mask had been.

"Your mother told me I'd likely find you in here. It's nearly time for dinner," Bremerton said in a conversational tone.

"I'm ready. I just needed a few moments away from the crowd," she replied.

He smiled, but it stopped short of his eyes. "I'm sure you did."

He reached a hand toward her throat, and Caroline flinched. Bremerton made a *tsk*ing sound. "Your necklace is askew. Hold still while I straighten it. We can't have you at dinner looking less than the beauty you are."

Two could play at this charade. She swallowed her nerves and said, "Thank you."

"There," he said. "The virgin huntress is as she should be."

Caroline could almost breathe again.

Bremerton looked more closely at her. "Or nearly as."

Before she could make a sound, his hand shot out. She felt a tug at her bodice, and then he held up the lace that Annie had added to Caroline's costume. He dropped it at her feet.

"It had come loose, somehow. But no loss," he said. "You shouldn't hide the bounty nature has given you." He held out his arm. "Are you ready?"

"Yes," she said with a calm that wasn't even skin deep.

They were out of the south wing and nearly to the dining room when Bremerton spoke again. "I'm sure you recall our conversation from last week. What is the only thing you need to do before I give you the world, Caroline?"

"Ask," she said.

"Correct. Ask." She could feel him looking down at her. She kept her gaze forward and her face serene. "But I'm sure even you are sophisticated enough to realize that you cannot ask for a lover until you've given me an heir."

SIXTEEN

"I STILL DON'T UNDERSTAND WHY LORD BREMERTON failed to propose last night," Mama said to Caroline as their carriage neared the Newport polo grounds. "Let's hope he's feeling more inclined today."

"He'll be playing polo," Caroline said. "I don't think he's going to pop out a proposal on horseback."

"Don't use that tone with me, young lady," Mama said. "And improve your posture. I've had no more sleep than you, yet I'm managing to look rested and content."

"Yes, Mama," Caroline said, though to her, Mama looked more driven than content. She sat ramrod straight with her dark green parasol held rigidly above her head like a fireworks rocket ready to launch. Since Caroline couldn't work up the energy to hide her exhaustion, she brought her parasol down to better shield her face.

"I wish you'd have worn pink," Mama said. "Your yellow is making you look sallow."

Small wonder. The whole family had been awake until seven this morning, when the last of the guests had departed Rosemeade after a dawn breakfast. Caroline had been allowed a three-hour nap before Mama had started drilling her about the night's events. According to Mama, the lack of a marriage proposal had marred what would have been a perfect evening. From Caroline's perspective, that had been the night's saving grace.

"Are you certain Bremerton didn't broach the subject of marriage in your conversations?" Caroline's mother asked yet again.

"I'm sure."

Mama shook her head. "I simply don't understand this."

Caroline had no intention of illuminating her mother, when she'd worked so hard to keep her in the dark. From dinner on, Caroline had stuck by Bremerton out of self-defense. They had appeared to be the perfect courting couple. Only Jack, who'd left just after dinner, had reason to know differently.

"It was right of me to insist that we arrive early," her mother said as they pulled onto the polo grounds. "We're going to be in the front row, and Lord Bremerton will be sure to see you."

It was a Newport tradition for lady spectators to stay in their carriages while they watched a match. The view was better, and they stood less chance of injury if the play left the field.

"Keep an eye out for him and see if you can draw his attention before the match begins," Mama instructed after she'd made sure the coachman had negotiated their way into a prime viewing spot.

"Yes, Mama," Caroline said while willing herself to be inconspicuous.

The polo club was fielding two teams this afternoon, one led by Mr. Carstairs and the other by Eddie. Mama, naturally, had chosen Carstairs' side of the enormous field, since Bremerton played for him. Directly opposite them, Harriet Vandermeulen sat in a barouche with Alice Hayes. Harriet happily waved. Caroline figured she must have been dropped from Harriet's adversaries list after Harriet had seen her with Bremerton last night.

Eddie and five other men stood on Harriet's side of the field, with their grooms and ponies behind them. Eddie's string of ponies were his pride. He'd had them shipped in from England. Caroline spotted his two favorite mounts—tall, matching bays who were proof that polo ponies were not ponies at all. Both horses were saddled and ready to play.

Caroline smiled as she watched her brother talk to his teammates, who all wore bright blue-and-white striped jerseys. Only three of the men would play with him, and two would stand as reserves. She easily picked out Charles Vandermeulen from the group. Two were the Arnott brothers, and another looked to be Robert Conable. She wasn't positive who the broad-shouldered player with his back to her was, though he looked markedly like Jack. But Jack wasn't a polo regular, so that was unlikely. Caroline willed the man to turn or at least move so no one else stood in her line of vision.

Bremerton was riding up. He wore the black-and-navy striped jersey of Mr. Carstairs' club team, along with the obligatory white polo jodhpurs and brown riding boots.

"Good afternoon, Mrs. Maxwell . . . Miss Maxwell," he said with nods to both of them.

"Good afternoon, Lord Bremerton. Caroline and I are looking forward to seeing you play," Mama said with a bob of her parasol that made Bremerton's mount shy.

The Englishman easily reined the horse in. "It should be an interesting match. Field conditions are rough after the showers that passed through this morning."

"I am sure it will be no challenge to you, and that your team will win," Mama said.

Caroline bit back a sigh. Mama had fully switched her allegiance.

"Thank you," the Englishman said. "While I've gotten to know my teammates better in the few days I've been here, both the greatest challenge and greatest reward lies in playing as a unit."

"That's so true," Mama said, nodding approvingly.

Caroline kept her eyes downcast so she wouldn't roll them.

"I regret today will be my last time to play here," Bremerton said. "It's a gray day in more than just the weather. I received some unfortunate news this morning. My father, who has been in ill health for some time, is doing poorly. I'll be leaving Newport tonight and sailing Saturday on the *Lucania,* from New York."

Caroline kept a composed face, but inside she danced a jig. "I'm sorry to hear about your father."

"That *is* a shame," Mama said. "But if you don't sail until Saturday, surely you can stay in Newport at least another day?" She hadn't even bothered to hide her panic.

Bremerton shook his head. "I'm afraid I also have business I must see to in New York." He paused. "Is there any possibility your family will be in London soon? We had little time to get to know each other, and I'd like to extend our acquaintance."

Caroline's happy music stopped.

"What a wonderful coincidence!" Mama said. "Mr. Maxwell and I were talking just this morning about making a visit to our London residence."

Her mother was lying, and even Bremerton knew it. He had no other reason to look so self-satisfied.

"But Mama, Helen and Amelia have commitments well through August," Caroline said. "It doesn't seem fair to make them leave Newport when nothing is as special as a summer by the sea."

"They're very excited at the prospect of travel," her

mother replied without looking Caroline's way. "I take it, then, that you will be in London, Lord Bremerton?"

"Yes. I will be staying at my father's home until I can assure myself that he is on the mend."

"Perfect!"

If Caroline hadn't already heard about Viscount Bellingham's poor health, she would have been certain that Bremerton had manufactured it to force her away from Jack. And she had her suspicions, just the same.

"Would you mind, Mrs. Maxwell, if your daughter and I spoke a moment in private?" Bremerton asked.

Mama rose as though ready to spring from the carriage. "Of course not."

"I don't want to disturb you, ma'am," he said.

The Englishman grasped his pony's reins in one hand and gave a flick of the other in the direction of a groom in Carstairs' team colors. The boy hurried over. Bremerton dismounted and turned the pony over to him. At the same time, Mama had prodded the coachman to help Caroline down and then to go fetch Eddie.

"Perhaps over this way," Bremerton said to Caroline when she'd reached the soggy ground.

He held out his arm. She took it, feeling as though she were on a leash, like Mama's little Pomeroy. Taking a leisurely pace, Bremerton led her in the direction of the polo club's rustic clubhouse.

"This morning it occurred to me that you might think I plan to tell your father what I witnessed in the conservatory last night," Bremerton said.

"And I'm sure that also occurred to you last night when I stayed pinned to your side."

He laughed. "I hope you retain your sharp wit once we are married."

She glared at him, no longer willing to hide her emotions. "Is your father actually ill?"

He stopped walking, but did not let her go. "Caroline, you wound me. Of course he is. And because I wish to be considerate of your feelings and not leave you in doubt, I want you to know that the scene in the conservatory didn't dissuade me. I still plan to pursue our eventual marriage."

"How could you? You know I have feelings for someone else."

"That is unfortunate for you," he said crisply. "But in the history of marriage, you are hardly unique. I am sure you'll find someone to take the Irishman's place in your affections once you're settled in England. It might even be me."

She couldn't quite decide if he'd meant that to be humorous. "Why should it matter to you, when you have no feelings for me?"

"I'd say that *no* feelings is overstating the case. I do have *some*. And after what I saw last night, I even have a certain amount of optimism that our marriage won't be a complete bore."

Caroline could feel heat rising on her face, but she refused to give him the satisfaction of witnessing her embarrassment.

"*Are* you planning to tell my father what you saw?" she asked.

Bremerton, who'd been looking across the field, returned his attention to her. "Why should I, when everything is going in my favor? Your Irishman seems to be forever on the losing team."

Jack turned away from Caroline and Bremerton and focused on his borrowed pony's tack. Watching the supposed couple would only make him want to go over there and knock His Lordship free of a few teeth for upsetting Caroline. And while the Englishman and he were bound to tangle sooner or later, this wasn't the place.

Eddie approached. He looked as sour as Jack felt.

"Sisters are a damned bother," he said. "You should be relieved you don't have any."

"What's the matter?"

"Because Caroline didn't close the wedding deal with the Englishman, I've been conscripted to go with Mother and the girls to England, immediately. She won't even ask Father . . . says he was difficult enough about coming to Newport." He made a low sound of disgust. "That means I'll have at least seven days at sea on the *Conqueror*. Seven days of pitching and rolling and heaving and . . ." He swallowed hard, and Jack laughed.

"It's not funny, damn it," Eddie said.

"Yes, it is. You're making yourself seasick on dry land. You know, I've seen you hanging upside down off a galloping pony to make a shot. If that doesn't make you sick, why does a ship?"

"Because I'm in charge of the pony and not the ship."

"Then have your father give you a captain's hat."

"That's not funny," Eddie said, though Jack was sure he'd caught a smile. But now Eddie was looking at him in a highly speculative way. "I've got an idea. You said you're out of capital for acquisitions, right?"

"Temporarily," Jack admitted.

"Then now is the ideal time for a beer tour of England. Pack your bags and come with me! When I'm not busy acting as the male of the Maxwell family, we'll drink our way through every pub and brewery we can find."

If Caroline was going to be around Bremerton, Jack didn't want to be an ocean away. The beer was just a damn nice bonus. "Sign me on."

"Done!" Eddie said.

"Are you two ready?" Charles Vandermeulen called to them. "Mount up and get moving!"

"Mama, the match is starting," Caroline said. Now that she knew Jack was playing, she wanted no distractions, which meant her mother had to stop fussing.

"I don't have time to watch," Mama said as she dug through her small bag. "Do you have anything I might take notes on?"

"No," Caroline replied. "You barely gave me time to grab a parasol before we left, let alone pack an office."

"Save me your snippiness and watch the match, then," her mother said. "I'll compose my packing list in my head."

Caroline nodded absently, already focused on the action. She had always wanted to learn to play polo, but even Eddie, who'd taught her how to shoot and spit when she'd been little, had drawn the line at this sport.

Bremerton was driving the play to the opposing goal, as Jack tried to defend. The Englishman scored easily, and the spectators on his side applauded. Jack hit the ball back in play for his team. The game moved more toward the center of the field, where Caroline could see the players' faces and catch an occasional word.

Bremerton said something short and apparently unfriendly to Jack as he leaned in and drove Jack and his pony off the line he'd been taking toward the ball. Jack recovered and positioned himself to take a pass from Charles Vandermeulen. Then Jack quickly took the ball to the other end of the field. Once again Caroline's view was of behinds and backs. But when it was Jack's back— and behind, for that matter—her vantage point had its compensations.

As play continued, the field went from soggy to sodden, with mud flying from beneath the horses' hooves.

The ball was no longer white, and the same was becoming true of the players' jodhpurs. When the action returned to the middle of the field, and close against her sideline, Caroline leaned out of the carriage as far as she could, trying to make the experience more immediate.

"No closer!" Mama ordered. "You'll get dirty!"

Caroline looked away. "I'm too far off for that."

When she turned back, both Eddie and his pony were on the ground in a tangle of legs and leather.

Without realizing she'd moved, Caroline was on her feet. "Eddie!"

"What happened?" Mama cried.

"I don't know!"

The pony was up, but Eddie still lay there. The other players had moved away, so she could see her brother's face. He was conscious, but his grimace spoke of pain.

"Gamble, get me down!" Mama cried to their coachman.

Caroline stayed her with one hand. A gentleman was already running across the field, black leather bag in hand. "Wait, Mama. Let the doctor get there." She couldn't imagine Eddie being very pleased to have Mama hovering over him.

Jack had dismounted and was kneeling on the ground next to Eddie. Whatever Eddie'd said had Jack smiling. Caroline could nearly breathe again. If Jack could smile, Eddie would be fine.

His Lordship was a lying bastard. Jack knew this to be true, but there wasn't a thing he could do about it. Not only had the Englishman intentionally cut Eddie off, he'd done it while trying to bring Jack down.

"Not much of a cowboy, are you?" Bremerton had taunted after scoring. Jack suspected then that Bremerton had been in the conservatory last night. And today

His Lordship was looking for some on-field revenge. But what really capped it was that instead of checking on Eddie's welfare or even expressing a word of regret, Bremerton was busy debating with the umpire exactly what penalty should be called for this "accidental" injury.

Jack focused on Eddie. The club's doctor was asking him the usual questions to be sure he hadn't lost his senses. Eddie knew who he was, where he was, and he was also damn sure his leg was broken.

"Don't let them cut off my boot," he said to Jack. "These are brand new . . . first wearing."

First Eddie had been making sure Gertrude, his favorite pony, hadn't been harmed. That, Jack appreciated. The boots, however, could go.

"You're a millionaire. Buy another pair," Jack said as he helped settle Eddie onto the stretcher that others had brought over.

"Bring him to the edge of the field until the ambulance arrives," the doctor directed.

Jack looked up. They were right next to the Maxwell carriage. Caroline's face was tight with worry, so he flashed her a reassuring smile.

"It's his leg, but he's more worried about his boot," he called to her.

She nodded and looked more relaxed, but Agnes Maxwell continued to wring her hands. No one could ever claim she wasn't a devoted mother.

"Well, damn. I've thought of one bad thing," Eddie said to Jack as they brought the stretcher back to the ground.

"Besides the fact that your leg is probably broken?" Jack asked above the commotion as the carriage next to the Maxwells' moved out to make room for the arrival of a horse and ambulance.

Eddie sucked a pained breath between his teeth as the

stretcher was jostled. "A broken leg gets me off the *Conqueror*."

"How's that bad?" Jack asked.

Eddie motioned Jack closer. Jack asked the doctor and others to step back for a moment.

"Bremerton did this on purpose," Eddie said in a low voice. "He might not have meant to hurt me, but he meant to hurt you, and I've got no idea why. There's something wrong with him."

Jack nodded. "I know."

"Here's the problem. My mother's not going to delay that trip to England unless I turn up dead from this, and I don't plan to."

"Good news, there."

"I need your help, Jack," Eddie said. "My father won't be ready to sail when Mother wants to go, and I don't want just Mother and Caroline up against Bremerton for even a week. My mother wouldn't know Satan if he showed his horns and tail, and Caroline is too inclined to go it on her own. You need to travel to England for me."

Jack had already figured this out. He'd planned to be there with or without Eddie's blessing. But now, at least, he wouldn't have to explain to Eddie why he'd decided to go even when the beer tour was dead.

"Of course I'll go," Jack said.

Eddie's tension eased. "Good. You need to be in London exactly when Caroline is. I'll act pathetic about letting you down, and square it away with Mother for you to sail over on the *Conqueror*. But I'm not so sure I can push her sympathy far enough to get you into the Grosvenor Square house."

"That's not a problem," Jack said. "I happen to know a nice widowed lady with a home in London."

Eddie nearly smiled. "Of course you do. You know all the nice ladies. And right now, I want a nice doctor with a big bottle of laudanum and some gin to wash it down. Then I'll let them cut off the damn boot."

Jack laughed. "Hang on. And Eddie?"

"What?"

"I'll keep Caroline safe."

His friend nodded, then gave a pained but real smile. "Tell her not to forget her six-shooter."

Jack glanced up at Caroline, who was occupied by sending a furious stare in Bremerton's direction.

"She'll be well armed, I'm sure."

Three hours later, Jack had been home and gotten O'Toole busy with the details of packing up Jack's life and readying to board a ship. Then Jack had stopped to confirm that Eddie had been properly seen to. While his leg was a clean break and would heal well, the boot had been a total loss.

Eddie had been right about his mother, too. The *Conqueror* would be sailing on Saturday morning, with or without Jack, and definitely without Bernard and Eddie. The only reason Agnes wasn't leaving sooner was that the balance of the ladies' wardrobes had to be brought from New York to Newport. And Agnes had her tail in a knot because the much larger and faster *Lucania* would beat them to England.

All Jack had left to do was persuade Flora to allow him to use her London town house. He bounded up The Reefs' steps, intent on getting these last details wrapped up and pleased to have some time to himself with Flora. He needed some of her female perspective when it came to Caroline.

The Reefs' butler greeted Jack and led him to the back terrace, where he found both Flora and Da in white wicker chairs, very close together. So close, in fact, that Jack was pretty sure that he'd seen Da pull his hand away from where it had been resting over Flora's, on the arm of her chair. Jack started to say something teasing, but set aside the comment. He could hardly tell Da to mind his own business when he was minding Da's.

Flora rose. "So you're back."

"I actually returned yesterday but had a ball to attend."

She smiled. "Yes, I saw the throngs at the Maxwells' gate and the glow from their cottage."

"It almost looked as though someone had set a torch to the place," Da said.

"It must have, if you could see it all the way from Touro Square," Jack said drily. He'd wondered where Da was when he'd left for the ball last night. And he was glad he hadn't looked for him when he'd arrived home just past one in the morning. Some things a son did not need to know.

"Please sit," Flora said, gesturing at a wicker settee that was placed at a right angle from where she and Da sat.

"Thank you," Jack said. "I've come to ask a favor of you."

"You know if it's within my power . . . such as it is . . . it's yours," Flora replied.

"You mentioned not too long ago that you have a home in London. I was wondering if you'd let me stay there?"

"Of course. Are you planning a vacation?"

"I wouldn't quite call it that. I promised Edward Maxwell I'd accompany his mother and sisters to London."

"When are you going?"

"Saturday morning," he replied. "I've been told that the Maxwells' yacht makes the crossing in seven or so days, so a week from Saturday, I should be in London."

"I knew this had to be about that Maxwell girl," Da said. "Are you not through collecting her yet? I'd think you'd have her all wrapped up by now."

Flora gave Da a curious look but ignored his question. Jack did, too.

"Why is Edward not going?" Flora asked.

"Bremerton broke Edward's leg in a polo match today," Jack said. "It was intentional, even if he got the wrong target."

"Were you the target?" Da asked.

"Yes," Jack said. "Bremerton is going back to England. He has managed to fool Agnes Maxwell well enough about his nature that she's packing up Caroline, Helen, and Amelia so that she can continue to push a marriage between Caroline and Bremerton."

"This is *not* good," Flora said, frowning.

Jack nodded. "It isn't. I'm genuinely worried for Caroline at this point." He didn't add that he was falling in love with her. Flora had already guessed that, and Da didn't need to know.

"You know," Flora said, "I believe I have had enough of Newport. It's time for another sea change. I'm going to book passage to England."

Jack appreciated her concern for Caroline, which he knew was behind this announcement. However, it presented a problem for him. "If you can then recommend a place for me to stay—"

"Don't start with that," Flora said, cutting him off. "London is not Newport. Clem and I spent half our time there. I have my friends, and they know who I am and what they may expect. Believe it or not, they like my unconventionality."

"Oh, I'm believing it," Da said.

"I was speaking to your son," Flora said firmly.

"But I'm wondering whether these friends so like your unconventionality that they will embrace you even with two Culhanes under your roof?" Da asked.

"Are you saying you want to go to London?" Jack

asked before Flora could answer. Because of some happenings in his village when he'd been a child, Da had no fondness for all things English.

"I am," Da said.

"But you hate the English."

"Not all of them," his father replied with a wave of his hand. "Though it is sounding like I wouldn't mind seeing this Bremerton put in his place."

Jack couldn't argue with the sentiment, but he did have other questions. "How will you work from there? You've already set business aside for more days in Newport than I thought you were capable of."

"Oh, I'm capable of slowing down . . . with the right person," Da replied, looking over to Flora, who was doing her best to look stern. Her acting talents were slipping, though. Jack could see she was losing her heart to Da all over again.

"And I'll work better than you on your best day," Da said to Jack. "London isn't my favorite place, but it's not bogside, either. If I've managed to keep a fortune afloat from a village the size of a flea's arse in Donegal . . . and I did for a month when my mam, God rest her, was on her last days. I'll be set fine."

"Patrick, I don't recall saying whether you may stay at my home," Flora said calmly.

"May I?" Da asked.

"No."

Da looked completely shocked. *"No?"*

"You have made your intentions clear, Patrick Culhane," Flora said. "You have told me that you're courting me the way I should have been courted by you all those years ago. Suitors do not sleep under my roof."

It was killing Jack, but he bit his tongue.

"Fine, then," Da said. "I'll get myself a suite of rooms at a hotel, but you can't keep me from London."

"I'd suggest the Savoy, on the Strand," Flora said primly.

Jack couldn't hide his grin.

Da glared at Jack. "Smile all you want, boyo. Because you'll be staying there with me."

SEVENTEEN

As far as Caroline was concerned, brothers were miraculous beings. Saturday morning had dawned better than she would have thought possible, all thanks to Eddie. Who but Eddie could have persuaded Mama to bring Jack on the *Conqueror*? And who but Eddie could have presented Caroline with a shiny new six-shooter and bullets to replace her beloved Colt that Mama had confiscated on Thursday?

If Caroline had to go to England, at least she was going with a man and a gun. Matters could be worse. So of all the females now gathered in Rosemeade's Imperial Salon, only Mrs. Longhorne was in tears. And she was nearly inconsolable.

"I am leaving a great deal of wedding planning in your hands, Mildred," Mama said to her friend. "I ask that you follow my list to the letter. There should be no deviations, no matter how small they might seem to you. I have a vision of how this ceremony should be."

If Caroline had believed for an instant that there would be a ceremony, she would have been offended by her mother's overstepping. But as it was, planning would keep Mama occupied while Caroline sniffed out Bremerton's secrets. He could not hide in his own land. People there knew him, and from what Peek had said, they didn't necessarily like him, either.

"I won't deviate a bit, Agnes," Mrs. Longhorne said as she dabbed her eyes with a violet-embroidered handkerchief. "And I am honored that you're entrusting me with this."

"I wish I could be here and we could work side by side. We are a most formidable team," Mama replied, looking a little watery herself. "Even with the church arranged for, there's so much to be done, but I can hardly send Caroline on her own."

"Of course not," Mildred agreed.

"Promise me that you'll find the very best craftsman for the cherubs to be placed in the festoons on the end of each church pew."

"Of course," Mildred said.

According to Mama, Caroline was to have a February wedding at St. Thomas's. Thus, the cherubs.

"Each figure must be detailed, lovely, and covered with enough gold leaf that it could be taken for solid gold. And I want the faces to look real," Caroline's mother added. "None of those blank-eyed pudding faces."

"You could use Caroline's and Bremerton's likenesses from when they were children," Helen suggested in a peppery tone.

Mama didn't seem to pick up on Helen's attitude, though. "That's a very original idea. Well done! But I think we're going to have difficulty getting a childhood portrait of Bremerton here on such short notice."

Thank heaven for that, Caroline thought. If it were to be in the least accurate, any childhood portrait of Bremerton would have him pulling the wings off butterflies.

"Mama, Lord Bremerton hasn't even proposed yet," Amelia said. "What if he finds someone he loves more?"

"He will be proposing to Caroline, or he would not

have invited us to London, Amelia. And who do you think would be more appealing than Caroline?"

"No one, Mama," Amelia dutifully replied.

Mama might have missed it, but Caroline had caught the wistful look in Amelia's eyes. Were Caroline an innocent sixteen and had not seen Bremerton's true colors, she might have felt the same way. But she was older, wiser, and battle-hardened. She resolved to tell Amelia about the dangers lurking out there for an heiress. While Helen was aware, Amelia remained blind, and Mama would never arm her properly.

"Mildred, please start contacting florists today," Caroline's mother said. "We're going to need tall, potted cherry trees just beginning to blossom. Since it will be February, they will have to be forced."

That, at least, was a neat fit, Caroline thought. Both the bride and flowers would be forced.

"Yes, yes," Mildred said, nodding. "I know exactly whom to contact."

Berta entered the room. She was dressed in her gray traveling dress, complete with heavy cloak. Caroline, who had opted for her lightest travel dress in gabardine, wanted to perspire just looking at Berta.

"Ma'am, the carriages are ready," she said to Mama.

"Is the staff at the harbor?"

"They are all aboard ship, ma'am."

Mama nodded briskly. "Very well. Please gather up Pomeroy and place him in his travel basket, Berta."

Mrs. Longhorne sniffled again.

"And Mildred, the lilies must be pure white," Mama said. "No cream at all." She smoothed her kid gloves and briefly touched the brim of her hat, as though to confirm that its tilt was perfect. "If you have any issues whatsoever, send me a telegram."

"I will," Mrs. Longhorne said.

Mama turned her attention to the girls. "Let's be on our way. Caroline's future awaits her on bended knee!"

And with luck, Caroline thought, Bremerton would never rise again.

"One man owns this?" O'Toole asked Jack as they stood at the *Conqueror's* polished teak rail awaiting the Maxwells.

"Yes," Jack said.

O'Toole snorted. "What does he do with it all? It's a waste. Most of my village would fit in the servants' quarters. Did you know there are over fifty workin' for the Maxwells on this ship alone? And I'm not countin' the maids and whatnot who paraded on after us."

Jack had thought he was numb to great wealth, but he was wrong. He had never before been aboard the *Conqueror*. At almost three hundred feet long, the black, steel-hulled beauty was indeed a floating village. But she was also fast, built especially to beat a Vanderbilt yacht. And Jack, who generally wasn't interested in that kind of fiscally insane competition, appreciated the results of Bernard Maxwell's obsession. He planned to tour the engine room as soon as possible. Whatever Maxwell had going on with those twin steam engines would translate well to an efficient brewery. The more heat Jack could throw, the more beer he could make.

The rest of the ship kept pace with its engines, too. Earlier, Jack had been shown to Eddie's private stateroom, which even Eddie hadn't seen since the ship had been refitted. If he had, he would have been damn tempted to fight down the seasickness and cope with the bad leg. The room was a small-scale gentleman's club, finished in dark woods and hunting tapestries. It even boasted a built-in humidor packed with cigars and a bar cabinet offering a selection of whiskeys Eddie would kill for.

And then there was the bed. If anything on this ship was—as O'Toole had said—a waste, it was a bed that big for just one. As tempted as Jack had been to imagine Caroline sharing the massive four-poster, he refused to let his mind travel in that direction. For the next seven days, he would be Saint Jack. Brotherly Jack. A Jack above reproach. He didn't need to give Agnes Maxwell a valid reason to cut Caroline off from him. Agnes tended to do a good enough job with no reason at all, and Jack needed to stick close to Caroline.

"Damned if there's not more of them comin'," O'Toole said from his spot on the rail next to Jack. "Would you look at that?"

The Maxwell women had just exited one carriage, and the servants, another. Jack quickly spotted Caroline in a light blue dress with a small matching hat perched on her head. The breeze made the puffy arms of her dress ripple as she scanned the ship with one hand cupped over her eyes to shade them from the sun. Though he was amidships and at least one hundred feet away, he raised a hand in subtle greeting. Her wave was less restrained and resulted in her mother quickly shooing her up the gangway.

"So your attention has turned from the Goelet governess?" asked a dry English voice from behind Jack.

He knew it was Peek, so he didn't turn. O'Toole did, and yelped. This must have been the boy's first sighting of the governess.

"My attention is on the dockside, Miss Peek, and not on anyone in particular," Jack said.

"There is no point in lying, Mr. Culhane. I am not a naïve miss," Peek said as she came to stand next to him. "And I am fierce in defending my charge."

"I am sure you are."

"Which is why I find myself in the unusual diplomatic position of coming to you, from whom I am duty bound to protect Miss Maxwell, and seeking your help."

"What sort of help?"

She looked O'Toole up and down. "I would prefer not to speak in front of your servant."

"Then we won't be speaking at all," Jack said with a shrug.

"Very well," she replied. "If you feel this youth is that inconsequential, I shall speak."

O'Toole stiffened, and Jack briefly settled his hand on O'Toole's tweed-covered shoulder. Like most young men, O'Toole hadn't yet learned how to choose his battles.

"I told Mrs. Maxwell yesterday that I had recently made inquiries about Lord Bremerton with an acquaintance of mine," the governess said. "And while she was not interested in the results, I am quite sure you will be."

"Bremerton is no friend of mine," Jack said.

"I fear he is no friend of Miss Maxwell's, either."

For the first time, Jack could hear actual concern in the governess's voice. She was more than a woman fixed on keeping an unblemished work record intact.

"What did you learn, Miss Peek?"

"My friend, a fellow governess, says that Lord Bremerton's estate in West Sussex is declining at a startling rate. Her employer recently hired the former Bremerton housekeeper. Lord Bremerton could not keep up on wages, and the house was daily growing barer of art and silver."

"Which is why he's so fixed on Miss Maxwell," Jack said. "More men than His Lordship view marriage as a means to pay their way out of debt."

"It seems neither you, nor Mrs. Maxwell, can understand. These are belongings that would have been in the family for generations, and not for Lord Bremerton to do with as he pleases. Bremerton's grandfather is a man of great wealth and pride. His Grace must be unaware that this is happening, and it would behoove him to know."

"I don't travel in the same circles as dukes, Miss Peek."

"But you travel closer than I. And you seem to have a great interest in Miss Maxwell. I hope that you will use this information. I fear her mother will not."

"Thank you for sharing it," Jack said. If nothing else, he would see what Flora might be able to find out through her friends.

"That does not mean I won't be watching your behavior with Miss Maxwell," the governess crisply added. She walked away toward the *Conqueror.*

Jack smiled. "I would expect no less."

O'Toole gave a low whistle. "I don't know how you rich find the time to make money, with all the time you spend sticking your noses in each other's business."

Jack laughed. "You don't know the half of it."

The weather was perfect, the ship a marvel, and by Wednesday dinnertime, Caroline was losing her mind. Not only had her mother *not* taken to her quarters as Caroline had eagerly anticipated, but she was at the head of the table.

"There must be more plum tartlets," Mama said to the waiter, a tall and stoic Scandinavian. "Go back and check."

The waiter inclined his head and retreated. Mama, who had eaten three already, frowned impatiently at the man's back. "One would think he was in a funeral procession, the pace he's walking."

"You seem in good spirits this trip, Mama," Caroline said, hoping to spare the waiter more criticism.

"I believe the sea air is agreeing with me," her mother

replied. "Peek suggested that I should spend time keeping my eyes on the horizon and putting fresh air in my lungs. It's working wonderfully! And Pomeroy seems invigorated, too."

Caroline glanced at the little mop who sat on a tapestry pillow by the dining room's arched entry, and tried to discern whether the dog was invigorated or not.

"Did you know your father even designated an area for Pomeroy's constitutionals?" Mama asked. "He has his own strip of sod from Rosemeade to use while we are at sea."

"I'm not certain that's proper dinner conversation, Mama," Amelia said.

"Ah, but we are in a land of no laws," Mama replied.

"Not to mention no land," Helen muttered just under her breath. Caroline, who sat next to her, caught it. Jack must have heard from his seat opposite her, too, because he ducked his head to hide a smile.

"In this rugged environment, I have decided I'm free to speak as I wish," Mama decreed.

Rugged? Caroline was the only one missing a comfort while aboard ship, and that was Jack. Meals were the only time she saw him. There were other opportunities, but he'd actively avoided them.

Mama cast a gimlet eye on Jack. "Did your father win a house in London on a hand of cards, too?"

Caroline wanted to sink beneath the linen-covered table, but Jack just laughed. "No, he did not, Mrs. Maxwell."

"Then where are you staying?"

"At the Savoy," he replied.

Mama sniffed. "Really? How unexpected."

Jack started to say something but stopped. Caroline gave him credit for his self-restraint. Hers had reached its limit.

She pushed back her chair. "If you'll excuse me, Mama, I am feeling the need for some of that fresh air."

"Get your cape, first," Mama said. "And take Pomeroy with you."

Caroline scooped up the dog and headed down the thickly carpeted hallway, past the corridor that led to her room, and outside to breathe freely. Evening had come, but it was far from dark as she took the deck. She set Pomeroy on his feet and smiled when he chose the rail instead of his designated spot as the place to leave his mark.

"Let's stay back from the edge," she said to the little dog when he was done. "Mama would never forgive me if you went overboard."

"But if I did, she'd breathe easier."

Caroline turned. Jack was right behind her.

"Well, hello," she said. "Does this mean you're through avoiding me?"

Laughing, he held a hand to his broad chest. "A direct shot, Artemis."

"Of course," she replied and then began to follow Pomeroy, who was heading toward his piece of home sod. "And I note you're not denying the charge."

"I'm not," he agreed as he pulled even with her. "But I have my reasons."

Caroline didn't comment. They walked in silence until they had reached the bow, where Pomeroy was rolling with great abandon on his grass, paws in the air and a tiny canine smile on his face. Caroline rubbed her arms. Mama had been right about the cape. It might be July, but there was a bite to the air this far out at sea. It seemed to Caroline that it was growing rougher, too.

"Here," Jack said as he settled his black evening jacket coat over her shoulders. She wanted to draw it close to her face and see if it carried the tempting scent of male and sandalwood she recalled—and had dreamt of—since a week ago in Rosemeade's conservatory. Instead she gave him a polite, but not *too* forgiving, thank you.

"Bremerton was trying to harm me when he broke Eddie's leg," Jack said in a strangely calm tone. "None of what happened was an accident."

Caroline swung around to face him. "What? Do you have proof? If you do, you must tell Mama immediately."

Jack touched his hand to her face. "Sweetheart, if I had hard proof, we wouldn't be on this ship."

Caroline had heard the bad news, but at that moment, she didn't care. Her mind couldn't seem to work past the fact that Jack had just called her sweetheart.

"Sweetheart?" she asked.

An expression close to regret passed across his face. "That's what I said."

"You don't seem very happy about it."

"What part of falling in love with a woman who's being married off to an almost duke should make me happy?"

Caroline couldn't stop her smile from growing until it nearly hurt her face. "The love part?" She moved closer to him. "Doesn't that make you even a little bit happy?"

"If I could guarantee you'd smile like this every day for the rest of your life, it would make me damn happy."

"I will," she said. "I promise." Her heart raced with excitement. "How could I not? When we get to England, I'll send a telegram to Papa and tell him I need him there immediately, and then we'll . . ."

Caroline trailed off. What *would* they do? If her mother had scoffed at the idea of Jack marrying Harriet Vandermeulen, she'd go apoplectic at the idea of him as a son-in-law. She would refuse, and Papa would let her have her way.

Jack nodded. "That's exactly where I run dry of ideas."

She reached out to settle her hand against Jack's chest. She wanted to at least feel his heartbeat and let herself know this moment was real.

He stepped back.

"We can't," he said, tipping his head toward the port side of the ship. Peek stood there, far enough away that Caroline couldn't complain that the governess was being obtrusive, yet close enough to stand guard.

"I don't care about her," Caroline said. "Not anymore."

Jack moved away. "I don't, either, but here is what I do care about. . . . I care to be close enough to you in London that I can help if Bremerton becomes dangerous. And if word gets to your mother that I am more than just Eddie's friend, that won't happen. I can't risk that. Bremerton isn't just some feckless lord, Caroline. He manipulates, and he believes he's above all rules. If you cross him, he'll strike back."

"I know," she said, thinking of the way the Englishman had dragged her into Mrs. Longhorne's folly for simply asking a few questions. "Truly, I do."

EIGHTEEN

THURSDAY EVENING, JACK MADE HIS WAY DOWN THE hallway to his room. It wasn't easy going. Last night's increasing wind had turned out to be the outer edge of stormy seas, and tonight the *Conqueror* was working its way out the other side.

Dinner had been a solitary affair with not a Maxwell in sight, and the soup course had been foregone. Now all Jack wanted was to read the book he'd borrowed from the ship's library. He timed his reach for his door handle to the vessel's roll and stepped inside.

"Papa didn't build this ship for rough seas," Caroline said from her perch on the center of his bed. "And you don't have any food in here."

Because he had no other option, Jack closed the door. "You'll find the food in the dining room, though you're underdressed for dinner." She wore a ruffled, long-sleeved white cotton robe that covered her from chin to toes, and yet somehow she managed to look sensual.

"I have ball gowns with half this amount of fabric." She gave a wiggle of her bare toes. "Did you know that in France it was once the style for women to receive their male admirers *en déshabillé,* wearing their finest night clothing? Flora told me all about it."

Jack set the book he carried on one of the room's two armchairs. "I'll bet she did. But you might have noticed that we're not in France."

"We're someplace better. According to my mother, we're in a land of no laws."

Caroline's dark hair had been plaited into a thick braid that lay over her right shoulder. Jack's fingers twitched as he thought about slipping the braid from its thin bit of ribbon and seeing her hair fully down. "Much to my regret, there is no such place."

"There is, right here," she said as she patted the burgundy-colored coverlet stretched across the bed.

"What are you doing here, Caroline?" It was an obvious question, but he needed to hear her answer.

"I've been waiting for you. You promised me a bed. One with just the two of us, and the rest of the world be damned. And that's what we have, even if it's one that pitches and rolls."

Jack shucked his evening jacket and threw it over the back of the armchair.

"You need to go back to your room," he said while he undid his white necktie and sent it to join his jacket. "Someone is going to find you here."

"No, they're not. Mama's love affair with the sea is over, and she has taken to her bed. Even Helen and Amelia aren't leaving their rooms, and Annie tells me that Peek hasn't been seen. And of course I spent all day playing shut-in so I could have some freedom."

"Only you," he said.

She smiled. "I know. But I realized last night after Pomeroy and I had left you on deck that I had forgotten to tell you something very important."

"Which is?" he asked as he settled into the other armchair.

"I love you, Jack. And this time I'm not saying it out

of frustration or anger, but only because it needs to be said." Humor fled her eyes and was replaced by something more poignant. "I have loved you for as long as I can remember. I know it seems sudden, my being here like this, but you have no idea how long I've been waiting."

And she had no idea the effect her words were having on him. "We need to keep waiting."

"The night of the ball, Bremerton told me that after we are married and I give him an heir, I am to ask his permission to take a lover."

Jack didn't want to begin to sort through the levels of wrongness in that statement. "Bremerton is an idiot, and you're not going to marry him."

She hesitated. "But what if we can't find a way to stop this? I can't turn my back on my family and what they expect of me, and I can't bear the thought of not knowing what it's like to make love with you."

His heart slammed at the thought, but someone had to remain in control. Unfortunately, that was him. "Unlike your almost duke, I'm discovering that I'm very traditional when it comes to you. Our first time making love will be after we're married, and not before." He stood and walked to the side of the tall bed and braced his palms on it to balance against the ship's rocking. "And I give you permission to shoot me with that six-shooter of yours if I ever bring up the subject of taking lovers . . . not that either of us will have reason to want to."

"So you have no intention of making love to me tonight?"

"None," Jack said.

She smiled. "Fine. Then take off your vest and shirt."

"What?"

"One should always have a fall-back position when negotiating, and that's mine."

Jack laughed. There was no woman on Earth he'd ever want more than Caroline.

"What do you have to offer in exchange?" he asked. "I don't drop shirts and vests for nothing."

"I'm on your bed. I'd consider that a more than adequate accommodation," she replied.

"Ah, but you were there before the dealing began."

"That was highly imprudent of me," she said. "How about this?" She undid the top three buttons on her frilly robe, exposing more white cotton, pin-tucked, beneath.

"That's no gain at all," he said. "Your hair. I want your hair down."

She played at deliberating for a moment. "In exchange, I will get both the vest and the shirt, correct?"

"Yes."

"Fine."

Jack watched as she untied the thin white ribbon that bound her braid. Ribbon gone, she drew her fingers through her hair, and the braid unraveled like bands of dark silk.

"There," she said, once it was flowing over her shoulders. "Done."

She waited expectantly while his fingers, suddenly clumsy, worked at his vest buttons. He shrugged free of the garment and dropped it onto the bed.

"Halfway there," she said. "Let's move it along."

Jack smiled. "As you wish. I'd hate to deprive you of the upper hand." After a short struggle with his stiff collar and cuffs, he was quickly rid of the shirt.

Caroline frowned at him. "I feel cheated," she said as she took in his fine cotton undershirt. "I had expected much less beneath."

"It's never wise to bargain without all the required information," he replied. "But to prove I'm a generous man . . ." He unbuttoned the undershirt, drew the fabric free of his trousers, and pulled it over his head.

Caroline's mouth went dry. There were perfect marble contours of the male torso, created by a sculptor long dead, and then there was Jack. Warm, living, breathing Jack.

"Very generous," she said.

She wanted to place her mouth against the pulse that was jumping in his throat. She wanted to touch the dusting of dark hair across the center of his chest. And she wanted to feel emotions she couldn't even put words to.

"Have we reached the end of our negotiations?" he asked.

She shook her head no.

He smiled. "What, then?"

"Your shoes."

He glanced down at his feet and then back to her. "Really? Then your robe goes."

Caroline couldn't hide her smile. "If it must."

She worked her way up to the bed's ornately carved headboard so that she had something to hold on to. Disrobing would have been awkward in calm seas. An unsteady bed was making it worse. By the time she'd unbuttoned the robe the rest of the way and freed herself from its yards of fabric, Jack's shoes were long gone.

"And now?" he asked.

"What would it take to get you on the bed?" she asked.

"I'll agree to that concession to move along the negotiations."

Jack was there before Caroline could even thank him for his consideration. He settled on the open spot next to her, head on the pillow and smile on his face. Caroline, who was still kneeling with one hand gripping the headboard, looked down at him. He would have appeared relaxed and companionable if she hadn't been able to see the tension just beneath his skin. And what skin it was. She took after her mother and had a creamy hue, unlike her paler sisters. But Jack was darker yet, as though he'd spent time with nothing but air between himself and the sun.

Caroline didn't want to bargain anymore. She wanted to touch, and so she did. She let her fingers trail from his shoulder and across his collarbone. Jack drew in a deep breath, as though he was steeling himself for some trial.

She settled her palm flat against his chest so she could feel the heartbeat she'd craved last night. His was strong and steady, not racing as she knew hers was.

"You're really quite amazing looking," she said.

His mouth turned upward in a brief smile. "Thank you."

She laughed. "No. Thank *you*."

Feeling bolder, Caroline ran her hand over the muscled strength of each arm, then traced down his ribs and the flat muscles of his stomach. His breath was coming faster, and she could see that he worked to keep himself still under her touch. One unsteady hand still on the headboard, she bent closer. Her hair swung free of her body, and Jack lifted his hand to touch it.

"I knew it would be like silk," he said.

She bent down to kiss him, and everything changed. Jack moved quickly, settling her on the mattress as he rose above her.

"I did better at holding still than I thought I would," he said.

And he was clearly done with that. His mouth met hers in a kiss that wasn't gentle or patient, but made of sheer demand. Caroline answered with a few demands of her own, and it was both heaven and torture the way he touched her. His hands were quick and sure—a touch here, a touch there, but no one place long enough to satisfy her.

"Jack," she said between kisses. *"Please."* And with him, asking wasn't a form of debasement, as it felt with Bremerton. She was Jack's equal. That made the asking a gift.

"Please, what?"

She shook her head. "Please . . . I don't know. Please, everything."

He moved a little away, leaning on one elbow while he stroked her hair. She kept one hand on his arm, not wanting to lose contact with him.

He looked down at her for a moment, then said, "It won't be everything, sweetheart, but I'll make it memorable."

Really, despite her earlier bold words, what he offered was as far as her ability to flout convention would allow her to go. "Yes."

He folded back the fabric and kissed her at the top of the valley between her breasts. He worked his way lower. She let her eyes slip closed so she could just feel. As the ship rolled and Jack worked his magic on her, time and the outside world went away. If she and Jack failed at losing Bremerton—if this was all she was to ever have with Jack—it would almost be enough.

Caroline drew Jack's mouth to hers and kissed him. "I believe I want a small wedding, and I'd like it very soon."

He framed her head with his hands and kissed her again before saying, "I don't recall proposing, Miss Maxwell."

"You will," she said with complete certainty. "Because otherwise, how am I ever going to learn *you* by touch?"

* * *

Twenty minutes later, Caroline left Jack's room. Even if she felt completely different, she'd taken the time to be sure she looked the same as she had earlier in the night. The hallway was quiet and her gait only a little crooked as the ship pushed its way through the last of the rough weather. She stopped at her mother's double doors and listened. All was still. Caroline moved on. Two more doors, and she would be safe. Then Amelia's door swung open. Caroline jumped and Amelia yelped.

"What are you doing?" Amelia asked, her eyes wide.

"I was checking on Mama," Caroline replied.

"How is she?"

"I don't know. I put my ear to the door, and it was silent inside. I decided not to bother her."

Amelia gave her a very superior smile. "Maybe just like you, Mama's out sneaking around in her night-clothes."

"What do you mean?"

"I went to visit you earlier, and your room was empty."

"I've been in the library." It seemed a safe lie, since Amelia would never voluntarily enter that room.

"In your nightclothes?"

"No one saw me. They might, however, see both of us if we stand here chatting much longer." Amelia was a smaller version of the white, ruffled confection Caroline knew she looked like.

"Then come in," her sister said. "I'm lonely, and there's no one to talk to around here."

Caroline glanced longingly at her door. So close, yet so far.

"Just for a few minutes," she said.

Amelia's room was an homage to the color pink in its many riotous shades. Caroline found it unsettling, but it was her sister's favorite hue.

"So what would you like to talk about?" Caroline asked as she seated herself in a pale pink armchair embroidered with bright pink daisies.

"It doesn't matter what," Amelia replied. She hopped up on the edge of her canopied bed. "I'm just tired of being the invisible Maxwell on this trip. Mama dotes on you, Helen is off in her own world, and you ignore me."

Apparently, Amelia was in a mood.

"Why don't you pick the topic?" Caroline suggested.

"Fine. Have you ever been in love?"

That was what she got for not driving the conversation, Caroline thought. "When I was five, I loved my first pony, Henry."

"I'm not talking about ponies," Amelia said. "We're well past that age. I mean with a gentleman. Are you in love with Lord Bremerton?"

"No," Caroline replied.

"Why not? He's handsome and polite, and he dotes on you, too."

"I'm not in love with him for countless reasons, but I'll start with the most important. He and I don't suit."

Amelia looked at her suspiciously. "I saw you at the ball and at Harriet Vandermeulen's picnic. It looked as though you got along very well."

"What one sees of a couple in public isn't necessarily what it's like when they're alone," Caroline said. "When it's just the two of us, the ease and politeness are gone. I'm a business transaction to him."

"Maybe that's because he knows you don't love him."

Caroline sought a diplomatic way to explain this to her sister. "Lord Bremerton and I are just different sorts of people, Amelia. It's like the color pink. It's perfect for you, but not for me."

Amelia considered the matter for a moment and then said, "I think Jack Culhane is your color pink. He suits you. You two laugh at each other's quips. You smile when he walks into a room, and you follow him with your eyes when he leaves. He is your pink."

"If those are the standards for pink, I suppose you could say that," Caroline said. She would have said Jack was her whole rainbow if it would have removed the cross look from Amelia's face.

"That doesn't seem fair to Lord Bremerton. You're his color pink, and I think you're Jack's, too. I'm just tired of you hogging up all the pink. You can't be two men's pink. It's not fair. Something should be done about this. Soon you'll be every man's pink and there will be none left for me. And it's my favorite color!"

Caroline rose. "I'm going to bed. There's nothing I can say to you tonight that will make you happy. Sleep, and we'll talk later."

Amelia glared at her.

One thing was certain—Caroline would not wear the color pink tomorrow.

Friday's breakfast started out decently. The seas had calmed, and though Caroline was the only Maxwell eating, at least the others weren't looking too green. Jack was working his way through his eggs and sausage.

"Captain says we are to make harbor just after noon," Agnes Maxwell said. "The storm slowed us only a little. We'll be in plenty of time to catch the afternoon train to the city."

"Good. I can't wait to get off this ship," Amelia said while using her fork to chase a melon cube around her otherwise barren plate.

Agnes disregarded Amelia and focused on her eldest daughter. "Caroline, if Lord Bremerton's father is in relatively good health, I expect there will be invitations awaiting you. You are to accept them all."

"Of course," Caroline said.

Jack willed her to look across the table. He wanted to send her some silent reassurance, but she kept her eyes downcast.

Amelia dropped her fork with a clatter.

"Amelia, that was unnecessary," her mother said. "Where are your manners?"

"Where are Caroline's manners, Mama?" Amelia replied.

Jack set down his fork—quietly. The best eggs in the world wouldn't be worth witnessing sibling warfare. He placed his napkin on the table and readied to make his escape.

"See? She's doing it right now," Amelia cried.

"Doing what?" Agnes asked.

"How can you miss it, Mama? She follows every move Jack makes. She hangs on his every word. She has a perfectly nice man in love with her, but Jack is her pink."

Jack froze. Either he was losing his mind or Amelia was speaking in tongues.

"Amelia, what are you talking about?" Agnes asked.

"Caroline is in love with Jack, Mama. She told me so last night."

Caroline's face turned white. "I said nothing of the sort!"

Amelia stood. "You did. You know you did. You said Jack was your color pink!"

Jack pushed back from the table. "If you'll excuse me," he said at the same time Helen was rising.

"Both of you, stay," Mrs. Maxwell commanded. "Caroline, what is this nonsense Amelia is talking?"

"I visited with Amelia in her room last night," Caroline said in a level voice. "She was feeling ill and a little cross. We talked. She asked me if I loved Lord Bremerton, and I said I did not. And then she lost her temper."

"I did not lose my temper!"

Amelia would have been more credible if she weren't shouting now, Jack thought. He kept his mouth shut, though.

"Mama, we were talking about love," Amelia said. "I love the color pink, and Caroline loves Jack. That was the conversation, and *I* have no reason to lie," she added with a glare in Caroline's direction.

Agnes Maxwell gave Jack a baleful look. "You may leave the room now, Mr. Culhane."

Jack rose. "Thank you."

He had a feeling those were to be the last words he'd be permitted to say to a female Maxwell for some time to come.

NINETEEN

JACK KNEW THERE WERE FAR WORSE FATES THAN BEING exiled to the Savoy Hotel. On Tuesday afternoon, though, he couldn't think of a single one. While Caroline was no doubt fending off Bremerton at some luncheon or another, Da and he sat glumly at the hotel's bar. They were among the few patrons there, since it was a freakishly sunny London day. Most everyone else was outside on the hotel terrace or walking in the gardens alongside the River Thames.

"I'll bet you've never been outsmarted by a sixteen-year-old," Jack said to his father.

"You'd be losing that bet. I raised you, and I'm guaranteeing that you got away with plenty that I don't know about."

"Point taken," Jack said before taking another swallow of what was probably the worst lager he'd ever tasted in his life. Then again, that could have just been his poor attitude working its way to his taste buds.

"Care to tell me what happened?" Da asked. "You've been stewing for days."

He'd actually done some brewery work, too, but mostly Da was right. And the days felt more like an eter-

nity. "All I know is that I stood accused and was con-
victed of being Caroline's color pink."

"Pink? What does that mean?"

"Apparently that she loves me."

"Then why did she just not say it?" Da asked but then
gave a dismissive wave of his hand. "Never mind. I know
the answer. The Maxwells are a mad lot. Mad as a pack
of rabid dogs."

Breakfast last Friday had not been the most sane thing
Jack had ever seen.

"So does the girl love you?" Da asked.

"Yes, but that's not relevant at the moment."

Jack's father looked at him as though he'd just said Ireland wasn't the center of the solar system. "Not relevant?
It damn well is relevant any time a woman will unbend
enough to admit she loves you. Try saying it and then
having your words handed back to you on a platter, along
with your own head."

"It wasn't a good crossing, I take it," Jack said. His
father had been doing his share of silent stewing, too.

Da snorted. "Between Flora cutting me off cold the
first night and me playing cards with a thieving English
lord who wouldn't honor his debts, there's been none
worse."

Jack had a very uncomfortable thought. "Tell me it
wasn't Bremerton."

Da nodded. "It was. Flora chose the *Lucania* because
it was the only ship with a Saturday departure, and
damned if the Englishman wasn't in first class, too."

"There had to be several hundred people in first class,
and you befriended *him*?"

"Intentionally," his father said. "I'm going to have my
eye on *any* British git who's after harming my son." He
made a low sound of anger as he pushed his empty

whiskey glass toward the inner lip of the polished mahogany bar. "Damn British bastard!" Realizing the bartender was right there, he added, "Not you, of course."

The bartender nodded and pulled out a bottle of Da's favorite, Jameson. When he went to fill the glass, Da instructed him to leave the bottle.

"Did you tell Bremerton who you were?" Jack asked.

"Just my first name, but it wouldn't have mattered if I did. To him, I was just another uncivilized Paddy. The name went in one ear and then out the other." Da took a sip of his whiskey. "I set him up well, too. I let him win long enough that my money was in his pocket, but two days later, when I started winning, all he offered me was a marker for the debt. The man couldn't hold his liquor, either. He was all puff and noise about the heiress he's about to marry. That would be your Maxwell girl, wouldn't it?"

"In theory, yes," Jack said.

"You'd best be making sure it doesn't happen in practice," Da replied. "He said how this time, he was doing it right. No manipulation or back talk allowed."

Jack knew Caroline would not manipulate unless cornered, but that was little solace, considering Bremerton got a thrill by trapping. And as for the back talk, that, unfortunately, was Caroline's stock-in-trade on a good day. But the words *this time* sat worst of all. Jack was sure he'd never heard Caroline mention that Bremerton had been married before. And as concern jolted through him, he was equally sure that he was done feeling sorry for himself. The hell with being exiled by Agnes Maxwell and sitting in a great pool of self-pity with Da. He had things to do.

"I have to leave," he said to his father. "Will you be okay here?"

"I've made it this far on my own," he said. "I'm sure I'll make it fine a few hours more."

For Caroline, the very best thing about being in London wasn't the fine architecture, the accents, or the sophistication of the city. It was knowing she would never be seated by Bremerton at a social function. As a lord and grandson of a duke, he was a distant face at the well-titled end of the table. Caroline sat with her kind—American heiresses and other such foreign riffraff.

Today's large luncheon was hosted by Lady Reynolds, whom Caroline had never met before. Lady Reynolds's silver hair stuck out from her head at all angles, and she had a fondness for white face powder. If Caroline hadn't been feeling marginally charitable, she would have compared her hostess to a plaster death mask. She'd certainly given Caroline a cold, dead stare today. She'd announced that she had known Bremerton since he'd been a child and certainly hoped Caroline recognized the honor of being escorted by him. Luckily, life among the riffraff was proving far warmer.

"How was Newport?" asked Marjorie Smith, a fellow heiress whose mother had brought her from New York a year ago and refused to let her come home until she was wed. "I miss it so."

"It was as lovely as ever," Caroline said. "I hope to be back there soon."

Marjorie looked at her speculatively. Or perhaps she was just squinting. Marjorie's mother insisted she did not need spectacles. Marjorie's unfortunate habit of striking up conversations with potted palms suggested otherwise. "But all the talk is about an impending engagement between you and Lord Bremerton."

"The talk is very premature," Caroline said. "We're

just getting to know each other. Had you met him before today? If you can share any stories, I'd be curious to hear them."

"I'm afraid I don't have anything to tell," Marjorie said with a shake of her blond head. "He is quite handsome. I'm sure I'd recall meeting him, if I had."

"And here I was certain that you knew everybody," Caroline said. "I wonder how Bremerton never came onto the scene?"

"It is quite remarkable," Marjorie replied as she took another look up the long table. "My mother and her friends make sure I have all the proper introductions. Maybe he's considered improper? Wouldn't that be dark and romantic?"

Caroline answered with a bland smile. If being bullied and subtly threatened was part and parcel of dark and romantic, she could do without it. Just then, Bremerton leaned forward and looked down the table at her. Caroline pretended interest in her overcooked squab.

"Excuse me, Miss Maxwell?"

Caroline looked over her shoulder to see a footman in the Reynolds's forest green livery.

"Yes?"

"There is a messenger waiting for you in the front hall. It is of some urgency."

"Thank you," Caroline said. "I'll be right there."

She hoped it wasn't Mama. This morning, Caroline had tried to talk to her calmly about Jack and what Amelia had said. Mama had taken to her bed complaining of chest pains, and Berta had sent for the doctor. After seeing Mama, the doctor had delivered a strong warning to Caroline to be sure that nobody overexcited her mother.

"If you'll excuse me," she said to her nearest fellow diners before following the servant. She could feel

Bremerton's gaze hard on her as she left the room, but she didn't look his way.

Her shoes tapped a quick rhythm across the glossy oak of the hallway floor. She slowed, though, when she came to the black-and-white marble entryway. There stood Jack. He smiled. She smiled back. Enormously. Caroline thanked the footman, who retreated to the far end of the hall.

"How did you know I was here?" she asked Jack in a low voice.

"I had O'Toole slip over to your town house and get your weekly schedule from Annie."

"Excellent job."

"Thank you. I plan to work hard to live up to the honor of being your pink," he replied with a teasing smile.

She winced. "I'm sorry. That was completely mortifying. You caught us at our worst."

"That was nothing," Jack said. "Wait until you catch my father when he's in a mood." He glanced toward the footman. "Can you make your excuses and leave? We need to talk."

"I'll be right back."

Caroline returned to the dining room and apologized to Lady Reynolds, saying that she was needed at home. Bremerton offered to escort her, but Caroline quickly told him that her mother had sent a carriage. His response was cordial enough, but suspicion was obvious in his pale eyes. There would be repercussions for this escape, but she'd gladly pay the price.

In no time at all, she was outside with Jack. He ushered her into a waiting hansom cab, slid open the trap door in the cab's roof, and gave their driver a Mayfair address. Jack and she sat close together on the cab's single seat. No one on the street could see when Jack held her hand. His warmth worked its way up her arm and to her heart.

"Where are we going?" she asked as they pulled away from the curb and into the traffic.

"Not far. We're going to have a visit with Flora," Jack said.

"Flora is here?"

"Yes. She and my father both crossed on the *Lucania*. It seems we're too interesting of a show not to follow."

Caroline smiled. "I'm glad they're here."

"I'm glad Flora is, but the jury's still out on Da," Jack said. He flashed a quick smile that spoke of his love for his father. "I've been picking up some news on Bremerton and want to see if Flora might be able to help us."

"I'm assuming the news isn't all sunshine and joy," Caroline said.

Jack gave her hand a reassuring squeeze. "It's nothing we can't handle."

She decided that, in this case, she was fine with delaying the inevitable and didn't press for more. Her time was better spent simply holding Jack's hand and enjoying the sunny day.

Just a few minutes later, they pulled off the busy main thoroughfare and onto a quieter, elegant residential street. The cab stopped in front of a redbrick town house that wasn't the largest but was immaculately kept. Jack handed their fare up to the driver, who then opened the cab's doors. Jack exited, helped Caroline down, and then up the steps to the town house's main entrance. A black-suited butler opened the door, and soon they were on their way to Flora.

She rose as they entered the room and approached them, arms extended, in a cloud of ivory taffeta and violet perfume. "Caroline, how wonderful to see you."

Caroline embraced her friend. "And you."

Flora turned her attention to Jack. "You're looking well, Jack. How's your father?"

"Holding up the bar at the Savoy right now, I believe."

She smiled. "He'll be done with that by sundown and over here to give me a piece of his mind." She looked at Caroline. "Jack's father proposed marriage while we were aboard ship. Some nonsense about having the captain perform a ceremony so we could get it over with. It was the most unromantic proposal I've ever received, and I have received my share."

"I'm sure he's seeing the error of his ways by now," Caroline replied.

"He's long overdue," Flora said. "But enough about Patrick. Welcome to my home, and, please, have a seat."

Once they were settled, Jack in a jewel blue armchair and Caroline and Flora in a pair of matching floral ones, Jack spoke.

"So was Da the only one to cross paths with Bremerton on the way here, or did you, too?" he asked Flora.

"I saw your father with a gentleman who I was told was Bremerton, but I kept my distance. I had no idea what Patrick was up to, and I preferred to keep it that way."

"A wise choice," Jack said to Flora. To Caroline he said, "During the crossing, my father took it upon himself to try to wring some money and information from Bremerton. He got a gambling note that Bremerton will never pay up on and one odd statement that we need to pay some attention to. Has Bremerton ever mentioned being married before?"

"No, never," Caroline replied. "He's not exactly generous with personal information. The one time I tried to ask him anything, he scared me off the conversation."

"Scared you, how?" Jack asked.

"It doesn't really matter," she said. "Now that he's broken Eddie's leg, we know to take him seriously." She considered how to find what they needed. "If he were married, it would have to be in *Debrett's*. The copy I was working from in Newport was outdated, but he hadn't been wed as of 1890. I don't suppose you have a more current copy here, Flora?"

"I won't allow that odious book through the door."

Caroline laughed. "I'd call that a prudent policy."

"Do I want to know what *Debrett's* is?" Jack asked.

"No," the women replied in unison.

"I'll have my governess, Peek, follow up on this," Caroline said to Flora. "I'm sure she has a fresh copy already."

"Also, if he was married, someone in that part of society would have to know about it," Flora said. "I'll do some asking through my friends."

"While you're at it, see if you can find out anything about his life in West Sussex. Rumor has it that his house is being stripped of valuables," Jack said.

Caroline looked his way. "Your father certainly didn't get that from him."

"No, Peek provided the local gossip," Jack said. "We know Bremerton's a gambler, since he bit on Da's nightly card game, but that doesn't mean that's where his money is going. The more details we can gather, the better."

"Well, for a man with an ill father, he's very social," Caroline said. "In the day he was here before me, he managed to make a two-inch-thick stack of invitations appear at my house. I'm sure I'll learn more as I attend all these functions."

Jack looked at Caroline. "I need you to be careful when you deal with him. His exact words to my father were that he planned to do marriage correctly this time. He wasn't going to tolerate manipulation or back talk."

Flora looked at Caroline and shook her head. "Oh, my, he *has* picked the wrong woman, hasn't he?"

* * *

An hour and a half later, after some real lunch and more talk with Jack and Flora, Caroline returned to the Grosvenor Square house. Amelia was lurking in the front hallway.

"Where have you been?" she asked.

Though it was evidence of a character flaw, Caroline hadn't yet fully forgiven her sister for last Friday's drama. "At last count, I didn't have to report to you."

Amelia stopped Caroline as she tried to walk past. "You have good reason to be upset with me, but you have to trust me when I tell you that you don't want to go upstairs. Mama is beside herself."

"What this time?" Caroline asked. She didn't want to be insensitive about her mother's health, but she suspected that the woman was going to outlive them all.

"Lord Bremerton is in the parlor. Helen is currently entertaining him. I ran out of things to say, and he's saying as little as possible."

Caroline blew out a sigh. She'd been expecting to pay for escaping Lady Reynolds's, but not on the same day. She thanked her sister, stood taller, and went to face the Englishman.

"I'm relieved to see that you're well," Bremerton said as soon as she'd walked in the parlor door. "Your family has been alarmed."

"I'm fine," she said to him, and then told Helen she was free to leave.

"If you're sure?" Helen asked.

Caroline nodded, and Helen departed, but not without a few looks over her shoulder. She also left the parlor door open. Caroline appreciated the thought.

She went to stand in front of the sofa upon which Bremerton sat. She'd noted that he hadn't risen when she'd entered the room. That, she supposed, was to express his extreme vexation. He had forgotten that she did not particularly care whether he was vexed.

"I'm surprised to find you here, Lord Bremerton," she said.

"Not half as surprised as I, to find that you were not."

He'd delivered the words in a silkily smooth voice that made her pulse jump more than if he'd expressed anger.

"I had some personal matters that I needed to attend to," she replied.

"Yes, I saw the Irishman with you outside Lady Reynolds's. I'd say they were some very personal matters, indeed."

Caroline worked to keep a calm demeanor. "We aren't engaged. There's no understanding between us at all. I am free to see my friends and conduct my relationships as I see fit."

He rose. "Let's not make a mistake regarding where we stand, Caroline. I have spoken to your father and obtained his consent to a marriage. All I have yet to do is propose to you."

Before she could even draw a breath to respond, his hand snaked out and wrapped around her wrist. She refused to give weight to his behavior by fighting back, so she let her arm go limp.

"I would ask if he took you to his suite at the Savoy, except I know he did not," Bremerton said in a perfectly calm voice. "You visited with a Mrs. Flora Willoughby, I'm told."

"You're having me followed?"

"I'm merely looking out for your safety as you visit your future homeland."

"Your consideration is unnecessary," she said.

"But it's quite necessary." He pulled her closer. She thought he was about to kiss her, but he did not. Instead, he brought his mouth to her ear and said in a low voice, "I would be most upset to find you were no longer a virgin."

Her breath caught in her throat as he pushed her away. She'd just regained her balance when he said, "I look forward to seeing you at the museum gala tonight." He tilted his head and assessed her from head to toes. "Wear diamonds, Caroline."

"I could set my watch by you, Patrick Culhane," Flora said to herself that evening as she waited for Soames, her butler, to show Patrick into the front parlor. It was not quite five, and Patrick had apparently simmered as long as he could.

He entered the room, hat in hand, but with anything but a contrite look on his face. "I know I went about things wrong on the ship, Flora, but refusing to talk to me at all is like sending a man to the gallows for trespassing."

"Good evening to you, too, Mister Culhane. May I offer you any refreshments?"

He tossed his hat onto an oak side table and said, "No thank you, but you may offer me a second chance."

Flora smiled in spite of herself.

Patrick grinned. "I take it that was polite enough for you?"

"It was better than telling me to get ready for a ceremony in front of the ship's captain because we're growing older and have no time to waste. You, I must point out, are growing older faster than I. The clock isn't winding down on me."

He laughed. "Cruel woman."

"Only when it's deserved," she replied, but softened the words with a smile.

"I've come to ask you to accompany me to dinner on

Saturday night at the Savoy's River Restaurant," Patrick said.

"You can't possibly have a reservation for this Saturday," Flora replied. "With Chef Escoffier's fame, it takes months to obtain a table."

He smiled. "Would I be lying about something that will prove itself come Saturday?"

"No," she admitted grudgingly.

"So will you or won't you?"

"I will," Flora said. "After all, who could pass up . . . Escoffier?"

Patrick grinned. "I know my strengths, and cooking's not among them. But there are things I do well, you might be remembering." He walked to her, took her hand, and kissed it. "I'm sure if you do some thinking between now and Saturday, you'll remember what one of them is."

With that, he was gone.

Flora stood where he'd left her, remembering every single, last thing that Patrick Culhane did to perfection.

TWENTY

CAROLINE HAD WORN DIAMONDS ON TUESDAY NIGHT, rubies on Wednesday, pearls on Thursday, and sapphires on Friday. She had danced when told to dance, spoken only on command, and shared no opinion that differed from Bremerton's. Yet according to the Englishman, she was still falling short of what he expected of his future wife. Peek had said that the men in Bremerton's family outlived their women. Caroline was certain this was because they drowned them in demands. But she came from hardy American stock, and she fully intended to have a future that would not include being told what to wear every day of the week.

Saturday evening had arrived, and Annie was in Caroline's bedroom helping her into a pale green Worth ball gown with iridescent beading that would complement tonight's demanded emeralds. While Annie worked, Caroline shared information to pass on to Jack through O'Toole, who had become their conduit.

"Also tell him that Bremerton's late wife could have been French," Caroline said. "He told someone last night that he'd been touring the French countryside when his brother passed away, and that word didn't get to him in time for him to attend the funeral." She looked over her shoulder at Annie. "The man has an excuse for everything."

"Except for the way he treats you," Annie said as she gave the dress one last tug. A few threads snapped somewhere in the layers of fabric Caroline wore, but the gown sat smoothly, when it had refused to cooperate before. Annie came around to face Caroline. The maid stood, hands on hips, and surveyed her.

"Perfect, of course," she said. "I wish I did poor work. I hate having a hand in this, night after night dressing you up for that man. I feel like I'm fattening you for the kill."

Caroline smiled. "That's not the most flattering comparison, but it's apt enough. I promise you, though, that I have matters under control." And that was true, so long as she did exactly what Bremerton wished, and did not risk seeing Jack.

"Miss Caroline," Berta said from the bedroom doorway, "Lord Bremerton awaits you downstairs."

"Thank you, Berta," she said. "I'll be down in just a moment."

Mama's maid left. Annie hurried to the dressing table and retrieved the emeralds. "I don't know how you can be so calm, Miss. You know he's doing this on purpose. Yesterday he was fifteen minutes early, and today twenty."

"He's doing it to get me to react. Therefore, I won't," Caroline said as she looked in the standing mirror and used two jeweled hairpins to place the dress's small, matching feather aigrette into her hair.

"Oh, you'll react one day. You're just storing it up." Annie smiled. "You're not the sort who's destined for sainthood."

Caroline laughed. "Definitely not. I'm planning on developing a headache just around midnight, so expect me home not long after."

"I'll be here, waiting to hear how another night with the devil went."

The devil was in the parlor, dressed to perfection in his cutaway tail coat. "You are timely."

"I try to oblige," she replied.

"I would like a moment to speak with you before we leave," Bremerton said. He gestured at a small chair Mama had had upholstered in a Chinese tapestry. "Sit."

Caroline's dress, with its voluminous skirts, was not made for comfortable sitting. Once she had herself adequately perched, Bremerton moved in front of her. He stood less than a foot away, which forced her to crane her neck in order not to be staring at parts of him with which she'd prefer to remain unacquainted.

"Is there something in particular you wish to speak to me about, Lord Bremerton?"

"I want you to call me Marcus."

"If you wish." Caroline clasped her hands together in her lap. She'd begun to shake. She knew what was coming next.

"You've had a week now to meet those whom you would be seeing in my social milieu," he said. "You have performed adequately."

He seemed to be waiting for her to say something. She gave him a cheery smile. "Thank you. Maybe you should give me a treat, as my mother does her lap dog."

He disregarded her comment. "At this point, I see no reason in delaying my request for your hand in marriage."

Again he stood silent. Caroline watched him.

"Well? What is your answer?" he finally asked.

"I don't recall being asked a question," she said as she sorted through the possible ways she might be able to escape or delay him.

His expression went from disaffected to annoyed. "If it soothes you to be asked in the form of a question . . .

Miss Caroline Maxwell, will you do me the honor of marrying me?"

She wanted to give him a blunt and irrevocable no. That, however, would only serve to inflame warfare among her parents and herself. Even her father, who was an indulgent man, would not tolerate outright rebellion. She drew in a breath and stepped onto the narrowest tightrope she had ever tried to tread.

"I recognize the great honor you've bestowed upon me, but I would hope you understand that I can't give my consent at this moment. The marriage of a daughter is a joyous thing, and yet my father is an ocean away. I'd like to have him here."

"Your father has already consented."

"True," she replied, wishing the Englishman would move far enough away that she could stand. Her neck was beginning to seize up. "However, that was all business. I'm speaking of the emotional aspects. I want to see my father's eyes when he knows I am to wed." And if it was to Bremerton, she wanted Papa to grasp the level of sacrifice she was making. "I would also point out that I haven't yet seen where you live, Lord Bremerton—"

"Marcus," he said in an icy tone.

"Yes, well . . . I would think that if a woman is to marry, she should have some sense of what her lifetime surroundings are to be, and what she can do to create a place of comfort for her husband. You've said that all I need to do is ask, and you'll give me the world. I don't ask for the world, but I do request these two small things."

He stared down at her for what must have been at least a minute. His hands clenched and unclenched a few times. Caroline knew he wouldn't dare to strike her in her own home, but she stiffened just the same.

"I expect your father to be here in under a fortnight,"

he said. "And if you wish to see Chesley House, you shall see it."

She exhaled a breath she hadn't even known she'd been holding. "Thank you."

He looked down at her for a moment longer, a muscle at the side of his jaw working. "I will make your excuses to the Felker-Hugheses this evening. I am quite sure you must be overwrought."

If he thought missing a ball was punishment, he knew nothing about her. Caroline nodded, and Bremerton turned and walked from the room. Once he was gone, she remained in the little Chinese chair and considered her options. Like the verbal tightrope she'd just treaded, they were stretching thin.

Caroline looked up as someone entered the parlor. It was Mama, and she wore a dinner dress instead of her recent shut-in garb. Her mother started when she noticed her.

"What are you still doing here?" Mama asked, her hand to her chest.

"Lord Bremerton was worried about my health and told me to stay in tonight."

Her mother came closer. "Are you ill?"

"No, I had just asked him to defer his marriage proposal. He believed that I had to be ill."

"He offered and you *declined*?"

"No, Mama," Caroline said in a calming tone. "As I just said, I deferred."

"This is dreadful!"

"No, it's reasonable. I want Papa here, and I want to have seen Bremerton's house." Caroline estimated those two events would buy her another three weeks. "That's not so very much to ask."

Her mother seemed to calm herself as she paced in front of the fireplace.

"Well, we'll do what we can to speed this along. Your father should be here by Monday," Mama said. "He's crossing on the Vandermeulens' yacht with them. I had asked him to leave the *Conqueror* at my disposal for a speedy return to New York to complete wedding plans . . . should you be a decent enough daughter to let that come to pass." She began breathing quickly, but getting no air in. "You, however, have not! How could you do this?"

Her mother's calm had been very short-lived. Caroline didn't want to think how Mama would have taken it if she'd said no. She rose and reached out a hand in a conciliatory gesture. "Please relax. There's no crisis." Except Papa arriving early, she thought.

Her mother held a hand to her chest. "There *is* a crisis! Any well-bred young woman would have accepted. I'm sure he's off looking at other potential wives tonight!"

Mama clearly underestimated the lure of the Maxwell millions, but pointing that out would do little to help.

"Please, you really do need to breathe, Mama."

"I can't!"

"Do you want me to call for your doctor?"

"No! I wish you to stay out of my sight unless you're coming to tell me that you've accepted Lord Bremerton. Now, please leave me."

"Yes, Mama," Caroline said. She kept her head high all the way to her bedroom, where she cried. How could Mama not see Lord Bremerton for what he really was?

Jack sat at the bar in a smoky pub some distance from the Savoy. Talk and laughter bounced off the building's low, beamed ceiling. The air was thick, and the ale, the richest Jack had ever tasted.

Da was taking Flora out to some fancy dinner tonight, and had even gone so far as to have a new tuxedo made.

Jack was good with his unremarkable clothes and a platter of roasted beef and boiled potatoes. At least, as good as he could get knowing that Caroline was with Bremerton yet again.

The Englishman had been efficient in ensuring that Jack couldn't secure invitations to any of the events he'd been taking Caroline to. Jack had asked Flora to try through her friends, and he had reached out to some college acquaintances who now lived in London, but he'd come up dry. He had, however, caught some unsavory tales about Bremerton.

Rumor had it that His Lordship owed a great deal of money to a man one didn't want to cross. The only reason he still lived was that he was a duke's direct heir. The potential of eventual repayment beat the nuisance factor of killing him.

The noise level in the pub suddenly dropped. Jack looked toward the door. Bremerton had entered. His evening clothes made him as obvious as a peacock in a flock of sparrows. He slowly scanned the crowded tables. Jack turned back to his food. The Englishman could afford to work to find him.

Bremerton soon elbowed his way between Jack and the man seated to his right, who looked damned unhappy with the intrusion. Jack kept eating.

"This would be your sort of place," Bremerton said.

"Best ale I've ever had," Jack replied. "Want me to buy you one?"

"You're not in the least curious why I'm here, are you?"

Jack speared another bite of potato and shrugged. "All we have in common is Caroline. And as to why I'm not surprised to see you, why should I be? I know you're having me followed." He inclined his head toward a scarecrow of a man with a pockmarked face and tweed cap. He'd been sitting by himself and nursing the same ale for some time. "Your man isn't very subtle."

"But he comes cheaply and he's not averse to violence," Bremerton said.

Jack heard the threat, he just didn't care. "In his line of work, he'd better not be. So what do you want?"

"I want to make it clear what the consequences are if you do not leave England immediately."

"And those would be?" Jack asked after making Bremerton wait while he ate a bite of beef.

"Fatal."

Jack laughed. "Unlikely unless you hire better than that," he said, hitching his thumb toward Bremerton's puny hired muscle. "And we both know you're flat out of money."

"Are you drinking something or just taking up my space?" the bartender demanded of Bremerton, who ignored him.

"I don't mean fatal for you," Bremerton said to Jack.

He gave Bremerton a brawler's grin. "We both know you're not touching Caroline until you're married."

"But Flora Willoughby is expendable."

Now Jack was angry. "I'm beginning to lose my patience with you."

The bartender smacked his palm on the bar. *"Oi!* Order or get your overdressed arse onto the street."

Jack wanted that arse to land another place. He stood and knotted his left hand into Bremerton's cravat and sunk his right into his gut. The Englishman's knees buckled. He staggered into Jack's neighbor as Jack threw some money on the bar.

"He can finish mine," Jack said and then left the pub.

Flora loved formal restaurant dinners. She knew the order of cutlery for twelve courses and could handle escargot tongs without a slip. She reveled in epicurean delights and felt that fine French burgundies were nectar of the gods. Tonight, though, as she sat in the Savoy's River Restaurant with Patrick, she might as well have been gnawing on squirrel and swilling grape juice. Flora was inexplicably nervous. And Patrick, who generally did not do well in places as opulent as this, remained completely calm.

She had never seen him looking more handsome, either. His tuxedo was so well cut that she wanted to remove the bow tie and loosen a few buttons on it. Just to relax him, of course, and not because she happened to be craving his closeness. She'd been over two weeks without even a kiss, and she was far hungrier for that than she was the *filet de poule au trouffes* sitting on her plate.

Patrick took a sip of his wine and looked at her evenly. "Is the food not pleasing you?"

"It is," she said. "Very much."

He smiled. "I'd be believing you more if you'd take a bite."

"Oh . . . of course," she said. Flora cut an infinitesimally small piece of the chicken and nibbled on it. "The sauce is heavenly," she said once she finished.

He smiled. "There wasn't enough on that fork for a hummingbird to taste."

The waiter came to remove the course, and Patrick asked him to delay bringing the next one. Flora imagined the chef would be heaving a cleaver if they waited too long, but she was glad for the break. Too much was coming at her, too quickly, but from the determined look Patrick now wore, it wasn't going to stop.

"When I last saw you, I told you to think about what I do well," Patrick said once the waiter had left. "And instead of asking what you thought about, I'll tell you what I know I do well."

He leaned closer. "I'm an incredible lover." A playful smile tugged at the corners of his mouth. "But you already know that, and I won't bore you by pointing out the obvious."

Flora said a silent word of thanks for all the years she'd been on stage. She kept her expression the same as if he'd been talking about the weather.

"And I'm a good provider," he said. "I'm not afraid of hard work, and don't plan to stop until I'm in my grave. I'll be slowing a bit now, as it's time to turn to other pleasures, but I'm guessing that your wealth outstrips mine, anyway . . . not that I want a penny of it."

He paused and smiled. "And I know I'm a good da. You just have to look at Jack to know that. Should you want a child, I'd be honored to be his or her father."

His words made her want to weep, but then she'd miss the rest.

"And now here's what I've done poorly with you, Flora, and I swear I never will again." He hesitated, and she knew how difficult he'd always found it to admit fault.

"My Maeve was a fine woman," he said. "I loved her with all my heart. And when she died, I thought I could never love another. But then I met you, and though Maeve had been gone a long, long time, I felt guilty for loving you. And scared by how much I did, too. I pushed you away when I should have been holding you close. I was a fool."

Flora gave up and used her napkin to dab at her eyes.

"And then, after that, I was a liar when I told you in Newport all I wanted was your friendship. I want it all. I want your cries when I'm loving you. I want your temper when I've crossed you. I want you now and tomorrow and every day of my life." He nodded. "There, now. I've almost said it."

She smiled over her tears. "I can't believe there's anything else to say."

"There is. I was an eejit to try to rush you on the ship. Whatever wedding you want, we'll have. In London, New York, or Newport, it's yours. So will you marry me, Flora Willoughby?"

"Tully," she said.

Patrick looked at her blankly. "What?" he asked.

"Tully. Isn't that where you were born?"

"Aye."

"I want to get married in Tully. No fuss and no frippery."

A slow smile worked its way across his handsome face. "You're meaning this? Tully, County Donegal?"

"Yes, I am."

He tipped back his head and laughed. "You're going to keep me guessing, aren't you, my love?"

Flora smiled. "For as long as we both shall live."

Well past midnight, Jack sat in his father's suite waiting for Da to arrive. A fire burned in the small grate, cutting though the dampness rising off the River Thames. Jack knew he should be feeling more tired than he was, but anger sustained him.

Da came in, untying his white bow tie as he walked. He smiled when he saw Jack. "Congratulate me, son. I'm going to be a husband again."

Jack rose and shook his father's hand. Da pulled him into a hug and patted his back as though Jack was the one who'd done something monumental. His father stepped away. His nose was red at the tip and his eyes looked suspiciously watery. He cleared his throat twice before speaking.

"It's a grand night," he said. "And that was the most

important bargaining I've done in years." He paused and laughed. "Hell, bargaining? I gave it all away, and I'm glad I did."

Jack smiled, though he had a tough time making it reach his eyes. "So is the bride Flora?"

"Of course it's Flora," Da blustered. "Who else might I be after marrying?"

Jack went to the cut crystal carafe that waited on the room's sideboard. He poured Da a glass of what had to be Jameson's finest. He poured a splash for himself into a tumbler, too.

"I know," he said, handing his father a glass. "After all, who else would have you?"

They toasted each other.

"Who else, indeed," Da said. His father had a swallow of whiskey and watched him keenly. "Do you want to tell me what happened or am I to guess?"

Jack resettled onto the red-and-gold striped settee. "Bremerton paid me a visit tonight while I was having my dinner and ale at the Boar's Head Pub."

"I can understand how a man like that might put you off your beer, but if he was with you, at least he wasn't squiring about Caroline."

"True," Jack said. "But he was making threats."

Da sat next to Jack. "Well, I know they weren't against you, because you wouldn't be caring. What did he say?"

"He threatened Flora."

Da's jaw twitched as he digested what Jack had said. "He knows how to hurt you then, doesn't he?"

"He chose the best available target," Jack agreed. "Could you get Flora away from England? I know that Culhanes stand and fight, and once you're gone, I'll do that for both of us."

Da let out a long, weary sigh. "I'll have us gone as soon as I can persuade Flora to pack." He gave a tick of a smile. "It seems we're getting married in Tully. Clearly, she hasn't seen the village church. I'd wanted you there, and Flora will be expecting it."

Jack nodded. "Get her off this island, then tell her we'll celebrate together in New York."

Da nodded. "I'll book passage Monday morning."

"Thank you."

"So," Da said after they'd both stared awhile into the meager flames, their minds clearly elsewhere, "what are you going to do about the Englishman?"

"First, I'm going to Bernard Maxwell and asking to marry Caroline. I found out tonight through O'Toole that Maxwell is to be here by Monday," Jack said. "Maybe he'll shock the hell out of me and say yes."

"If he had the sense of a donkey, he would," Da said. "But I'm thinking the Maxwells and sense parted ways a long time ago. Excepting Caroline, of course," he added.

"Of course."

Da shook his head. "Who'd have thought I'd marry again?"

Jack smiled. "Me, now that you and your sense have joined up again. I'm happy for you, Da."

He nodded. "And soon I'll be for you."

Jack would make it so.

TWENTY-ONE

CAROLINE'S FATHER ARRIVED AT THE GROSVENOR Square house on a very rainy Monday afternoon. Jack, who sat out front in a hired cab, decided it would improve his chances if he at least let Mr. Maxwell dry off before he made his call. He impatiently lingered another fifteen minutes or so and then rang the bell. The butler, as stoic as O'Brien back in New York, disregarded the fact that Jack was damn wet as he ushered him to the parlor. Bernard soon joined him.

"Good afternoon, sir," Jack said to Caroline's father as they shook hands. "Thank you for seeing me so soon after your arrival." The older man looked weary, likely worn down from travel with the Vandermeulens. The family never stopped talking.

"I was wondering how long you planned to lurk outside," Bernard said. "I saw you when I was coming in. You do know that Edward didn't make the crossing with me?"

"Yes, sir," Jack said. "I'm here to speak to you."

"Well, speak, then," he said genially.

There was no point in delay. "I'm here to ask for your daughter's hand in marriage, sir."

Mr. Maxwell stared at him as though he'd just announced his intention to sink the *Conqueror*. "You wish to marry *my* daughter?"

"Yes. Caroline," Jack added to be perfectly clear.

"But I just spent days listening to talk about how you're about to propose to Harriet Vandermeulen."

"It was just that, sir . . . talk. It will be cleared up now that the Vandermeulens have arrived. I love your daughter."

"You always struck me as the sensible type," Bernard said. "You accompanied Caroline over here, son. You know the trip was made to settle marriage matters with Lord Bremerton."

"I know that was your wife's intent, and possibly yours. I came to keep her safe from Bremerton."

"What do you mean, *safe*?"

"He isn't who he pretends to be," Jack said. "I've heard talk that concerns me."

Caroline's father shook his head. "You can't be about to hand me the same tale as Edward did about Bremerton trying to injure someone on the polo field? I checked with the match umpire and a dozen other witnesses. The field was wet. Accidents happen."

"They do, but that wasn't one. He was trying to hurt me."

"You? Why would he even notice you?"

"He had reason," Jack said. Admitting to Bernard Maxwell that he'd been kissing his daughter wasn't going to win Jack a bride.

Mr. Maxwell's congeniality was wearing thin, and his bushy brows were coming close to meeting above his nose. "Whatever issue you have with the Englishman has nothing to do with Caroline. She's at no risk."

"I believe she is. I'm asking you to wait before you send her to visit Bremerton. Please listen to what I've heard and see if you can prove or disprove it. I've been working to get to the people who can help me do the same, but it's been difficult. They're not interested in opening their doors to an American they've never heard of before."

"You can save yourself the effort. Caroline and her mother already left for West Sussex on the morning train," Mr. Maxwell said.

Which had to be why O'Toole hadn't been able to get to Annie last night or early this morning, Jack thought. "That makes it all the more urgent to find out the truth about Bremerton," he said aloud.

"You're at best a friend of my family. Caroline's marriage arrangements are none of your business."

"They couldn't be more my business, sir. Your daughter loves me, too. We could marry without your consent, but she also loves you and your wife and wants to please you. I respect that. Caroline told me about the husband list Mrs. Maxwell wrote. I'm asking you to put it aside and consider Caroline's future. Give us your blessing, and don't put your daughter in a position where to make you happy, she has to sacrifice her own happiness."

"I'm going to be blunt about this because I don't want you harboring hope. Look at Caroline's family, and then look at yours. We've been at the pinnacle of American society longer than your family has been in America. You're a fine friend for my son, but you're not of the stature to marry a Maxwell. Do you hear what I'm saying?"

"Yes, sir, though with great respect, you're dead wrong," Jack replied. "But let's address that later. First, I want Caroline safe. I'd like you to listen to everything I've heard about Lord Bremerton."

Jack stood his ground as the older man deliberated Jack's request.

"You accept defeat well," Caroline's father finally said.

"I suppose I can listen. Sit." He sat in a brown leather wing chair, and Jack took the one opposite him.

And as he told Caroline's father all that he knew, Jack didn't share one essential truth about himself: He didn't believe in defeat at all.

Caroline sniffled. The carriage Bremerton had sent to the train station smelled of mildew and had been bothering her nose. At least her discomfort suited the wet day and served as a counterbalance to her mother's relentless cheerfulness. As they approached Chesley House, it was safe to say that Mama's heart problem had miraculously cured itself.

"Well, it certainly is a large enough place to keep you busy," Caroline's mother said as the country house grew from a distant dot on the landscape to a looming presence. The long, three-story building was a drab sight. Its gray stone blended into an equally gray sky, and the reflecting pond in front of the structure only amplified the effect.

"Lord Bremerton has done well for himself," Mama said, continuing the same one-sided conversation she'd had going since she, Annie, Berta, and Caroline had boarded the train this morning.

Caroline shook her head. "The house, as well as the title, are on loan from his grandfather. He owns neither."

"Please at least try to be cheerful," Mama instructed as they bounced along on a gravel road in need of attention.

"This is my new cheerful," Caroline replied. "You didn't let me wait long enough to see Papa, and you didn't bring Peek. So, all things considered, I'm quite sunny."

"I can hardly help it if the Vandermeulens' yacht is slow, and you know that Peek was needed to watch over the girls in the city. We could hardly ask them to leave, when it's not even August and anyone of import remains there."

Caroline wouldn't have wished her sisters here. Especially not Amelia, who had finally realized that not only was Bremerton not the romantic figure she had made him out to be, he wasn't even particularly nice to her. It was better that both girls stayed in the city and perhaps even ran a little wild while Mama was elsewhere. The July timing was convenient for Bremerton, too. There would be little to do but sit on this moldering property and look at each other.

"I had no idea you had become so close to Peek that a mere week without her would put you in this mood," Mama said. "She is quite devoted. I will keep her on for Helen and Amelia."

Fondness hadn't driven Caroline's desire to have Peek along with them, necessity had. Peek knew people locally and could have been instrumental in finding out about Bremerton's supposed French wife. Now Caroline was on her own, and time as well as the Englishman had become her enemy.

"All I ask is that you not hover now that we're here, Mama," Caroline said. If she had only Annie for help, she needed room to maneuver. "You've gotten what you wanted, now please give me the freedom to adjust to my new life."

"Of course," her mother said, and then pointed out the window. "Oh! Look at that lovely little folly of a ruined thatched cottage! Isn't this the most romantic landscape?"

Caroline sighed. The cottage her mother was admiring was no landscape accent, but the real thing. And still occupied, too. Mama was so in love with the notion of England that she painted everything in rosy hues.

The carriage jolted to a stop and a young man who'd been standing at the front of the house came forward to help Caroline and her mother. At least the rain had stopped pelting down. Caroline shook out her blue travel cloak and skirts once she reached the gritty limestone gravel drive.

The boy led them up the house's three broad steps, which were in need of a good sweeping, and held the door open for them. Neither Bremerton nor a servant waited in the cavernous entry hall, a space dominated by a large, curving stairway that must have been quite impressive in its day. Now it looked suspect, as did the hall. Its plaster walls were discolored, and while a few small oil paintings still hung, more notable were the dust outlines where larger pieces had once been.

"You'll have such fun decorating this place," Mama enthused.

If Caroline were the sort of person Mama was, and took actual joy out of gathering up as many of the world's treasures as she could to use as props, that might have been true. Caroline preferred to see things in their natural surroundings, where context made them all the more understandable. And these surroundings certainly confirmed her beliefs about Bremerton.

He appeared on the upper hallway. Caroline suppressed a shiver that came from both the house's chill and her own nerves. It was as though thinking his name had summoned the devil.

"Welcome," he said as he started down the stairs. "I wish we would have had a better day. Chesley House shows poorly in the rain." His deep voice echoed against the bare walls.

"It's a lovely property, with great potential," Mama said.

Caroline kept her silence as Bremerton made the ground floor. He wore country tweeds that, although the fit was perfect, didn't suit him at all. He was playing yet another role, and this one less convincingly than his city persona.

"That's kind of you to say, Mrs. Maxwell. There's much that requires attention here," he replied. As he did, he watched Caroline in a way that made her immediately decide that Annie would be sleeping in her room with her.

"Your maids and trunks should be along shortly," he said. "In the meantime, my housekeeper should be here to show you to your rooms. We'll be having dinner with two of my neighbors and with Lady Carew, my great-aunt on my mother's side, who acts as hostess here at Chesley House, since I am yet unmarried."

"I look forward to meeting your great-aunt," Caroline said. "I'm sure we'll have a lot to talk about, since she's known you from childhood."

"I'm sure you will," Bremerton replied smoothly. And even if Mama had been paying closer attention, she probably wouldn't have caught the flash of cold warning in the Englishman's eyes. She was already convinced that he represented perfection.

The housekeeper, a harried-looking woman somewhere in her middle years, arrived.

"Mrs. Parker, if you would please show our guests to their rooms?" Bremerton said. To Caroline and her mother he added, "I'll give you time to settle in. We'll meet in the dining room at eight."

"Right this way," Mrs. Parker said, leading them to the stairway. "As you'll see, we have neither gas nor electric on anything but the main floor. Lord Bremerton says the stone walls are much too thick to accommodate such conveniences. There are candles and oil lamps in your rooms to help you get about in the night."

"It's all so very romantic," Mama said. She clearly had not thought through the stone situation far enough to understand this meant that in the winter, the upstairs rooms were heated only by fireplaces. Caroline would hold out hope for plumbing.

Mrs. Parker stopped at a door and swung it open. "Miss Maxwell, this will be your room."

Caroline stepped inside. Mama and the housekeeper followed. The room was large and had clearly once been very elegant. Now it possessed that same aura of slow decay as the rest of the house. The rosewood dresser was new, but had nothing in common with a four poster bed that was at least a hundred years older, or with the small sofa in front of the fireplace that looked as though it had been upholstered with a local cow. The green draperies hung listlessly, and the rug was worn down to its backing in spots. And this was likely the best of the guest rooms, which Caroline would have been accorded as Lord Bremerton's future fiancée. At least, though, it had a chaise on which Annie could sleep, and it was clean.

"Thank you," she said to the housekeeper. "It will do quite nicely." She turned to Mama, who had picked up a chipped china shepherdess figurine and turned it upside down to look for its maker. "No need to linger, Mama. I'll see you at dinner."

As soon as the two other women had departed, Caroline closed the door and began pacing the room. There was work to be done to get her into Jack's arms, and she was ready to begin.

Jack usually loved Mondays. They were the start of a new work week, and rich with potential. This Monday, however, had been rich with something else entirely. He'd taken enough of a hit from Bernard Maxwell that he figured he might as well just keep going and deal with the mess of politely explaining to Harriet that there would be no marriage proposal. It was his fault for not having done it sooner, but he hadn't wrapped his mind around the girl's unbelievable tenacity. She'd crossed the ocean with not even a shred of the encouragement that had sent Agnes Maxwell into a frenzy of packing.

Jack had learned from Mr. Maxwell that the Vander-meulens had also taken suites at the Savoy. If nothing else, that made Jack's wrap-up of the worst Monday on record efficient. He'd had a note delivered to Harriet's rooms, asking her to join him on the terrace at six. She approached now, dressed in a lavender gown with more fluff and lace than Jack had ever seen. Her hat was no shirker when it came to ornamentation, either. He spotted three small, stuffed birds among the silk leaves and would bet that a couple more were hiding in there somewhere.

"Hello, Jack," she said. "How wonderful that you're in London. I had no idea you'd be here." Harriet was an unskilled fibber. Her voice wavered and her eyes darted.

"I thought we could take a walk in the embankment gardens now that the rain has stopped," Jack said. "But it's still wet. How about if we have a seat at one of these tables?"

"Do you like to walk?" Harriet asked.

"It gets me from place to place," he said with a smile.

"If you like it, then we shall walk," she replied. "It's most healthful." She gripped her skirts and raised them until he could see the pointy toes of her white kid boots. "Shall we?"

They walked down the outer stairway, toward the garden. Harriet stopped at the puddle stretching across the expanse of the ground at the stairs' base, stubbornly set her jaw, and marched over it.

Jack would have offered once again to turn back, but he got the sense that once Harriet was set on a course of action, she was going to see it through to the end.

"As you know, your father approached me some weeks ago and suggested that marriage to you was an option I should consider," Jack said as they passed beneath an oak tree.

Harriet stopped. "Yes, I am aware of that."

"I was honored," Jack said, stopping too. "You're a beautiful young woman from a fine family."

Harriet looked up at him. He'd expected to see some sort of feminine softness in her eyes. Instead he saw the fierce spark that came with the thought of impending victory. He was damn sure he looked the same way every time he bought another brewery.

"Thank you," she replied in a sweet voice.

"And as much as I was honored, I determined not to follow through on your father's suggestion."

"Well, that's not true. We've danced together and had meals together," she said.

A breeze pushed through the oak tree, sending the droplets of rain that had clung to its leaves down in a miniature shower. Harriet glared up at the tree.

"Shall we move on to stand by the river?" Jack asked.

"No," she replied angrily. "We'll stay here. Are you denying that we danced together?"

"No, but you danced with a great many men, and spoke with them at your picnic, too. I was just part of your legion of admirers."

"Yes, well, you're the admirer I've chosen," she said.

"The choice has to be mutual, Harriet," he said in a firm but kind voice. "And I've fallen in love with someone else."

"Love? What does love have to do with marriage for people such as us?"

He smiled. "You sound exactly like I did, and not all that long ago. I looked at marriage as I did any other business transaction."

"Well, naturally," she said.

"Someone has proven to me that I was wrong, and I'm betting that when you least expect it, some man is going to come along and do the same for you."

Harriet made an annoyed little sound. "That's

nonsense. And you've put quite a knot in my plans. I have every intention of being married this winter."

She walked to the water's edge, and Jack followed. A small sailboat slowly worked its way toward them, its sails just catching the scant breeze. Harriet glared at the boat, too, though Jack got the feeling it was really intended for him.

"If marriage is your intention, I'm sure you'll succeed," he said.

She looked at him. "You're here in London, and you came with the Maxwells, which means you're in love with Caroline."

He nodded. "I am."

"But you can't be in love with her. She's supposed to marry Lord Bremerton. You're supposed to love me. Think how much more convenient that would be."

"I'm new to this love thing, but even I can guarantee it has nothing to do with convenience."

"And yet you're in love." She shook her head. "You're not who I thought you'd be."

Jack smiled. "I'm not who I thought I'd be, either."

But he liked this new man a whole lot more.

Caroline and Mama weren't overdressed for dinner so much as they were too newly dressed. As the small party sat gathered around the dining table, which had an unfortunate slope toward Caroline, she assessed the state of their wardrobes. Lady Carew wore a gray silk gown with an enormous bustle that had been the height of fashion twenty years ago, but no longer. The two women from the neighboring family—Miss Daisy Ridley and her widowed mother, Mrs. Olive Ridley—were dressed in more recent clothing, but Caroline still felt too glittery and new by comparison. Even Bremerton's evening clothes were more subdued than his city wear.

Mama, of course, didn't seem to notice. She and Bremerton talked on about ways in which the house could be improved and who their favored architects were. From time to time, Bremerton would glance Caroline's way, but it seemed that since he believed victory—and her funds—were his, there was no need to feign interest in her in front of others. Caroline was fine with that.

"This is all highly irregular," Lady Carew announced in a loud, quivering voice from her seat at Bremerton's right. His great-aunt was quite elderly and, Caroline feared, no longer fully in possession of her faculties.

"What, Auntie?" Bremerton stopped to ask.

"I do not understand why we have these foreigners at my table. They are from America, you say?"

"Yes," Bremerton replied.

"It's a land of heathens and savages. They all live in mud huts."

Caroline looked downward to hide a smile, but Mama was puffing up like an adder. Bremerton motioned to the waiter, who was the same boy who'd opened the front door for them earlier. "My aunt would like some more wine."

"It sounds as though you and Lord Bremerton are to marry," Miss Daisy Ridley said to Caroline. Daisy was close to Caroline's age and possessed of a ruddy glow that Caroline saw most often on her centaur female friends—those who would sooner die than be parted from their horses.

"There are no plans at this point," Caroline replied.

"You are not the first American girl to come to the county," Daisy said. "I simply don't understand it, though. Why would you possibly want to move so far away from both your mother and your home? And why would your mother want you to?"

Since Caroline was plagued by precisely the same

questions, it was difficult to come up with an answer that wouldn't make her mother look like an ogre or she like the family member that must be shed at all costs.

"It's complicated," Caroline said.

"Nothing in this world is so complicated that it can't be broken down just like my horse's tack," Daisy replied. "And you seem to have your wits about you more than the other Americans I've met. Break it down for me."

Caroline drew in a breath and was ready to give it a try, but Lady Carew interrupted.

"You!" she cried, pointing a finger at Caroline. "You in the yellow with all the jewels."

"Yes, ma'am?"

"Why are you here?" she asked, her rheumy eyes narrow.

"Your nephew invited me," Caroline replied.

"Miss Maxwell has come to Chesley House to decide if the house and I suit her," Bremerton said to his aunt.

"Whatever for?"

"The general intention is that we should wed."

"Wed?" his great-aunt asked. "What did you do with the last one?"

"What last one, Auntie?"

"Why, your wife, of course. I saw her scurrying around here from room to room." She pointed at the waiter. "Go find her now. We cannot be served until she is at the table, too. And who seated me in the wrong place? I am to be to your left, Marcus. Your wife is to be at your right."

Daisy moved closer. "Disregard her," she said in a low voice. "She has declined greatly since Lord Bremerton and she arrived. It's quite sad."

Caroline nodded. "I understand." But she also understood that Lady Carew, while old, wasn't necessarily mad.

"Are you going to reseat me?" Lady Carew demanded. She pointed at Mama. "Make her move."

Mama's jaw had gone slack. Caroline couldn't recall ever seeing her this shocked.

"Perhaps dinner in your room would suit you, Auntie?" Bremerton suggested.

"Yes, and tell me when you're rid of the foreigners." She glared at Mama. "This is all most irregular, bringing around this odd lot."

Bremerton rose and motioned to the waiter. "We shall escort you to your room," he said to his great-aunt.

Caroline couldn't wait until she was back to hers, either.

Two hours later, the jewels were off, the dress rehung, and Caroline sat in her dressing gown on the edge of her bed, running a brush through her hair. Annie was in her nightclothes, having snuck away from her room next to Berta's to keep watch for Bremerton.

"I will never complain about my lodgings in any of your houses again," Annie said.

Caroline had never actually seen the servants' quarters in either house. "Why? Are your rooms back home not satisfactory?"

Annie laughed. "Well, I have my own room, even if it fits no more than a cot and an old wardrobe. That's better than what I had with my family. But here?" She shuddered. "I opened my door and a rat ran out. I would have sent someone after it, but the thing looked like it was ready to starve to death on its own. I'm telling you, there are parts of this house no one has touched in years. And as for the rest, the devil can have it."

Caroline slipped off the bed and put her brush next to her mirror on the nightstand. The candle there flickered with the breeze she'd made. "I've noticed they're running even thinner on servants than the situation Peek described."

Annie nodded. "There's Mrs. Parker, the housekeeper, Charlie, the waiter and footman and I think gardener, too. Then there's Cora, the only maid, and her husband, who's both coachman and groom, and a cook. Small wonder no one can keep up."

"Who has been here the longest?"

"Only Cora and her husband were here when the last Lord Bremerton was alive. Charlie's new, and not nearly so fun to tease as Jack's O'Toole." Annie sighed. "A week here is punishment."

A knock sounded at the bedroom door. Caroline held her finger to her lips.

"Is that you, Mama?" Caroline called.

No one answered for a moment, but then Bremerton identified himself and asked if he might step in. Caroline walked to the door and put her hand against it.

"That would be very improper," she said through its hard surface.

"Culhane has seen you in less."

Caroline winced at the reference. From behind her, she heard a hiss. Annie had risen and was ready to spring. Caroline shook her head and mouthed the word no.

"I am asking if you would please stay on your side of the door," Caroline recited like a schoolgirl saying her verses.

"For now, I will allow that," Bremerton replied. "Tomorrow, I am hunting in the morning. You and your mother may occupy yourselves here. Don't disturb my aunt. As you've now seen, she's not well."

"We will do as you wish."

"And, Caroline?"

"Yes?"

"Tell your maid to go back to her room. We sleep with neither Irishmen nor servants."

TWENTY-TWO

CAROLINE MADE CERTAIN THAT BREMERTON WAS OFF slaying birds before she went to breakfast the next day. Wearing her simplest morning dress, she walked to the dining room. Though it wasn't even eight, the table had been cleared of all settings. She stood there feeling lost until Cora, the sole maid, came in, dusting rag in hand. The tall and slender woman, who looked to be a handful of years older than Caroline, quickly cleaned but showed no apparent interest in finishing any one task.

"I was wondering if it would be possible to get breakfast?" Caroline asked.

The maid jumped like a nervous cat. "I'm sorry, but that would be up to Mrs. Parker."

"Is Mrs. Parker available?"

"She stepped out of the house."

The information had been given hesitantly. Caroline decided to put the maid at ease. "My name is Caroline Maxwell. And I believe you're Cora?"

"Yes, miss."

"It's a pleasure to meet you, Cora."

"Thank you, miss."

"So I am to wait until Mrs. Parker returns?"

"Yes, if you care to try to have breakfast," Cora said

as she picked up one dented candlestick from the buffet and wiped beneath it, but then cleaned around its mate. "But the master's rule is that once the master has eaten, the meal is over."

"I see," Caroline replied over her grumbling stomach. "Thank you, Cora."

"Yes, miss. Is there anything else I may do for you?"

"Nothing at all, thank you." Caroline made her way from the dining room to the stairs and was about to go up when Mama came rushing down. She was dressed in her dark blue travel garb, and to Caroline's knowledge, no travel was planned.

"Where were you for breakfast?" Mama asked.

"I was still in my room."

"You'd better hurry tomorrow. The meal was over and done with before my tea could steep." Her mother kept looking up the stairway as she spoke, and she seemed as skittish as Cora had, too.

"Where are you going?" Caroline asked.

"How did you know I was going someplace?"

"Your clothing."

"Oh, yes. Of course. London."

Caroline's relief was infinite. "Thank heaven! Give us ten minutes, and Annie will have us packed."

"No need. You're staying here." Mama pulled a telegram from her small purse. "Your father has instructed me to return to London at once." She handed Caroline the paper. "As you see, it's addressed to me, alone, and it says only 'Return London Now.' There's no mention of bringing you."

Caroline handed the telegram back.

"You know he meant me, too, even if he didn't spell it out," she said. Papa was always ridiculously frugal when writing a telegram. It was as though he guarded the family fortune one word at a time.

Mama returned the message to her purse and then gave Caroline a sharp look. "Have you accepted Bremerton's proposal?"

Now she understood her mother's game. "No."

"Then it's not time for you to leave. I hope to persuade your father to return here with me tomorrow so he can witness your engagement. Lord Bremerton thought it was a fine idea."

Of course he did, because that meant Caroline would be alone tonight. "Mama, you can't just leave me here without a chaperone."

"You have Annie," her mother said.

Caroline was speechless for an instant. "You wouldn't even trust her to go to Harriet's picnic with me, and yet you'd leave us here, alone?"

"You'll be fine," Mama replied. "Even you can't find much trouble, here in the middle of nothing. And if you're looking for a titular chaperone, there's Lady Carew. Your reputation is safe."

Berta teetered down the stairs, carrying Mama's smallest travel trunk.

"To the carriage, Berta," Mama commanded before coming to Caroline and taking her hands. "You're twenty-one years old. I was married and had you at that age. Surely you're independent enough to spend less than two days on your own."

If Caroline had been anyplace but there, she'd have been popping champagne corks and celebrating her freedom. But tonight, she'd be turning the lock on her bedroom door.

"Travel safely, Mama."

Four hours later, Bremerton was still harassing birds. No lunch was to be served until he was done. Annie had even gone to the kitchen to ask for bread and cheese, but with no success. Now she was off trying to sweet-talk Charlie into asking for her. Caroline was in her bedroom contemplating the healthful aspects of fasting when Cora appeared in the doorway and asked permission to clean.

Caroline put thoughts of hunger away. She sat at the dressing table and pretended to sort through her jewelry. Really, she watched Cora through the mirror. At first, Cora darted glances in her direction, but eventually she began to clean, and with more thoroughness than she'd shown downstairs, too.

Caroline decided it was time to speak. "Would you mind if I asked you a question?"

"No, miss," Cora replied without looking her way.

"Last night, Lady Carew said something at dinner about Lord Bremerton having a wife."

"Lady Carew is often confused."

"Yes, but I don't think she's confused about this. And I do wish that you'd sit and talk to me."

"I can't sit, miss."

"Would you at least take a moment from your work? I'm alone here except for Annie, and both of us see that things aren't normal in this house."

"You've got the right of that," the maid said under her breath.

"I promise this isn't just a visitor's curiosity. Lord Bremerton has proposed marriage. I feel I have a right to know about him and his past, even if he refuses to tell me." Caroline stood and walked to Cora. "You're married, aren't you?"

"Yes."

"And you love each other."

She nodded. "Very much, miss. My Jamie and I ran off, even though we knew I'd lose my job for having done so. Maids cannot be married. But the last Lord Bremerton's wife, she told the housekeeper not to let me go. Lady

Beth was a kind woman. We all hated seeing her leave Chesley House after Lord Percival died." Her mouth worked for a moment as though she was trying to hold something in. "And I don't like following the orders Lord Bremerton gave about you. It's not right, not feeding you. I could hardly work while telling you that."

"Thank you," Caroline replied. "I'd guess that not feeding me isn't the only strange thing you've seen around here."

Cora's expression grew darker for a moment. "I've seen plenty."

"A friend of mine heard whispers that Lord Bremerton might have had a wife," Caroline said. "Having loved and lost someone isn't usually the stuff of rumors. I'm sure you can see why I'm worried."

"I want to help you," Cora said in a rush. "I do, but this is the only job I'll be getting unless Jamie and I part." She shook her head. "I can't do it, miss."

If Caroline had had a house of her own, she would have offered the couple employment. But she didn't, and wouldn't before they starved. But she did have something.

Caroline returned to the dressing table. Papa had said that a woman's jewels were insurance against many things in life. Hers might be insurance against marriage. She selected a heavy gold brooch set with diamonds and rubies, and brought it to Cora.

"I want you to have this," she said. "It's your assurance that if you choose to leave here, you and Jamie can start a new life."

The maid shook her head. "I can't be taking that. I'd be accused of theft."

"I'll write a letter of gift," Caroline said. "Please. All I want is to have the same freedom given to you. I want to marry for love."

She held out the pin again. This time, Cora hesitantly

took it. She held it cupped in her hand and looked at it for a moment, then sighed as she handed it back. "I can't do it, miss. But I'll tell you what I know about Lord Bremerton's late wife, and that will be my gift to you."

Caroline felt nearly weak with relief. "Thank you."

Cora knotted her hands together and began speaking. "When Lord Bremerton took over the house, he came straight from France and brought with him a wife. She was French and spoke not more than a few words of English, but she was very beautiful and full of smiles for the first days she was here. Then something happened. I don't know what, but her smiles were gone and she spent most of her time avoiding the master. I don't suppose that's surprising, considering his nature."

"No, it's not," Caroline agreed.

"Not more than a week later, Lord Bremerton told Jamie to saddle a horse for his wife. They were going to explore the countryside. Jamie chose a mare he knew was safe, but Lord Bremerton said his wife needed a mount with a spirit to match hers. He insisted on a filly that was hardly saddle-broken." Cora gave an angry shake of her head. "The master said the horse bolted and his wife died. He called it 'a most tragic accident.' I call it near close to murder. I always think about how horrible it must have been for her, in a land where she couldn't speak the language, had no friends, and then died not a fortnight later."

"What was her name?"

"Adele."

"Is Adele buried in the village churchyard?" Caroline sought proof of events that even her doubting mother would accept, but more than that, she wanted to feel as though Adele had found peace.

"No," Cora replied. "His lordship said he wished her returned to her family. I'd like to believe he did that, but I can't. He's not a kind man."

Caroline had nothing to say for that, now knowing she'd received only a negligible dose of his unkindness. "Did his wife meet any of the neighbors?"

"No," the maid said. "His lordship was in mourning for his brother, so they didn't socialize."

"Lady Carew had to be here, at least."

"She wasn't here, either. She didn't come until after Lord Bremerton was alone."

"So she couldn't have known Adele, then," Caroline said to herself.

"I think Lady Carew sees things the rest of us don't, miss. And I think those things are real."

If that were the case, Caroline wished she could see Bremerton's wife, too. She wanted to know what truly happened. "Where did Adele spend her time?"

"Mostly, she'd be in the east wing's library or out walking the grounds. It was all so very sad."

"Thank you for telling me about this," Caroline said.

"You've a right to know," Cora replied. "And Jamie and I are the last here who can tell the tale."

Caroline held out the brooch again. "Please, take it."

Cora deliberated for a moment, then accepted it. "Thank you. You've changed our lives."

Caroline smiled. "And you might just have saved mine."

Jack wasn't sure what he was doing in the Maxwell parlor at three on Tuesday afternoon, and he hadn't been impressed by Bernard Maxwell's terse summons, but he was there, just the same.

"I owe you an apology," Caroline's father said as he walked in the parlor door. This was the first time Jack had seen Maxwell looking worn down. Jack didn't like it.

"You were right about Bremerton," the older man said. He pointed to the wing chairs where they'd sat yesterday. "Have a seat."

"I'll stand, thank you," Jack replied. "What have you heard?"

"Enough that I immediately sent word to Agnes to get back here. I expect them soon." Maxwell shook his head. "I can't believe how damned hard it was to get in to see Endsleigh. At home, people come to me." He tapped his chest. "*Presidents* come to me. The old man's staff made me sit in a long hallway for over an hour before I was allowed an audience. All that time, the dead dukes of Endsleigh were staring down at me. Even the damn paintings had a superior attitude."

"It's not such a rare thing," Jack said, deciding to take that seat after all.

"We're not like these people, Jack."

He smiled. "And yesterday you were telling me that I wasn't like you."

Whatever Maxwell had planned to say in return was lost in the commotion of Agnes Maxwell rushing into the room. She pulled up short when she spotted Jack.

"What is he doing here?" she asked her husband while she unbuttoned her blue cape, shrugged it off, and handed it to a waiting footman.

"He's my guest," Bernard replied. "Where's Caroline?"

"Still at Chesley House."

Bernard shot from his seat. "What?"

"But only for a very short time," she added. Her voice quavered in the face of her husband's anger. "I am hoping you'll return with me on the morning train. Caroline won't accept the proposal without you there."

"She won't be accepting the proposal at all," Bernard replied.

Agnes stiffened. "How can you say that, after all of my work?"

"Not another word," her husband said.

She closed her mouth.

Bernard looked at Jack. "Endsleigh told me a few tales from Bremerton's early youth that make me believe he not only harmed Edward, but has done worse. And since Bremerton stepped in line to inherit, his grandfather has learned more. Not only does Bremerton gamble money he doesn't have, but he's being blackmailed. The duke has no proof, but he suspects the blackmail has to do with the death of his grandson, Percy, as well as the death of Bremerton's first wife, Adele. The duke would rather see the title extinguish than eventually go to Bremerton, but he can't control that."

"I should never have left Caroline there, not even for a short while," Agnes said. "I don't know what I was thinking."

Maxwell turned back to his wife. "Neither do I. There will be much more discussion about who and how my daughters may marry from now on."

She nodded.

"Where, exactly, is Caroline?" Jack asked her.

"At Chesley House, outside the village of Arundel, southwest of here."

"We need Caroline out of there tonight," Agnes's husband said.

"But there's no train service past Petworth until morning. I checked at the station before coming home," Agnes replied.

Jack rose. "If you'll excuse me," he said to the Maxwells.

"Where are you going, son?" Bernard asked.

"To Chesley House."

TWENTY-THREE

WHAT WOULD A WOMAN WHO SPOKE ONLY FRENCH want in an English library? Caroline closed the door behind herself, pulled open the dusty gold curtains to let in the afternoon summer sun, and began trying to answer that question.

She sat behind the mahogany desk and started pulling open drawers. Other than a few worn pen nibs and the odd scrap of paper, the desk had been cleaned out. She moved on to the bookshelves. Someone many years ago had loved botany. A third of one wall was filled with old texts. If Adele had read Latin, she would have been in heaven. However, in Caroline's circles, Latin-reading women were fairly scarce. And given Bremerton's need to control, she doubted he would have wed a woman more intelligent than he. She laughed to herself when she realized what she'd just thought. Of course he would marry a bookish heiress. She was proof of that.

Caroline pulled a volume at random. It had been shelved for so long that its top was thick with dust. Holding in a sneeze, she replaced it and tipped out a few others to see if they, too, were long unread.

Satisfied that botany and Latin hadn't been Adele's

lures, Caroline moved on. She'd nearly decided that the Frenchwoman had merely chosen the library for its out-of-the-way location when she came upon a small foreign language section.

"Yes," she murmured to herself as she ran her fingers along the works of the philosopher Descartes, translated from their original Latin to French. Whatever the language, they remained heavy reading. Smiling Adele would have fancied something lighter. Caroline smiled, too, when she saw a copy of *Les Trois Mousquetaires*. Trying to think like Adele, she pulled the book from the shelf, dragged the desk chair into the sunlight, and began to read. She'd just gotten to d'Artagnan's first skirmish with the Comte de Rochefort when Annie shot into the room.

"Here you are! You'd better hurry, or dinner is going to pass you by, too. Bremerton is gobbling his food just to be sure you go hungry."

Caroline closed the book. Hesitant to leave a good story behind, she brought it along to the dining room. Bremerton looked up from his plate as she entered. All she could think was, *So this is what a murderer might look like. One would never know.* She decided to be as she always had been with him—somewhat south of polite. If she started fawning now, he would suspect something was awry.

"I didn't know we were to dine early," she said to the Englishman as she slipped into her seat and set her book on the table. "Then again, you didn't tell me."

"What is that you're reading?" Bremerton asked.

"Alexandre Dumas," she said. *"The Three Musketeers."*

"In French?"

"Well, yes," she replied.

"You speak French?"

"Yes, and German. And I read Latin and some Greek, besides."

He made a disinterested sound. Caroline nipped into her chicken while she could. Nerves had only increased her appetite. This was plain food, but after a day of going without, it tasted like ambrosia.

"We'll be taking a ride tomorrow," Bremerton said. "I thought you might like to see the countryside and perhaps visit with the Bentons before your mother and father arrive."

"I don't think so."

"What?"

"Let me put that in British terms. I wish to never ride with you."

His look of surprise quickly faded. "Your choice. Stay here, then."

"I will," she said before eating five green beans in quick succession.

Bremerton set down his fork. Charlie stepped forward and cleared the plate. He looked Caroline's way before turning and walking at a snail's pace toward a tray he'd placed on the buffet. Caroline was grateful for the brief reprieve. She bolted as much food as she could before Charlie returned and pulled her plate.

Bremerton, who had been watching her, said, "After that show, I'm sure you don't wish for dessert."

"I couldn't eat another bite," she lied cheerfully. "In fact, if you'll excuse me, I believe I'll retire to my room and read for the evening."

"Of course. I'll be by to check on your welfare later."

"That's quite unnecessary," Caroline said as she rose and reclaimed her book from the table.

"But it will happen all the same," Bremerton said.

Caroline left the dining room and found Annie waiting for her in the hallway.

"Did you get any food in?" Annie asked.

Caroline smiled. "An impressive amount. Thank you for the warning."

They climbed the stairs, and once they were back in the bedroom, Caroline took a look at the cowhide couch and decided to forego sitting on that in favor of reading in bed. Annie settled onto the chaise with a piece of lace she was tatting. She said it was going to be for her wedding dress one day, if she was ever mad enough to marry. If all marriages turned out like poor, dead Adele's, it would be madness. But Caroline still held out hope for Jack and true love.

The light in the room was growing dimmer. Caroline set aside her book to turn up the flame on the oil lamp she'd moved bedside. When she picked up the thick book, a folded piece of ivory-colored paper slipped out of the back pages.

"What have we here?" she said.

Annie looked up from her lace. "It looks like a piece of paper to me."

Caroline unfolded the paper. She drew in an excited breath as she realized that the slightly crooked writing on the stationery was in French. Adele had been writing a friend named Dominique.

"Oh, no," she said as she read Adele's confession that she had lied to Bremerton about being an heiress.

"What is it?" Annie asked.

Caroline scanned the rest of the letter, which had never been completed. "This was written by Bremerton's late wife. She'd lied to him about her wealth. When they arrived at Chesley House, she realized he was in financial straits and had likely married her for her money. She had just confessed to Bremerton when she'd written this. He had become enraged. She was hoping he'd come to love her and forgive her. She felt terrible about her deceit."

"He killed her, didn't he?" Annie asked after a stretch of silence.

Caroline hadn't had time to share with Annie what she'd learned from Cora, so she quickly updated her.

"Money and pride are the two most important things in Bremerton's life. Adele struck at both of those," Caroline added. "And if he didn't kill her, why would he be trying to hide both her life and her death?"

Caroline could feel Adele's lingering presence so vividly that she understood how Lady Carew might see her. And Caroline felt danger, too. She set aside the letter and rose from the bed. "Is the Colt that Eddie gave me still hidden in the trunk below my corsets?"

"I didn't move it," Annie said. "That thing scares me."

Caroline went to her trunk and carefully uncovered the revolver. It was nearly identical to the Colt Single Action Army her mother had confiscated, only this time Eddie had bought her one with a shorter barrel that he teased her by saying made for a more ladylike weapon. So long as it still shot bullets, it could be as ladylike as it wished. Caroline took those, too, from the trunk. She carefully loaded each chamber and set the hammer in the safety notch. Then she went to her dressing table and dumped all the jewelry from its case, placed the gun inside, and closed the top.

"Is that this season's new accessory?" Annie asked.

"The most useful yet." Caroline sorted through the jumble of jewels on the tabletop and selected a sapphire necklace. "This can serve a few purposes, too."

She held it up for Annie to take. "We're leaving tonight. I want you to go to the nearest house and bargain for the use of a horse and any type of cart. It doesn't matter what, so long as it can get us to Arundel. We can't trust that we'll be able to get a horse from here."

Annie shook her head. "I don't want to leave you here."

"And I don't want both of us to be trapped here," Caroline said. She waggled the necklace. "Take this and get moving."

Annie did, but not without a worried backward glance.

"Don't worry," Caroline said. "I'll do this as safely as I can."

It had all sounded so simple, Jack thought. Take a train to Petworth, find a horse, and ride like the wind to Chesley House. Except the train to Petworth had stopped in every village along its tracks, plus once for sheep across them. He had willed himself to be calm. From Bremerton's perspective, everything was going just as he'd planned. He had his heiress and he was training her to be biddable. So long as those two facts did not change, Caroline was safe.

Even after Jack had made Petworth, the only horse he'd found was more about passing wind than letting him ride like it. It had been ten and more miles of hard, slow road, but he'd reached Arundel's outskirts before sundown.

"Excuse me," he said to a cluster of men lingering outside a pub. "I'm looking for Chesley House. Can you tell me where to find it?"

"Chesley House?" said one. "Never heard of it."

"Yeah, you have, you fool," said another. "It's one of the Duke of Endsleigh's places." Except he'd said duke as though it was pronounced like book, which snagged up Jack's attention.

"*Oi*," said a third man, waving a hand Jack's way. "Did ye not hear my question? Are you a gennleman like the duke?"

Jack grinned. "Not on my very worst day."

"That being the case, we'll tell you. You need to stay on this road, south near all the way to Littlehampton," the second man said. "You won't miss the place. It's a big pile o' stone."

Jack reached into his pocket and pulled out some coins. "Thank you," he said as he tossed them to the men. "The next one's on me."

And on he rode, near south to Littlehampton, wherever the hell that was.

The sun had been down long enough for the stars to begin to show when Bremerton's knock sounded at the bedroom door.

"Come in," Caroline called from her seat at the dressing table. She turned and watched as Bremerton stepped inside.

"Where's your maid?" he asked.

"You told me to have her sleep in her room, so that's where she is," Caroline replied before facing the mirror.

She picked up a diamond earring and held it as though deciding how it would look on her. As she returned it to the dressing table's surface, she watched the Englishman walk a circle of the bedroom. When he was done, he stopped behind her and put both hands on her shoulders. For the first time, she managed not to shiver at his touch.

"It seems my stableman and maid have come up missing. Might you know anything about that?" he asked.

"No."

"Interesting. I was certain you would. Mrs. Parker told me it happened just before dinner. You'd been around the house all day, and you have a way of stirring things up." He paused. "Now Mrs. Parker and the waiter seem to have disappeared, too. Good help is so hard to find."

Caroline looked away from the mean curve to his smile. "I am sorry to hear that."

He let his hands slip from her shoulders and bent forward to give a negligent flick at one of the rings that sat in the jewelry she'd been sorting. "So many riches and not enough days in a life to show it off."

She let her gaze meet his in the mirror. "Should I interpret that as a threat?"

"No, I was merely making a comment on your wealth." He turned and walked away. Caroline relaxed marginally.

"So you speak French and interpret threats," Bremerton said. "And I would guess by my missing servants that you now know I once had an interest in things French."

"If you're referring to your late wife, yes."

"I'm sure you have questions," he said as he settled onto the cowhide couch. "Do ask."

"I've learned that you prefer it when I don't."

"As you wish. Then I'll ask again, where's your maid? I know she's not in her room."

"Then maybe she's in the kitchen," she replied, praying that Annie was now outside with their transportation.

He rose. "I am not fond of liars."

"And I'm not fond of having you in my room," she said in a calm voice. "You've been here, you've checked on my welfare, and now I'm asking you to leave."

"And if I choose to stay? I think at the very least I deserve to see you as the Irishman has."

Caroline reached into the jewel case as though looking for another piece, but pulled out her gun. She pushed away from the dressing table, turned, and raised it at him.

"My brother Eddie taught me how to shoot and spit," she said. "Of the two skills, I prefer shooting."

"Then put it down. There's no need for drama,"

Bremerton said in a smooth voice that Caroline was sure had swayed others, but not her.

"You can loom and threaten, but if I pull this little gun, you call me dramatic. That's hardly sporting of you," she said. She paused a moment, trying to decide if that was really the sound of hooves on stone she was hearing outside. She thought it might be.

Caroline stood and advanced a step on Bremerton, who held his ground in the middle of the room. "Eddie taught me to always leave the chamber at the firing pin empty so there wouldn't be any nasty accidents if I dropped the gun. But I was feeling a little distracted when I loaded this tonight, and do you know what silly thing I did? No?" she asked in the face of Bremerton's continuing silence. "I loaded all six chambers. Let's hope I don't drop the gun. But just in case, I'm going to suggest that you stay well back. We both know about those tragic accidents, don't we, my lord?"

"You have lost your mind."

"Maybe," she said cheerfully. "And since I have, I'm going to make some demands. Until Annie arrives with our horse, you are to stay where I can see you, and with your hands in the air."

"What?"

"As they say in the Wild West of my country, reach for the sky." She narrowed her gaze. "And I do mean now."

Bremerton raised his hands.

"Thank you."

A commotion sounded from someplace downstairs. Annie had to be back. But then Caroline heard a male voice calling her name. She laughed with joy.

"We have a guest," she said to Bremerton. "It's the love of my life."

He didn't appear very impressed.

"Upstairs, Jack, and grab a candle," she called. "You're going to want some light."

Jack bounded up the stairs two at a time, and the candle he'd just lit smoked and flickered as the air pushed past it.

"Which room are you in?" he called.

"Keep coming this way!"

He was close enough that he could see light spilling from a room on his right. Jack stepped in and froze.

"Hello, Jack," Caroline said, both her eyes and a gun trained on His Lordship.

"It doesn't look as though you needed a rescuer," he said conversationally.

"Appearances can be deceiving. I was actually a little vague on this part of the plan. I'd been expecting Annie, but as you can see, she isn't here. And sooner or later, I was going to have to either shoot this man or run."

Jack grinned. "I vote for shoot him."

"My decision was leaning in that direction," she replied.

"For what it's worth, your plan would have worked . . . more or less. I passed Annie on the lane a way back." He paused. "Did you know that goats can pull a cart?"

She laughed. "She bartered sapphires for goats?"

"And a very small cart." He circled Bremerton. "How do you feel about violence?" Jack asked Caroline.

"I seldom condone it."

"Ah. Too bad." He moved directly in front of Bremerton and was amused to see Caroline reposition herself so there was nothing between her and her potential target. "Then we'll do it like this . . ."

"I'm giving you one shot at me," he said to Bremerton. "Totally free."

"Jack . . ." Caroline said in a hesitant voice.

Jack grinned at the Englishman. "Take it, you git."

Bremerton swung, but Jack ducked.

"Missed," he said, right before he broke the bastard's nose. Jack and Caroline watched as the Englishman crumpled.

"Do you have anything I can tie him up with?" Jack asked.

She stopped aiming at Bremerton long enough to gather a fistful of fat strings from a trunk.

"Corset lacings," she said. While Jack trussed up the Englishman, Caroline aimed her gun.

"I don't think he's getting up," Jack pointed out.

"I'm just being careful," she said. "And about the violence, I said I *seldom* condone it. For him, I would have made an exception. You didn't need to let him swing first."

Satisfied with his knotwork, Jack stood. "I knew he couldn't hit me. Now, how about if you put down that gun so I can propose?"

Her eyes grew wide. She carefully placed the gun on a curio shelf. Jack walked around Bremerton, who was beginning to stir, and took a knee in front of Caroline.

"Caroline, you are my love, my laughter, and the most frustrating woman I'll ever meet. Would you please do me the honor of being my wife?"

Her eyes were misty, but her smile was bright when she said, "Jack Culhane, what took you so long?"

EPILOGUE

ENGLAND WAS WELL BEHIND THEM WHEN THE Maxwell women, Bernard, and Jack sat down to dinner on the *Conqueror* two days later.

"I have an announcement to make," Caroline said to her parents once the champagne was poured. "My husband list is down to one name, and that is Jack's. We plan to marry this winter, and there will be not a single cherub anywhere in the church. We very much want all of you there, though."

Her father's face had turned ruddy with emotion. "I've been waiting years to walk you down the aisle, Pumpkin."

"Bernard," Mama said before Papa started laughing.

"I know, I know. I can't call her Pumpkin."

Mama sighed. "I had so hoped for a duchess in the family, but Bremerton is well off the list."

Before they had left, Papa had sent a packet to the Duke of Endsleigh with all the information that Caroline and Jack had uncovered on Bremerton. If he ever did inherit, he was likely to be a duke behind prison bars.

"But, you know," Mama said, "there are so many nice English gentlemen, and Helen and Amelia have yet to marry. . . ."

"Oh, no," Helen said. "Don't even begin looking at me like that. I have no desire to live in England."

"France, then. Or Italy," Mama exclaimed. "You'll make the most beautiful bride!"

Jack placed his hand over Caroline's where it sat on the tabletop. They smiled at each other. Caroline had found the place she most wanted to be, and that was with Jack. They would have the perfect life and the perfect wedding, complete with chocolate cake.

Love

IN A NUTSHELL

In loving memory of Bubba Gimp,
the coolest special needs coonhound to walk this earth.
And also of Ceili, his wonderful Westie mama dog.
There will never be another pair quite like you!
—Dorien

ONE

KATE APPLETON NEEDED A JOB. AGAIN.

Actually, *need* didn't come close to describing the hunger and sharp bite of desperation speeding her steps across Depot Brewing Company's parking lot on that crisp October afternoon. Just as the town marina to the right of the microbrewery was growing empty of boats, Keene's Harbor, Michigan, was growing empty of tourists and their cash. And, at this moment, Kate needed cash. She had moved to Keene's Harbor a couple of weeks ago, eager to change her parents' dilapidated lake house into a thriving bed-and-breakfast. They had moved to Naples, Florida, and the harsh reality was that it hadn't been used in years, except as a nut storage facility by a family of industrious squirrels. Ironic, since a homemade plaque proclaiming the house "The Nutshell" had adorned the front entrance since before she could remember.

In any event, the house needed a lot of work, and her parents were less than enthusiastic about pumping tens of thousands of dollars into a home that was already underwater on its mortgage. To make matters worse, they'd gotten a letter from some lawyer last week that the bank had gone into bankruptcy and the mortgage had been sold to some private investor. He'd offered to release Kate's parents from the debt in exchange for the property. It was actually a fairly generous offer, considering the market, but Kate was trying to build a life for herself in Keene's Harbor. And dammit, her family home wasn't for sale. Depot Brewing wasn't just Kate's last shot at employment. It was the last shot at her dreams.

Crimson maple leaves crunched beneath her leather boots as she marched toward the handsome yellow brick and sandstone building and checked off her plan of action. She would be firm, yet polite. Honest, yet not to the point of over-sharing. And she would go straight to the top, to the guy who could make her, or— Forget that. She wouldn't consider the possibility of someone breaking her. And she wouldn't consider walking away without a job.

Kate drew in a breath, pulled back her shoulders, and wrapped her hand around the hammered-bronze door handle of her new workplace.

Matt Culhane sat holed up in his small and admittedly cluttered office behind Depot Brewing Company's taproom. He wanted one last look at his inventory spreadsheet before the after-work crowd showed up. Not that he begrudged his customers their fun, but he should have chosen to stay put in his dungeon of an office in the back of the microbrewery rather than move into the portion of the building housing the newly constructed but noisy restaurant. He was deciding whether to work out a trade with one of his brewer buddies for some Chinese hops when he heard Jerry, his hospitality manager, greet someone in the taproom.

"Is Matt Culhane in?" a woman asked Jerry. "I need to talk to him. His office is in the back, right?"

"Yes," Jerry replied. "But . . . Wait, you can't—"

"Thanks so much for your help," the woman replied. "I can find my way."

Kate knocked once on the open door and swept into the office, closing the door behind her and leaving Jerry standing on the other side openmouthed and clearly flustered.

Culhane's first thought was that she was a woman on a mission. His second thought was that he was intrigued. She was just over five feet tall, and had short-cropped blond hair, big hazel eyes, and a wide mouth that he suspected would light up a room when she smiled.

Matt rose, rounded his desk, and extended his hand.

"Hi, I'm Matt Culhane."

Kate took his hand and gave it a firm businesslike shake. "I know. I'm Kate Appleton. I don't have a job. And it's your fault. Twenty minutes ago, I was fired because of you."

"Because of me?"

"Yep. From Bagger's Tavern, down on Keene Avenue. It was all because of your skunky beer."

Before he could respond, she planted herself in the one guest chair that didn't have files stacked on it.

Cute but crazy, Matt thought, following her lead and returning to sit in his chair behind his desk. And oddly enough, it did nothing to diminish his attraction to her. "Harley fired you?"

"He did," Kate said.

"Did he say why?"

"Apparently, I'm no longer to be trusted behind the bar, because bad beer passed from tap to lips. I don't think that's fair. And when I look at the whole mess, I figure it's your responsibility. It was your beer," she replied in a patient tone. "I moved to Keene's Harbor three weeks ago and lobbied like crazy to get even that part-time bartending job. Then I lost it over bad beer. Now I have nothing. Every store downtown is owned locally, and every owner runs their place alone in the slow season."

Matt smiled. "That's to be expected. A town built to hold several thousand summer visitors can be pretty empty come the cool weather. Why'd you move here in the off-season?"

"Well, let's just say my options were extremely limited. I needed an inexpensive place to stay, and the mortgage payments on my parents' lake house are a heckuva lot less than any decent rental."

Actually, she was a few months behind on the payments. Between her crapola job at Bagger's and the endless repairs on the house, her savings were pretty much gone. She'd talked to the bank and they'd agreed to let her catch up over the next six months, but that was before they'd gone belly-up. Kate drove the thought from her mind, replacing it with the happy memories that had inspired her to move to Keene's Harbor in the first place. "I'd spent summers here as a kid and loved it. I thought I could come up with some sort of job."

Apparently, she had some history around town, and she also looked to be in the general ballpark of his age. Still, it was no surprise their paths hadn't crossed earlier. He'd stuck with his townie pack. In his high school days, the summer girls weren't worth the snobbishness some of them had thrown at the locals while sunning on Lake Michigan's long stretch of beach.

"So you're a summer person," he said. He wasn't into line-drawing anymore, but he couldn't resist teasing just a little, trying to provoke the same little flush of emotion to her cheeks he'd seen when she first walked into his office.

"Thanks, but I think of myself more as a Citizen of All Seasons."

"Works for me. Where's your parents' place?"

"It's on the lake about two miles north of town. It's old, big, and drafty. And it's a huge money pit, which brings us back to the aforementioned skunky beer," she said, obviously trying to drive the conversation to a destination.

Matt was curious enough to give her the room to run. "I'll agree that Harley serves my beer, but I'm not going any further than that. The keg could have been bad for a lot of reasons, including dirty tap lines, bad tapping, or the fact that it was past its expiration date. But the bottom line is that I didn't tell him to fire you."

"Just the same, honor compels that you give me a job."

Another surprise bombshell. "A job?"

"Yes. And I'm available to start immediately."

Lucky me, he thought. The woman was clearly crazy, and yet strangely appealing in her overly earnest, convoluted reasoning.

"Supposing, for the sake of discussion, that we were hiring right now," he said. "Other than a couple of weeks at Bagger's, what's your work experience?"

She folded her hands in her lap, a gesture more appropriate for a navy blue interview suit than jeans and a puffy, off-white down jacket still zipped up to her chin. He wondered what she was going to wear when it *really* got cold around here.

"I have a B.A. in Drama from a small college in Ohio."

This time he couldn't fight back a smile. "I didn't ask about your education. I asked what you can do. Before you came to Keene's Harbor, did you have a job?"

"Yes."

He waited for more, but it didn't appear to be coming.

"And?" he asked.

"I was an assistant editor at a business magazine head-quartered downstate, outside of Detroit."

"And?" he prompted again.

"I moved here."

"As you said, with very little in the way of options. What happened to the job?"

"The skills aren't relevant to what you do here, but if you really need to know, I was let go."

"Why?"

"It wasn't directly performance-related, so again, I don't think it's all that relevant."

He was hooked. He had to know. He was sure it was something worth hearing.

"Spill it," he said. "Lay it on me."

Kate bit her lower lip. "I had a little incident changing the black ink cartridge for the printer I shared with a couple other people. Maybe it was because we'd switched to a generic brand, or maybe it was because someone— perhaps with the name of Melvin—had messed with it, but whatever the case, I got ink all over the front of my dress. And then while I was in the bathroom trying to soak what I could from the dress, the fire alarm went off."

"Sounds like something you'd see on Cinemax after midnight."

"Let's just say that when presented the choice between potential death and a bit of semi-nudity smack in the middle of downtown Royal Oak, I let the skin show."

"You didn't have much of an option."

She raised her right shoulder in a half shrug. "True. As it turned out, someone—perhaps with the name of Melvin—had pulled the fire alarm. There was no fire, but between the scene on the street and the fact that the video from the building's security camera somehow hit the Internet and went viral, my boss let me go. He said I had become a liability to the magazine. No one could take me seriously. And so someone with the name of Melvin got my job."

"That stinks," Matt said.

Kate nodded in agreement. "It did. But I learned a few good lessons, including always use brand-name ink and watch out for guys named Melvin."

Matt laughed. Kate Appleton might be an involuntary exhibitionist, but so far she'd shown herself to be smart and quick with an answer, and she wore her emotions on her face. His gut told him she was possibly a little nutty, but beyond that a decent person. And Matt generally went with his instincts.

"Now, about that job?" she asked.

He leaned forward, elbows on desk. "I'll start by saying that the bad beer at Bagger's was a problem on his end of the system. Granted, there's a remote possibility it happened here, but that part of the process is under tight control, so I'm not talking to you to redeem my honor or anything like that."

She nodded. "Okay. So long as the talk involves a job, I'm listening."

Kate Appleton did not appear to be a believer in the theory of leverage, in that he had it and she did not. Still, she was bold. He appreciated that about her. And, at the moment, she might just be exactly what he needed.

"There have been some incidents over the past few months," Matt said, lowering his voice. "They didn't start out as anything big or all that awful. In fact, for a while there, I just kind of put it down to a streak of bad luck."

"What kind of bad luck?"

He leaned back in his chair and considered when it all started. "Well, call it ego, but I'd like to think that last spring, my first failed batch of beer in years was more than just a slipup on my part. Since then, it's been small stuff . . . misrouted deliveries, flat tires on the delivery trucks . . . that kind of thing."

"All of which, pardon me for saying this, could be put down to employee screwups."

Matt nodded. "I know, but they're happening more and more often. I really think one of my employees is trying to sabotage my business."

Kate leaned forward in her seat. "What makes you think it's an employee?"

"Access. Whoever is behind it knows my schedule and my business. And most of the incidents have occurred in employee-only areas, where a customer would be immediately noticed."

Kate raised her eyebrows. "So you want me to help find some deranged lunatic with a beer vendetta."

"I'd hire a private investigator, but this time of year, it would be nearly impossible for a stranger to go unnoticed for more than a day. You, on the other hand, are not a total outsider. And between the impressive performance you just gave convincing me to hire you and your degree in drama, I'm guessing you can act a part if you have to. That makes you a great candidate for the job I have in mind."

She tilted her head. "And that would be what?"

"I'd be hiring you to be a floater. If someone is out sick or there's a crunch in a certain area of the operation, you'd be the one to step in."

"Even though it's likely that eighty percent of the time, I won't know what the heck I'm doing?"

"I get the sense you're a quick study."

"Absolutely. Definitely. I'm your girl. And since I'm so smart, I get the sense that I'll be more than a floater."

"Your job will be to tell me what's going on around here. What am I missing? What don't people want to say to my face? Who have you seen that shouldn't be here?"

"You want me to be a *snitch*?"

"How about a secret agent?"

She sat silent a moment, trying on the phrase for fit. "I like it. I'm Appleton. Kate Appleton. Licensed to Snoop."

"Good. You'll be my eyes and ears. If someone in Keene's Harbor has a grudge against me, you'll let me know."

"Sounds doable. From what I heard behind the bar at Bagger's, folks around here still do love to talk."

"Well, don't take the buzz too literally. The colder the weather gets, the bigger the stories around here grow. Town is pretty quiet after Labor Day, and we need something to keep life interesting."

"Fair enough. How much are you offering for the position?"

"Minimum wage," he replied.

"I'm sorry, but don't think so. I'm desperate, but not shortsighted. Sooner or later, someone is going to figure out that I'm bringing gossip back to you, and at that point, I'm not going to be worth anything."

Matt grinned. "So what do you suggest?"

"How about minimum wage and a $20,000 bonus if I'm directly responsible for finding your saboteur?"

"You're kidding."

"Nope."

Matt considered his options, and they were limited. He couldn't hire a full-fledged townie any more than he could a PI. If word got out that some crazy was targeting Depot Brewery, it could scare away a lot of customers.

Kate smiled. "Hey. It's no more than you'd pay to a PI, and I only get paid if I actually solve the mystery. And it could end up costing you a lot more to just ignore the thing and hope it goes away."

Matt paused to consider her argument. The truth was,

the "accidents" were starting to add up and had already cost him more than $20,000. "Okay, deal."

Kate beamed. "I promise I'll be the best secret spy you've ever hired."

At a quarter to nine on Friday morning, Kate parked at the far end of Depot Brewing Company's lot. She exited her ancient, beloved green-and-slightly-rust-spotted Jeep and pocketed her keys. Since she had the luxury of a handful of minutes, and Mother Nature had granted Keene's Harbor yet another blissfully sunny day, she checked out in more detail her new place of employment.

If Kate could whistle—which, sadly, she couldn't—this place would merit a nice long and low one. Small wonder the tourists flocked here like it was nirvana. An outdoor patio, now closed for the season, was surrounded by evergreens that must have cost Matt Culhane a fortune to have transplanted onto this sandy spit of land. She could picture the patio full of people, laughter, and music in the summertime. And she could picture Culhane here, too.

As the microbrewery's name implied, this had once been Keene's Harbor's railroad depot. Kate's dad, who was a history buff, had told her that this town had been built on the lumber trade. In a few decades, though, most of the area was logged out. A few decades after that, the rail spur to the harbor was abandoned. All that had been left was a wreck of a building that Kate recalled as a prime spot for the underage summer kids to drink a few super-sweet wine coolers.

Since she hadn't been alone at this party spot, she'd bet she wasn't the only one who got a kick out of Matt Culhane turning it into a microbrewery. He'd obviously added on to the small depot, but whoever had come up with the design had made sure that the original architecture still shone through.

Kate was unsure whether it was okay to go through the "employees only" door near where she'd parked, since there was a huge semi backed up to an open garage-type door next to it. She opted for the public entry.

Now that she wasn't wrapped in a haze of determination and desperation, she noted the mosaic in front of the entrance. Set into the concrete was the Depot Brewing logo—a steam locomotive surrounded by a bunch of whimsical items, including what looked to be a happy three-legged dog.

Kate stepped over the image, feeling that the dog had suffered enough without being trod upon. "You're a pretty cool dude, three legs or not."

"His name is Chuck, and he's my dog," Culhane said, suddenly standing in the open doorway. "Well, the real one is. That one's tile, so I don't think he'll be answering you."

She couldn't work up a single word in reply. The man was flat-out gorgeous. A muscled, dark-haired, blue-eyed, one-dimple-that-he-could-apparently-produce-at-will kind of gorgeous. She'd noted this yesterday, too, but anxiety had kept her on her game. If she'd babbled in the face of male hotness, she would have walked away empty-handed. Today, she had a job and her words were fleeting.

"I—I like dogs," she finally managed. She thought of her former dog, Stella, and felt a little lump forming in her chest.

"Good. And I like dog people. Why don't you come on in?"

Kate did, trying hard to cut back on the staring. She was sure he was wearing the same slightly faded chambray button-down shirt and pair of well-fit jeans as yesterday afternoon. New to his features was the shadow of a beard. His dark brown hair looked either tousled with sleep or the lack thereof.

"You're seriously tall," she said.

He laughed. "To you, maybe."

Pull it together, Appleton, she thought. Get a grip!

"Point taken," she said. "From the vantage point of just over five feet, pretty much every guy's a giant. You look tired, too."

Matt ruffled a hand through his hair. "We pulled an all-nighter."

"An all-nighter doing what?" she asked, immediately wishing she hadn't, because the answer might be personal. Her long-dormant libido stirred at the possibilities.

"Come this way and I'll show you," he said. "It's not all that exciting."

Cross orgy off the list.

"We just got into bottled beer in addition to kegs and growlers, so we don't have a regular bottling line yet," he said. "That means we have to rent a portable line every couple of months until I think sales justify the expense of a permanent one. It will take another addition or a move of the whole facility to do it, so for now, we make do. And we also do it after hours so that our regular business can cruise on."

Matt ushered her past his office, through a set of glass doors to a room with enormous stainless-steel tanks, and then through another door into a brightly lit storage room with a truck well. The kind of industrial orange, temporary lighting she'd seen sold in building warehouse stores shone up the ramp and into the back of the semi.

"A bottling line on wheels," Matt said.

"Very cool," she said, thankful to have something other than Matt to focus on while she regained her business manners. That done, she turned her attention to the people busy checking her out. About twenty exhausted-looking souls sat at tables someone must have dragged in from the taproom.

"Everyone, this is Kate," Matt announced. "Kate . . . everyone."

"Hey, Kate," a few of them said. Most just raised a glass of beer in a weary greeting.

Kate fought hard not to gag at the thought of beer as a breakfast staple. She liked the idea of herself as a yogurt-and-fruit girl, but the reality was she was more the cold pizza type. Especially when she was PMSing.

"Kate's coming to work with us as a floater," Matt said to the assembled crew.

That brought on a little more enthusiasm.

"Good, a new victim," a midnight black–haired young woman said.

Kate thought the employee looked too young to work with beer, except for the tattoo of a bare-chested cowboy riding a neon-colored dragon wrapping its way from her wrist up her arm. Either she'd forged her mother's signature for that beauty, or she was at least eighteen.

"Does this mean that Hobart and I are breaking up?" the young woman asked Matt.

"For this weekend, at least."

She squealed, then ran and hugged her boss.

"It's up to Jerry if Kate stays there, Amber," Matt said, gently unwinding her and taking a step back. "But you worked hard last night, and I know you're sick of Hobart."

Who the heck is Hobart? Kate thought, scanning the crew for a guy who looked remotely like he might have the misfortune to be named Hobart.

Matt turned to Kate. "Let's go to my office. We might as well get the paperwork out of the way. Then you can report to Jerry."

"So he'll be my direct supervisor?" she asked as Matt ushered her back the way they'd come.

He nodded. "He manages food services, which will include you for the time being. He's the guy you met out front during our unscheduled job interview yesterday afternoon."

"Oops. I sort of bulldozed right past him. I probably didn't make the best first impression."

"Jerry can be pretty forgiving, and you'll like the rest of the crew, too. About half of the people you saw back in the storage room work for me, and the rest are temps who come in for the bottling. We finished up over two hundred cases just a little while ago. Most of the other employees, except the summer staff, you'll meet today."

Matt opened his office door. "Come on in. It shouldn't take long to get this squared away, then we'll get you a uniform."

Kate glanced around, taking in the framed photos on the cubicle-style walls, which didn't quite make it all the way to the ceiling.

"My family, mostly," Matt said. He waved one hand toward another shot of a pack of helmeted and uniformed men bearing sticks. "And my hockey team."

She smiled. "That, I'd figured out."

Kate pulled her driver's license and social security card from her wallet and handed them to Matt. "You need these, right?"

He settled in behind his desk. From its front, she guessed it was a vintage oak piece that had been left to molder in the closed-down depot. Its top looked as though a file cabinet had disgorged itself onto it. Working in a measure of chaos definitely didn't throw this guy.

Kate sat and watched as Matt studied her license.

"Turn it over," she said, knowing exactly what he was

thinking. "I'm divorced. My name is changed back to Appleton on the back."

He glanced up at her. "Divorced? Sorry."

"Don't be," she said. "It was for the best."

Except for that messy little glitch whereby both she and the ex, Richard, had lost their savings. The McMansion he'd so desperately wanted had turned out to be worth less than a soggy chicken patty when they'd gone to sell it. Even tougher on Kate had been handing over their poodle, Stella, to the ex because he'd ended up in a place more suitable for dog ownership and the court had awarded him guardianship. Kate had fought hard to keep Stella, but the truth was, Richard had a more expensive lawyer, and she lost. She couldn't bear to think of Stella too much these days.

Matt pulled a form from one of the stacks of folders covering his desk. "Yeah, well, from what I've heard from friends, it had to be a pain to go through."

"Well, it's survivable, but let's just say I'm convinced that if you look in the mirror and say *Richard Slate* three times, he'll magically appear and kill you with annoying small talk. Although that wasn't what ended the marriage. I trusted him completely, and he cheated on me. Even after I caught him, the weasel denied the whole thing. You know what he said after I told him I wanted to leave? Nothing. He just shrugged his shoulders and went back to his sudoku puzzle."

"So your married name was Kate Slate."

Kate winced. "It seemed like a good idea at the time. How about you? Ever married? Dating anyone?"

He glanced up. "Why? Interested?"

"Not a chance. I've got enough complications to handle without dealing with men."

"What kind of complications?"

Kate pushed her hair back. "Well, for starters, my parents have given me four months to turn our broken-down lake house into a B&B, or else they're going to turn it over to the jerk who bought the mortgage. I have a $10-per-hour job and $15,000 worth of repairs. I'm going to be a homeless dishwasher if I can't make this work."

Matt admired an entrepreneurial spirit, especially when it was nourished by an impractical dream. Everybody had rolled their eyes when he announced he was going to build a brewery.

"I know you've got the stuff," he said. "And the lake is a great place for a bed-and-breakfast. Just put one foot in front of the other."

Easy for him to say.

"Knock, knock," a guy said from behind Kate.

Matt looked over and gestured him in.

"This is Jerry," he told Kate. "But then, you've already met."

"In passing." She gave Jerry an apologetic smile.

Jerry looked tired and overworked, though he was a good-looking guy. He was probably somewhere in his midthirties, and of medium height, with dark brown hair and a goatee. But at the moment, even that goatee was slumping, and his brown eyes looked worried.

"She practically knocked me to the ground," Jerry said. "It was sort of embarrassing."

For both of them. Kate didn't believe in flattening guys, except when strictly necessary. And even though Jerry-as-a-victim had been unavoidable in her quest to get to the big boss, she could still feel the Appleton Curse of a neon blush rising. When she'd been little and playing Go Fish with her mom on The Nutshell's back porch, the blush had been the tip-off to a fast move on her part. And now it only grew brighter under Matt's steady gaze.

He smiled at her. "Kate, why don't you wait for Jerry out in the taproom? He and I have a couple of things to cover."

Kate recognized a gift when handed one. She said her thank-yous, saved her fence-mending with Jerry for later, and beat a hasty retreat.

So Kate Appleton blushed. Matt liked that about her. There was something fascinating about being bold enough to run over a guy and yet a day later, be contrite enough to blush.

"She's presentable and all that, but kind of pushy, don't you think?" Jerry asked Matt as soon as Kate had cleared the room.

"I think she's going to do great. And you're twice her size and her supervisor. If she can pull one over on you again, you deserve it."

Jerry looked a little brighter at that thought. Considering the matchup, Matt wasn't one hundred percent sure he should look so happy.

"So Amber says you want Kate with Hobart this weekend."

"Yeah. Amber could use a break, but after that, you can move Kate around as needed."

Jerry stroked his goatee. "Huh. Anyplace."

Matt began recalculating the odds on that particular matchup. Kate might have Jerry in the gutsiness department, but Jerry was nothing if not a dogged and steady guy. And he could also be a little sneaky, in a good-natured sort of way.

"So go to it," Matt said.

After Jerry took off, Matt looked at his weekend schedule and sighed. He had just enough time to head home, shower, and change before he had to drive an hour north to Traverse City for the weekend. He was getting tired of being on the road all the time, even if it did mean his business was growing in a tough economy. Much as he was proud to keep so many people employed year-round, he wanted his life back. He wanted some romance in his life, and maybe even love. He had a good feeling about Kate. She was going to help him find his saboteur, and maybe a lot more.

TWO

By the time Friday's lunch rush hit full swing, Kate knew too well what Hobart was. Instead of being paired with an unfortunately named coworker, she stood in front of Depot Brewing's noisy, sloppy, and steamy commercial dishwashing machine. Hobart had been named for its maker. It had a four-foot-long stainless-steel prep counter running at a right angle to its boxy entry and a staging area for clean racks of dishes at the exit. The machine was bulkier than her Jeep. More demanding, too.

"Hot!" called one of the line cooks as he dropped a dirty skillet onto the end of the prep area.

"Thanks," she replied from her side of the counter, but he had already hustled back to his station.

Every inch of the white tile–walled kitchen had been designed for food production, and the staff worked it to the max. Elbow-to-elbow, the three line cooks held their territories in front of the stove, grill, and fryer. Servers darted in to pick up orders, the barback hauled glassware, and pretty much everyone brought Kate more work. Her job was to clear the food debris and paper trash from the gray plastic bus tubs delivered to her. Then she had to rack all the dirty ware, send it into Hobart, and circulate the clean stuff back out for use.

"You've never done this before, have you?" a male voice asked.

She glanced up from her duties to see Steve, one of the servers, watching her. Tall and slender, with a dark tan and blond highlights in his hair, he looked like a surfer dude.

"Nope," she said.

"Definite bummer, but you're gonna have to speed up. We're almost eighty-six on forks."

"Eighty-six?"

"Out of."

"Gotcha," Kate said, moving a silverware rack into the cleaning line.

Jerry, who was currently MIA, had demonstrated the job to her well enough. In fact, it had seemed easy before crunch time came. But Jerry must have left something out of his instructions, because this just wasn't working out the way it should. In the battle of woman versus machine, the machine was kicking her butt.

"Do you have any tips on how I can go faster?" she asked Steve.

Steve's mouth widened into a goofy smile. "Nothing much I can say right now."

Something was up. Something no one had shared with her. Not that she could do much about it, other than feed more dishes through Hobart. Without thinking, she used her arm to wipe sweat from her forehead, forgetting that hot sauce and ketchup were smeared on that particular arm.

"Careful, there. You don't want it to end up in your eyes," Laila, the most senior of Depot Brewing's servers, said as she made room for another tub of dishes. The silver-haired woman pulled a clean napkin from her server's apron, and handed it to Kate.

Kate wiped her forehead. "Thanks."

"I've been in this business a lot of years," Laila said. "Worked most everyplace in town, too."

Kate nodded. She'd seen Laila's plump and smiling face in an old staff photo behind the bar at Bagger's, right next to Harley Bagger's vintage lighter collection.

Laila adjusted her apron and patted Kate on the shoulder. "Over the years, I've collected some nuggets of wisdom, and I'd like to share three with you."

Kate brightened, despite the fact she probably still looked like an accident victim. "Really? What?"

"First, don't go anywhere with empty hands. There's always something that needs tending."

"Okay."

"Second, comfortable shoes are a must."

Kate looked down at her food-speckled, white leather sneakers. "Got that covered. What's the third?"

Laila grinned. "How about we let you stew on that until you get caught up?"

Yup, Kate smelled something, and it wasn't just the hot sauce she'd been wearing. The scent was that of a rookie dishwasher being roasted. But she could appreciate a little gamesmanship as much as the next girl. And when inspired, she could engage in some, too.

The clock on the wall opposite Kate inched its way to three P.M., one hour before her quitting time. The kitchen's rhythm had slowed from its earlier frantic beat to a busy yet congenial hum. The line cooks cracked jokes and laughed with one another. The servers took brief breaks, chugging soft drinks and counting their tip money. And Kate finally caught up.

"Awesome job! I can see the counter," Steve said as he approached with a heavy load of dirty dishes.

"But not for long," Kate replied. "Where was this stuff hiding?"

"Hiding?" He set down the bus tub. "Dude, it wasn't hiding."

Just like Steve wasn't hiding another goofy grin. Now, at least, she knew what was up.

"No biggie," she said. "I'm game. Bring it on."

And he did. Two more tubs soon joined the first.

"Is that the end of it?" she asked.

"Dunno. There might be more," Steve said before ambling off.

"How's it going?" Laila asked when she arrived with yet another stack of dishes a couple of minutes later.

Kate gestured at the mess. "Could be better. I'm not sure I get the rhythm of this place."

"And that, my new friend, is where the third nugget of wisdom comes in."

"Which is?"

The older woman smiled as she added her contribution to the mess. "Ask Steve once you've caught up."

Another dishwasher might have whimpered, but not Kate. She was made of sterner stuff. Craftier stuff, too. After feeding another couple racks into Hobart, she took a quick glance around the kitchen. The servers and the cooks were all out front, too wrapped up in their current conversations to be paying attention to her. She quickly stowed the three remaining unwashed tubs on the floor, in the open area beneath Hobart's exit ramp.

She'd barely had time to hide her grin, too, when Steve arrived with another load. He did a double take at the clean counter.

"Wow! Did you really get through all those dishes, Tink?"

"Tink?"

"Short for Tinkerbell. You made that stuff disappear like magic."

Tink wasn't the sort of nickname she wanted to encourage, but she'd have to deal with that later.

"Just doing my job," she said, knowing that his view of the dirty tubs was blocked. "And Laila said you'd share her third restaurant hint with me as soon as I was caught up. So how about it?"

"No can do," he said with a nod to the dishes he'd just delivered.

She'd been expecting this.

Kate gave Steve her best smile. "You know, that's one awesome-looking orange-and-white VW van with all the old surf shop stickers out in the employee parking area. It's yours, right?"

"Down to her tires," he answered with obvious pride.

"I thought so!"

"Betty's the real deal. I found her in a junkyard when I was seventeen, and . . ." His brows drew together. "Hey, why are we talking about her right now?"

"Steve, order up!" one of the line cooks called.

"In a second," he answered without looking away from Kate.

"Now, before it's cold!" the cook bellowed.

"Betty looks like you keep her nice and neat," Kate said.

"I do."

"Then you'd probably be real sad if all these dirty dishes ended up in her, wouldn't you?"

His tan seemed to fade. "No way. You wouldn't."

If her mascara hadn't already been sweated off, she would have batted her eyelashes. "I might."

"Yo, Steve!" the cook shouted. "Now!"

Steve briefly looked his way. "Yeah, just hang on, would you?"

"Sounds like you're pretty busy," Kate said. "I, on the other hand, have plenty of time to go out to the parking lot and bring Betty a little gift. Or you can tell me Laila's third nugget of wisdom."

The cook had started hissing something unintelligible in the secret language of angry fry cooks.

Steve winced at the sound.

"So what's it going to be?" Kate asked.

Steve hesitated for just a second, appraising Kate with a friendly stare. "You're tougher than you look, Tink."

It was nice to hear. For so many years, Richard had told her that she wasn't tough. Her moving to Keene's Harbor and her nutty plan to turn a broken-down family vacation spot into a B&B was all about showing that she could survive—and more than that, succeed—without anyone's help. She had something to prove to herself and the world before she was ever going to let a man back into her life.

"Thanks, Steve," Kate said.

Over at the grill, the cook seemed to be speaking in tongues.

"You might want to hurry this along," Kate said.

Just then Jerry strolled into the kitchen from the tap-room area. Unlike Kate, he looked well rested and free of food stains. "Sounds like you have an order up, Steve," he said.

Steve bolted for his food, glancing back over his shoulder at Kate and Jerry. "Understatement."

Jerry toured the dishwashing area, then gave Kate a crooked grin. "Looks like you have a couple of stragglers. Are they there for a reason?"

"Persuasion for Steve."

He laughed. "So I've heard. I've been getting Hobart

updates out in the taproom. Those dishes you've hidden have been doing double-duty today."

"What do you mean?"

"Yesterday, you rushed by me. Today, I kept you rushing." He hitched a thumb at the bus tub still on the prep counter. "Servers are supposed to clear the trash before dumping everything else in the tub. I figured for today, that job should be shifted to you." He paused, smiling. "See, Laila's final nugget of wisdom is do unto Jerry as you would have done unto you."

Kate laughed. "Golden, all the way."

Now she got the rhythm of Depot Brewing, and she had a feeling she was going to fit right in, too.

Early Saturday afternoon, Matt stood in the parking lot of his latest purchase, a decrepit Traverse City motel called the Tropicana Motor Inn. Next to him stood Ginger Monroe, his local office manager.

"A flamingo mural? Are you sure about this place?" Ginger asked, flipping her aviator sunglasses from the top of her bright red head down to her elegant nose as she surveyed the motel's front wall.

"If I weren't, I wouldn't have bought it."

"I can't believe I never noticed the painting before. Those birds are wrong in every possible way."

Matt didn't respond. So far as he was concerned, a glam-looking twenty-five-year-old who had a burning love for 1950s fashion and B movies shouldn't freak out over flamingos. Those quirky birds and she were kindred spirits.

"Their beady eyes are following me," she said.

"Then look away."

"I can't. Trying to avoid looking at this place is like turning away from a train wreck. I don't know what you're thinking."

He grinned. "That's half the fun of working for me, isn't it? And I'm working on building a sister restaurant on the lake in Keene's Harbor. If you think this motel's going to be work, you should see that place."

Ginger laughed. "All the same, how about if I just wait for you at the truck? And much as you might want to stand here all morning admiring your buddies, remember you have a meeting back at the office in ten minutes."

"Don't let Ginger hurt your feelings," he told the fading birds after she'd walked away.

In truth, the flamingos *were* his buddies. They amused him as much now as they had when he'd been a kid and his parents would bring the family here on vacation. With five kids to clothe and feed, and a business that had never exactly cranked out money, the relatively cosmopolitan atmosphere of even sleepy Traverse City, and the Tropicana Motor Inn, had been a treat. His mom said the mural made her feel as though they were in the Caribbean instead of on Grand Traverse Bay.

Ginger was dead-on about the train wreck part, though. The city had grown in popularity and wealth, but the Tropicana hadn't been so lucky. The former owners had moved to Florida five years ago, believing they could sell waterfront land to a developer in a heartbeat. Not so. The real estate market had gone south directly after them.

Matt had kept an eye on the languishing property while he'd worked to find the cash to cut a deal. Earlier this year, he'd played with the numbers and figured out how to both retain the motel's character and make it work. Last week, he'd finally been approved for a resort liquor license. After renovations and the addition of a restaurant, this place would be a gold mine during tourist season. As would the property in Keene's Harbor he planned to renovate.

Matt was all about envisioning. While he'd negotiated

this deal, he'd imagined himself kicked back on the new restaurant's terrace, saluting his bird buddies with an ice-cold beer. Weird, though. Right now, as he pictured it, a small and curvy blonde named Kate had planted herself in the middle of the vision. He'd had a lot of daydreams about the brewery over the years, but they'd always been *his* daydreams. Just him and the brewery. He kind of liked having Kate there.

After checking his watch, Matt headed back toward the truck. The last thing he wanted was to be late for a meeting with Travis Holby. Like Ginger and the Tropicana flamingos, Travis was an original. A sometimes cranky original. He was also a prodigy of a master beer brewer and key to restoring this motel. For that, Matt would deal with the guy's quirks.

Nine minutes later, Matt pulled up to the office building housing his third-floor walk-up office space on Traverse City's Front Street. It was small but had a great view over Grand Traverse Bay, the long natural harbor separating Lake Michigan from the town. The largest city in the area, Traverse City was a grown-up version of Keene's Harbor, with a sleepy population of 15,000 in the off-season, swelling to the breaking point with tourists and summer people in July and August.

Travis had made himself comfortable in Matt's office, taking up residence in the reception area from the seat behind Ginger's desk. "You're late, Culhane."

Matt fought back a smile. You had to admire the kid's style. "Last I checked, this was my office. So I'm not late. You're early."

Travis gave Matt a flat stare that usually came from the kind of man who had teardrops tattooed at the corner of his eye. And while twenty-something Travis was missing that particular mark, he did have his share of tats and piercings, including a gauged ear that made Matt wince every time he looked at it. The younger man was both wiry and wary, like a cage fighter. Sometimes he had the combative attitude of one, too.

Ginger entered the office on Matt's heels. "He's not late. And I'm betting you got here early just to snoop around."

Travis did his best to look indignant. "I'm not snooping."

Ginger cut her eyes first to Travis and then to Matt. "I really should start locking the door."

"You did," Holby said. "I just didn't feel like waiting in the hallway."

Matt glanced back at the door. No visible signs of damage. The guy was good.

Travis smiled proudly. "Don't worry, I've been keeping myself amused."

And there was plenty of stuff filling the office for Travis to amuse himself. Matt had to admit that he'd been kind of annoyed when Ginger had stuck a television and a mini-fridge in the outer office. He'd kept his mouth shut, though. She worked here forty hours a week, managing his books, taxes, and investments. He spent most of his time at the brewery, so if he made it up to T.C. three times a month, that was a lot.

Travis picked up a bag of potato chips from Ginger's desk and popped one into his mouth.

"Those were in the drawer," Ginger said.

He popped another potato chip, daring her to complain. "Jalapeño. Spicy, just like you."

Matt had no idea what was going on between Holby and his office manager, but this clearly was not the first time they'd met.

Matt inclined his head toward the closed door to his private space. "Do you want to head into my office?"

"When I've got football on the TV and your amber ale chilling in that fridge? Hell, no."

Matt looked over at Ginger. "Why don't you head on home? I'll catch up with you on Monday."

"Okay." She shot Travis another glare. "Not a single crumb or you're a dead man."

"Sorry about that," Matt said after Ginger had left. "She's not usually so—"

"Locked and loaded?" Travis said. "Don't worry about it. Actually, I'm surprised she didn't body slam me."

Matt dragged over one of the guest chairs so he was seated next to Travis. "I take it you know her?"

"Used to date her. She dumped me for cause."

Matt didn't especially want to know the cause. He was sure he'd either done it or had it done to him at one point or another.

"Thanks for coming into town and seeing me."

"No point having you drive all the way out to Horned Owl."

Which was part of Travis's problem. He'd sunk a ton of money into a brewery and taproom so far off the beaten path that visitors needed to drop a trail of bread crumbs in order to find their way back to the highway.

Matt stood, got two ambers from the fridge, and handed one to the younger man before sitting. Travis opened the top-right desk drawer and pulled out a bottle opener.

"You've got this place scoped out, haven't you?" Matt asked.

The brewer opened his beer with a well-practiced motion. "It's good to know what weapons a woman can use against you."

Matt's thoughts traveled the road south, back to Keene's Harbor and Kate Appleton. Weapons like wide hazel eyes and a mouth made to linger over? Oh, yeah. That was good stuff to know.

Travis waggled the opener in front of Matt's nose. "You coming back from wherever you are?"

Unfortunately, yes. He took the opener and dispatched his beer cap.

"I've learned there's no good way to start a conversation like this, so I'm just going to put it out there," Matt said. "Word is, you're having cash-flow problems."

Travis took a long pull on his beer. "Bull. Where'd you hear that?"

Matt shrugged. "You know how it goes. There aren't that many of us in the business, relatively speaking, and we've all got bar gossip down. They were just a couple of passing comments, but enough that I wanted to talk to you."

Silent and clearly torn between anger and embarrassment, Travis turned his attention to the television. Matt did the same.

After the Spartans completed a fourth-down conversion that was a work of art, Travis asked, "If I do have a cash crunch, why would you care?"

"A few reasons. First, I like your product. And you remind me of me, ten years ago. You've got all the enthusiasm of a homebrewer and, unfortunately, all the business skills of one, too. But I think, given some time, you're gonna kick ass."

"If I'm so hot, why didn't you hire me as a brewer when I came to you four years ago?"

"You and Bart working together?" he asked, referring to his brewmaster. "One or both of you would have been dead inside a month."

Bart was one of Matt's closest friends, and also the only guy out there who could consistently kick Matt's butt at poker. Bart's competitive streak didn't stop at cards, either. When it came to beer, he was as determined to remain top dog as Travis was to attain that status.

Travis scratched the spider tattoo on the side of his neck. "Suppose I was having money troubles, just what is it you're proposing?"

"A loan and a leg up," Matt said. "There's a niche market I think you can fill. And I also think you can help me. You have both the skills and the edgy attitude for a project I'm working on."

Travis shook his head. "So you think I'm good, but not good enough to make it big?"

"Not yet."

"You pulled it off."

"Yeah, but I also screwed up plenty along the way. Why not ride along on a little of what I've learned, like how you're killing yourself by changing up recipes so often? It's like you've got beer ADD."

"So what? I like creating."

"You probably also like keeping the lights on and heat running in your brewhouse, too."

"Yeah."

"Winter is coming. Business might be so-so at best for you right now, but in another month, no one is going to follow that donkey trail out to your place. What then?"

"I'll deal with that when I get there," Travis said.

"Wrong. Too late then. You always have to have a plan."

"I can think on my feet. It's all good."

"You can also fall on your ass. Out of curiosity, how much do you need to get through the winter?"

Travis took a swig of his beer, clearly considering the matter. "Thirty grand."

Yeah, the guy had major *cojones*. "Okay, how much do you need if you don't spend February in Mexico or whatever you've factored in there?"

"Twelve to fifteen grand, assuming prices stay stable," he said. "I don't suppose Ginger has that much cash hidden in a secret compartment in her desk?"

"No, but for the right terms, I can scrape it up."

"So, deal."

"Any money I lend you is going to come with an interest rate of five points above prime. And no complaining about the rate, because it's more than fair. It's a gift. If you're at the point I was when starting out, your equipment is leveraged to the hilt and you have no other assets."

"Close," Travis admitted. "I've got my car and my house, both of which are mortgaged."

"Okay, then. For any outstanding loan, you pay me interest only for twenty-four months, with the balance due at the end of that time. I don't cut into your cash flow with principal payments, and in exchange, I get the exclusive right to feature your beers in a restaurant here in Traverse City. You can sell by bottle in markets, but I'm it otherwise."

Travis's pierced eyebrow met his unpierced one. "Small point, but you don't have a restaurant here. Best I can tell, you've got nothing north of Keene's Harbor."

No shock that Travis wasn't aware of Matt's activities. Under the radar was generally his style. Exactly four people on the planet knew about his Tropicana buy, and that he was already corporate angel to another struggling brewpub in this city's warehouse district: Bart, Ginger, his lawyer, and his accountant. And Matt trusted all of them not to spread news until he was ready to have it spread. What Matt did outside of Depot Brewing was his business and his way of stepping out from under the microscope that could be Keene's Harbor.

"I'll have a place for your beer by next Memorial Day," he said to Travis. Assuming spring actually arrived in April and he could get the footings dug. That was a dicey proposition near the tip of Michigan's mitten.

"What happens if I can't pay you back?"

"I'm not through with the conditions yet. You also have to agree to have Bart come up and do a one-week consult with you on your recipes. They're original, for sure, but rough yet."

Travis pushed out of his chair. "No way am I consulting with that jerk."

Matt fought to hide his grin. His reaction would have been the same, back when. "Huh. And yet you wanted to work for him."

"I was desperate."

Matt didn't reply. Travis would do the math and see he was desperate now. To point that out would cut into the guy's spirit, and Matt liked that spirit, warped as it was.

Travis stalked over to the television set, blocking Matt's view. No problem. Travis could contemplate wherever he wanted. He drew down his beer and thought about taking the rest of the jalapeño chips. Except, as he recalled, Ginger also usually had some locally made sourdough pretzels in her stash. He leaned over and reached into the appropriate drawer.

Travis swung around and faced Matt when he was halfway through his second pretzel twist.

"For fifteen grand upfront, I can kiss up to Bart," Travis said.

"Twelve grand."

While Matt was fair, he wasn't into giving away money. "And just so you know the final deal points, before you get dime one, you need a business plan. A real one on paper and with financial projections that I have approved. And if you default any principal payment, I get a controlling interest in Horned Owl Brewery."

Travis went slack-jawed. "So if twelve grand is all you end up lending me, you think that should entitle you to run my life?"

"If you can't pay me back, maybe you need someone to run your life for a while. And at least I'm giving you a fair shot at making it."

"The last four years of my life are worth more than twelve grand."

"I can't deny that," Matt said. "But that's the price of a start-up. Hell, I did the math on what I was earning per hour after my first year and almost crawled under my bed. It was depressing and unfair. But you have to look at it from my side now. If Horned Owl fails—and I don't think it will—all that money buys me is some recipes, beer names, and label art."

"So why are you doing it?"

Travis still looked skeptical, and Matt didn't blame him. This was a big step.

"There's no scam here and no motive other than to get your beer out there for people to find," Matt said. "I'm going to have a place for that soon, and you are straight-up the best brewer for the spot. And like I said, you remind me of me." Minus the tattoos, the piercings, and the attitude. Okay, add back in the attitude. Ten years ago, Matt had been happy to brawl for the sake of brawling, just as Travis was.

Matt gave the idea a final push. "Tell you what, think about it for the rest of the weekend, and if you're interested, give me a call on Monday. I can have my lawyer draw up the paperwork for you to take a look at. For now, let's catch the end of the game."

Travis settled in, and both men drained the last of their Rail Rider ambers. Matt had done all he could. If Travis Holby was the man Matt estimated him to be, he'd take this deal even if it chafed his pride, and he'd also pay back the money as agreed.

"No need to wait until Monday," Travis eventually said. "Let's do it."

"Okay," Matt replied.

Though he'd kept up a mellow front for Travis, Matt was feeling damn good. Someone had once bailed him out, and now he got to pass along the favor and make a few bucks in the bargain.

THREE

AT TEN ON MONDAY MORNING, KATE LOBBED AN OPEN case of uncooked chicken wings into the Dumpster behind Depot Brewing. Misfortune had sunk its teeth into Matt Culhane. Or at least into his walk-in cooler.

"I'm telling you everything was okay when I left last night," Kate said over her shoulder to Jerry.

Jerry's face was locked tight with anxiety, a muscle twitching at the side of his jaw. "Can you prove it? Someone screwed up and hit that cooler's power switch. I'm betting it was you."

She turned back to grab something else to toss from the cartful of spoiled food. Jerry wasn't looking much better than the tray of tepid slider patties. Having had her work life pass before her eyes on a couple of occasions, she knew the expression of someone staring down unemployment. And because it must suck to be him at this moment, she decided not to take it personally that without cause or investigation he'd pinned the blame on her.

He'd also called her in five hours early. Niceties such as hairstyle and matching socks had fallen by the wayside as she'd scrambled to get to the brewery.

"Jerry, I know I had the least experience of anyone last night, but honestly, my lack of experience makes me even

our office? The one whose walls stop about six feet
f the ceiling? Think not."

Then come to the market with me. I have to pick up
to cover us until the frozen stuff thaws and our re-
ement shipment arrives this afternoon."

Harborside Market?"

"Yes, why?" He hesitated. "Are you worried about the
y you look?"

"No, even though maybe I should be a little. What's
rrying me is that anything I know about the locals in
is town, I learned from Marcie at the market. Harbor-
de is the place to see and be seen. If I go there with you,
ople will think . . ." She rolled her hand, sending him
to what she felt was an obvious conclusion.

"That we're shopping?" he asked.

"No, they'll think we're more than employer and em-
oyee."

His grin widened.

"What?"

"You are a summer person, aren't you? Among the lo-
s, you don't have to do anything to start gossip. It's
f-seeding. The second I hired you, it started."

"But it's unsubstantiated."

"I don't think a trip to the market constitutes a mar-
e proposal."

"We do need to talk, but I want it to be away from
n," she said.

liflower, then I'll na   lot in   after
that, it's anarchy."

"Oh, no. The display is perfect. I'm just distracted."

The market door opened. Instead of Matt, Junior Greinwold, the town's beloved but totally inept handyman,
shuffled in. As always, balding, slope-shouldered, and
ulky Junior carried a blue six-pack cooler. He'd been

more careful. I've told you what I saw. What happened
after that, I don't know."

Before last night, she also hadn't known that Jerry was
in the habit of leaving the kitchen and taproom in the
hands of the crew and disappearing when Matt was elsewhere.

"Someone has to have seen something," he said.

Kate lobbed a five-gallon jug of mayonnaise that was
now both heart attack and food poisoning by the table-
spoon. It made a satisfying thud as it hit the bottom of
the Dumpster.

"Possibly," she replied, though she had her doubts.

Jerry sighed. "I need to go in and clear more food. Just
keep tossing."

Kate couldn't begin to imagine how much money
Depot Brewing had lost overnight. She couldn't put the
cooler incident down to carelessness, either. Not only had
the unit's power switch to the right of the door been
turned off, but the door had been left open, too. From
what she could gather from the brewery gossip, without
both of those events, the cooler would have held its temperature within the allowable range until morning.

She also knew that the walk-in's door was tough to
leave open. Kate had scared the bejeezus out of herself
Saturday evening when she'd wheeled in a cart with the
bins from the salad prep area and the door had shut. On
the bright side, her panicked scream had made the cooks'
nights. So what if her brain had shut down when the door
slammed? So what if there was a latch on the inside, too?
Everyone had issues, and maybe hers was a touch of
claustrophobia, especially when trapped inside a giant
stainless-steel refrigerator.

Her attention was drawn by the clank and rattle of a
cart being wheeled across the asphalt. Steve and Amber
had arrived with more spoiled food for the Dumpster, and

Kate knew this was prime sleuthing time. She kept her head down and continued to clear her cart.

"So where do you think Matt is?" Amber was asking Steve.

"I'm thinking more about what he's gonna do when he gets here. Someone is dead meat."

Amber grimaced. "I'm glad I got cut early. I'm off the hook."

Steve nodded. "And the dude trusts me, for sure."

"So where do you think he is?" Amber asked again.

Steve shrugged. "Maybe he has a secret girlfriend. Like a married one."

"I'm sure that's not the case," Amber said, turning on her heel and huffing off, back to the building.

"Another babe under the spell of Matt Culhane," Steve said to Kate. "I've been asking Amber out for weeks. She always says she's too busy, but I know if *he* was asking—"

"I find it hard to believe he would date an employee," Kate said.

Steve shrugged. "You never know in the restaurant business. Late nights. Lots of beer and parties. And he's got one or two women hanging around here who are borderline stalkers."

Kate thought it sounded a little like jealousy on Steve's part, but Matt was a pretty hot ticket. "Are you saying Amber might have sabotaged the cooler because she's obsessed with Matt?"

Steve looked shocked. "No way! She just has a huge crush on the guy. But who doesn't? I mean, every female in a hundred-mile radius drools over him."

Matt stepped forward to take a tub of blue cheese from Kate and pitch it into the Dumpster. "Talking about me?"

Kate hadn't realized he was there. She allowed herself a glance to see if his sex appeal had diminished over

the weekend. She decided it definitely ha[d] back to Steve before she turned to stone [a]ever a woman did when staring into the f[a]tion.

"We can handle this," Matt said to Steve. you head inside?" He waited a moment and g[a] at Kate. "Interesting look you've got going know you were into tractors."

She had no idea what he was talking abo tors?"

"Your choice of headwear. It makes quite ment."

Kate absently touched the crown of her head. been able to find in the way of hair protection w[h] had ordered her to the brewery had been a fluf ered hat of her mom's or a green-and-yellow Jo[h] tractor–emblazoned bandana that she'd une[a] the linen closet. She'd chosen the bandana.

"I was short on time, and Jerry sounded [h] hysterical. Desperate times and all that. Sp which, you know this wasn't an accident, rig[h]

"Yes. I'm just glad it's not the weekend. V fighting chance to pull it together for a Mon If this had happened on a Saturday, we would[n] time to prep the volume of food we'd need." "How'd you survive the weekend?"

"I have a new boyfriend named Hobart. H become very close."

Matt smiled. "I'm going to hate to break

"Don't even think about moving me aw bart. Everyone's back there at one point or all of them talk. You move me, I miss all o

"You'll have to tell me what you've hea[rd]

"I will, when we can find the time alon[e]

"Let's step into my office when we're d

"Okay, we'll compromise," she said. "How about a ten-minute head start for me, and then we meet at the market?"

"So we're just bumping into each other?"

"Totally casual."

Five minutes later, Kate pulled into an open parking space near Harborside Market, which was weirdly named, since it stood seven blocks from the water. After grabbing her keys and hopping from her Jeep, Kate walked past Keene's Wine Bar/Bookshop, with its pastel-bright and cheerful Victorian façade. The sporting goods store, with its canoe-shaped sign and manly dark wood exterior, had a placard out front advertising its evening fly-tying class. She skirted around that and moved on.

Kate arrived at the quaint market, which still had an original leaded-glass panel of intertwined green vines and red roses above its broad plate-glass window. Inside, she saw the usual gathering of locals, some shopping and some just shooting the breeze.

The market's automatic door opened as she approached. Even if she hadn't agreed to meet Matt, the scent of freshly baked cookies would have lured her in. And as always, everything in the store was perfectly faced, stacked, and alphabetized. Kate had heard the occasional first-time visitor whisper that it was a little eerie, but she liked it. It gave her comfort to know that

"It's quirky-looking, but it tastes the same as regular cauliflower," a woman's voice announced from behind her.

Kate turned to see Marcie Landon, the market's owner. Marcie had ash-blond hair cut into a sleek bob and had been blessed with classic features that left people guessing her age. Not that she held still long enough for a guess to be made. The woman zipped around so quickly that it seemed she was everywhere at once.

"What does?" Kate asked.

"The cauliflower," she repeated as she came to stand beside Kate. "It's purple, but the flavor isn't any different."

"Oh. Okay."

"Since I started carrying it a few months back, all you summer people have raved over it."

"Great," Kate replied, amused that she was still lumped with the summer people long after summer had gone. She'd heard somewhere, though, that it took three generations of full-time residency to be considered a townie, and she was well short of that mark. But speaking of townies, she wondered where Matt was.

"They're all about the same weight," Marcie said.

Kate blinked. "What are?"

"The cauliflowers. You're staring at them. I did worry that there was a certain hypnotic quality to this display. Maybe I should . . ." She trailed off and gave an appraising look around the produce aisle. "But if I move the cau-
____, I'll have to move the peppers, and after

helping Kate patch up her house, fixing broken toilet seals, regrouting leaky showers, and other minor assorted broken things until she could afford to hire a real contractor. She still didn't know what he kept in the cooler.

Kate had begun checking out brussels sprouts still on the stalk when the door swung open again. This time, it was Matt. He grabbed a cart and headed her way.

He pulled his cart even to her. "Funny meeting you here."

"Amazing coincidence."

"So what do you say we shop together?" he asked.

"Sounds like a plan."

He closed his hand around her basket's metal handle. "Here, let me take that for you."

Kate grasped her basket tightly. "No, I can carry it."

Matt grinned, "Are you sure? Letting go can be a helluva lot of fun. Good for you, even."

"Are we still talking about my basket?"

Marcie popped up at Matt's side. "Well, look at you, Matt. Aren't you the chivalrous one, taking Kate's basket."

Kate let go of the basket and Matt took an involuntary half step backward. Marcie gazed speculatively, first at Matt and then at Kate. "So how long have you two known each other?"

Matt was seemingly oblivious. "Since I hired Kate last week."

Marcie settled a hand against her heart. "So, no long-ago romance rekindled? That means you felt a spark right away. How sweet."

"There was no spark," Kate said.

A bold-faced lie, of course. But her feelings were hers and she wasn't sharing her spark with the whole town. Or even Matt.

"Nonsense," Marcie said. "I have an eye for these things. I could tell immediately with each of Shay Van-Antwerp's three husbands. There's always a spark."

"Cheese. I need cheese," Matt said.

Kate figured that was as good a change of topic as any. She whirled around and took off for the deli counter, followed by Matt.

Matt stopped dead halfway to the counter. Junior Greinwold was peeking out at them from behind a soft drink display.

"Hey, Junior," Matt said.

Apparently, Junior didn't spy often. He stammered something, grabbed a couple of plastic two-liter bottles, and bolted.

Kate turned to Matt. "You know Junior? He's been working at my place. He seems like an okay guy, but I have to say the way he holds on to that blue cooler like it's made of gold is a little creepy."

Matt resumed walking toward the display case filled with cheese. "He's a good guy. Hangs out at the brewery. The cooler's probably filled with my beer, but nobody really knows for sure. And don't worry about Marcie, either. People love to talk in this town."

She shook her head. "I don't care about the gossip. What I care about is having my job made tougher."

"Tougher how?"

"Tougher, as in nobody is going to talk trash in front of me about you or Depot Brewing if they think we're an item."

"I could give you back your basket," he offered. "You know—the symbolic handing over of the cauliflower to mark the end of our affair?"

Kate tried not to smile. "Funny. But I'm being serious here. There's no point in handicapping myself."

"True," Matt said. "I should have thought about that."

They'd arrived at the deli counter, as had Marcie, Junior, and a couple of women Kate had seen at Bagger's Tavern every now and then. Somehow, she doubted they all craved cold cuts.

Marcie hustled around the counter and nudged aside the teenage boy working there. "I'll take care of this." She gave Matt a cheery smile. "What can I get you?"

"Three pounds of Swiss and two of American, sliced medium, please."

Marcie didn't move. "It's been a while since I've seen you dating anyone, Matt."

"Work keeps me busy," he said.

"Then it's nice to have found someone right there at work, isn't it?"

Matt was unfazed. "About the cheese?"

"Sammy, three Swiss, two American, medium," she called to her helper without letting her gaze waver from Matt. "Really, I've never seen you look at any woman the way you do at Kate."

Kate tried to respond but had to pause to catch her breath first. Was that true?

"I am not dating Kate," Matt said. "I have no plans of dating Kate. She's an employee and that's all."

That might have been true, and even what Kate wanted, but darned if the words didn't feel harsh. She glanced at her watch and pretended surprise at the time. "Speaking of which, I need to go home and get cleaned up for the dinner shift." She retrieved her mutant cauliflower and focused on Matt. "I guess I'll see you at work this evening?"

"No, I have dinner with my family tonight."

"Good," she said, and she meant it, too.

Kate needed some time to get her "this is only work" attitude in place. It was that or give in to the spark she refused to feel.

* * *

Matt sat looking at the dining table, worn and scarred from decades of family dinners. Lots of happy memories were contained in those scars and, even though he and his sisters were adults with their own lives and dining room tables, there was something comfortable and special about that particular table that drew them all together for the occasional family meal. So here he was, women to the left, women to the right, and his dad at the far end.

In just about every way, Matt was a younger mirror of his salt-and-pepper-haired dad. Now, they got along great. When Matt had been in his teen years, however, there had been some friction. It hadn't been anything bad—just the usual stuff involved when a kid's testosterone level jumps ahead of his common sense.

When he was a kid, his friends had always told him he was lucky to have the "cool mom" in the neighborhood, and he agreed. He liked that she had bowled in the same Thursday bowling league for the past thirty years, walked three miles every day, and was an eagle eye of an archer. He did, however, feel that pretty soon they were going to have to stage an intervention when it came to her holiday decorations. Every year, for each holiday, she tried to outdo herself. This year, she'd added an assortment of bunny figurines dressed in Halloween costumes parading down the center of the dining table like a zombie army. And last year's creepy wrought-iron bird figures still glowered at him from the bay window's sill.

This house had been in the family since it was built in the late 1800s, back when the Culhanes had money enough to build a three-story, seriously ornate Victorian. The locals still called it the Culhane Mansion. Matt found the mansion reference to be overkill, just like his mom's decorations. He frowned at the bunny in a tiger costume lurking by his water glass.

Matt's mother leaned forward from her seat to his father's right. "Is something wrong, Matt?"

Matt opted not to insult the bunnies. "Tough day at work."

The buzz around the table quieted and Matt knew he'd made a mistake. All his sisters and his mother focused their attention on him. His father pretended to be lost in thought, abandoning Matt to his Inquisitors.

Matt's sister Maura, nine months pregnant, gave him a concerned look, implying that he lived in a constant state of chaos. Her four-year-old, Petra, sensing something interesting was about to happen, stopped coloring and gave Matt the same look.

"What happened *now*?" Maura asked.

Petra looked up at her mom and then to Matt. "Yes. What happened now?"

"The walk-in cooler had an issue last night. We lost a lot of food, and I had to scramble to make today work. Did it, though."

Maura looked relieved. "Now that Dad's sold the business, you really should have him help out at the brewery. God knows you could use it."

Matt smiled. His family might be overprotective, but they all looked out for one another. "Got it covered. I added staff last week."

Petra put down her crayons. Her face was covered with tomato sauce. "Is it a girl or a boy? Boys smell sometimes."

Matt's sister Rachel laughed. She was the family's baby and undisputed princess. She was also the only one in the family with curly hair. Matt's mother always said it was her mischievous nature that made her hair curl.

She turned to face Matt, her hand resting on her hip. "That's an excellent question. How does your new employee smell?"

Matt concentrated on chewing his food.

Petra looked around the table. "Boys have a penis and girls have a bagina."

"Come on, Matt," Rachel said. "We all want to know if your new staff member has a bagina."

"Jiminy Cricket. I'm eating pizza. Do we really have to talk about baginas?"

Rachel put her index finger to her lips and studied Matt. "You know what I think?"

She paused for effect. "I'm reading a book about body language right now, and yours is very closed. As if you don't want to talk about baginas at all."

Matt put his hands flat on the table. "That's what I just said. I said it two seconds ago."

Rachel leaned over to Maura. "Matt's always been very excitable when it comes to baginas." Everybody at the table nodded.

"Anyone I know?" Lizzie, his second-youngest sister, asked. She was his best friend as a kid and the tomboy who'd always kept up with him. Her brown hair was still cut short, and her years of playing sports with Matt and his friends had given her an athletic body that looked great in her Keene's Harbor police uniform. Matt's friends hadn't shown a lot of romantic interest in her back then, but they sure did now.

Matt grabbed a slice of pepperoni from the pan. "I don't think so. She's new to town. Her name's Kate Appleton."

"Hmmm . . . Is she Larry and Barb's youngest?" his mother asked.

Matt looked up, intrigued that his mother might know Kate's parents. "I don't know."

"Short, cute, long and curly blond hair?" his mother asked.

In Matt's estimation, Kate had also gone from cute to sexy. Not that his mom needed to know that. "Short, with short blond hair."

"I'll bet that's Kate, all grown up. And you'd know Larry if you saw him," his mother said. "He always used to have his Saturday morning coffee with the group in the hardware store."

Maura smiled at her brother. "Matt didn't like working Saturday mornings. It cramped his Friday night style."

"Well, back when we'd spend our Friday nights together at Bagger's Tavern, I remember Barb being quite the social butterfly. Great singing voice, too," his mother said.

"As I recall, Larry was a bigwig in the auto industry," his dad added.

"Advertising," his mom corrected.

"Cars," Dad said.

His mother patted his father's hand where it rested on the table. "No matter. They were good people, though they haven't been around much in recent years. They own that big old house, The Nutshell. Sits right at the end of Loon Road, on the cusp of the lake, and has a great view of the bird sanctuary across the way."

Matt stopped eating. "That's Larry and Barb's house?"

He knew the house well. He owned the mortgage. The owner was three months behind on the loan and his lawyer had already begun the foreclosure process. He was the jerk evicting Kate Appleton from her bed-and-breakfast.

Matt wanted to ask for more details, but he knew that would tip off his family to the fact that Kate had caught his attention, and in a big way, too. Matt looked toward the front windows, where the iron crow ornaments were silhouetted in the setting sun. He pushed away from the table and went to get one.

"Mind if I take this?" he asked his mother.

"Of course not. Are you actually going to start decorating your house? I could come over with the spare decorations up in the attic, and—"

"Thanks, but all I want is the bird," he said before she could offer up anything else.

Matt returned to his seat, moved the bunny away from his water glass, and put the crow in its place. The ornament was really kind of creepy, with feet too big to ever work and corroded spots that gave it a diseased look. No matter. Kate was either going to understand the spirit of his peace offering or think he was nuts.

FOUR

NIGHT HAD FALLEN. KATE SAT ON THE OVERSTUFFED floral chintz sofa in The Nutshell's circa 1976 living room. She'd left the room's beach-facing windows open enough that a crisp breeze pushed through them. As a teen, when she'd been feeling a little blue, this couch had been her landing spot. While Kate wasn't blue, exactly, she did feel the need to decompress. Between the cooler incident, the market nonmeeting, and a wild dinner shift that had followed, she was tapped out. A half-eaten bag of chocolate chips and an equally depleted bottle of white wine, along with its glass, sat on the oak coffee table in front of her. She'd had a decompression fest.

To make matters worse, there was something wrong with her living room floor. The floorboards on the western side of her house, next to the master bedroom, had buckled, bowing upward. She had noticed it a week ago and moved a heavy armoire to the affected area in order to flatten the wood. But it had only gotten worse, much worse.

Kate suddenly felt a twinge of late-night loneliness. She picked up the telephone and dialed her friend Ella Wade. Ella answered on the third ring.

"Chocolate chips and Chenin Blanc for dinner aren't necessarily signs of a pity party, are they?" Kate asked.

"I think that depends on the hour and the quantity consumed," Ella said.

Kate rested the phone between her ear and her shoulder while she corralled a few more chips. "Started early, and lots of both."

"I'm sorry to say, then, that your meal has all the earmarks of a pity party."

Kate smiled at Ella's answer. They had become friends as teenagers, sneaking Strawberry Breeze wine coolers behind the then-abandoned train station. Ella had always been the brainy one of the pack. Kate had gone on to a middling college and lots of parties. Ella had cruised through Harvard and then moved on to Stanford for law school with every intention of becoming a professor. She'd changed course a couple of years ago and joined her family's law practice in town. Ella's family had been lawyering in Keene's Harbor since the late 1800s.

Kate dug around in the bottom of the bag for a chip. "I'm going to continue to think of my meal as decadent pampering."

"A handful of chips is pampering. A bag is pity-scarfing. I heard that plastic crinkling. What's going on?"

"I'm never going to get this house fixed. What do you know about warped floorboards?"

"Sounds like you've got a water leak. The water gets trapped under the wood, causing it to expand, and it buckles to relieve the pressure."

Kate sucked in her breath. "Great. A water leak. I'll call a plumber tomorrow and see if he can find the problem."

"So," Ella said, "not to change the subject, but I had

lunch at Bagger's yesterday. How'd you get Matt Culhane to give you a job?"

Kate refilled her wineglass. "Equal parts desperation and determination. And the end result seems to be a whole lot of suffering on my part."

"I don't see how a person could suffer too much with Culhane to look at," Ella said.

"The suffering comes from running Hobart, the dishwasher from hell. As for my boss, I'll admit he's a stellar decorative item, when he's around. But really, after Richard, I'm not looking at men as anything more than decorative. There are good substitutes for any of their other uses."

"Ouch! That's a little bitter."

And a lot easier to say to Ella than it would've been to Matt when he was handling her cauliflower, but Kate was determined to keep her head on straight.

"I'm going to continue to think of it as a practical attitude," she said. "As a species, men are great—some of my favorite people. But I need to sort out a whole lot of stuff before I date, let alone do anything else, ever again."

"Okay, I can agree with that. I've taken the celibacy pledge until I can bring in enough work to support the salary Dad insists on giving me. Not that there's anyone around here to date, in any case. Except Matt Culhane," Ella added in a teasing voice.

"So, anyway, how's work?" Kate asked.

"Pretty much how you'd expect it to be when working with a father, a brother, and two cousins. Wonderful, except when it's not. And then, at least we all still love each other. The other day—"

Kate was distracted by the crunch of tires on the gravel drive out front of the cottage. She set aside her wineglass and stood.

"Hang on," she said to Ella. "I think someone's here."

"Out there? You're kidding."

The drive to The Nutshell was a good, winding stretch off the road just inland from the shore. People didn't end up at her door by accident.

"Wish I were," Kate said.

A ratty black T-shirt emblazoned with the words SEX AND BEER in fat white block print, and plaid flannel sleep pants so worn that they were frayed over her knees weren't exactly "meet the visitor" wear.

Then again, who could possibly be visiting her? Her wine buzz was swept away on a sea of adrenaline.

"Don't hang up," she whispered to Ella.

"Why would I? And why are you whispering?"

Kate nudged aside the lighthouse-themed curtain that covered the front door's window and peeked outside. A pair of truck-height headlights shone directly into her eyes. She let the curtain drop and turned the door's dead bolt.

Her visitor's vehicle had come to a stop. "Don't know," Kate said to Ella. "I'm just a little edgy. You're the only one who'd be out here, and you're there."

"Okay, you have a point," Ella said. "Should I dial the police on my cell?"

"A lot of good that will do when I'm way out here."

The truck's headlights were off. Kate scurried to the kitchen and grabbed the biggest knife she could find in the knife block.

"Single girl. Lake house. Mysterious midnight intruder. This is so straight out of *Friday the 13th*," she told Ella.

Kate glanced at the serrated bread knife in her hand. Great. She'd have to saw the prowler to death.

A knock sounded at the front door. Kate considered this a good sign. So far as she knew, homicidal maniacs didn't knock. Then again, she had limited experience with homicidal maniacs.

"Jeez, this is like one of those horror movies!" Ella said. "Don't go to the front door. That's the equivalent of the stupid babysitter who goes down into the basement. Just hide."

Kate approached the door. "My car is out front, Ella. The lights are on in my house. Clearly, I'm here." Funny how calm she sounded when her heart was slamming its way out of her chest.

Another knock . . .

"Do you have the knife?" Ella asked.

"Yes."

Kate ducked below the door's window. She had no intention of losing the element of surprise. Slowly, carefully, Kate moved the curtain. Inch by inch, Matt Culhane's face appeared, lit to glowing perfection under the porch light.

"Oh, no." Kate let the curtain drop.

"Who is it?" Ella asked. "Freddy Krueger? Your ex, Richard?"

"No. Worse. It's Culhane."

"You're kidding!"

Kate rolled her eyes. "Nope. He's here in all his glory."

"Really! All his glory? Nice."

Matt knocked again and called her name.

"I have to go," Kate whispered into the phone, and disconnected over Ella's pleas to stay on the line and eavesdrop. Then holding the phone and knife in one hand, Kate released the dead bolt and opened the door just enough to peek out.

Big, strong guy, eyes full of ambition, and a smile that was full of humor—at himself and the world—the kind of humor that only comes with a healthy dose of self-confidence. Yep, it was Culhane all right.

"Hey," Matt said.

Kate tried to process how best to get rid of the knife, which now seemed a little excessive. "Gosh, this is a surprise. How'd you find my house?"

"Well, that's an interesting story."

That got Kate curious.

"I don't suppose you'd consider letting me inside?" he asked.

Good grief, she thought. She was a wreck. Almost-empty wine bottle, ratty clothes, hair from hell, and she had a bread knife in her hand.

"I thought we were going to talk tomorrow?" she said to him.

His smile was crooked and endearing. "I decided I like tonight better. And I come bearing gifts." He reached into his pocket and pulled out a weirdly shaped object.

Kate squinted down at the thing, uncertain what it was.

"Is it chocolate?" she asked.

"Sorry, no chocolate. It's metal."

"Metal what?"

"A metal crow."

Kate reached to accept the gift, inadvertently brushing her hand against Matt's. A little tingle of heat rushed through her, leaving a breathless lump in her throat.

The knife in her other hand dropped to the floor, interrupting the moment. "Come in. I was having a glass of wine. Can I get you anything?"

He stepped inside. His gaze shifted from her to the knife at his feet, then back to her. He took his coat off and casually hung it on the rack. "No, thanks."

Matt followed Kate into the living room. "So, why aren't you drinking beer?" he asked.

Kate hastily cleared the coffee table of the remnants of her Not a Pity Party. "I've never been much of a beer drinker. To be honest, I hate the stuff. Have a seat."

Matt settled on one end of the sofa, and Kate took a spot on the opposite end, leaving a fabric field of poppies and chrysanthemums between them. She was glad for the space, because he looked good. Really good.

"Let me get this straight," Matt said. "I hired someone who hates beer to work in a microbrewery?"

"It looks that way."

"I think I need a more detailed application form." He pointed at her shirt. "Should I assume you hate both the things listed there?"

She glanced down at her SEX AND BEER T-shirt, then back at Culhane, who gave her a grin.

"Neither of them are at the top of my priorities these days. But this is a song title, and the shirt's from Milwaukee 2006 Summerfest."

"You sound pretty certain about that no sex or beer thing. I think I'm going to have to take you up on the challenge."

Her heart stumbled. "You're talking about the beer, right?"

"Of course I am. I have my priorities, too."

Yeah, and not for a minute did Kate believe it was beer. Okay, truth was she *hoped* it wasn't beer.

"So what is it we *really* had to talk about?" she asked.

"First, you were right and I was wrong."

Kate laughed. "That's always a good start."

He pointed to the ornament. "And this comes with the admission. I'm not much for eating crow, so I thought I'd give you one."

She examined the weird little metal bird. "Thank you, but it looks more like a raven to me."

"My family vote came out in favor of a raven disguised as a crow."

She couldn't have heard that right. "Your family voted?"

Matt shrugged. "Long story. It begins with my birth. Let's just skip it and move on to me saying that I was nuts to have thought we could talk at Harborside Market."

"It's okay," she said. "I think everyone in town is now pretty clear on the fact that you're not attracted to me."

"I'm not that good an actor," he said. "*No one* believes it."

Kate bit into her lower lip.

Matt studied her for a beat. "I just admitted I'm attracted to you, and I can't read your reaction."

"Flustered," Kate whispered.

He blew out a sigh. "I get that a lot. Why don't you give me a quick rundown of what you learned this weekend?"

"Well, first, I learned that Jerry doesn't seem too devoted to the concept of management once you leave town. He shows up for a little while, tells the staff to follow the usual program and call his cell should something break, burn, or blow up. Then he leaves."

Matt raised his eyebrows ever so slightly, but he said nothing, so Kate plowed on. She might as well get all the bad stuff out of the way. He'd wanted an unfiltered report, and she would deliver it.

"Well, Steve thinks you've got some secret affair with a married woman, but I think he was just saying that to enhance his own romantic life."

"I don't think I want to know how that could possibly enhance his romantic life. And for the record, married women always have been and always will be off-limits."

"I haven't known you long, but you seem like a stand-up guy to me," she said. Still, time would tell.

One life skill Kate had been working to develop was a keener eye for dishonesty. She'd missed the early warning signs with Richard, but eventually she'd caught on. Now she was at least marginally older and wiser, both of which rocked. And while she still planned to open her heart and trust, she'd do it with some initial caution. She wasn't up for another loss of love or poodle.

"Is there anyone else I should know about?" Matt asked.

Kate shook her head. "It sounds like you're golden with the rest of the staff. I didn't hear anything, except a passing mention from Laila that her son couldn't get a job with you."

"He'd have to apply for a job first, which he won't, because he likes his winters off from his marina job."

"I got the feeling Laila believes he *has* applied."

"Well, employee applications are confidential, so I won't be clearing that up," he said. "That's it, then?"

"Yep."

Matt nodded. "Any thoughts on who might have sabotaged the walk-in fridge?"

"That's tough. It could have been anyone. Laila and Steve were in and out. The cooks were there. And so were the bartender, the busser, and the barback. It could have been Jerry, until he went on walkabout, or whatever it is he does. No one saw it happen and all of them had access. Add to that, it probably happened after hours, which means the back door was open while the trash was being hauled out. The walk-in is on a straight path from that door. It's highly unlikely that the crew would have missed someone slipping in, but it's possible."

"True, but I'd rather believe the nearly impossible than think my own employees would mess with me."

"I understand. But until someone is caught pulling one of these stunts, everyone's on the list. And I know this is technically none of my business, but maybe if you shared a little info with your staff when you take off, they wouldn't pass their free time coming up with the Top Ten Bizarre Reasons Matt Culhane Is Missing."

"You're probably right," he said. "But I shouldn't have to tell everyone my every last move. For all the time I'm there, I deserve some privacy when I'm not."

"It was just a suggestion."

"I know, but I'm used to running my show my way."

"Sorry. I'm hardwired to just put it all out there."

"So I've noticed," he said. "I think it might be one of your better qualities."

They smiled at each other, and she found herself considering how it would feel to close the distance between them on that flowery sofa and kiss him. It would feel good, she thought. *Really* good.

It was like a dreadful out-of-body experience as she witnessed herself begin to lean toward him like a teenager crushing on a new boy. The lean was immediately followed by panic, and Kate shot to her feet and set the metal bird on the coffee table. "It's getting late. I'm sure you're really tired."

Matt rose and reached out to touch her hair. "I could never be *that* tired."

Holy Moses, Kate thought, the panic mingling with flat-out lust.

"Before this goes any further," he said, "I have something I need to tell you. I'm the guy who owns your mortgage."

For a moment, Kate thought she'd misheard. "What?"

"I didn't know it was your house before tonight, I swear. I'm really sorry, but I have a lot of money already invested in this, too, and I made a fair deal with you and your parents."

"You think it's fair to take my home?"

"Kate. It's falling apart and nobody would pay what I'm offering."

Kate felt her blood pressure hit the stroke zone. "It doesn't matter what somebody would pay, because it's not for sale. I'm going to get the money to fix the place somehow, and I'm going to turn this place into a home and a business."

Matt shuffled his feet and looked into Kate's eyes. "Look. I'll give you until Thanksgiving to get caught up on your mortgage. Just ignore the foreclosure papers."

Kate's eyes were as wide as saucers. "Foreclosure papers! You're serving me with foreclosure papers?"

"Not anymore. At least, not right now."

Kate turned Matt around and hustled him to the door. "I don't have much of a choice. I'll take the deal. And I'll see you at work tomorrow. The sooner I find your saboteur, the sooner I get my bonus and the sooner I can pay you. Good night!"

Kate listened to the crunch of gravel as Matt's car drove off. She hated him for taking her house, but she had to admit he'd been honest with her, and even generous giving her until Thanksgiving. She leaned her forehead against the door and gave up a sigh. The worst part of the whole hideous mess was that she had very friendly feelings for him. Feelings that might be misinterpreted now. She worried that he might have a hard time sorting out her genuine attraction from a cheesy attempt to bail on a mortgage payment.

FIVE

MATT AND HIS THREE-LEGGED DOG, CHUCK, HAD HUN-
kered down to watch the flames dance in the large fieldstone fireplace that anchored the great room in Matt's log
home.

Chuck gave his standard contribution to any conversation: a thump of his tail against a pine floor scarred
from his constant quest to discover if the darker knots in
the wood might actually be hidden dog treats.

Matt stretched his arms across the back of the brown
leather sofa. He took in the family photos that sat on the
fireplace's rough-hewn oak mantel. Chuck starred in
more than one of the shots.

Five years ago, Matt had found Chuck tied to a newspaper box outside a gas station. Apparently, someone had
stuck him there the prior night and no one had laid claim
to him during the course of the day.

Matt liked to think of himself as a practical guy. He'd
known that a three-legged hound, no matter how much
he otherwise appeared to be bred to hunt, was going to
be ornamental at best. But one look at that dog's chocolate brown eyes and hopeful expression, and there had
been no way he could have left him behind.

"That was my lucky day," Matt said to Chuck. Chuck

was a good listener when Matt needed to unload. And Chuck could be counted on for unconditional love any time of the day or night. "I don't know why I'm letting Kate get to me," Matt said.

Chuck tilted his head, probably trying to pick out words he knew, like "food" and "treat."

"But that's not what's messing me up. There's something more about her. Look at the way she took on Hobart like it was her life goal. And the way she's straight with me, too. No sugarcoating. I like her. A *lot*, if you know what I mean."

Chuck started to snore as he fell into a doze. He had been neutered a long time ago and had absolutely no idea what Matt meant.

Matt's thoughts turned from Kate to his business problems. As the old saying went, it wasn't paranoia if someone really was out to get you. The flat tires and messed-up deliveries he'd dealt with, but the open walk-in had cost him some serious money. He had been trying not to take it personally, since whoever was doing this had a certain level of insanity going on, but this *was* personal.

Matt headed into the kitchen. He opened the fridge and pulled out the orange juice jug, only to discover that at some point or another, he'd stuck it back in there empty. At least that way it matched the rest of his fridge's barren expanse. He left the empty jug on the counter and swore he'd remember to get food tomorrow. Or eat at the restaurant again.

The phone rang and caller ID told him it was Lizzie. Guess she wasn't through with him for the evening. He could ignore her, but it would do him no good. As a Keene's Harbor police officer, she'd been known to pull him over when he'd ducked the rest of the family for too long. He picked up the phone. "Hi, Lizzie."

"You blew out of the house so fast, I didn't get the

chance to give you your ticket for Friday night," Lizzie said.

Ticket.

Matt didn't like that word in any Keene's Harbor context, be it parking or speeding or, far worst of all, admission. And even though this was Lizzie on the phone, he was damn certain that she was referring to the dreaded admission ticket to whatever Friday night benefit was planned at the Brotherhood of Woodsmen's Hall.

"There's a fund-raiser for Lester Pankram," she said.

Matt winced. Lester was a nice old guy, but thrift had gotten the better of him. He'd been driving his tractor along the shoulder of a road when he'd seen a beer can. Hot for the ten cent refund, he'd stuck his tractor in neutral and hopped down. Blind to anything but that shiny can, he'd failed to note the road's downhill slope and had pretty much run himself over. He'd come out of the incident with a broken leg, the sure knowledge that he'd become a Town Legend, and a Friday fund-raiser that would be held to help cover his medical expenses.

"I'm working Thursday and Friday this week," Matt said. "There's a private party at the brewery on Thursday, and we're always slammed on Friday night."

He rolled away from the nearly weekly fund-raisers the way Lester should have from his tractor. For some reason, at these events the older folks in town found it amusing to reminisce about the many dumb-assed moves Matt had made as a kid. The talk came with multiple elbows in the ribs, wry winks, and laughing. A lot of the stuff was funny when he heard it the first time of the night, but by the fifth or so time around, he found himself remembering why he'd decided to build his home deep in the woods. And why he liked to send an anonymous envelope of cash to the fund-raiser's beneficiary.

"Let your staff do what you pay them for, and come

to the fund-raiser," Lizzie said. "You can meet and greet there, too."

"Thanks, but I'll pass."

"How about you don't, this time? You skip ninety-nine percent of these things. It makes you look like a hermit."

He smiled at the gap in her logic. "Only if you can find me to see me."

"I'm not joking, Matt. This is a town tradition, and we Culhanes have been part of the town forever. Dad wants you there with the rest of the family, even if he's too proud to say it."

That was the thing about Lizzie—she'd always known just how to get to his soft spot. She had none of the noise of his other sisters and ten times the efficiency. Matt didn't want to disappoint his dad. He loved the man, even if he had never been able to pull off working side by side with him.

"I'll stop by," he said. "But no way am I staying the whole night."

"That's up to you. All I did was commit to getting you there."

Matt sighed. No doubt another of his siblings had the duty of making him stay.

He wandered out of the kitchen and back to his spot in front of the fireplace, where Chuck slumbered on.

"Anything else?" he asked his sister.

"It would be nice if Depot Brewing dropped off a keg for the event, don't you think?"

"I wouldn't have it any other way."

At least then he could be sipping some of his favorite Scottish Ale while being retold the tales of his youth.

"Great. And Matt, pick up Mom and Dad on the way to the hall, okay?"

His mom and dad were fully capable of driving to the hall, not to mention circumnavigating the globe.

"What? You don't trust me to show up?"

Lizzie laughed. "I just know you."

"Fine, I'll pick them up. But so long as we're horse-trading, do you want to do me a favor?"

"What?"

"When you're on night patrol, take an extra loop by Depot, could you?"

"Do you want to tell me why?"

"It's nothing big, just enough small stuff going down that I'd like a little extra attention."

"Define small stuff," she said in a voice that was now one hundred percent business.

"One set of flat tires on delivery trucks and an open freezer door. The first definitely took place after hours, and the second, maybe. Either way, an extra drive-by or two would help."

"Okay, I'll make sure we swing by more often. There's not as much to patrol this time of year, anyway. And I'll see you on Friday, right?"

"Wouldn't miss it," Matt said.

He disconnected and looked down at Chuck.

"Dude, I'd trade places with you in a heartbeat."

Chuck briefly opened one droopy hound eye as though to say "no way," then cruised back to napland. The canine king would not be deposed.

In bed but not sleepy, Kate reached for the phone to pick up her conversation with Ella.

"I just wanted to let you know I was alive," she said when her friend answered.

"When you didn't call back right away, I figured maybe you were putting Matt Culhane to one of the better uses God intended."

"It was briefly tempting, but no."

"Do tell."

"I'd rather not," Kate said. "It wasn't one of my better moments. How about if we take a look at my big social picture, instead? I remain in social limbo. I need to start getting out and meeting more people."

"That, I can help you fix. This Friday there's a fundraiser at the Woodsmen's Hall. Why don't you come along with me? It's nothing all that thrilling. There's beer, potluck, and gossip, but it'll give you a chance to meet a few more people."

Kate smiled. "I think you've just given me incentive to survive the rest of the week at work."

Including Thursday's private Halloween-themed party being thrown by Shay VanAntwerp. Jerry had told Kate she'd be doing a lot of detailed prep work for the gathering. Kate didn't know what that meant, but she expected it wasn't good.

"Don't get your hopes up too high about this fundraiser," Ella said, then yawned. Too late. Kate was primed.

Wednesday had been little more than a blur of frenzied work as the Depot crew prepared for Shay VanAntwerp's annual extravaganza. It was now Thursday evening, and Kate was exhausted. She stretched the cramped fingers of her left hand and looked at the jack-o'-lanterns leering at her from tables set up in Depot Brewing's loading dock area. Wednesday morning, she'd viewed Jerry's assignment of creating fifty pumpkin carvings as a gift. This was her fun, artsy reward for having become BFFs with Hobart. For the first dozen works of art, she'd been all about the details, shaving away paper-thin bits of rind for perfect translucent accents. Frankenstein and Dracula came to life, along with a tribute to Stella, her poodle. As she'd worked, Kate had enthusiastically separated pumpkin seeds from guts, thinking that salty roasted treats at each of the party tables would be an ideal accent to Culhane's fabulous brew. But by the afternoon, her gag reflex had kicked in, and washing slimy mutant gourd seeds had fallen off her list of volunteer activities. She had left work and taken a series of long hot showers, both before bed and after she'd woken this morning. No luck. She still smelled like a giant pumpkin.

By 5:30 P.M., Kate no longer cared how she smelled and her artistic impulses had begun to sputter. No more tiny tools for her, just a nasty, sharp filet knife.

"Almost done?" Laila asked as she entered the storeroom.

"Just three more to go."

"No time. You're going to have to put them aside and help set up. The early comers are starting to trickle in."

Kate looked at her watch, which she'd set on one of the table's edges to avoid most of the pumpkin carnage. "But the party isn't supposed to start for another half hour."

"Free beer tends to make for overly prompt guests."

"I hadn't thought of that. All the same, I'd really like a shot at finishing. I swear, with my new minimalist approach, I'll be done with the last three in a flash."

"Okay, then. I'll gather up some help to have the finished ones taken out, and you keep carving. Everything needs to be done before Shay arrives. The good news for us is that she always arrives late," Laila said, filling a cart with grinning heads and leaving Kate alone in her pumpkin kingdom.

Figuring the time had come to kick the assembly line into high gear, Kate grabbed the big butcher knife she'd borrowed from the kitchen and stabbed it into the top of the first of the three intact pumpkins. It sunk in quickly and deeply. The act was weirdly satisfying. She seemed to be developing a very real disrespect for pumpkins.

"You look like a natural."

Kate glanced up to see Matt watching her from the

doorway. She pulled on the knife, but it had gone in too deeply and wasn't coming out. She tried to rock it back and forth. No luck. "I'm not sure that's a good thing."

He approached her. "Problems?"

If one counted among them a heady overappreciation of a man dressed in something as simple as a black polo shirt and jeans, she had exactly two at the moment.

"The knife is stuck."

"Let me see if I can help."

Matt came around to her side of the table. Wow, but he smelled good. She caught a hint of woods and green fields. And, unlike her, he didn't have a bit of pumpkin slime on him.

Kate moved her hand away from the knife, but not quickly enough. They touched, and she swore she felt an electric tingle as her hand involuntarily began to close around his. The sensation was far more satisfying than stabbing into a pumpkin. Good news on the mental stability front.

Matt wrapped his hand around the knife's handle and winced.

"Sorry," she said. "I guess everything's a little messy at this point."

With his free hand, he brushed a fleck of pumpkin from her cheek. "So it is," he said, "but it still looks good."

He turned his attention back to the pumpkin and pulled the knife free with an ease she envied.

"Tell you what," he said. "Why don't you get a bunch of these outside to line the front walk, and I'll finish up the last three?"

Kate shook her head. "No, you don't have to do that. It's my job, and I'm all about finishing what I set out to do."

"You're not just talking about pumpkins, right?"

"I moved to Keene's Harbor for a reason. To start a new life and build something I can be proud of."

"And I'm the guy trying to take that away from you? It's not personal. It's business. And it was in the works a long time before you even moved to Keene's Harbor."

Kate crossed her arms. "Look. I know that. But that doesn't mean I like it. And I'm going to find your saboteur, collect my $20,000 bonus, and buy back *my* house."

Kate didn't want to even think about the fact that a contractor had spent an entire day at her house trying to locate and fix her water leak. She didn't have the money to pay him, either. Yet. And she wasn't about to ask her parents for help. She wasn't even sure they had the money, what with her father retired and living on long-held investments.

"Right now, all I want to do is carve a pumpkin," Matt said. "Cut me a break here."

"Well, since you put it that way, I could use a break, too. I'm pretty much pumpkined out."

He smiled. "Consider yourself sprung."

Kate grabbed a cart and loaded it with four jack-o'-lanterns. She made her way to the front of the house, where costumed beer lovers had already gathered. Once there, she slowed her pace enough to check out the guests. The event, like her emotional state, was high school all over again. The women had taken the borderline bawdy path to apparel, while the men had gone for minimal effort. Among the male ranks, there looked to have been quite a run on Grim Reaper costumes. Kate counted five of them in the crowd already. Two Grims were tall and skinny, and the other three of more well-fed dimensions.

The taproom was in full Halloween mode, too. The front windows were edged with strands of orange lights that glowed warmly against the dark wood trim. Tealights adorned each table, adding to the festive look. And an appetizer bar had been draped with orange linens and decorated with absurdly grinning skulls that shone from within. Kate wished she could stay and mingle, but there was work to be done.

She thanked one of the tall-and-skinny Grims as he held open the front door for her and the pumpkin cart. A sharp blast of wind greeted her. No doubt a storm was brewing out on the lake. Chilled, she hustled the cart over the mosaic mural, then hung a left to the end of the jack-o'-lantern line that Laila had already started.

Once Kate had her pumpkins in place, she patted her pockets for a light. She had none, of course. She turned her back to the wind and headed to the bar to snag a pack of matches. Inside, she spotted Laila chatting with a Grim Reaper. Market owner Marcie Landon was with them. She was very fittingly costumed as a tape measure. The bit of tape showing from the front of the bright yellow box was probably marked to perfect scale. The tall-and-skinny Grim definitely liked Laila, hovering close enough to be in her personal space. Laila didn't seem to be objecting, either. She was laughing at something the Reaper had just said. Kate smiled, waved, and moved on.

Outside again, she hunkered down by the first jack-o'-lantern and pulled out her pack of matches. Two sputtered and died even before she could get them to the tealight waiting inside, and the next two were snuffed by a draft coming through the pumpkin's eyes.

"Okay, then," she said to herself and sat down cross-legged on the sidewalk. Clearly, she would be there awhile.

"You need a lighter."

Kate looked up past a pair of sensible white server sneakers and standard Depot uniform to Laila's serene face.

"I don't suppose you have one?" Kate asked.

Laila pulled out a rectangular silver lighter adorned with what looked to be crystals. She flipped it open with a distinctive click, bent down, and did in two seconds what Kate hadn't accomplished in four matches.

"Sometimes the old things are the best," Laila said.

Kate smiled. "Obviously, you haven't seen my house."

At eleven that night, Kate lay in bed, unable to sleep. The contractor had found her leak. Evidently, when Junior had regrouted the shower tile in her master bathroom, he hadn't inspected the shower pan. It had completely failed. Even worse, he'd reset the toilet without a proper seal, and raw sewage had swept underneath her bathroom floor. The water damage from the shower and toilet had infiltrated her living room, causing her floor to warp. The contractor was coming back tomorrow to pull up her water-damaged floor and tile. Kate had tried to call Junior several times but he wasn't answering—probably in his best interest, given the problems he'd caused.

The good news was that it seemed like a pretty simple fix, and the contractor thought he could do it for a couple thousand dollars. More than Kate had but doable, especially with the bonus money she planned to earn.

Kate set aside the magazine she'd been leafing through. An article on "Ten Ways to Drive Him Wild" wasn't what she needed to get Matt Culhane out of her head. Indulging in each of those ten with him might do the job. But she wasn't going there.

Kate's cell phone rang, and she jumped at the unfamiliar sound. She hadn't received too many phone calls since her big move away from the city.

"Hello?"

"Hey, Katie-bug!"

"Dad?"

"I know it's late, but I picked up this new phone today that does everything but clean the pool, and I wanted to be sure I had your number right."

Her father sounded pretty chipper—about one double Manhattan's worth was her guess. She could picture him sitting in a lounge chair out back of their Florida house, with the pool lights and stars shining. He was probably wearing his favorite navy cardigan and blue-and-white seersucker trousers. And Mom was probably inside pining for the days of wholesome television and good old-fashioned family values. Kate loved her parents, but it was like they'd just been freed from a 1960s time capsule.

"You've got the number right, Dad."

But he'd never called it before, always opting for the landline when she'd lived back downstate. And she hadn't heard from either her mom or her dad since that highly uncomfortable family dinner three months ago, when she'd had to admit how broke she was. Of course, she hadn't called them since then, either.

"So as long as we're chatting, I was wondering how . . . The Nutshell is?" her dad asked.

"The house is fine, Dad."

"No issues with the plumbing? I know we're due for a new septic system."

"It's all good," she said.

"And that loose step on the way down to the beach?"

"I nailed it back down," she fibbed.

Fact was, she hadn't ventured to the water. All she'd done since she'd landed in Keene's Harbor was focus on finding a job and nailing down her future. Beach walks had seemed like a luxury she hadn't earned just yet.

"Well, that's just great," her dad said with more enthusiasm than the conversation warranted.

"Are you and Mom okay? There's nothing going on down there that I should know about, is there?" she asked.

"We're fine, Kate. Just fine! How's the refrigerator?" he asked. "Do you need any help stocking it?"

They'd finally reached the real purpose of the call.

Kate was glad no one was around to witness her embarrassment. The last time her dad had asked questions like this, her brother, sister, and their respective spouses had been watching. Kate had felt like the loser-girl on a reality TV show.

"I promise I have more than diet soda and shriveled-up apples in the fridge," she said.

She still had that head of purple cauliflower, after all. But so long as she loaded up on the cheap employee meals at work, shopping was optional.

"Just checking. I know things have been tight."

"It's okay. I found a job."

"Really? What are you doing?"

"I'm washing dishes and doing prep work at Depot Brewing."

The line fell quiet for a beat.

"That's great! It's a tough job market out there. You should be proud. If you come up short, let me know and I'll slip a care package your way. Just like your old college days."

Ugh. Kate knew he was trying to be positive and supportive, but she was right back to feeling like the loser-girl. Kate wanted to be there for her parents, like her siblings were. Not the other way around.

"Thanks for the offer, but I'm doing great," she said. And it was true, if "great" could be defined as able to splurge on a fake cappuccino the next time she put gas in the Jeep.

"Just say the word, Katie-bug . . ."

She wouldn't, though. Her parents were retired, and money didn't grow on trees. They probably had a woefully out-of-date concept of how much money was needed to get the house in shape. But more important, Kate had something to prove. Not to her parents, but to herself. She could stand on her own.

SIX

On Friday night, Matt walked into Woodsmen's Hall with a parent at each elbow. The crowded room was filled with laughter and the blended smells of three dozen casseroles that probably all included crispy fried onions. This was an old-school Keene's Harbor food-and-gossip fest, right down to its location. Other than getting an occasional refresher coat of paint, the long and narrow single-story hall hadn't changed in a hundred years.

Matt felt pretty okay with being there until he saw Deena Bowen over by the beer table. In her bright blue V-necked dress, Deena was as much a knockout as she had been on the one date they'd had together. One date had been more than enough for Matt but not for Deena, and a woman scorned is a woman to be feared. Matt turned his head before Deena could catch him looking. It was the same technique he used when faced with a black bear in the woods. Deena and that bear bore a lot in common, personality-wise.

"You're dragging your feet, son," Matt's father said.

"Just soaking it all in."

"Come along, Patrick," his mother said. "I want to see what's over in the silent auction.

"Harley Bagger has offered up a couple of lighters

from his collection, and Enid Erikson was donating some of those fun toilet paper covers—you know, the ones with the dolls' heads and frilly dresses?"

His parents headed to the back of the hall, Dad with less fervor than Mom. Matt stuck to the front. One of those blank-eyed dolls would be staring at him from the back of a toilet at his parents' home soon enough. Mom would probably give him one for Christmas, too. Unfortunately, Chuck could sniff out chewy plastic items the way most of his breed could raccoons. The doll would be history.

Matt stopped and talked with Bart, his brewmaster and buddy, about the upcoming hockey season. They were defending league champs, and Bart had his eye on a prospect to be sure they stayed that way. Matt gave Bart a fist bump and took the slow route toward the three refreshment tables. The first held soda and mixers, followed by high-octane punch, and then beer. He stopped and chatted with as many folks as he could. He wanted to give Deena time to move on.

Clete Erikson, the town police chief and husband to toilet paper doll-maker Enid, was manning the brew table. Clete reminded Matt a little of Chuck. Not that Clete was missing a limb. He just had the same droopy hound features.

"Hey, Chief," Matt said.

Clete returned the greeting and slid a red plastic cup of beer Matt's way. "Guess you're wanting one of these."

"Sure am."

Matt took a sip and scanned the stream of new arrivals flowing into the hall. And then he saw her. Kate was a flash of scarlet sweater and spiky blond hair, so obvious among the less vivid colors surrounding her. The night was looking up.

* * *

"It's the townie mother lode," Kate said to Ella as they worked their way into Woodsmen's Hall. The place was packed, which made it all the better to be with Ella. Kate's friend was gorgeous. She was tall, with straight black hair that just swept her shoulders. She also possessed a figure that Kate envied but didn't want to work to attain. Crowds just kind of parted for Ella.

"This is also the safest place on Earth," Ella said.

Kate could see why. She'd already spotted a handful of police officers and most of the volunteer fire department, all of whom she recognized from her brief stint at Bagger's.

As Ella and she wove through the throng toward Ella's unstated destination, Kate said hello to the people she recognized. She was pleased to even get a few return greetings that didn't come with that confused "Where do I know her from?" look in the eyes.

"Where are we heading?" Kate asked her friend over the noise of the music that had just started.

"Beer table for the first stop," Ella said.

"I don't suppose there's a wine table?"

Ella shot her a dubious look. "You're not serious, are you?"

She had been, but she'd never admit it.

Ella had a conspiratorial look in her eye. "I have a plan for you."

"And beer is part of it?"

"If you don't want a beer, just make sure you grab something to drink, because you're going to need it."

"That sounds marginally dangerous."

"If it's only marginally, we're doing pretty good," Ella said.

They rounded food tables packed with the kind of calories a sensible woman would avoid, but which Kate considered staples. She looked away from the temptation, but suddenly the evening's danger factor rose. Matt stood at the beer table, and something way hotter than hunger for ham casserole rippled through Kate.

"Hi, Matt!" Ella called.

Matt *very* slowly turned his attention from Kate. This was a first, since usually when Ella called, guys hopped to.

"He's into you," Ella said to Kate in a low voice.

Kate shook off the moment. "Punch sounds good. Really good." She moved on to the table directly to the left of Matt.

Ella lined up with Matt, got a cup of beer, and chatted a little with Clete Erikson.

Kate investigated the punch. Clearly, this was the grandma drink, complete with the obligatory island of orange sherbet slowly melting in a sea of bright pink liquid studded with chunks of melon and strawberry. Not her beverage of choice, but still about ten thousand spots ahead of beer. She ladled herself a big plastic cup, trying to avoid the fruit. If anyone was going to have the bad luck to create a scene with a public fruit-choking incident, Kate knew she'd be that person. To make up for the fruit, she added a little more punch, plus some of the orange stuff.

She glanced over and caught Matt watching her, a broad smile on his face.

"You sure you want to drink that?" he asked.

"Not really, but I'm going to give it a try, anyway."

"Note the people lining up for the beer and note the continuing absence of people at your table. What does that tell you?"

"That Keene's Harbor is a haven for beer snobs?"

He grinned. "Live and learn."

She raised her cup of sludge in a sketchy toast. "That's my general plan."

Ella, who'd been watching, fought back a laugh. Kate

glanced into her cup again. It wasn't the prettiest stuff she'd ever seen, but it couldn't be *that* bad.

"We need to get moving," Ella said. "We'll catch you later, Matt."

With that, she snagged Kate by the wrist and began hauling her and her foaming punch back past the siren-like lure of the casseroles.

"You still sing, right?" Ella asked.

The summer they were sixteen, they had nothing better to do than drive around town and sing along to the radio. Kate had a shiny new driver's license and a less shiny hand-me-down car. And when they'd needed money for more gasoline, Ella had played the guitar and Kate had sung on the street corner until they had change for a few gallons or the police told them to close up shop.

"Not even in the shower. I keep the water temperature set too low to carry a tune," Kate replied.

They passed through what was obviously a silent auction area. Kate halted at a collection of old vinyl albums up for bid. Her parents had stuck their ancient stereo at The Nutshell. There was nothing Kate would like more than to mix a little retro Jimi Hendrix and Janis Joplin in with the Frank Sinatra and Barbra Streisand already in residence.

Ella nudged her along. "No time to window-shop. You've got music of your own to make."

Kate noticed the small stage at the back of the long hall. About a half dozen people were in a line to the stage's left, and Marcie Landon was onstage aligning a microphone stand behind a monitor of some sort. She seemed to be giving the arrangement the same OCD level of scrutiny she gave the shelves at her market.

As they came closer to the group, Kate started picking out the particulars. Junior Greinwold, with his trusty blue cooler at his feet, was flipping through an aged three-ring binder while a guy and another woman Kate didn't recognize were peering at it from either side of him. A liquor-tinged memory of a party in someone's basement and a lot of really bad versions of "Pour Some Sugar on Me" came back to her.

Kate stopped dead. "Karaoke? No way!" Ella settled a hand on Kate's arm and drew her to the edge of the room. "You wanted to know how to become part of the town again, right?"

"Yes."

"Then rule in karaoke."

"You're kidding. I thought the only place you could still find it was in ratty college bars."

"It's become the favored competitive sport in Keene's Harbor. See those chairs?" Ella pointed to three chairs lined up at the far edge of the dance floor in front of the stage. "Judges. Olympic scoring. The whole thing. Now, come on."

Kate looked around. "Isn't there an arm-wrestling or kielbasa-eating challenge I could do instead?"

"Just get on up there," Ella said.

"What, alone? You're going to make me do this and you're not singing?"

"I still can't carry a tune, but you can. Do this, Kate. I'm telling you it will help."

When she'd asked Ella for help in being accepted as one of the locals, she'd been thinking of something that might have taken a bit less effort and potential for humiliation on her part. But she trusted Ella. And what had dignity ever gotten her, anyway?

"Okay, then. Just stick by my side until I get a song under my belt."

"I'll be your personal assistant, I promise," Ella said. "Let me hold your drink for you."

They joined the field of karaoke Olympians.

"No cuts," said a woman at the back of the line.

Kate blew out a sigh. "No problem."

Ella drew Kate back a few steps, her voice lowered. "That's Deena Bowen. She's about five years older than us, so you missed out on her when we were kids. She's also the town's undisputed karaoke queen, among a couple of other less perky titles."

"Such as?"

"Psycho revenge queen. She's always verbally gunning for Matt, and from what I've heard, they only had one date. Though I guess she lobbied long and hard even for that one."

"She's a little spooky. Do you think she'd ever do more than just bad-mouth him?" Kate asked Ella.

"I don't know. She's bitter, for sure, but I think she's just acting out over a whole lot of bad stuff in her life." Ella paused long enough to give her a teasing smile. "Why? Are you worried about being in the line of fire if you date him?"

"You don't have to be dating a guy to want to see him stay in one piece." She inclined her head toward Deena. "And you have to admit she's somewhere south of hostile. It rolls off her in waves."

Ahead of Deena, Junior was pacing back and forth, shaking his arms and repeating "ma, me, mi, mo, mu" as his apparent warm-up exercise. Deena hissed at him to shut up before she had him sedated. Junior picked up his cooler and walked away from Deena to practice next to Kate.

"How's it going, Junior?" Kate asked.

Junior glanced at Kate and hugged his cooler. "Fine."

"Don't you want to know how things are going for me?"

Junior hugged the cooler even tighter. "I guess so."

"Well, I'm glad you asked. I've been trying to call you

for two days. The 'improvements' you made to my toilet and shower leaked all over my entire house. The contractor was there today. Do you know what he found when he pulled up the floor?"

Junior looked a little ashamed. Kate suspected it wasn't his first plumbing disaster. "Dooky."

"That's right. Lots of dirty dooky and mold. There were guys in hazmat suits in my house for eight hours containing the 'affected' area with plastic sheeting and setting up negative air blowers to suction all the mold outdoors."

Junior bit his lower lip and shoved his hands into his pockets. "I heard they can be a little noisy."

Kate's eyes were as big as dinner plates. "It sounds like a hurricane is blowing through my house."

"Everyone, come line up back here," Marcie said from the stage, rescuing Junior and gathering the group behind a white wooden latticework screen that had been decorated with plastic ivy.

Not the most attractive ivy Kate had ever seen, but she was glad for whatever cover from the audience she could find. She needed to get her stuff together before facing them.

"For the benefit of the new entrant, I'm going to repeat our standing rules," Marcie announced.

Kate gave a quick wave in acknowledgment to the other contestants now scoping her out. Happily, only Deena looked like she meant to inflict bodily harm. Everyone else nodded or waved back.

"There are six of you singing. We will determine the order of competition in the first round by pulling numbers from the bingo cage." She patted the cage in question, and the balls in it quivered. "Lowest number goes first. Two competitors will be eliminated in each of the first two rounds, leaving two finalists for the kamikaze challenge."

Kate raised her hand like the obedient student she'd never quite been.

"In a moment, Kate," Marcie replied. "The judges' scores are final. No bribes will be accepted or threats tolerated." She said the last with a pointed stare at Deena. "And tonight's winner will receive the grand prize of five pounds of venison burger provided by Harley Bagger."

If Kate was going to sing for her supper, she would have appreciated something non-Bambi-like, but she wasn't here for the chow.

"You had a question, Kate?" Marcie asked.

"What's the kamikaze challenge?"

"In the final round, a song will be selected at random for you from the playlist."

Deena snickered. "As if you have to worry."

Marcie gave Deena a glare. "And no sabotage, either. Now, if you'll excuse me . . ." She walked back out to the microphone, leaving Kate and the other singers hidden behind the plastic jungle.

"And tonight's judges, chosen at semi-random from among our guests, will be . . ." She looked down at a sheet of paper. "Starflower Creed, Shay VanAntwerp . . . and Matt Culhane."

SEVEN

MATT FLIPPED THROUGH A STACK OF ALBUMS BEING offered in the town's garage sale of a silent auction. Actually, if he thought he could consistently find a stash of music like this in local garages, he'd be joining his mom on the Saturday morning circuit. Next to him stood Lizzie. She must have pulled the short straw in the "keep Matt here" challenge, because she hadn't left his side in the past ten minutes. And somewhere at the very back of the room, Marcie Landon was calling names over the sound system.

Matt picked up his head at the sound of something all too familiar.

"Did I just hear my name?" he asked Lizzie.

"I don't know. Did you?" His sister's smile was nothing short of smug. This was never a good sign.

Again his name drifted above the crowd. "Matt? Matt Culhane?"

"That's definitely your name," Lizzie said.

"It is. But I have the option of ignoring it," he said, testing Lizzie's level of investment in whatever was going down.

His little sister tried to hip check him away from the

album collection. "Come on," she said. "Let's go see. Maybe you've won something."

He held her off long enough to write a bid on the vinyl collection big enough to scare off competitors. He knew that wasn't the silent auction spirit, but he wasn't messing around. There was a pile of Doors and Jefferson Airplane in that stack.

Marcie waved her hand, urging him toward the stage. "Matt, there you are!"

"What am I here for?"

She laughed as though he'd made a joke. "Ladies and gentlemen, our third judge is now taking his seat. Let the karaoke competition begin!" she said with a flourish and hurried back behind the screen.

"You set me up," Matt said to Lizzie.

"Fact. But think of judging as an exercise in civic duty. We all have to do it. It's your turn, and now that you're trapped, I can go have fun."

While thinking of a fitting revenge to eventually spring on his sister, Matt made his way to the open judge's chair. He settled between Starflower and Shay.

Starflower, one of the silver-haired elders of the Creed Commune outside of town, said, "Remember, Matt, peace comes from within."

She didn't generally offer up platitudes without a purpose.

"I take it you've judged these before?" he asked.

She gave a slow nod of her head, closed her eyes, and began humming to herself. Matt wondered if he was catching a whiff of something less legal than the scent of Starflower's lavender oil, which she sold in a shop the commune owned in town. Matt preferred to find his inner peace the way he'd been raised—family, friends, and hard work.

To his right, Shay VanAntwerp flicked her perfectly straight and shiny blond hair over her shoulders. "I was told we'd be up on the stage. That's the only reason I agreed to judge."

At least she'd been given a choice.

Besides, Matt understood Shay's stage addiction. She'd been Little Miss Keene's Harbor for four years running when they were kids. After that, Shay had been hooked. If there was a sash or crown to be won, she was in the race. Matt had always thought that if Shay redirected all that energy and determination, she could govern a small nation. Kind of like Kate. He wondered what she was making of this whole scene. If it was odd to him, it had to be downright surreal to her.

Deena Bowen was truly psycho.

"You cheated," Deena said.

"How could I cheat? Marcie drew the numbers," Kate replied.

"You came in here earlier and rigged it."

"Why would I do that?"

"Because everybody's out to beat me. But just because you get to sing first doesn't mean you're going to win. It doesn't give you any advantage," Deena said.

"Another good reason I wouldn't come in and play with a bunch of bingo balls, don't you think?"

Deena's hostility aside, Kate was looking forward to getting this first number done. She hadn't sung in front of strangers since she was sixteen, and the idea of doing it now had her a little rattled. And the idea of having Matt judge her was even more uncomfortable.

"Ready?" Marcie asked.

Kate nodded. Because her mouth was as dry as the dunes overlooking Lake Michigan, she poked her head out from the far side of the jungle screen and signaled Ella for the punch. Kate chugged half and winced. The concoction was so sweet that she swore her blood had just turned to syrup.

Ella gave her a weird look as she took back the cup.

"What?" Kate asked.

"You feel okay?"

"Nervous, and now probably borderline diabetic."

Ella waggled the cup. "That's okay. You won't be feeling anything very soon."

"What do you mean?"

"This is trash-can punch. Beneath all that sugar is enough overproof rum to pickle a sailor. All I can say is good thing I drove."

"Thanks for sharing. If I'd known about the punch, I'd have started drinking earlier."

"Kate," Marcie said. "Curtain time."

Except for the crucial lack of a curtain.

Palms clammy and heart slamming, Kate stepped out from behind the latticework jungle and walked tentatively to the microphone. She allowed herself a glance toward Matt, then wished she hadn't. As surprise and then pleasure paraded across his face, Kate had to quell a truly chicken-feathered urge to jump from the stage and chug the rest of that overproof courage. But if this was what it took to be initiated into Keene's Harbor, no way was she going to back down.

"I'm going to give you a little 'Crimson and Clover' . . . Joan Jett style," she said into the microphone.

Kate didn't care that half of the hall still talked and laughed as the music started. All that mattered was reaching the end of the song. She hadn't lied when she'd told Ella she hadn't been singing, but more than the chilly shower had been stopping her. In the space of one year, she'd lost her marriage, her home, her dog, and her job. She wasn't exactly depressed, but she was just flat-out busy trying to rebuild her life and her identity. Most of the time, she just felt too tired to sing.

But as she eased into the song, Kate recalled one cool thing about singing. When singing, she didn't have to be Kate of the somewhat screwed-up life. She became whatever character she chose to take on. And tonight, she chose to be a rocker seductress.

Kate let herself go with the song's sensual sway and began to kick out the lyrics with conviction. This wasn't about winning Bambi meat or even town approval. It was about living in this moment. It was about feeling the slow, sexual surge that made her grip the microphone stand with both hands and make love to the crowd.

When the song finished, Kate dropped her gaze to the plywood stage and blew out a sigh of relief. She was fairly certain she hadn't sucked. Except the hall remained weirdly silent. Okay, maybe she was delusional. Maybe she really had sucked. Just when she was sure that was true, applause and a couple of whistles and howls kicked in.

Kate smiled at the crowd and said her thanks. Then she caught Matt looking at her with an intensity she'd never gotten from any other man. Not even from Richard. She felt as though the stage was rocking and rolling beneath her feet. It wasn't the not-so-grandma punch, though. This was a punch of another kind, one of sheer hunger and absolute sexual certainty.

Matt wasn't messing around.

Now Kate got why women trailed after him as though they'd lost their favorite plaything. Still, she refused to fall for him, no matter how hot that landing might be. Without even looking at the scorecards the judges now held aloft, Kate escaped the stage while her legs could still carry her.

Matt was a goner. He was ready to serve himself up to Kate however she wanted him. Preferably naked. And even more preferably, tonight.

Matt listened to a damn fine version of "My Wild Irish Rose" by Junior and an equally scary rendition of "Do Ya Think I'm Sexy?" by Deena. But all of that was second to wondering how he could get Kate alone. He *really* liked her. Ironically, that made things more complicated. Not that he was going to let that stop him. Or even slow him down.

Marcie stepped onstage, aligned the microphone to her satisfaction, and announced the second round finalists. Kate had made the cut.

Starflower leaned over to speak to Matt. "We get a ten-minute reprieve before they start the next round."

"You mean a break?" Matt asked.

"No. Definitely a reprieve," she said. "I'm stepping outside to meditate and make myself one with the evening peace."

Or peace *pipe*.

As for Matt, he planned to meditate on how to make progress with Kate.

The overproof rum had kicked in and was burning through Kate like jet fuel. She didn't feel buzzed so much as energized. Sometime around midnight, when both the alcohol and the sugar had wreaked their havoc, she knew she'd be parched and cranky. And no doubt still sleepless. Too late for regrets, though. She looked out at the people gathered behind the judges, and Kate the Performer took over. It was round two of the Great Karaoke Olympics, and Kate was into it.

"Marvin Gaye's 'Sexual Healing,'" she said into the microphone.

Kate ripped into the song, enjoying her time in the spotlight, loving the lyrics, loving the music, thinking that life was full of moments just like this. Unexpected, surprising moments. And Kate realized that unless you put yourself out there, you could very easily miss them. Maybe it was time to take some more risks with her life.

A low howl drifted into the room from somewhere outside. The sound slowly raised in both pitch and volume, and people began to turn and head toward the door. Kate knew her voice wasn't chasing them off. She'd witnessed this scene before at Bagger's Tavern. The place could go from full to empty in sixty seconds flat when the town's volunteer firefighters heard the alarm sound.

"Fire," Ella mouthed from the base of the stage. She pointed toward the door, and Kate nodded in acknowledgment. Ella was one of the handful of women who served on the town's fire department.

More people filed out, but Kate kept singing. Now she knew how the band on the *Titanic* had felt. A woman who looked kind of like Matt leaned over his shoulder and said something to him. He stood. Kate didn't like the grim look on his face. She finished, skipped her bow, and made a moderately graceful jump from the low stage.

"What's going on?"

"There's a fire at the brewery," Matt said. "Could you come with me?"

"Of course," she said, because she'd decided not to let herself lust after Matt Culhane, but she darned well liked him.

Matt looked at the crowd gathered in his parking lot. In Keene's Harbor, the only thing that drew a bigger crowd than a Friday night fund-raiser was a good, old-fashioned Dumpster fire. There was such a weirdly festive atmosphere that he half expected to see the spectators pull out marshmallows and start toasting them. Of course, the spectators would have to fight their way through the most massive contingent of first responders that Matt had seen since the Independence Day fireworks debacle of '90. Since he'd been intimately involved in the accidental early start to that annual celebration, he'd watched that group from afar.

"Is the whole town here?" Kate asked.

"More or less."

He found a spot for his truck, and immediately noticed an ambulance parked at the brewery's employee door. The vehicle's back door was open and the interior was lit. Inside, a familiar figure lay on a stretcher.

Matt sprinted over to the ambulance. He'd barely reached it when Kate joined him. For a little thing, she had a long stride.

"Give me a second," he said to her.

"I'll be right here."

Matt didn't recognize the two paramedics working on Laila. All the same, he climbed into the back of the ambulance.

One of the paramedics was inflating some sort of air cast around Laila's ankle. "You'll have to get out, sir," she said.

Laila tried to prop herself up on her elbows, despite the paramedics' orders to stay still. "He'll stay right where he is. Work around him."

"What happened?" Matt asked.

"Twisted it hard." She winced as she tried to settle more comfortably on the stretcher. "I had stepped outside for a second to use my phone when I saw the fire. I called 911, but the fencing around the Dumpster was already burning. I tried to run a hose from the loading dock door. The hose ran me, instead, I guess. Broke my phone when I went down, too."

"Don't worry about the phone. I'll get you another one," Matt said. "Let's work on getting you fixed, okay?"

Laila had been with him since the day he'd started serving food. Yeah, she could be a little bossy, but he'd learned more from her than he could have from any number of highly paid consultants. She was family, plain and simple. And he felt sick that she had been hurt trying to help him.

"We're ready to roll," the larger of the paramedics said.

Matt touched Laila gently on her shoulder. "Can I do anything for you?"

"Get ahold of my son, Joe. Tell him where I am and that someone's going to need to come get my car."

"No problem. And I'll be over to the emergency room in just a while."

"Don't you dare. You've got enough to deal with right here. Clete already shut you down for the night."

At that news, Matt bit back on a couple of his favorite curse words.

"The Dumpster was too far from the building for a spark to fly. And even if one did, the roof's metal," he said.

"I know," Laila replied. "But you know Clete. And Steve went to look for Jerry to argue the closing, but Jerry was nowhere to be found."

"Don't worry," Matt said. "Just focus on getting yourself better and let me deal with the rest of this, okay?"

"I will."

He gave her hand a squeeze, which was about all the affection Laila would accept.

"Hang in there," he said before climbing out.

Kate still stood watching the firefighters spray down the smoking Dumpster and fence.

"Arson is a definite buzzkill," she said without looking his way.

She'd voiced what Matt had been thinking since they'd pulled into the parking lot. If not for all the other incidents, Matt would have attributed it to Steve sneaking a cigarette by the trash. Matt had snagged him doing that countless times.

"It is. And I know I'm lucky it wasn't worse. Laila's fall was bad enough."

"She'll be okay, though, right?"

"I don't know if her ankle is sprained or broken, but she'll recover." He paused. "And probably demand to come back to work long before she's ready, too."

"Speaking of which . . . Besides Laila, who was on staff tonight?"

"The usual. Amber and Steve were in the dining room. Ruby was busing dishes. Pat, Renaldo, and Manny were in the kitchen. And Jerry was supposed to be here, not that he is." He paused a second. "Before I left for the hall, Nan and Floyd were in the brewery working on one of Bart's new beer recipes. I don't know if they're still around. So what it comes down to is any one of my own employees could have done this to me."

"Or maybe just a random firebug. I'm betting Keene's Harbor has a pyro or two," she said. "What's frustrating is that I'd like to say everyone at the fund-raiser can be dropped from the suspect list but it's too easy to make it here from the hall to say that for sure."

Matt understood frustration. He was frustrated that his night's business was literally going up in smoke. He was angry that someone had made jerking him around their new hobby. And he was furious with himself for permitting them to mess with his ability to coolly sort through the facts.

Kate briefly settled her hand against his arm. "Hey, this isn't going to go on forever. It's going to be okay."

"Now would be a good time for it to end."

"Agreed," she said. "Should we talk to the fire chief?"

"That's up next."

"Mind if I come along?"

"Not at all. A set of objective ears is good. But you should know that Norm's more about putting the fire out than any kind of investigating. That's one of the quirks of having a volunteer fire department."

"Still, if you tell him about all the other things that have happened, he'll have to see a pattern."

"You and I might, but unless you've been living through it, it's a tough pattern to see." He led her to the back of the fire truck, where Chief Norm stood talking to Clete Erikson.

"Sorry about this, Matt," Norm said as they neared.

The fire chief had been of average size in his active days as a charter fishing boat captain. Retirement had caught up with him, though. Now he was shaped like his favorite bowling ball. Still, he remained surprisingly agile.

"Thanks for getting the fire put out," Matt said.

Norm nodded. "A few of us are going to stick around awhile in case any hot spots flare up."

"Great. Will you start your arson investigation tonight or wait for first light?"

Norm looked surprised. "It's a Dumpster fire, Matt. What makes you think it's arson?"

"The fence was burning. You can't believe that the entire enclosure sparked and went up without an accelerant."

"Son, what does a Dumpster hold but trash?" Clete

asked, but gave no time for an answer. "The ember from one cigarette butt could have set it off. I'll interview your employees, but I don't see any point in rattling the whole town with talk of arson."

"The town will be talking anyway," Kate said.

The police chief turned his head. "What did you say?"

"I said that the town will be talking anyway. That's what Keene's Harbor does, especially when the topic is as high-profile as Matt and Depot Brewing. They bring more money to this town than any other five businesses combined. Failure to investigate won't make the talk go away. It will just get worse."

Clete moved a step closer to her. "Well now, little lady, I'm not sure what business any of this is of yours."

She looked up at Matt. "Little lady? Did he just call me *little lady*?"

Yeah, that had been a critical error on Clete's part, Matt thought. And Matt was happy to urge her on. If anyone could help him quickly shake loose an investigation, it was Kate. "I believe he did," Matt said.

She turned back to Clete. "I might be little and I might also be a lady, but I am *not* a little lady any more than you're the ghost of John Wayne. And even the ghost of the Duke playing a sheriff blindfolded would know this is arson. If you and Chief Norm aren't interested in investigating it, I'm sure someone is."

Clete was more puzzled than annoyed. "Didn't anyone ever tell you that you can catch more flies with honey than you can with vinegar?"

"She's right, Clete," Matt said. "If you don't step up, I'm going to have to call the county sheriff's office and bring them in. You don't want that."

There wasn't enough light to catch the look in Clete's eyes, but Matt was betting it wasn't a happy one. Somehow Kate had hit his hot button without even knowing it. Or maybe she'd sensed it. Keene's Harbor wasn't flush with money. Clete lived in fear of the town cutting back on its police coverage and using county services.

Clete stood taller, probably trying to make up for the fact that he was in civilian clothes. "Norm, if you're going to be staying, could you put crime scene tape around the Dumpster area once it's cooled down?" He turned to Matt. "Could you tell your employees to stay in the restaurant until I can interview them? Site photos and talking more to Laila will have to wait until the light of day."

"Thanks, Clete," Matt said.

He glanced at Kate, who wore a victorious smile. Their methods might vary, but Matt appreciated another person of action when he came across one. And he was appreciating Kate Appleton more by the minute.

Kate looked at Matt's profile in the dim illumination of his truck's dashboard lights. The guy was wiped out, and she couldn't blame him. He turned onto The Nutshell's winding drive, then pulled up beside her Jeep.

"Home again," he said.

She took in the silhouette of her childhood home and felt comfort ease into her bones.

"I am," she said.

That much, at least, felt very right. She smiled at the thought and the man who had triggered it.

"Did you get dinner?" she asked.

"I never made it over to the food tables."

"Why don't you come in? I don't have much outside the key food groups of chocolate and wine, but I'm sure I can pull something together."

"Thanks, but I need to get back to the brewery and make sure everything's under control, then look in on Laila. How about if I take a rain check?"

"Sure," she said, even though she felt a little disappointed. She reached for the truck's door handle. "Good night, then."

Kate was about to exit the truck when Matt spoke again. "You're not scheduled for tomorrow, are you?"

"No."

"Then I'd like you to take a road trip with me. I'll pick you up around eight."

"Where are we going?"

"A motel."

"*A what?*"

He smiled. "You heard me. We're going to a motel, among other places. But it's business. You can relax . . . for the moment."

Kate was guaranteed not to sleep at all.

EIGHT

A COUPLE MINUTES BEFORE EIGHT ON SATURDAY MORN-
ing, Matt pulled into Kate's driveway. He reached for the
closest of the two travel mugs of coffee he'd brought along.
As he took a swallow, he also took advantage of the opportunity to check out The Nutshell in the daylight. He'd
bought the mortgage on the advice of his financial advisor,
and his interest had been in the land and not the house.

Last night, when Kate had cornered Clete, she'd in-
voked the ghost of John Wayne. Matt had found it tough
not to laugh, since he'd often thought Clete purposely cul-
tivated the look and attitude. But if Matt were to talk
ghosts and The Nutshell, he'd have to say the Rat Pack,
with Frank Sinatra leading the charge, would hang out
there.

Once upon a time, this had been a top-of-the-line
cottage, but that time had passed. The Nutshell's upkeep
had to be a bear by virtue of its size, not to mention its
windy perch over Lake Michigan. Though Kate had limited Matt's indoor tour the other night, he'd guess the
house held at least six bedrooms, and probably more.

The place's white paint was pulling away from its
trim, its entry porch had begun to sag, and its silvery ce-
dar shingles were becoming gap-toothed in places. The

Nutshell had character, though. He liked that it was as quirky as its current resident.

The front door swung open, and Kate appeared. She wore dressy boots, snug jeans, a clingy red V-necked sweater, and had a huge brown leather purse slung over her shoulder. Matt slipped from behind the wheel and rounded his truck. He opened the passenger-side door for her and waited while she climbed on board.

"Was it this big last night?" she asked, clicking her seat belt into place as they pulled out of her drive.

"What?"

"Your truck. Last night is kind of a haze of stage fright, adrenaline, and punch, so my memories are fuzzy. But it's like *Land of the Giants* in here. My feet barely even reach the floor." Her smile was brief, but it still made him feel good. "So the standard question would be: Tell me, Culhane, are you compensating for something with this monster vehicle?"

He grinned. "I've never worried about compensating."

"Really?"

"Want to check?"

"I'll take your word for it," Kate said.

That was a flirtatious warning shot across her bow, she thought. She'd set it up, and he'd followed in kind. It was fun, but she didn't want it to go further just yet. She dug through her purse and pulled out a pair of oversized sunglasses.

"I probably shouldn't talk again until I've had my second coffee," she said. "Anything before that is the insomnia speaking."

"Do you really have insomnia?"

She nodded. "I'm having a little mold problem. The place is filled with negative air blowers, and there are guys coming today to remove the damage and HEPA vacuum the place."

Matt raised an eyebrow. "Mold problems can be really hard to fix. And expensive. Are you sure you don't want to bail now? I was going to raze the structure anyway."

Kate felt her jaw drop. "Excuse me— You want to destroy my family's lake house so you can build some tourist trap of a restaurant? Are you serious? I will never, ever, ever let you get your hands on my house."

"I think I pushed a button best left alone for now," Matt said. "Would you consider coffee as a peace offering?"

She reached for the mug in her cup holder. "Coffee would be a wonderful peace offering. Sorry I snapped. If I don't catch more than three hours of sleep in a row soon, I'm going to be giving Deena Bowen a run for her money in the cranky department. And it isn't just the blowers. I wasn't sleeping too well even before they arrived. All night long the house is filled with creaks and groans and whispers. At four in the morning, it sounds downright haunted. Not that I have issues or anything." She took a swallow of coffee. "But enough of my neuroses. Why not tell me where we're going besides that motel you mentioned."

"First, we've got to head to my office," he said.

"Bad news, then. We're heading in the wrong direction."

"My Traverse City office."

She turned her face his way, and he had to focus on the road not to smile at how cute she was in the big glasses.

"Okay," she said. "So you *do* have a secret life. Are you a spy? Is this one of those 'I'm going to tell you but then I have to kill you' road trips?"

Matt laughed. "You stand a better chance of being bored to death by my secret life. All the same, it's mine and I choose to keep it among certain people. Now that I'm making you one of them, no sharing this with Ella or anyone else."

"Deal," she said. "And thank you."

"For what?"

"For letting me be in the know. I've been kind of low on friendships since I moved here, and I like having one with you. It's . . ." She lifted one shoulder in a small shrug. "I don't know, really special, I guess."

It was to Matt, also, but he didn't want to make the moment sappy. He went for one more kick of caffeine before setting the mug back in its holder. "Today, among other things, I have to pull the plug on a business relationship that hasn't worked out."

"What kind of business? Is it at least something dangerous or exotic?"

He smiled at the excitement in her voice. "Sorry to disappoint, but he's another microbrewer. I gave him a rescue loan a few years back. The guy brews some great beer, and I didn't want to see him go under. But good beer isn't enough to be a success."

"Do you lend money often?"

"When I feel it's right. I wouldn't be in business today without the help I got when I started."

"That's pretty cool of you, actually."

"Don't let word get out. I like it better being viewed as the tough guy in town."

"So you have a full second life as a business investor."

"It wasn't in the plan, but accidentally, yeah."

"So why not at least tell the people at Depot what you're up to? It could save you a lot of grief."

"The more success I've had . . . at least, success from a Keene's Harbor viewpoint . . . the tougher it's become to have any privacy. And you have to remember that I'm the guy they've had stories about since I was eight years old and painted a bunch of the town dogs bright orange at the start of hunting season."

She laughed. "Makes sense to me."

"It did to me, too. Especially since I'd lost a family pet to hunters a year earlier. But a legend was born, and it's only gotten worse. I guess on one level, it's cool that everyone cares enough to watch me. But on another, it's tough to be under that level of scrutiny, even if it comes with a whole lot of love."

Kate had last been to Traverse City when she was sixteen. Back then, it had been a quaint place of cherry festivals in the summer and hot cider in the winter. Now, as she looked up Front Street, she saw it had become the home of bistros, film festivals, and Pan-Asian food. The city had grown up while she did, and apparently with fewer glitches than she'd experienced.

Matt pulled around a corner and then into a city parking lot behind a three-story redbrick building. Kate grabbed her bag and tried to find a graceful way to exit his ginormous, but apparently noncompensating, truck.

"I'm going to leave you with Ginger, my office manager, while I finish up business with Chet," he said as they headed toward the building.

"You have an office manager? How many people work for you up here?"

"Just Ginger, and I let her choose her title. So long as people do their work, I'm happy to call them Galactic Emperor or Most Royal of Personages or whatever they want."

Matt led her up to the building's metal security door and opened it. "I'm leasing the space from the yoga studio below. It's cheap rent, since it doesn't put out a fancy public face, but I don't need one of those."

They reached the third floor and Matt opened the door to a suite marked only with its number and ushered her in. Behind a desk in the moderately sized reception area sat a movie star–looking, twentysomething redhead. She

wore a red wrap dress with a plunging neckline, red lipstick that matched the dress, and just the right amount of
mascara to show off thick black eyelashes over her green
eyes.

"Kate, this is Ginger Monroe," Matt said. "And Ginger, this is Kate Appleton."

Ginger gave Kate a blatantly inquisitive look. "Hi."

Kate returned the greeting, but tried to keep her
curiosity under control.

"Is Chet here?" Matt asked Ginger.

"I sent him into your office. You might want to consider a bulletproof vest before you go in."

"That bad?"

"Oh, yeah."

Matt shot a dubious look at the closed door. "Then he
knows why he's here. I'll be out in a couple of minutes."
He paused. "Or maybe even sooner."

Kate settled into a guest chair and Ginger pulled open
a desk drawer and brought out a semi-full bag of salt-and-
vinegar potato chips. "Want some? They've got a good
bite."

"I love them, too, but I'm all about coffee at this hour,"
Kate said.

Ginger nodded. "Okay." Without pausing a beat, she
added, "So, are you Matt's new girlfriend?"

"No, I just started working for him last week."

Kate suddenly realized how much longer it felt, and
not in a bad way. No, this was more a *What did I do with
myself before all this craziness?* feeling.

"Interesting," Ginger said.

The conversation was starting to feel a little interesting to Kate, too. "So, Ginger, have you two ever dated?"

Ginger raised her eyebrows. "No! My dad would kill
him. Dad was Matt's high school football coach down in

Keene's Harbor. Matt was a big star, but that was ages ago. I was just a kid. And then Dad changed jobs and we moved up here."

"Matt was a football star? Figures."

Ginger grinned. "Doesn't it? He was hot stuff. I guess he had a full ride to Michigan State, but then messed up his knee during baseball season his senior year of high school. He lost the scholarship and ended up working around town before he took off for a couple of years. Everything turned out fine, though."

Just then the younger woman's eyes widened, giving Kate an instant of forewarning before Matt's office door slammed into the wall, and a short, heavy man whose skin color had risen to a shiny puce marched out of the office.

The purple man was sputtering so much he could barely choke out his words. "You'll pay, Culhane," he said.

Matt followed him out and remained admirably impassive. Kate wanted to learn how to do that, though she suspected she lacked the talent.

"I agree this is tough, Chet, but you know I've been more than fair," Matt said.

The older man's breathing was ragged, and he opened and closed his hands into fists. "Another six months wouldn't have killed you. Instead, you're killing me."

"You have four weeks before I'll be filing anything. Just work on those other possibilities, okay?"

Chet told Matt in graphic detail what *he* could work on, then stormed out.

Doing the right thing and doing the easy thing didn't seem to be lining up too well for Matt these days.

"I would have given Chet more time if I could have," he said to Kate, who sat next to him in the truck as they headed to his next appointment. "But I need to think about my cash reserves and my business. The slow season is coming on. It's going to hurt to take any more financial hits. I hate to be a survivalist, but it's better it's Chet's business than mine, especially when he's been in default for over a year."

"There's nothing else you could have done," she said.

"But there is. I should have pulled the plug on his financing last year. I built up expectations that I'd just keep letting this slide." He shook his head. "Big mistake."

Kate's eyes narrowed. "Does that mean you're thinking of pulling the plug on our deal? You gave me until Thanksgiving to come up with the money, and if you try to back out, I'll make Chet look like Gandhi."

Matt laughed. "You caught him at an off moment. He's not usually so purple."

"Good news there, or he'll be among the spirits pretty soon. One little vein in the brain goes *ping,* and it's all over."

Matt knew the feeling, even if he hadn't yet achieved Chet's color of purple. All the same, bringing a measure of calm and sanity into his life was now part of his game plan.

"True," Matt said. "And the good news is that no one is purple at our next stop, though Travis is pretty tatted up."

"And tatted Travis is . . ."

"The owner of Horned Owl Brewing and my newest project. Great concepts, but bad business decisions. Bart is spending today and tomorrow with him to go over his beer recipes and maybe tweak 'em where they need tweaking. Nothing too big."

He wasn't about to clue her into the other activity about to take place at Horned Owl. One that had occurred to him early this morning. Matt wasn't totally up to speed on it, but he knew that surprise was crucial. . . .

NINE

KATE FELT AS THOUGH HER FILLINGS WERE GOING TO fall out as Matt's truck slammed and rattled down a pitted gravel road in the middle of nowhere. "Are you sure this is really the road to the microbrewery?"

"Positive," Matt said. "It's also the first of three issues that have been tanking Travis's business."

Kate couldn't wait to see the other two.

"Do you think maybe you should slow down a little?"

"No way. Then we'd feel every rut in the road."

Being airborne didn't seem much better, but Kate also knew not to mess with a man on a mission.

"Hang on," Matt said, skittering around a hairpin turn. "It gets a little rough right here."

Kate's gasp was involuntary, and she wasn't real thrilled about the grin that appeared on Matt's face in response as she fought the urge to brace her feet against the dashboard. "Very Indiana Jones of you," she said. "I should have brought my bullwhip."

Matt's eyebrows raised a half inch. "Do you have a bullwhip?"

Kate smiled sweetly. Ms. Mysterious.

"Kinky," Matt said, "but I can deal."

He swerved around an unusually deep rut, barely

missing a tree. They made a hard right turn onto a narrow ribbon of a drive. All that marked it as more than a trail was a huge, sour-faced plastic owl on a post.

"Horned Owl issue number two," Matt said. "If you've got a customer ambitious enough to come back here, get a sign. Don't scare them off with a weird fake owl."

Now that they were traveling at normal speed, Kate took a look around. She imagined that the woods were lush and green in the summer. On this crisp autumn day, though, the maples were turning crimson and yellow, with the oaks not far behind. Only the scrubby jack pines still held much green.

"The scenery's a good prize for making it back this far," she said. "It's gorgeous."

The woods had thinned, and a meadow lay ahead. At the far end sat an unassuming double-wide home. To the right of that by a hundred yards was the most amazing barn Kate had ever seen. It might have been painted a traditional red, but the structure's hexagonal shape and the white cupola topping it were showstoppers. Someone had also added expanses of windows and a pergola-shaded terrace that angled off one of the back sides.

Kate blew out a whistle. "Definitely not issue number three."

"Except for the location, it's perfect." He parked next to a silver car that Kate had seen almost every day in Depot Brewing's lot. "Ready to go in?"

Kate climbed out of the truck. "First, let me play tourist."

She dug her phone from her purse and backed up until she found the perfect spot to take a picture of the barn. She liked that Matt was in the shot, too.

"Smile," she said. And even though he was laughing, she kept the picture. "This is turning into a pretty nice day."

"Hold that thought."

They walked up a stepping stone path to the micro-brewery's entrance.

Inside, a taproom of sorts had been partitioned from the work area by low walls made of silvery barn wood. Above the dividers, Kate spotted a couple of tall stainless-steel tanks back in a corner, much like the ones she'd seen at Depot Brewing. The beer-making end of the business remained a mystery to Kate. Bart Fenner, Depot's brewmaster, was notoriously protective of his portion of the domain. For all that Kate knew, fairies and elves made the beer.

Matt scanned the room. "Travis? You guys back there?"

"Yeah, hang on."

Travis emerged, and Horned Owl's issue number three was obvious. Kate doubted that Travis meant to be scary, but the nose and eyebrow piercings and a squinty-eyed stare did the job. The full-sleeve tattoo on his right arm actually served as a happy distraction. He appeared to be younger than Matt, but that didn't mean he wasn't old enough to have done some hard time.

"Travis, this is Kate, my newest employee. Kate, this is Travis Holby, owner of Horned Owl Brewing."

Travis fixed his stare on Kate. "What's Culhane got on you that you ended up working for him?"

Kate laughed. "It's more what I have on him."

Travis smiled, and the tough guy aura disappeared. Kate noticed for the first time that once you looked past the piercings, he had a true baby face, complete with pudgy cheeks.

"This is a beautiful place you have here," she said.

"Thanks. I've busted my a—, uh, back, putting it together. Why don't you have a seat?" Travis gestured to one of the three rustic-looking tables with low stools that served as seating in the taproom. "Hungry? Thirsty? Can I get you anything?"

Kate took the offered seat, but turned down food and drink.

"Hey, Bart," Matt called. "Why don't you come out here for a minute, too?"

Bart entered the taproom, and Kate thought there was no way she'd ever seen him at Depot Brewing. He wasn't the sort of guy a woman forgot. In fact, he nearly gave Culhane a run for the money in the looks department. But where Culhane was a rugged kind of hot, Bart had the exotic thing going. Looking at him was like taking a sexy trip to the South Pacific. He was tall and seriously muscled, with dark skin, soulful brown eyes, and black hair.

"I heard you sing last night," Bart said. "You're really good."

"Thanks," she said. "It had been a long time since I sang in public like that."

Matt smiled at her and her heart skipped a beat. The smile was intimate, as though they were the only ones in the room. She couldn't help fantasizing just a little about what she might do to enhance the moment if it wasn't for Bart and Travis's presence.

Bart sat down next to Travis but turned his body toward Kate. "I hear you have some issues with beer."

"It's more like beer has issues with me."

"When was the last time you tried it?"

"When I was in college."

Bart smiled, showing even white teeth. "So it's safe to say that it's been a couple of years?"

"Absolutely."

"What kind of beer?"

Kate shrugged. "I don't know. What kind do they typically serve in fraternity basements out of red plastic cups?" *Why was this beginning to feel like she was being set up?* "I try not to think of that night. But even though the details are fuzzy, the lasting impression is that it wasn't good."

Travis shook his head. "You know, you seem like the open-minded type. You put up with Culhane, you've stopped staring at my piercings, and yet you're judging all beer based on one bad, unfortunate game of beer pong."

"Believe me, I'd do the same with a rattlesnake, too."

Bart laughed. "It can't have been that bad."

"Okay, no, because I'm still alive." Kate glanced at each of them. "This is some sort of non-beer-drinker intervention, isn't it?"

Nobody answered, but the light of hope continued to shine in their eyes.

"Come on, Kate, what you drank was goat pi—, uh, urine, compared to what we make," Travis said. "This is craft beer, the nectar of the gods."

"Nectar?"

"Try my peach beer," he said.

The hair on her arms rose. "I'm not so sure about that."

"No peach, then, but at least try something while you're here."

She was, to some degree, a captive audience. And not wholly unwilling, either. It *had* been a lot of years, and there remained the remote possibility that the whole beer incident had grown in her mind. Maybe it hadn't been that truly awful.

"And consider this," Matt said. "I can't move you to the front of the house until you've learned to speak beer. So unless you and Hobart really do want to establish an exclusive relationship, you should give this a shot."

Kate had come to see the downside to dishwashing. Running Hobart meant standing at Hobart. To be a good secret spy, she needed more mobility.

"Okay. Let's do this thing." She looked across the table at Matt's co-conspirators. "I'm assuming you already have this arranged."

"It's going to be an experience to be savored," Bart said as Travis left the table.

Kate looked doubtful. "On my planet, that would be lounging in a Jacuzzi with a glass of wine and a good book." She could feel Culhane go still next to her, and she thought she should probably stop mentioning anything even remotely involving nakedness. Her imagination had already tossed the book and substituted her boss stripping down and making the tub blissfully crowded.

Matt gently touched Kate's hand. "All beer is made of four basic ingredients."

She drew on her last memory of beer. "Is skunk spray one of them, because that would explain the smell."

"Not even close. We're talking water, barley, hops, and yeast."

Travis returned to the table with a cooler bearing the Depot Brewing steam locomotive logo and a plastic cup. He set the cup in front of Kate and then got busy in the cooler.

"Those are hops," Bart said.

She squinted into the cup. "It looks like rabbit food."

"Check out the scent."

Kate took a whiff and immediately regretted it. The hops smelled like a mix of cheap perfume, soggy dog, and grass blades. She wanted to sneeze, and possibly gag, but could do neither with any measure of diplomacy. Instead, she rubbed the tip of her nose and tried to blink back the extra moisture in her eyes.

Matt fought back a grin. "I get the feeling you're not fond of hops."

Travis lined up three smaller cups. Each was filled

with the same grain, but of varying shades. "This is all barley," he said.

"Barley is good. My grandmother made soup from barley."

Matt smiled at her, and she began to relax again.

"Note the lighter and darker colors," Bart said. "Different degrees of roasting will add varying aspects to the beer. When we boil up the wort—"

"The what?" she asked.

"The wort."

"That sounds a little creepy," Kate said. "Like something on a witch's nose."

Culhane laughed. "That's what the boiled mix of barley, hops, and water is called. Brewers make wort. After that's done, the yeast will make the beer."

That, too, brought images to Kate's mind she would have been happy to skip. "Before I get too much scary input, how about if we move along to the tasting?"

Bart reached into the cooler, brought out a bottle of beer, and set a small glass in front of Kate. It was taller and bigger than a shot glass, but not by much. If this was all she had to drink, she just might survive.

Bart handed her the bottle. "This is Dog Day Afternoon. It was one of Matt's first beers and is still one of the brewery's most popular."

Kate smiled at the label's black pen-and-ink drawing of a goofy hound who was trying to look fierce. "That's the same dog in the mosaic out front of the brewery."

"Chuck's our mascot, even though Matt doesn't bring him around much. He's also Matt's longest lasting relationship . . . so far."

Both Bart and Travis were giving Kate suggestive grins as Travis took the bottle from her and poured for her. Kate focused on the tabletop.

"This is a summer brew," Matt said. "Technically, it's

a Kölsch style beer, which you'll need to know when you're on the floor. But really, just think about a beach day when you're ready for some shade and a cool drink."

Kate lifted the glass and tentatively sniffed its contents. She steeled herself. One sip from a Barbie-sized glass couldn't do all that much damage, could it?

"Come on, you can do it," Travis said.

She took a sip, expecting to hate it, but she didn't. In fact, she went for a slightly bolder sip.

"Not half bad," she said. "It's bubbly like soda but not icky sweet."

Matt grinned, obviously proud but trying to keep it under wraps. "It's a good starting point. Low in hops and lower in alcohol than some of the others you'll be trying. Ready to move on?"

"Almost." Kate drained the sample glass. "An unpretentious beer, lightly floral, and of earthy peasant stock."

"You joke, but beer tastings are a big part of how our business has grown," Matt said. "A little less attitude than some wine events, but we have food pairings and tasting notes, too."

"Really?"

"It makes sense if you think about it," Matt said. "What was your first impulse when Travis poured you that sample?"

"To smell it."

"Exactly," Bart said. "Let's try an IPA on her for bouquet."

"IPA?" Kate echoed.

Bart handed her another bottle. This one's label was nearly psychedelic and read Goa for the Gusto.

"India Pale Ale," Bart said. "So called because when the British Empire was at its peak, British ale had to travel a long way to get to Britons. Lots of hops were added to each barrel as a preservative, and the product ended up way different than it started out. It became part of beer history."

Kate handed the bottle back to Travis, who poured her a sample. She lifted her mini-glass and smelled the ale.

"Wow! It smells almost like a sauvignon blanc . . . all citrus." She drew in deeper. "Like grapefruit, and maybe a little lemon?"

Matt nodded his approval. "Exactly. Like all IPAs."

Emboldened by the so-not-beer aroma, Kate downed half the sample in one swallow, then had to fight not to gag it back up.

"Issues?" Travis asked.

Kate took several deep breaths. "Totally not my style. It tastes nothing like it smells."

She really could have used a food pairing. Something smothered in hot sauce to wipe out the flavors lingering in her mouth would have been dandy.

"For a lot of people, an IPA is an acquired taste," Matt said.

Travis rose and grabbed an empty pitcher from behind his pouring counter.

"Dump," he said.

Kate tipped out the last bit of beer in her glass. "Thank you."

"Technically, hops add both dryness and bitterness," Matt said.

"The bitterness I got. How about a little Dog Day to cleanse my palate?"

Travis gave her a refill. She downed it, then shuddered as the last memory of the Goa left her body.

Matt grabbed another sampling glass and set another bottle on the table. "Dragonfly Amber Ale. Time to move one step darker in the ales."

"So long as you leave the Chuck beer in easy reaching distance, I'm game," Kate said.

"Dragonfly Amber is the first of my beers to place in judging at the Great American Beerfest," Matt said.

"What's Beerfest?" Kate asked.

Travis's face was heavy with awe. "It's like the Olympics," he said.

Matt poured Kate a sample. "Caramel malted barley, smooth finish, and dry hopped to eliminate bitterness while keeping the dryness in place."

Kate tried a sip and found she had no problem at all with the Dragonfly. "Okay, now *this is* the nectar of the gods," she said.

Travis pumped his fist. "Another beer hater bites the dust."

They moved on to stouts and porters, and Kate loved them all. Clearly, she had misremembered her earlier beer encounter.

Once the guys had finished up with the tasting, they started discussing Travis's recipes. Kate tried to follow the conversation, except she didn't have the background to know whether his autumn pumpkin ale was "cutting edge," as Travis claimed, or "too out there to turn a profit," as Matt contended.

"Is it getting warm in here?" Kate asked.

The men paused in their conversation.

"Not that I've noticed," Matt said.

"Okay. Carry on."

Kate wandered over to the small tasting bar and began leafing through Travis's beer notes and advertising materials. The editor in her quickly returned.

"Does anyone have a pen?" she asked.

All she received in response were blank stares. They had moved on to addressing the level of nutmeg in Travis's brew. No big deal. Her purse, which always held a fistful of pens, was in the truck.

When she returned, she asked the guys, "Mind if I grab another Dog Day?"

"Go for it," Matt said. "We shouldn't be that much longer, though."

She pulled a beer from the cooler and went back to flyspecking Travis's notes. She'd finished her first mini-glass and was pouring her second when Matt joined her at the bar.

"Sorry this is taking so long," he said. "I need to take advantage of the time I can be up here. Travis isn't hot on listening to Bart, so I have to be the enforcer."

"No problem." She slid Travis's brochures closer to Matt. "I've been keeping myself busy. I cleaned up the copy and kicked up the language."

Matt gave her a funny look. "Your face is kind of red. Are you okay?"

"Yes."

Or at least she thought she was. Kate touched a hand to her cheek. She *was* hot. Like a core-temperature-reaching-lethal-range kind of hot.

"I think I'll step outside for a second," she said.

Whatever Matt had to say in return was left in the dust as she bolted toward the door. Once outside, she climbed into Matt's truck and flipped open the passenger's vanity mirror.

"Oh, man!"

The whole beer issue was coming back to her now. That youthful flirtation had ended not because she'd drunk too much and made herself sick, but because beer was her Kryptonite, something akin to severe lactose intolerance.

She wasn't red. She was Chet-colored.

Kate sat back and fanned her face. She knew what was

...es turned back on this week. Sorry there wasn't much hot water."

"It was perfect."

Actually, it had taken a while before she'd felt safe to go near the shower. First had come the belching with enough gusto to win a frat boys' contest. From her side of the bathroom door, she'd heard Matt saying that he'd be taking off for a while. Kate had figured he'd been engaging in chivalry or self-preservation. Either way, he'd missed the worst of the episode.

"I've brought you some stuff I thought you might be ble to use," he called.

She opened the bathroom door enough to reach out r arm and grab a plastic sack. "Thanks. That was re-y nice of you."

Though, again, it still could have been self-servation. Keene's Harbor remained over an hour ay, and her stomach still sounded demonically pos-

coming next. Her internal temperature would kick up even higher, her stomach would begin to ache, and finally she'd emit a rumbling last heard at Mount St. Helens. She had an hour and more in the truck with Matt on the way back to Keene's Harbor. No way could she pretend for that length of time that she had no idea where those noises might be coming from.

Damn.

Kate hopped from the truck to catch the October wind. If she could cut the heat, maybe she could kill the whole vicious cycle.

"Calm thoughts, cool thoughts," she coached herself as she headed upwind. "You can beat this."

Once she'd made the outer edge of Horned Owl's parking area, she pushed up her long sleeves and held out her arms for optimal wind exposure, slowly rotating like a deranged wind turbine. Still, she could feel sweat collecting between her breasts.

"I am so screwed."

She shot a look at the brewery's door. Thank heaven all was quiet and still. The guys could talk while she cooled. She returned to the truck and used the open passenger door as shield.

Kate pulled her arms from the sweater's sleeves. Inside the sweater's protection, she reached back and unhooked her bra. Those miserable years of middle school gym class had served a purpose, after all. She could still remove her underwear without showing a square inch of skin.

One hot-pink bra with black lace overlay was history in three seconds. Kate chucked it onto the truck's seat, then jammed her arms back through her sleeves.

"Please, please, please," she murmured. Just who outside of her own rebelling body Kate was begging, she didn't know.

Her digestive system emitted a groan that silenced the chickadees up in the trees. Temptation grew. One polite burp that no one other than her feathered friends would hear might fix the whole issue. But then she flashed back to her last beer episode. She'd been sucked in by that whole "one burp" theory, and the aftermath hadn't been pretty.

She pulled on her sweater's neckline until she got some good air between herself and the knit fabric. Then she took the sweater's bottom, looped it up through the top, and drew it back down. The rig held, even though her posture made a gargoyle look good. She turned and just about smacked into Matt.

"How long have you been standing there?" she asked.

"Long enough," he said. "Do I even want to know?"

"Probably not."

"You've been gone awhile," he said. "Bart and Travis wanted me to come out and check on you."

Which was a lie. They were negotiating the terms of a winner-takes-all arm-wrestling match over the pumpkin brew recipe. A rabid fox dropped into the middle of the room wouldn't have distracted them.

"As you can see, I'm kind of having a problem."

"Either that or you're into some voodoo ritual. What's up with your face, though?"

"My face?" Kate's voice rose an octave in alarm. "What's wrong with my face?"

"You've gone from red to spotty. Is it possible that you have an allergy to something in beer?"

She clamped her hand over her mouth in what he would have said was an expression of shock, except for the way her chest and shoulders heaved.

"You're not going to hurl, are you?" he asked.

Hand still over mouth, she shook her head no.

And even if [...]
wins. Got it?"

"Dude, that is so not fair," Travis said.

"When you can pay me back, we'll talk about fair. [...] til then, it's all about leverage."

Bart slammed Travis's hand to the tabletop, win[...] the match and illustrating Matt's point.

"Just like that," he said.

Back outside, Matt found Kate waiting for hi[...] truck. As he climbed into his seat, a pink-and-b[...] went flying into the back. He'd witnessed a bra[...] fore, but not in these circumstances.

"I think it's the hops," he said rather than [...] on the projectile. "I've seen it happen to peopl[...] the redness you started out with, at least—ju[...] bad."

Kate snorted, or maybe wheezed. "Great. [...] tombstone. Kate Appleton. Went to hell in a [...]

sessed. Kate riffled through the bag. Antihistamines, as promised, plus antacids.

So much for Matt Culhane ever being tempted by her again, she thought. She was gross—inside and outside. Arms wrapped around her bloated midsection, she regarded her spotty reflection in the bathroom mirror. This was what she wanted, right? Not to have to worry about any hot and messy sexual entanglement that took place outside the privacy of her imagination. Now that she faced that reality, the answer came back an edgy maybe not.

"Can I bring you anything else?" Matt called.

"No, thanks."

After antacids, what was left?

Matt believed in choosing his moments and in letting others choose theirs. When Kate decided to stick on her bug glasses and pretend to sleep most of the way back to Keene's Harbor, he'd respected that choice.

"Hey," he said when she finally stirred.

"Hi."

"Feeling any better?"

"Yes."

"Are you up to having a conversation longer than one syllable?"

"No," Kate said.

"All the same, can I ask you something? Did that happen to you the last time you drank beer?"

She didn't answer immediately. "Kind of, I think. I mean, I sort of recalled discomfort, but it wasn't this bad."

"In that case, I'm sorry. I never would have asked you to try it if I'd known this was what happened to you."

"My fault. Even with that vague memory, I shouldn't have risked it, except . . ."

"Except what?"

"Except I also did it because *I* wanted to, and because it seemed important to you. I mean, this is what you do. You've got great reason to be proud of all you've accomplished. Then, here I come and turn up my nose. I wanted to be . . . I don't know . . ."

"Nice?"

She sighed. "Yes, nice. You deserve that."

"So do you, Kate."

"I know, but it's been so long. It's like I can hardly recognize it. That long without nice in your life . . . and I don't mean that I was abused or anything . . . it was just the absence of nice. But, anyway, you forget how it feels."

He didn't know where she'd been, other than geographically, before she'd landed in Keene's Harbor. All he knew was that he liked it when she was happy.

"Okay," he said. "So, nice it is. And I'm moving you to the taproom on Monday. I need to have you someplace where you can keep an eye on Jerry when I'm not there. You were right. He takes off, and I don't know what he's up to. And Laila's going to be out a minimum of this next week with her ankle sprain."

"I can do that," she said.

TEN

EARLY MONDAY MORNING, KATE PULLED INTO DEPOT Brewing's parking lot. She was exactly on time for the training session Matt wanted to get in before the rest of the staff arrived. Matt, however, was not. With not a heck of a lot else to do, Kate exited her Jeep and meandered toward the building's front entry. She smiled down at the mosaic of Chuck and allowed herself a moment of yearning for Stella. She missed her dog every single day.

Pushing doggie thoughts from her mind, she glanced into the Depot's interior through the narrow window to the right of the front door. The large potted tree in the entry lay on its side. Kate moved closer and peered into the lobby. Opposite the tree, the low table that usually held brochures had been upended. She could have bought one tipped thing as an accident, but not both.

Running on sheer instinct, she pulled on the door's large bronze handle. The door swung outward. And because she was terminally curious, she stepped inside.

"Hello?" She paused to bring the tree upright. "Anyone here?"

Apparently not. She set the table on its feet, scooped up the brochures and replaced them. She also picked up a bit of string or something that the cleaning person must have missed. She tucked that into the front pocket of her khakis, along with a crumpled cocktail napkin. If she was going to tidy up, she might as well do it properly.

As she left the entry, Kate was greeted by a stale beer aroma she'd last smelled in Bagger's Tavern. Except unlike Bagger's, this place was all clean slate, wood, and ceramic tile. There was no obnoxiously absorbent carpet to be found.

Kate followed her nose to the taproom.

"This is *so* not good."

Every table and chair had been flipped. Beer was running, but with no pitcher or pilsner glass to catch the brew. She sprinted behind the bar and realized that not only had the taps been left running but every keg had been shot full of holes. A note had been spray painted on the mirror behind the bar in giant red letters: *You're Next.*

One foot hit where the rubber mats should have been, but weren't. Momentum carried her forward. The wet floor brought her feet out from beneath her. And then she went down. Hard.

Kate wasn't the most predictable woman on Earth. Still, Matt felt pretty sure if her Jeep was in the lot, she couldn't be too far away.

"Kate?" he called before he unlocked the brewery's employee door.

No answer. Odd, he thought. She wasn't in her Jeep, she wasn't waiting at the door, and she hadn't answered his call. He was hit with a shot of protective male concern. He walked from the kitchen down the short hall, being drawn to a sound he'd caught plenty before, but never at this hour. A beer tap was spitting, then blowing. He hustled to the taproom and stopped dead at the bar's back side.

"What the—"

Kate sat propped on her elbows, feet splayed out in front of her.

She looked up at him. "It's a little swampy back here."

"Are you okay?" he asked.

"Everything but my tailbone and dignity. I was just working my way back to my feet."

"Let me help you."

Matt scooped her up and held her tight to his body. He reached around her with his free arm and pushed each of the eight beer taps back into their closed positions. The act was a formality, since all the barrels were now drained. No wonder Kate had gone down. The keg system's drains couldn't handle the volume, and that floor was damn slick.

"You're soaked," he said.

"Half of me, at least."

He grabbed a clean bar towel from the stack on the counter and began to mop her off. He was somewhere in the vicinity of her backside when she took the towel from him.

"I think I can handle it from here," she said.

"Sorry," he said, but not with a whole lot of repentance.

She smiled. "So I see. You might want to grab a towel for yourself now, too."

"I've smelled like beer before," he said, but wiped his hands just the same. After he tossed the towel back to the counter, he gestured at the floor. "Sorry about this."

Kate gestured toward the vandalized mirror. "The note is what's really freaked me out. Is this the first time the saboteur's ever targeted you personally?"

Matt shrugged. "Yeah. This is sort of new."

"Well, personally, I can't wait to have a chat with the jerk who did this," Kate said. "But right now, I'm wet and gross-smelling. I'd like to go home and change before we start my training."

"No training today," Matt said. "We'll start fresh to-morrow."

"I don't want to lose a day over a bruised butt. How about if I go home and get cleaned up? I'll come back at lunchtime and observe for the afternoon. It's not going to do me or you any good to have me sit home."

"True," he said. "Are you okay to drive?"

"Yes. I'll take some extra towels so I don't soak my seat."

Once he had Kate safely to her Jeep and on her way, Matt pulled out his cell phone and called in the law. Ten minutes later, just as he'd finished mopping the spilled beer, Lizzie arrived.

Lizzie surveyed the taproom. "Someone sure was busy."

She set her clipboard down and pulled a digital camera from her uniform pocket. "I'm going to take a few pics."

"No problem."

"So tell me what you know," she said between shots.

Matt looked at the messed-up room and felt his frustration surge.

"Kate and I were going to meet here at seven-thirty. She got here first, found the front door unlocked, and the mess inside. Beer was free-pouring in here. She went behind the bar to catch the taps and fell. The mats were still rolled from the floor mopping last night, and the back of the bar had standing beer."

Lizzie pocketed the camera and picked up her clipboard. "The front door is usually locked, right?"

"Yes, unless someone screws up in a major way."

"Who has keys?"

Matt righted a café table. "Jerry, Bart, Laila, and I. No one else that I'm aware of. I closed last night, and I know for sure I locked that door, which means someone else has a copy."

"Or Jerry, Bart, or Laila were here just a little while ago," she said as she jotted notes.

"Laila's down with an ankle sprain from Friday night, so she's out. You can check with Bart and Jerry, but neither of them had reason to be here. Though Jerry isn't exactly up for employee of the month at the moment."

"What's up with Jerry?"

Matt picked up a chair. "I've been told that he's been leaving work when I'm not around. It could mean something, or it could mean nothing at all."

"Told by who?" Lizzie asked.

"Kate. She'll be back here at lunchtime if you want to talk to her. She's pretty sharp. I trust her observations."

"Okay, but why didn't someone else on staff tell you about Jerry before this?"

Matt shrugged. "I don't know for sure, but most everyone has been around for a long time. This place is family, and just like we did when we were kids, these guys tend to cover for one another. Which is why I don't want to believe that Jerry would sabotage the bar. We've been friends for too long."

"You don't have any real enemies, Matt," Lizzie said. "No matter who did this, it's going to be bad news, once we find out."

All the same, Matt wanted it done.

Lunch rush had arrived, and Kate was settled in at the taproom bar. She was one in a long line of females, most of whom were watching Matt pour beer as though he were making gold from lead.

Really, what was the big deal with beer pouring? And how had the jungle drums gotten word out so quickly that Matt was behind the bar? Kate figured they must have a calling tree or something.

"Just water for me, Matt, and a veggie quesadilla. Do

you think you could make that with whole wheat torti-
llas and goat cheese?" asked a dark-haired female three
women down.

"How about organic carrot juice?" asked the girl next
to her. "Do you have any of that, Matt?"

He answered each of their questions in the negative,
but with a style Kate envied. The next time around the re-
birth wheel (if the reincarnationists were right), she hoped
for a dollop of that charm. If she'd had to tell those women
no, they'd be howling for the manager. Or Matt. Because
he was all they wanted, anyway.

Kate took a sip of her iced tea and paged through the
microbrewery's training manual. The chart of which
glass to use with which beer was proving a little com-
plex for her current attention span. She never would have
thought that beer and a snifter could go together, but that
weird combo was the least of her issues.

Kate's tailbone had begun to ache, and her pride still
stung. Before she'd showered and returned to work, she'd
retrieved the crumpled white cocktail napkin and the
short bit of thin, braided string she'd picked up from
the floor and stuck into her pocket. Those two items
were the only clues she had. Until she was sure they
wouldn't trigger some sort of *aha!* moment, they would
rest in her dresser's top drawer.

"Kate, right?" said a voice from behind her.

Kate looked over her shoulder.

"I'm Liz Culhane, but everyone calls me Lizzie," the
woman said. "I'm also Matt's sister."

Kate smiled. "Right. I saw you talking to Matt the
night of the karaoke contest."

"I was a little more casually dressed then." Lizzie nodded to her police officer's uniform. "Mind if I join you?"

"Not at all."

Lizzie took the stool next to Kate. "It's nice to finally meet you."

"Finally?"

"My brother mentioned you the other night at dinner."

"Really?" Kate had tried to sound cool. She wasn't so sure she'd pulled it off.

"Yeah, in a Matt sort of way. Not with a whole lot of detail."

"Oh." Kate glanced at Matt. Though he was pouring a pitcher of beer, she could tell he was listening.

"And I also know you took a spill this morning," Lizzie said.

"I did, but I'm okay." Kate noted the other woman's clipboard. "I take it we're talking officially rather than personally?"

Lizzie smiled. "A little of both, I think."

Matt greeted his sister and set a glass of ice water on a coaster in front of her, then moved on to suggest items actually on the menu to the dark-haired woman, whose name was apparently Lana.

"On the official front, I'd like to ask you a couple of questions," Lizzie said to Kate.

"No problem."

"Matt said you got here before him. Was there anybody else around or leaving the Depot area when you arrived?"

"The last person I saw was Junior Greinwold walking down Keene Avenue with Harley Bagger. Otherwise, no one, which I'm coming to understand is pretty common this time of year."

Lizzie nodded. "It's quiet, which makes something like what's happened around here really stand out. And what frustrates me is that this building is like fingerprint soup. Even though it's the cleanest restaurant I've ever seen, it's still a public place. People are in and out all day long. Lifting prints would be pointless."

Kate nodded in agreement. "You know it's been more than the Dumpster fire and the vandalism, right?"

"Matt told me about some other events . . . flat tires, stolen supplies, and the open walk-in cooler."

"Plus the iffy Depot beer at Bagger's, though I have no idea if that was actually related. It's how I landed here, though. Harley fired me, and Matt hired me."

"Really? I thought he'd hired you because you two are involved."

A redhead one seat down from Lizzie aimed a surprised look Kate's way. Kate ignored it and focused on Matt's multitasking skills.

"How does he do that?" Kate asked Lizzie.

"ADD," she replied. "Mom always said Matt was either going to spend his life with a million tasks half done or learn to run the world." Her smile, so similar to her brother's, held a ton of pride. "It looks like he's taken the world-running route."

And he looked damn fine while doing it, too.

"Okay," Lizzie said. "One last official question for you. I know it's unlikely, since you haven't been back in Keene's Harbor very long, but is there anyone here who could have a grudge against you? Is it possible that yesterday's incident wasn't aimed at Matt at all?"

"From what Matt has told me, no one other than Jerry knew that Matt and I were going to be in early. I'm not tops on Jerry's list, but he wouldn't endanger his job to get rid of me. Beyond that, I've kind of been on the fringes of things since I came to town. Nobody much knows me. I don't think I've even had the opportunity to tick anyone off besides Deena Bowen, and I get the sense that it's not personal in her case. She's angry at the world."

"You've got that one half right. She might be ticked

off at the world, but she saves a lot of her ammo for Matt. I think after Friday night, you could have moved into target range."

"Do you mean by singing in the karaoke competition? That doesn't make sense."

"It does. I saw the way Matt was looking at you while you sang," Lizzie said. "And if I saw it from the side of the stage, guaranteed Deena saw it from backstage."

Kate glanced down the bar, where Lana was stroking the bar's laminated surface while talking to Matt.

She rolled her eyes at Lizzie. "Paging Captain Oblivious."

Lizzie followed Kate's line of vision. "It's always been like that for him. The less he pays attention, the more blatant they become. Growing up with him in the house and the high school versions of Lana at the door was weirdly entertaining. If nothing else, it gave me a good perspective on how I didn't want to be around boys."

"No doubt."

"Hey," Lizzie said. "This is kind of spur of the moment, but would you like to come have dinner at my parents' with me tomorrow? It's Spaghetti Tuesday, which means it's a family tradition that we drag along friends. My mom makes a salad and a huge pot of spaghetti. If it all gets eaten, great. If not, my sisters and I have leftovers to take home."

"What about Matt?" Kate asked, and just as she did, he came to stand in front of them.

"Matt's our backwoods recluse when he's not at work. He never comes to Spaghetti Tuesday."

Matt looked at Kate. "Contrary to what my sister says, I'm not a hermit. I'd actually been planning on spaghetti night. How about if I pick you up?"

Kate put her hand on the smooth bar surface and quickly pulled it back. "Sure."

"Great. I'll be there at six."

"See?" Lizzie said to him. "You're dating!"

A gasp rose along the girls' all-star admiration line, then all eyes turned to scrutinize Kate. In the space of thirty seconds, she'd gone from being unknown to notorious. But for spaghetti, family, and time with Matt Culhane, she'd deal. And happily, too.

Just before five that evening, Kate walked into the post office. She smiled at the sweeping stairway to nowhere, created when the building's second floor had been roped off due to declining town population. Despite the passage of time, the interior of the ornate sandstone and yellow brick building was like a trip back to the early 1900s. Or maybe just to high school, considering the way Deena Bowen was giving Kate the stink-eye as she approached.

Deena stepped away from the wall of brass and glass–fronted post office boxes.

"Hey," she said.

Kate had never heard that one syllable delivered with more crankiness.

"I hear you're going out with Matt," Deena said.

Kate wasn't going to get into the technical aspects of whether a family spaghetti dinner qualified as a date. She worked up what she hoped was a noncommittal shrug and moved on to her mailbox.

"He'll dump you. Just wait and see," Deena called after her.

Kate didn't plan to get to the dating point, let alone the dumping point. She let the comment roll off and turned her attention to the accumulation of mail in The Nutshell's box.

"Junk, bill . . . more junk," she said as she pulled items from the tight space. "And . . . trouble."

Her mother's custom periwinkle linen stationery was

unmistakable, as was her perfect cursive script—written with a black ink fountain pen, of course. So long as the letter wasn't directed to her, Kate found it cool that her mom kept up the dying art of handwritten correspondence. But when *Ms. Katherine Appleton* appeared on the address line, the envelope was often stuffed with ego-crushers. Not that Kate thought her mom meant to do that, but the end result remained the same.

Kate closed the box and took her load to the counter behind her for sorting. She dropped the catalogues filled with goods she couldn't afford into the recycling bin, tucked the electric bill into her purse, and opened her mom's letter. In the past, many of Mom's messages were like bikini waxes: best finished quickly.

The first few lines were about the weather and her mother's golf game. Then Mom offered a little chitchat about Kate's brother and sister and their respective brilliant toddler offspring, which led into the true purpose of the letter.

As I dream of Ivy League educations for my grandchildren, her mother wrote, *I can't help but feel a moment's sorrow that you didn't follow a more financially secure path. A business degree would have allowed for far more stability than a degree in the arts. It's a different world than when I was your age, Kate.*

"Doing what? Accounting?" Kate said to herself. She was fine with basic addition and subtracting, especially if she had a calculator. Start placing numbers in labeled columns, though, and she was a lost cause.

Kate had chosen the small liberal arts college her mom had attended, and it had been a good fit. She figured the love of history and art was something in her genes, something that she had inherited from her mother, but her mother might be right about changing times. Kate admitted to herself that she was struggling career-wise.

Ella joined Kate at the counter. "I've come to offer you safe passage." She hitched her thumb at Deena. "She seems to be lurking."

"No biggie. I'm getting pretty good with the end run when it comes to Deena, but I'm still not so good with this stuff."

Ella smiled and tapped the letter, which lay on the counter, just begging to be read to the very end. "Pretty handwriting, but I'm guessing it's not from a great-aunt leaving you a fortune?"

"It's from my mother, offering her perspective on where I went wrong. It seems I should have gotten a business degree in college."

Ella shook her head. "But you hate numbers."

"You know that, and I know that, but Mom considers it a trifle in the Appleton scheme for world domination."

"And yet you read on."

"Yes. Because my mom is probably right."

Ella pulled the letter from the counter.

Kate made a grab for it. "Hey!"

Ella held the letter in the air above Kate's shorter grasp.

"Seriously," Ella said. "I'm taking custody of this. I've known you since we were kids. That means I also know how good you are at beating yourself up whenever your mother makes a comment, no matter how well intended. What constructive thing would come from finishing this letter right now?"

"I could learn something."

Ella handed her the letter. "Learn something later. Put off reading the rest of the letter and come with me for loaded nachos at Bagger's. It'll be just like the old days. We can pig out, then go home and sleep."

Kate stuck the letter in her purse. "So long as I get extra sour cream and guacamole, it's a deal," Kate said.

ELEVEN

MATT WASN'T WHOLLY ANTI-TRADITION. FOR EXAMPLE, he got a real kick out of Christmas, especially now that Maura had given him twin nieces to spoil and had another baby on the way. Thanksgiving was a winner, too, since his dad and he had a turkey hunting contest each year. Spaghetti Tuesdays, however, had to die.

The rite had started in junior high, and he'd always been on the losing side. Even when he was backed up by half the football team, they were no match for his sharp-witted sisters. Over the years, Matt had developed empathy for those poor, wild Thanksgiving birds looking down the barrel of a shotgun. It had been a while since he'd attended Spaghetti Tuesday, but he had no delusions. His sisters would cut him no slack. And heaven help Kate if she wasn't on her toes. His sisters weren't mean, but they were mercilessly honest.

"Let me know the second you start feeling tired, and I'll get you out of here," he said to Kate as they approached the house.

"I appreciate the sentiment, but we're not even inside yet."

"The offer still stands."

She laughed. "Come on, Matt. How bad can it be?"

"It all depends on whether you're the diner or the main course."

They reached the porch, and Matt held the door open for Kate. The sounds of laughter and conversation rolled from the back of the house, along with the scents of garlic and spices from his mom's amazing spaghetti sauce.

Kate ran a hand over the oak banister that had been scratched and worn by generations of tough Culhane kids. "This house is awesome," Kate said.

"It is." Matt ushered her past the entry, through the living room and into the dining room, where everyone always tended to gather.

All eyes turned their way. Matt could feel Kate hesitate. He didn't blame her. His sisters were quite the crew.

"Everyone, this is Kate. Kate, this is . . . everyone."

His mother laughed and approached them. "Matthew. Have you lost all your manners?"

Matt gave his mom a hug. "I just didn't want Kate to feel like there's a quiz at the end of the introductions."

Matt's mom smelled of the rich, flowery perfume she'd worn for as long as he could remember. She looked great, too. Her silver-threaded dark hair had been twisted into a knot, and while her khakis and blue sweater were standard mom-clothes, she wore them with flair.

She held out a hand to Kate. "I'm Matt's mother, Mary, and you're Kate Appleton. I remember you as a youngster. You were such a cute little thing with all those blond ringlets!"

Kate shook his mom's hand. "It's a pleasure to meet you, Mrs. Culhane."

"Please, call me Mary."

"Okay." Kate handed Matt's mom the shiny gift bag she'd been tightly gripping. "I brought a little something. It's not much, but my mother taught me never to arrive with empty hands."

His mom pulled a bottle of Chianti from the bag and laughed. "This is exactly what Barb would have brought, too."

Kate's eyes widened. "You know my mother?"

"Of course. It's been years since we've had the opportunity to spend any real time together, though. Back before we all got too busy with children and life, there was a group of us that would get together at Bagger's now and then during the summer." She smiled. "In fact, I recall one night when your mother and I had a contest to see who could get the most tips while dancing on tabletops."

Kate was dumbfounded. "My mom? At Bagger's?"

Matt's mom nodded. "Harley's place was very different in those days. It was the trendy spot to go, like Matt's is today." She gave Matt's arm a little pat.

Matt liked that his mom was proud of him. He was proud of her, too. "Are you thirsty, Kate?" he asked.

His mom eased into hostess mode. "We have water, milk, soft drinks, coffee, tea, wine—and Patrick, my husband—he's out back with the men—mixes a mean dirty martini."

"Thanks for the offer, but a soft drink would be perfect."

"I'll be right back. Matt, introduce your sisters before the other guests arrive and it gets too confusing." Matt's mom gave Kate a sunny smile. "You know, I'm so happy Matt decided to bring a girl along. It's been forever!"

He just hadn't had the right incentive, Matt thought. For Kate, though, he'd be willing to do a year of Spaghetti Tuesdays. And that was just for starters.

Matt turned to the family table, where a hugely pregnant woman—and Kate thought that in the very kindest of ways—sat with a woman identical to her, except for the burgeoning belly. Opposite them sat Lizzie and a twentysomething woman with wildly curly light brown hair.

"Kate, you know Lizzie," Matt said. "Next to her is Rachel, and across from them are my sisters Anne and Maura. Maura's the—"

"Don't you dare say I'm fat," Maura cut in, then winced. "Sorry, rogue hormones. I know I'm only having one this time, but I swear I feel like it could be three. Especially today. Just call me Supercrank."

"I was going to say that you're the oldest among us, but I'm guessing that wouldn't have scored me any points, either," Matt said.

Maura smiled. "Not a one."

"Maura and Anne are twins. I was born next, Lizzie eleven months after me, and then Rachel last."

"We surrounded him," Anne said.

Kate had no doubt that they had . . . and still did to this day.

"Where are Todd and Jack?" Matt asked.

"Outside," Lizzie said. "Hiding, I think." She focused on Kate. "Todd and Jack are Maura and Anne's husbands, respectively. They have coming to Spaghetti Tuesday but never really making it into the house down to an art."

Kate sat in the open chair in front of her.

"If you want to go hang outside with the guys, that's fine," she said to Matt.

"No way. I don't trust anyone at this table not to fill you with lies about my youth."

Rachel leaned forward, smiling conspiratorily at Kate. "Lies? Why would we have to bother with that when the truth is so entertaining?"

Matt smiled. "See what I mean? I'm going to go grab a beer." He shot Rachel a mock stern look. "Try not to do too much damage while I'm gone."

"So," Anne said as soon as Matt had moved off. "Word

at the market is that you and Matt went away for the weekend."

Kate wondered if she was going to have to post a notice on the market bulletin board disclosing the truth of her nonrelationship with Matt.

"We were up in Traverse City for a day, but it was just business," she said.

"Business?" Maura asked. "What business does Matt have in Traverse City?"

Yikes! She'd screwed up already. But in her defense, she never would have thought that his family didn't know what he was doing.

"Well, sort of business. There were a couple of brewpubs he wanted to check out . . . a little comparison shopping, you know? Anyway, he asked me to go along. It was just a day trip."

"I don't know," Rachel said. "It sounds like a date to me."

Kate shook her head. "Trust me, it wasn't. I'm not dating right now, anyway."

"Why?" Maura asked.

"Maura! It's none of our business," Anne said. "But don't let that stop you if you feel like answering, Kate."

Kate laughed. She liked these women. In just minutes, she'd grown more comfortable with them than she was with her own sister, Bunny. Of course, Kate wasn't in the position of constantly being held up for comparison to the Culhane sisters, as she was to Bunny. And despite the goofy name her sister chose to go by in lieu of Barbara, Bunny was one fierce competitor: top of her class, rainmaker in her law firm, and very strategically married. Kate had never measured up especially well.

And Mary Culhane's story of Kate's periwinkle-stationery-loving mother dancing on a tabletop had been a mindblower. Her family had been all about proper manners and proper clothing and proper country clubs and schools back in Grosse Pointe. The idea of Barb Appleton table dancing was as improbable as Kate becoming an astronaut.

Right now, Kate might as well have been on Mars. No, not Mars. This place was warmer and a whole lot more hospitable, but still just as foreign.

"I got divorced about a year ago. After that, I decided until I get the rest of my life in order, dating can wait. Plus, I tend to make some pretty atrocious decisions when it comes to men. I've got a whole lot of stupid to figure out."

"Matt's not an atrocious decision," Lizzie said.

Kate gave a little involuntary smile. Lizzie was right. "Well, anyway, my life definitely isn't in order."

Matt returned from the kitchen with his beer and a tall glass of cola for Kate, then rounded the table to take the open chair at its head. "That's my motto: Matt Culhane—he's not atrocious."

Lizzie laughed. "So just how much of our conversation did you catch?"

"Enough." He took a swallow of his beer. "And to save Kate further embarrassment—and you guys a whole lot of extra snooping around—I do have a few business things going on in Traverse City. Remember that Tropicana Motor Inn that Mom and Dad would take us to?"

"Yes," all the sisters chimed.

"I just wrapped up a purchase and renovation deal on it."

Anne raised her eyebrows in amazement. "You bought the motel with the hokey flamingos painted on it? Now, *that* is an atrocious decision."

Maura scowled. "I like those flamingos!"

"So do I," Matt said. "The place was sitting vacant,

so I picked it up. And I'm just sharing this with you so you'll get off Kate's case about the two of us dating. And no more commentary about my flamingos or my dating choices, or I'll start dredging up your old dates."

Everyone was silent. No one wanted to discuss their dating history. It was Lizzie who changed the subject.

"Hey, isn't that annual beer festival thing in Royal Oak coming up in a couple of weeks? You should take Kate along."

Kate's somewhat homesick heart jumped. "Royal Oak? Really? I used to live there."

Matt nodded. "I remember you mentioning that."

He turned to Lizzie. "I'm going, but I have my usual road crew coming along."

"The groupies?" Lizzie asked.

"They're not groupies," Matt said, then gazed at his beer's label. Kate supposed he was just admiring his dog's smiling likeness.

"They follow you from event to event on their own money for the privilege of pouring your beer and hanging your banner. If that doesn't make them groupies, I don't know what does."

"There is the sexual connotation," Rachel said. "I don't think that applies." She paused, then added, "My university is teaching a class on the Grateful Dead as part of its cultural anthropology curriculum. Groupies would be an interesting topic, too."

"Rachel is working on her master's degree," Anne said to Kate.

Matt looked just a little annoyed. "All the same, they're not groupies. The thought of Harley and Junior as groupies could mess up a perfectly normal guy for life."

"I could pour your beer and hang your banner," Kate said.

"Actually, you can't pour his beer off-site since you work for him," Lizzie said before Matt could speak. "It's against state law for microbrewers."

Rachel pointed her finger at Lizzie. "Exactly. Which is why Matt has the groupies. Or sometimes one of us goes along, but with Maura due any second now, we're not up for a road trip."

"Other than Harley and Junior, who are your roadies, if I'm not allowed to call them groupies?" Lizzie asked.

"Mayor Mortensen and a couple of others have mentioned they'll be there, though they plan to catch a Pistons game, too, so I'm not sure how much actual pouring help they'll be."

"I could at least hang your banner," Kate said.

Anne smiled. "That definitely sounded suggestive."

"Okay, here's another thought," Kate said. "I could sell Depot Brewing merchandise."

"I don't bring merchandise," Matt said.

"You should," Kate told him. "If you sold hats and tees downstate, you could really get your name out there."

He nodded. "I'm betting you're right."

"Where in Royal Oak is the event?" she asked.

"In the Farmers' Market building, downtown."

"I used to work a few blocks east of there, on Washington Avenue."

"One street away from most of the restaurants and bars, right?" Matt asked.

"Exactly."

"They've mixed it up some this year with a private charity party thrown in on Friday night. Great for them, but I lose my whole day on Friday now, since I have to be set up earlier."

"So an extra set of hands would be good. I could help."

Kate wanted this so much, and not just to see Royal Oak, either. Kate wanted to be with Matt.

"I'd like that," Matt said, and their eyes held for a long moment.

"But really, guys. They're not dating. Not even a little bit," Lizzie said in a deadpan voice. "Can't you tell?"

Maura made an odd sound. "Okay, and I'm about to be not pregnant. Not even a little bit."

"What do you mean?" Lizzie asked.

Maura settled a hand on her belly. "I've been trying to be cool about it, but all of a sudden my contractions are getting pretty aggressive."

Matt stood up. "Contractions, as in labor?"

"Bingo. I thought it was just Braxton Hicks lead-up stuff, or we would have stayed home. After all, who wants to disrupt a perfectly good Spaghetti Tuesday?" She closed her eyes for a moment and blew out a slow breath. "Guess I was wrong. If this is anything like last time, it's going to be fast. Lizzie, could you go outside and round up Todd?"

"Sure," Lizzie replied, then headed out through the kitchen doorway.

"You can still take the girls for the night as we'd planned, right, Anne? They're upstairs playing in my old room."

Anne pushed back in her chair. "No problem. Let me get Jack and we'll go take care of things at your house."

Lizzie reappeared with a tall, dark, and semi-worried-looking guy Kate knew had to be Maura's husband.

He rounded the table and took Maura by the hand. "I told you those contractions were the real deal, babe. Your suitcase is in the trunk, right?"

"Todd, this is Kate. Kate, this is Todd," Maura said.

Kate had to give Maura major props for having good

manners during childbirth. She doubted she'd be able to show the same grace.

"Nice to meet you," Todd said to Kate, but his eyes never left his wife.

Kate gazed at the empty doorway after Todd and Maura left the room, smiling at each other, holding hands, and Kate realized she'd wanted that love and connection when she'd fallen for her ex. She might not have gotten it quite right back then, but she recognized a solid relationship when she saw one.

When she glanced away, she caught Matt watching her, and the warmth in his eyes had her heart skipping beats.

Matt's mom leaned her head out of the kitchen, ending the moment before Kate was quite ready to have it over. "Matt, could you and Kate take care of putting away dinner before you come over to the hospital?"

And then, suddenly the house was empty of Culhanes, except for Matt.

They moved into the kitchen, and Matt began putting plates away. "This is a new twist on Spaghetti Tuesday."

Kate helped him with the plates. There was something intimate about the two of them being alone in the house, she thought. A little exciting, too.

"Silverware goes in the drawer second down from the end," Matt said.

They worked in silence for a minute or so, then he asked, "So you've seen my crew. What's yours like?"

"Smaller. Different."

"Any sisters?" Matt asked while digging through the contents of a lower cupboard.

"One sister and one brother. Bunny and Chip."

"Seriously, those are their names?"

"Well, actually Barb and Larry, just like my mom and dad. Everyone calls them Bunny and Chip to save confusion." She pointed to a harvest gold–colored plastic bowl filled with salad greens. "Do you know where the top to this is?"

He rummaged through the bottom drawer, then paused to look up at her. "So among you summer people, when do adults become too old for names like that?"

"Never. The same holds true in the townie set. Witness Junior Greinwold."

Matt laughed. "Point taken."

He handed her the bowl's lid. "So how'd you luck out and end up without a nickname?"

Kate returned the salad to the fridge. "It was a near miss. Since mom and dad had already used up their own names, they could have moved on to the family parakeet's."

"Which was?"

"Spike."

Matt smiled. "I kind of like it. I think there might be some Spike in you. Remember, I saw you take down the fire chief," Matt said. "That was definitely a Spike moment."

Kate squelched a groan. "What should I do with the garlic bread?"

He handed her a box of aluminum foil. "How about if we take the bread and spaghetti to the hospital crew? I know Maura thinks this is going be fast, but I remember what it was like in that waiting room last time." He smiled. "All the same, it's totally worth the wait."

Kate hesitated in her wrapping.

"What?" he asked. "Maybe just the spaghetti should go?"

"No, definitely the garlic bread. But how about if I just help you get things packaged up? I'd feel a little intrusive being there. I mean, Maura and I just met."

Kate loved what she had seen of the Culhanes, but

whatever she and Matt had going on between them didn't make her family.

"Huh. I guess I wasn't looking at it that way," Matt said. "I was thinking more about how I'd like you to be there."

"You would?"

He came closer and tipped up her chin so that their eyes met. "I like being with you. I like having you next to me. Haven't you figured that out yet?" Matt lowered his mouth to hers and brushed a light kiss across her lips.

TWELVE

KATE HAD BECOME A HUMAN BATTLEFIELD. TEN DAYS of excitement over heading home to Royal Oak warred with ten nights' worth of nervous insomnia produced by the same trip. She'd been tempted to go with Matt to the hospital or his bedroom or wherever their kiss might lead, but in the end, she had him drop her off at her house before he went to find Maura and the rest of his family. The sun hadn't completely risen when Matt pulled up The Nutshell's drive. Kate, however, had been packed and ready for a good couple of hours. Preloaded with caffeine, she was waiting by the front door with her suitcase in hand. Matt exited the truck, took the suitcase, and stuck it in the backseat.

Matt opened the passenger door. "Do you want to lock up the house?"

"I can't lock it. I don't think we've had keys since my parents bought the place. All I can do is dead-bolt it from the inside. Let's just go."

"I don't want to be an alarmist, but since I just changed the locks at the brewery and hired a night guard, I'm tuned in to security issues. Keene's Harbor's a great place, but we have our share of crazies, too."

"All under control. *Avanti*."

Matt glanced at Kate. She was really ready. Almost too ready. "Is everything okay?"

Kate fidgeted in her seat. "Everything is perfectly under control."

The front door burst open and two or three workmen in hazmat jumpsuits ran out the door waving their arms frantically, screaming jibberish. Matt watched as they ran to the back of Kate's house and jumped into the lake.

Matt got out of his car and walked up to Kate's front door. There was a faint buzzing coming from inside her house.

He peeked inside the window. The entire living room was completely stripped of drywall, down to its studs. An angry swarm of bees filled a section of the exposed wall.

Matt walked back to the car and started up the engine. "Umm, Kate?"

"My house is completely filled with bees, isn't it?"

Matt nodded. "Maybe not completely filled. Some of the space is taken up with honey. I'm sure it will all be gone by the time we get back. Do you know what all this is costing? Are you sure you don't . . ."

"I know exactly what I'm doing. Just drive."

As Matt started down the road, Kate ran a mental tabulation of the damage and its cost. Two thousand to fix the leaky plumbing. Two thousand to fix the bathroom tile. Three thousand for the mold cleanup and another five thousand to replace the drywall and damaged floor. She wasn't sure how much bee removal cost. And she owed Matt at least $9,000 on the mortgage. If she didn't get the house fixed by Christmas, her parents were turning it over to Matt, and if she didn't get Matt paid by Thanksgiving, he was going to foreclose.

Matt sensed her thoughts and patted her leg with one hand. "Remember. Just one foot after the other."

Good advice, she thought. Panic was counterproductive.

"Run me through what we need to get done once we're in Royal Oak," Kate said. "I've already double-checked the boxes of merchandise and found one of those old-fashioned thingies to run credit card slips through. You don't want to lose the credit sales. And I really think we should have brought the hoodies along with the tees. It's autumn, after all."

Matt said nothing, but handed her a travel mug filled with coffee.

"What's next?" Kate asked.

"You tell me," Matt said. "You're my snoop. Anything new on that front?"

"Not a thing. Taproom work is harder than I thought. Servers are too busy to be good snoops. I did notice something about your menu, though. Who put it together?"

Matt lifted his mug from its holder. "I worked with a friend who used to be a regional manager for an upper-end chain."

"A woman?"

He took a swallow of coffee. "Yes, why?"

"Did you date her and dump her?"

Matt's eyebrows went up a fraction of an inch. "No."

"You must have ticked her off, at least. You have no fresh vegetables anywhere on your menu, aside from your iceberg wedge smothered in blue cheese dressing. Oh, and the mango poppy seed coleslaw, but don't get me started on that."

"No one else has complained."

"The customers who care the most are women—not your standard breed of beer lovers. And those women would eat fish bait if it gave them a chance at contact with you."

"What are you talking about?"

"Your lunchtime fan club. They know your schedule better than you do. Haven't you noticed the daily lineup?"

"I see them. They're nice people, but I'm not interested. And it's no big deal. Don't you see the way men look at you?"

Kate laughed. "No. I'm pretty pragmatic about my looks."

"And they are?"

"I don't know. . . . Kind of cute, I guess."

Matt glanced over at her.

"You're beautiful. And if you've missed men checking you out, I'll start letting you know when it happens. Like now. The more we're together, the harder it is for me to keep my hands off you."

Desire rushed through Kate's belly and she admitted to herself that she didn't want Matt to keep his hands off her. She took a beat to steady her voice. "Getting back to the vegetables. Do you have something against them?"

"No, in fact I like vegetables. Especially French fries."

She let that sit for a couple of miles and moved on to another topic. "You can never go home again. . . . Any idea who said that?" Kate asked.

"Nope."

"Well, I'm thinking it's true. You can't."

"Maybe for that unnamed person," Matt said. "But I do it every day. In fact, except for a short break long ago, I haven't left."

"Exactly. But I did, and now I'm returning. Today."

"And?"

"The magazine I used to work for will be there," she said. "The places I used to go will be there, and life will have rolled on without me. I'm going to be like a ghost."

"You look real to me."

Kate smiled. "But not to them."

Matt shook his head. "Kate, you've been in Keene's Harbor, not Brigadoon or whatever. You've made friends, found a job, even brewed up a little trouble, so it seems to me, you're doing great."

"The guy who took my job, he's got my office. And then there's Shayla the Homewrecker."

"Who?"

Kate gave a dismissive wave of her hand. "The woman my ex ran off with. She has my old bed, my ex, and even my dog. They all have lives, and I've been in a holding pattern. I don't have a clue what to do next."

He cut his eyes to her. "I'd suggest switching to decaf."

Kate realized she'd been jiggling her left foot at close to the speed of light.

"Kate, seriously, it's all going to be fine."

"But how can you say that? How do you know?"

"Experience, for one. And two, you're not the kind of woman to let opportunity pass you by. But that doesn't mean you need to dwell on things. How about you look at your time in Keene's Harbor as a gift? How about you slow down and appreciate the present? The best I can figure, the future takes care of itself."

"Nice philosophy, but I've seen how hard you work."

"I'm not saying I don't."

"I need a plan," she said.

He looked her way again. "Eventually you do, but not right now. There are no rules. There aren't any Plan Police waiting to nab you. Give yourself a break."

"Hmm," Kate said, liking the thought. No plan. She could live with that. And truth was, she didn't miss her old bed or her old job or her ex, but there was a hole in her heart for her dog. She desperately missed her dog.

Matt stepped back and took a look at the Depot Brewing Company booth. It was, as it should be, perfect. He and the road crew had set it up enough times in the past. It had taken some adjusting—and another table—to create Kate's merchandise area, but Matt considered it effort well spent. He should have started doing this sooner.

He also wished at least a couple of his sisters could be here, but understood why they weren't. The choice between a new nephew to pamper and working a beer festival was a no-brainer. He'd put in his share of time admiring baby Todd, too.

Harley stood beside Matt, checking out the booth. "Thirty minutes before the doors open," he said. "You've done good, son."

Matt smiled at his friend, who had as big a heart as he did a skinny body. When Matt had been a kid, he'd always mixed up Harley with the Scarecrow from *The Wizard of Oz*.

"I couldn't do it without you. Any of it." And Matt meant it. After Matt's dad had booted him from the hardware store for an admittedly bad attitude, Harley had given him a job. He had also given Matt loans and advice when he'd opened the microbrewery. Matt had been mad at his dad at the time, but now he realized his dad had done it to help him spread his wings.

"Glad to help." Harley stuck two fingers in his mouth and whistled for Junior, who was flirting it up with a pair of pretty hot-looking beer pourers a couple of booths down.

Junior gave Harley a wave.

"Now if you don't mind, I'm gonna go grab Junior," Harley said. "We need to check out that spread of fancy finger foods before we're trapped behind the booth. I think I saw shrimp."

Matt could have pointed out that the food was intended for the party guests, and not Harley and Junior, but his friend was among the ranks of old dogs who refused to be retrained.

After they'd taken off, Matt headed toward Kate, who was putting her finishing touches on the merchandise table. Just outside of Keene's Harbor she'd lapsed into silence. He'd understood . . . or thought he had. She had a lot on her mind, and she was going to process it in whatever way worked best for her. It was nice to feel comfortable and relaxed with a woman, even in a mostly silent four-hour car ride. He'd just turned on the music and moved into his zone.

He looked down at Kate's table. "How's it going over here?"

"Almost done." She was concentrating on adjusting a pile of T-shirts. "I'm using the 'stack 'em high and watch them fly' approach."

"It's your turf. Arrange it however you want. We should be getting our first takers in about half an hour." He held out his hand. "Come on, let's take a look around before the place opens for business."

Kate surveyed the booths lining one of the two long aisles that had been set up in the cavernous building. "I had no idea there were so many microbrewers."

"More every day," Matt said. "But it's like any other business. Right now, it's surfing a high, but it will level out again in a couple of years. Only the best will be commercial concerns, and the others will go back to home brewing, if they really have a passion for it, or just move on to the next fad."

The walk was a slow one. He'd been in the business long enough that he knew most of the exhibitors.

Between booths, Kate asked, "What are you, some kind of cult hero? I don't think there's a single person here who doesn't know you or want to know you."

"It's not that big a deal. We don't land under the same roof all that often, so when we do, we talk."

Matt stared into the crowd of people in front of him and saw that Chet Orowski was heading his way. Matt already knew through the grapevine that Chet hadn't been able to find any other investors.

Orowski stopped a couple feet in front of Matt, and Matt extended his hand in greeting, thinking this was as good a time as any to re-establish a cordial relationship. "Chet, it's good to see you."

Chet slapped Matt's hand away and poked him in the chest. "Culhane, you're a crook and a liar."

Matt stood his ground, waiting for Chet to finish. "Do you really want to do this here?"

Chet's face was flushed and his hands were fisted. "You bet I do." His pupils danced around his eyes like Mexican jumping beans and his voice got louder. "If I'm going to go down, it's going to be in a friggin' blaze of glory. I'm gonna stand behind my booth and tell everyone who will listen what a bastard you are."

Matt glanced out of the corner of his eye at the booths to his left. Yup, spectators were already lining up.

"And this is why you drove all the way from Traverse City and rented a booth in Royal Oak?"

If the guy was going to slander him, he could have done it in a much more cost-effective fashion, Matt thought. Chet really wasn't much of a businessman.

"Yes. No. I also did it to look for a partner. Someone honest. Someone who follows through." He glared at Kate. "Someone who doesn't waste all his time chasing after tail."

Kate stuffed her hands onto her hips, narrowed her eyes, and leaned into Chet's personal space. "Excuse me?"

Matt clamped his hand on Chet's shoulder. To everyone but Chet it would look like a friendly gesture. Only

Chet needed to know that this was a subtle warning of what could follow if he didn't tone it down.

"Now, Chet," Matt said. "We're all friends in this place, right?"

Chet went silent.

Matt made his warning marginally less subtle. "Right?"

Chet squirmed but Matt's grip on him stayed firm.

"Right," Chet gasped.

"And when we're among friends, we want everyone to have a good time, don't you think?"

Chet nodded enthusiastically, though Matt was pretty sure he'd spotted sweat popping out on the guy's forehead.

"Kate, here, is one of my friends, which would make her one of your friends by extension. You don't want to talk about a friend the way you just did about Kate, right?"

"Right."

"So how about you apologize to Kate—and to me, if you feel like it—and then we all get on with what's going to be a very good beer festival? After all, do good things and they come back to you."

"I—" Chet cleared his throat. "I'm sorry."

The words had been delivered without a helluva lot of sincerity, but Matt had no interest in pushing this scene a second longer than he had to. He released Chet's shoulder, then held out his right hand again.

This time, Chet did as he should have to begin with. He shook Matt's hand.

"No hard feelings," Matt said. At least not on his side. He wasn't going to speculate on Chet's.

Kate had been called a lot of things in her life: stubborn, nosy, and even some less nice stuff by her ex. But never had she been called *tail*.

She glared over her shoulder at Chet as Matt led her

away. In a perfect world, where she was all-powerful and could smite the bad guys at will, she'd still be back there giving Chet a new perspective on life.

Matt took her hand and gave it a friendly squeeze. "Don't let him tick you off. He's not worth it. Or if it would make you feel better, how about if later I lure him to the parking lot and you can give him a fat lip?"

Kate smiled in spite of herself. "I just might take you up on that."

He laughed. "I guess I should consider my audience when I'm joking around."

"I promise I won't hold you to your offer," she said. But she did hold his hand almost all the way back to the Depot booth, where she moved on to finish up her merchandise fluffing. And just in time, too.

Kate could time down to the second when cocktail hour was starting in Royal Oak's bars by the flood of private tasting guests into Farmers' Market. She saw plenty of familiar faces in the crowd. Back when she'd been at *Detroit Monthly,* she'd always gone out with coworkers for cocktails. Richard had worked late every Friday. Or so he'd claimed.

As people streamed by, she exchanged waves and greetings with casual friends. It felt good to see them, and that scared emptiness she'd been anticipating never materialized. She was no ghost; she was a new and improved version of Kate.

She looked past the guys checking out the Depot baseball caps and locomotive bottle openers and on to Matt, who was giving one awesome beer spiel. He was smart and funny, and his crowd was eating it up. Except one person. The guy was busy playing with his BlackBerry in exactly the same way that had made her insane from the day he'd bought the thing.

Richard.

Her ex's black hair was absurdly long, but his perpetual slight frown, English tweed jacket, khakis, and ever-so-retro loafers were just the same.

Kate felt trapped. Fight-or-flight instinct kicked in, and flight didn't look to be a viable option. Running out of the building wouldn't be very subtle, and she'd have to slip past him unnoticed to pull it off, anyway. Maybe Richard would drift off without seeing her.

She automatically made change for a guy who'd decided to buy ten bottle openers to give as family Christmas gifts. Somehow she didn't think Grandma was going to plotz with gratitude, but Kate wasn't about to stop the dude. After he was gone, she ducked under the table to grab more stock. She briefly considered hiding, except the space was a little tight and dark for her taste. And no doubt Matt would come looking for her. She'd rather not explain the whole ex thing to him.

Kate rose, and Richard spotted her. She wished she'd gone for full makeup instead of her usual mascara and lip gloss. It never hurt to look fabulous when seeing the ex for the first time since moving out of the marital home. But what she lacked in cosmetics, she could make up for in attitude. If Matt could talk nicely to Chet, she could do it with Richard.

Maybe.

Kate rounded the merchandise table and extended her hand. "Richard."

"Kate." His handshake was on the limp side, but at least he'd given it a shot.

"I'm surprised to see you here," she said. "You're not a beer drinker."

"This is a charity function that a client supports. I have to make a showing. But I'll say, you can't be nearly as surprised as I am. I'd heard you'd lost your job and had to move in with your parents."

"I have a job," she said.

"So I see. And Larry and Barb are well?"

"They're fine, I'm sure. They're at the Naples house until May, and I'm staying at The Nutshell."

"Really? The Nutshell? That must be interesting."

To anyone else, his comment would have sounded positive and sincere. Kate, however, knew how much he'd disliked both The Nutshell and Keene's Harbor. And she felt very protective of both.

Kate smiled. "It's wonderful."

"Really? Living in your parents' cottage and working in a brewery?" He glanced at his phone. "That's a far cry from what you used to do."

Kate wondered if Shayla was texting him, just as she had when Kate had been his wife. Water under the bridge, Kate thought. Shayla could text him all she wanted now. Kate had loved Richard, but his affair had taught her something. She couldn't be the person she was meant to be when she was with someone she couldn't trust. If she ever decided to marry another man, it would definitely be someone like Matt—someone who made her feel more herself than she did alone.

"I like it in Keene's Harbor. I always did," she said. "I'm happy there."

"How nice."

Funny thing, but he didn't look very happy about her being happy.

"So can I tell you a little about our beer?" she asked, knowing this would roust snobby anti-brew Richard.

"No thanks," he said. "I should move along."

Not quickly enough, she thought as he stepped off.

Then he turned back. "Oh, I forgot to mention . . . We had to give Stella away."

THIRTEEN

KATE FELT AS THOUGH SOME VITAL CONNECTION IN HER brain had just snapped. "Would you mind repeating that?"

A faint little smile was forming on Richard's usually passive face. "We had to give Stella away."

Stella had been their baby. They'd spoiled her like mad. When they'd separated, leaving her had been wretched for Kate, far more painful than leaving Richard. Stella had been faithful.

"What do you mean, *had* to?" Kate asked.

"Stella didn't take to Shayla. We couldn't have her biting all the time."

"Who, Shayla or Stella?"

"Very funny. Really, Kate, it's great that you still have your sense of humor to keep you going."

"And so you gave her away instead of sending her to me?"

"I didn't know where you were."

"My cell number hasn't changed."

Richard flipped his bangs out of his eyes like a pop star. "Don't be difficult. It's not as though you cared enough to take her in the first place."

"Don't even start with that stuff. I was ordered by the

court to surrender her to you, and you know it. You had the fenced backyard. I had the loft apartment and no dog park in walking distance. I didn't even get visitation rights, thanks to your high-priced, evil divorce lawyer. So tell me, who has her now?"

Her ex hesitated, and Kate knew this was going to be *no bueno*.

He looked down at his feet and Kate knew that for all his posturing, he felt bad. Richard had truly loved Stella, but Richard was a weak person. Richard was no match for Shayla.

"I'm not sure," he said. "Shayla handled it."

"Stella was ours before Shayla became part of the picture, and you let *her* handle it—whatever that means? How could you allow any of this to happen?"

He kicked the ground with his right shoe, then looked back up at Kate. "I'm engaged. Shayla wouldn't agree to marry me unless Stella went. She knows how busy I've been at work, so she just took care it. I'm sure she found Stella a good home. You should just move on, Kate."

Move on?

Stella had probably been dumped at the city shelter, where her chances would have been slim. Everyone wanted cute puppies, not seven-year-old ginger-colored miniature poodles who had just a bit of a bad attitude. But Kate wanted her with all her heart. She also wanted to shake Richard until his teeth rattled, or boot him one in the rear, or . . .

She wrapped her hand around the closest open beer from the pouring table. She didn't have a firm plan, but if Richard's ridiculous hair ended up looking like stringy black seaweed, that wouldn't be so tragic. Before she could do anything, though, two muscled arms gently wrapped around her from behind.

"Steady," Matt said low into her ear, drawing her closer. "Take a breath, sweetheart."

Kate's eyes were focused on Richard. "I want Stella *now*."

Richard's gaze darted from the beer bottle to Kate. "I told you, I don't know where she is."

Matt tightened his hold on Kate. "Why don't you set down the bottle?"

"He gave away my dog."

"I take it you know him," Matt said.

"This is my ex, Dick." Which he hated being called.

Richard turned to Matt and offered the same limp hand he had to Kate. "And you are?"

"Matt Culhane, Kate's boss."

"I should press assault charges against your employee."

Kate rolled her eyes. "For what? I didn't even touch you."

"Harassment. Intimidation," Richard said.

Kate's throat tightened. She was going to cry, but damn it, she wasn't going to do it in front of her idiot, rotten-to-the-core ex.

She pushed at Matt's arms. "I need to go outside."

Matt slid his arms away, and Kate hustled for the door. She walked blindly down the parking lot's first aisle, looking for some privacy and Matt's truck. It didn't take long to find something that big and red. She tugged at the passenger-door handle, but the vehicle was locked.

"Hang on," Matt said from behind her.

Kate turned and flung herself at him. "He gave away my dog to some stranger, Matt. I never should have let him have her."

Matt rubbed her back and gave her a chance to settle down. After a moment, she stepped back and wished for a tissue.

"I'm sorry." She wiped her eyes. "I feel awful. I should have never trusted him with my dog, but honestly, I didn't have a choice."

Matt unlocked the truck and opened the door for her. "Why don't you take a couple of minutes in some quiet? Harley and Junior have it covered inside."

Kate nodded and climbed in.

"I'll be back to check on you in a minute. I just have to . . ." He gestured back at the market building. Kate figured that could mean anything from "use the facilities" to "hide from the weepy woman." Either way, he'd been there when she'd needed him, and in her book, he was already a hero for that.

Matt had to sprint the forty like a high school kid to catch up with Kate's ex, but he did it. Richard was standing next to a black BMW, getting ready to leave.

Matt walked slowly up to Richard, trying his best at friendly. "That was pretty weird stuff in there."

Richard's mouth turned down. "It's always weird with Kate. Fire her now while you have cause."

"Thanks, but I'll handle my own employment decisions."

"Then keep her around, but you can't say I didn't warn you. She's a soul-eater."

Total bull, but Matt had the feeling this guy dished a lot of that. Matt got down to business. "So, Richard, I couldn't help overhearing you and Kate, and I've gotta say I think you know where her poodle is."

Richard took a half step closer to his car. "Why would I lie?"

"Good question, since you're pretty bad at it. You were obviously scrambling when you talked to Kate, and now can't meet my eyes. So what's up with the poodle? Susie? Sniffy? Whatever the mutt's name is?" Matt asked, figuring a little goading might work.

The color started to rise in Richard's face. "Her name is Stella."

"See? You care about the dog. It's obvious. I'm a dog guy, too, and have been for a lot of years. I get the relationship between man and canine. But I'm also a big fan of Kate's, so if there's something I can do to help her get her poodle back, I'm going to do it."

"Is that a threat?"

It was kind of funny that this professor-looking dude was ready to rumble, but Matt wasn't a rumbler anymore. He didn't have to be.

"If you're asking whether I'm going to beat you up over a poodle, the answer is no. If you're asking whether I'm going to put time and effort into getting to the bottom of this, the answer is yes. And when it comes to Kate, I have all the time in the world."

"Don't bother. Stella's fine."

"Really? And you claimed you don't know where she went. Want to tell me the real story?"

Richard hesitated, but finally made a sound of capitulation. "I found her in the city shelter where my fiancée, Shayla, had dropped her. I had some friends adopt her. I visit her all the time."

So he was cheating on his fiancée with a poodle. Matt couldn't say he'd encountered that before or wanted to again. Mostly, though, he wanted to ask how the guy could want to marry a woman who'd done what this Shayla had. But he already knew Richard's judgment sucked. After all, he'd let Kate go.

"Kate would be with the dog full-time," Matt said. "She loves Stella."

"I want Stella by me."

"She'd be better off with Kate." Matt paused. "And I think you know that."

After some sour-faced deliberation, Richard pulled a slim notepad and a gold pen from his breast pocket. He scribbled something on a piece of paper, tore it out, and handed it to Matt.

"Give me five minutes before calling," Richard said. "I'll need to talk to them first."

"You're doing the right thing," Matt said. He pocketed the paper and hoped this was the very last time he'd see Dognapper Dick.

Fifteen minutes later, after a call comprised of some detailed poodle negotiations, Matt stepped back into the party. Kate was at the merchandise table. She gave him a smile, but it wasn't up to her usual wattage. Mayor Mortensen and his wife, Missy, stood behind the beer table with Harley and Junior. Missy was as thin and cheery as Torvald Mortensen was rotund and generally glum. After saying hello to Torvald, Matt turned to Missy.

"Kate and I need to go take care of a few things," he said.

"I do?" Kate asked.

"You do."

Kate looked confused. "Okay, then."

"Do you think you could cover the merchandise table?" Matt asked Missy. "The party wraps up at eight."

"Absolutely. I'd love to help," Missy said. "Just let me get with Kate and learn the ropes."

While Kate and Missy talked, Matt made sure the rest of his troops knew what to do: all spare beer in the bins below the table, merchandise boxed and stowed, and everything wiped down and ready to roll when they opened again tomorrow at eleven.

"Come on," he said to Kate when Missy and she had finished. "We're going to sneak out on the boss."

Her smile was a little brighter. "That should be a challenge, especially for you."

"I'm pretty good at it."

Now if he could just pull off the rest of his plan.

After giving Kate some lame excuse about picking up supplies, Matt headed his truck out of downtown Royal Oak and south on Woodward Avenue. When they merged onto the freeway heading west, Kate started getting suspicious.

"What kind of supplies are we getting? They must be pretty exotic if you couldn't have picked them up someplace in Royal Oak."

"They're one of a kind," he said.

"Gotta be," Kate said before lapsing into silence.

Matt exited the freeway and, a few minutes later, turned into the subdivision he'd been told to look for. Two blocks down, first house on the left, he pulled into a driveway and parked.

"Friends of yours?" Kate asked.

"Not exactly."

She looked at the unassuming beige brick colonial with its perfectly clipped shrubs. "Okay, this is weird. I feel like I've been here before."

"It's possible," he said. "These are friends of Richard's."

"And you know this, how?"

"Your ex-husband and I had a talk. The usual guy stuff. We shared, we laughed, we bonded."

"No, really," Kate said.

"And he told me where your poodle is."

"Stella? *Here?*" She opened the truck door.

He settled a hand on her arm. "Before you go all Rambo, here's the deal. These people have had your poodle for almost six months. They love her and think of her as their own. They've even renamed her Bitsy."

"*Bitsy?* Granted, living here is better than what I'd imagined for her, but Bitsy? They probably have her in a pink ruffled collar and clipped with a little ball at the end of her tail. I need to go get her."

Matt held his palms toward her, trying to slow her down a little. "In a second, but first you have to listen. The only way they're going to let her leave with you is if she does it of her own free will."

He didn't add that if the poodle picked Kate, he'd be buying the couple a replacement dog. That was his bargain and his responsibility.

"You mean I have to sweet talk my own dog back to me when we haven't seen each other for over a year?"

He nodded. "That's the deal."

"It's insane."

"I know, but it was the best I could do." And that had taken some major persuading.

She drew in a deep breath, then slowly let it out. "Okay. I can do this."

They walked to the front porch, and Kate's finger hovered over the doorbell as she asked, "How am I going to handle it if she doesn't choose me?"

Matt spoke from the heart. "How could she not?"

As Kate stood waiting for the door to open, she finally recalled who would be on the other side—Myrna and Ed Savage. They were a nice couple about twenty years older than she. Ed was an accountant and one of Richard's clients. Kate had been to a dinner here once, years ago. She'd reciprocated, and that had been the end of any couples' socializing. She thought maybe Richard and Ed still golfed together, though.

The door swung open, and Myrna greeted them. She looked no happier to see Kate than Kate felt about this entire mess. But since this wasn't the Savages' fault, Kate took care to be super polite.

Matt's expression was a cross between amusement and ~~si~~gnation. "I just did what any other guy would have."

"Not Richard."

"No, not Richard."

There were a lot of things about her ex she could have ~~sh~~ared with Matt, but none of them really mattered.

"Luckily, he's not my problem anymore," she said.

Matt smiled at her, his eyes softened, and the room ~~gr~~ew warmer as those big bed fantasies charged to the ~~fr~~ont of Kate's mind.

"I'll clear the cart to the hall," Matt said.

Kate watched him push the cart out the door. This was ~~it~~ she thought. Here they were in a romantic hotel room. ~~Ju~~st the two of them . . . and Stella. Perfect, right? Wrong. ~~No~~t perfect. For starters, she was wearing a T-shirt that ~~ad~~vertised beer. Plus, she suspected her lipstick had got~~ten~~ gnawed off at Myrna's, and her hair was a wreck. He, ~~on~~ the other hand, was hot. His T-shirt molded sugges~~tive~~ly to his gorgeous body. His butt looked great in his ~~jean~~s. His hair was tousled just enough to be sexy, and ~~he ha~~d a manly five o'clock shadow going.

~~O~~kay, don't panic, she told herself. Get a grip. Should ~~she s~~tand? Should she sit? Should she lounge back onto ~~the be~~d? Should she get undressed? No, definitely no un~~dress~~ing. She wasn't ready for undressing.

~~Ma~~tt returned to the room, closed the door, and Kate ~~stoo~~d up from the bed.

"~~W~~ell?" Kate said.

~~The~~ir eyes met and held for a moment, and Matt ~~glance~~d over his shoulder at the door.

~~Eithe~~r he was checking to make sure it was locked, or ~~he~~ was planning on leaving, Kate thought. Best not ~~take~~ any chances on him leaving, she decided. It was ~~now or n~~ever, so she moved in and kissed him. Definitely

Myrna ushered them into the living room, where Ed stood waiting with a dog's travel crate at his feet. Kate caught a glimpse of Stella's ginger coat and her heart began to drum. She wouldn't be able to breathe properly until this was done and she had her poodle back.

"If you don't mind, I'd like to propose a few guidelines," she said to the couple. "How about if you're on one side of the room, and I'm on the other? Matt can put Stella—"

Myrna stood her ground. "Bitsy."

"The poodle," Matt suggested.

Kate pressed her lips together. "Matt can put *the poodle* in the middle of the room. Whoever she goes to first, keeps her."

"How do I know you're not cheating?" Myrna said, suspiciously sniffing Kate. "You smell like bacon."

Kate emptied her pockets onto the table. No bacon. Myrna sniffed again. "I think you still smell like bacon."

Matt picked up a can of Febreze from beside the couch. He generously sprayed both the women and stepped back. "Okay, then. Let's do it," Kate said, wiping her sweaty palms on her pants legs.

Matt retrieved the travel crate from Ed while Myrna moved to her husband's side.

Matt placed himself in the middle of the room. "Everybody ready?"

"Yes."

Matt opened the crate and withdrew Stella, who emerged with an obvious show of stubbornness. She didn't care that she weighed five pounds. She was mistress of her own domain.

Stella looked healthy, though she probably felt a little embarrassed by the hokey haircut—a pom on the end of her tail and balls on each hip, just as Kate had suspected.

Stella looked around, her brown eyes bright with

curiosity, and Kate focused on her poodle, willing her to look her way. *Please, baby. Please remember me.*

Matt set Stella down.

Myrna clapped her hands and made some kissy noises. "Bitsy-kins. Come to Mommy."

Stella looked Myrna's way once, then took a casual sniff at Matt's shoe before turning away from him, too. Kate smiled. Who wouldn't love a poodle that played hard to get?

"Come on, Bitsy. . . . Be a good precious babykins," Myrna cooed.

Kate figured that even in the time Stella and she had been apart, her dog couldn't have had a personality transplant. And that being the case, Kate knew just what to do. She plopped herself down on the beige carpet, her back to the beige wall, and feigned total disinterest.

Stella grew a tad miffed at Kate's nonchalance. She took one step, then another toward Kate, just as Kate had hoped. Now was the time for a little girl talk, Stella-style.

"Hey, Stella," Kate said. "You're looking pretty good. How have you been doing? Scare any Dobermans lately?"

Stella's ears perked up, and she ran to Kate and settled in her lap.

Kate nestled her cheek against Stella's soft fur. "You're the Best Dog Ever. I missed you so much."

And Matt was the Best Man Ever, Kate thought. He'd brought her back together with her Stella.

FOURTEEN

STELLA MUST HAVE BEEN ROYALTY IN A PR
Kate could find no other reason for the dog to
impressed with the hotel Matt had chosen. Ka
other hand, was wowed by the Townley Inn.
looked like something out of an English countr
all dark woods, plush carpets, and rich upho
her bed was a fantasy-worthy, feather-down
for lovers. At the moment, though, she sha
cranky poodle.

Kate sat alongside the dog at the end of
Matt sat opposite them in a desk chair he
their white-linen-covered room service ca
have been feeding her from the table," K
at the way she's turning up her nose at th
her. It's going to be tough getting her bac
food."

Stella was eyeing the final bite of te
plate. He speared the meat with his fo
huffed out a sigh as her last shot at
peared down Matt's throat.

Chicken breast with roasted aut
molished, Kate set her fork aside.
for Stella in the last ten minutes?"

not her best work, but then in her defense, she was a little rusty.

He tilted his head and looked at her. "What was that?"

She stepped back while finding some way to hedge her poor move. "A good-night kiss between friends?"

"Really?"

"More or less."

He looked at her with the same hot intensity he'd shown the night she'd sung in the karaoke contest. But this time she wasn't scared. At least not much.

"I thought we were closer friends than that."

"How close of friends?" she asked.

Matt didn't answer with words. Instead, he kissed her deeply. Intimately. Kate could swear she heard herself moan as his hand moved to the small of her back. She'd been starving for this.

For him.

There was no point in fighting it. Her willpower was shot. He was too sexy. Too near. Too perfect. She wanted his body heat and the feel of him taking her to that place she'd missed so much.

"Hang on, sweetheart," he said.

No problem, because she'd already wrapped her arms around his neck.

He scooped her up and settled her on the bed. He switched off the bedside lamp, and Kate reached for him. His weight settled over her, pushing her deep into the heavenly soft comforter.

She let her fingers flex into the muscles on the back of his shoulders as he claimed her mouth with his once again.

A low growl sounded. Kate was pretty sure it hadn't come from Matt, and she was almost certain it hadn't come from her. She nudged the pillow that Stella had to be occupying and got an angry grunt in response.

Matt moved on to kiss Kate's throat. She arched her neck and asked for more while she tried to work his shirt free of his jeans. She wanted to touch skin. *Now.*

Matt knelt above her and pulled off his shirt. Kate wished she had the patience to focus on his body's details but she was too far gone. She pulled him back down.

"We've got all night," he said.

"Not good enough."

"Trust me, it's gonna be good," he said in a low voice that made Kate's body hum in excitement.

Kate fumbled with his belt, thinking the damn thing was like some sort of Mensa brain challenge.

Stella let loose a series of high-pitched yips. Someone in the next room added a couple of firm raps against the wall.

Kate gave up on the belt. Her dog was going to ruin everything. "Stella, no!"

The poodle brought it down to a whine.

"Ignore Stella," Matt said, his lips skimming along Kate's neck, her ear. "Focus on me. Would it help if I howled?"

Stella went back to barking. The neighbor slammed on the wall, and the poodle amped it up to the point that Kate's ears rang.

Matt lifted his head and gave Stella a glare. "Stop!"

The poodle curled her lip, but obeyed.

"Now where were we?" Matt asked as he opened the top four buttons on Kate's chambray Depot shirt, his last word ending on a sharp breath of pleasure as he settled his mouth between her breasts. Kate murmured encouragement and Matt cruised on, making quick work of the rest of Kate's buttons.

"Gotta admire a man who's talented with his hands," she managed to say.

When Kate's shirt went flying, Stella let loose a snarl that sounded like it came from a Rottweiler.

Matt paused in his body exploration. "That wasn't a good sound."

Kate's poodle stared at them from one pillow over. The dog's eyes glowed in the dim light. And it wasn't an *I'm a happy dog* kind of glow, either.

"Settle down," she told Stella, but the poodle was focused on Matt.

"I'm sensing a turf war," Matt said.

Kate kissed him and popped the top button on his jeans. "No way."

Rrrrrrrrrrrrrf! Grrf. GRRF!

"No doubt about it. Your dog doesn't want me touching you," Matt said.

"She doesn't get a vote. Give me a second."

Kate unwrapped herself from Matt, corralled Stella, and tucked her into her travel crate, which sat beside the brocade love seat.

"Be good," she said to Stella.

Yip, yip, yip, yip, YIP!

Matt yanked a burgundy-colored throw from the love seat and dropped it over the crate.

Arooooh, roooh, roooh. Arooooooh!

The guy in the next room pounded the wall as though he planned to hammer his way through.

"Sorry," Kate called. "We're trying to get her to stop."

But Stella kept on in howl mode.

"I'm calling the front desk," the guy shouted through the wall.

Kate had a vision of security at the door. With the police. And the ASPCA. And just like her last legal run-in, she'd be only half-dressed.

Matt rolled to his feet. "This isn't going to work."

"I'm sorry. She's really a great dog."

"No problem. I understand where she's coming from. I feel exactly the same way about you as she does." He gave Kate a quick kiss over Stella's warning growl. "Lesson learned. Beware the overly protective poodle."

Saturday morning, Matt did his best to put Friday night behind him. He'd never seen a dog smirk, but damned if the poodle hadn't been doing just that as he'd left Kate's room. During a mind-clearing, wake-up run, he'd decided on a plan to win Stella over and clear the way for him to Kate's heart. Plus, he was far better off than Harley and Junior, who'd shown up for breakfast visibly and brutally hungover. Junior had turned gray at the sight of Kate's wheatgrass-and-mango smoothie, and had left the hotel dining room without ordering.

While Matt could stomach the idea of a wheatgrass smoothie, he couldn't deal with Kate's total silence now that they were on the road and headed for the beer fest. Stella was stowed in her crate, on the backseat, but probably still shooting him death rays.

"You're mighty quiet," Matt said.

"What would you like to talk about?"

"Last night."

"I didn't think guys talked about stuff like that."

"It's true. It's rule number five in the Code of Manliness handbook. I'm making a one-time exception."

Kate sighed. "Okay, so here goes. I'm kind of glad for the poodle alarm last night. I made myself a promise not to get involved with anyone until I figured out my life. For the first time, I feel like I might actually be making progress with that."

He had to give Kate credit. Not only did she have an impressive amount of willpower, she was also tenacious, passionate, and forthright. It was all he could do not to pull the car over and kiss her. But patience and planning had helped him succeed in business, and it would help him succeed with Kate. First things first. Win over the dog.

"I understand completely."

"You do?"

"Sure. I was lucky to be able to find my calling in a hobby I loved, but it was hard work figuring out how to build and run a business. It took all the energy I had. Right now, your business is your life. There's no reason to rush things between us."

Kate's body relaxed, and when she smiled up at him, Matt once again had to fight not to pull over to the side of the road. Sooner or later, Kate would come around, but how he'd help her get there was a more complicated proposition than charming the poodle. All he needed for Stella was a lamb chop in each pocket. Kate would take finesse.

They pulled into the parking lot at the Farmers' Market a few minutes later and noticed a police cruiser was parked in front of the main entry door.

"What do you suppose that's about?" Kate asked, looking at the cruiser.

"I suppose it's just life in the big city."

They entered the building and made their way back toward the Depot Brewing booth, stopping in the middle of the aisle, grimly gaping at the Depot Brewing Company banner hanging in tatters.

Harley, Junior, and Torvald Mortensen stood in front of Matt's booth with two police officers. A scarecrow manned the booth, dressed in a Depot Brewery T-shirt and hat. A huge jagged hunting knife was stuck in its belly and a corkscrew protruded from its right eye.

"The leftover beer from last night is gone," Junior said.

"We set up the tables again, though. They were all wrecked."

Matt clapped his friend on the shoulder. "Thanks, pal. I appreciate the help."

Matt, Harley, Junior, and Torvald answered the officers' questions while Kate sat on the floor, sorting through upended boxes. Matt was handing one of the officers his card when Kate joined them.

She held out a vintage lighter decorated with a black-and-white enamel eagle. "Sorry to interrupt, but I found this with the merchandise. I thought maybe it was Harley's?"

Harley barely glanced at it. "Nope."

"Are you sure?" Kate asked. "It looks like one from your collection."

"Sure, that's yours," Junior said. "I got it for you last Christmas."

Harley absently patted his pants pocket. "Huh. I must be worse off from last night than I thought. It's mine, all right. It must have fallen out of my pocket a coupla minutes ago when I was moving that stuff near the table. Thanks for finding it."

She handed it to him and turned her attention to Junior.

Junior clutched his blue cooler, searching for something to say. "I heard you've got bees in your house. You should be careful, because bees can be very dangerous."

Kate opened her mouth, thought better of telling Junior what she'd like to do with her bees, and snapped her mouth shut.

Matt asked the police what they knew so far, and it was nothing helpful. The building manager had opened the place at five to let in the cleaning crew. They'd done their job and left. The manager had stayed in his office. He'd also admitted to dozing off. Anyone could have slipped in at any point. Matt thanked the police and asked to be sent a copy of their report. Beyond that, he doubted that he'd hear from them again.

"Let's get to it," he said to his crew.

Harley volunteered to get the rest of the beer from Matt's truck while Torvald and Junior bought ice. It would be a shorter pouring day, but not a total wipeout. Kate got her hands on a ladder and roll of duct tape and began piecing the banner together from behind.

"Looks like you're going to need more tape," Matt said.

Kate leaned precariously from the top step of the ladder, trying to fix a torn piece. "I've got just enough. It's not going to be perfect, but it will do."

Harley rounded the table wheeling a dolly stacked with cases of bottled beer. His labored breathing made it clear that he was too hungover and out-of-shape to be a beer hauler.

"You're handling this situation like a champ," Harley said to Matt.

"I didn't know I had a choice."

"Most guys would be bitchin' and moanin'."

Matt smiled. "I've discovered it doesn't make much of a difference whether I do or don't, so I'm opting for don't."

Chet Orowski strolled up. "Looks like what goes round, comes round, huh, Culhane? I heard what happened to you." He looked at the scarecrow. "Looks to me like you screwed the wrong guy. You oughta be more careful."

"It's no big deal," Matt said. "We've still got some beer, the banner's okay, I'm thinking of using the scarecrow so I can ride in carpool lanes, and we're going to have fun. Because that's what we're in the business for, right?"

Chet threw up his hands, looking around the room, hoping for an audience. "Yeah, yeah, yeah. Great PR spin, but we both know the truth. Someone here hates you. I guess you're not the big star you thought you were."

"I've never thought of myself as a big star," Matt said. "I brew beer, and that's it."

Chet snorted. "Sure thing. You've got your pride the same as all of us, and now your nose is getting rubbed in it. It couldn't happen to a nicer guy."

Kate finished taping the sign and started down the ladder. The ladder rocked left and Kate leaned right, trying to keep from falling. For a long moment, both Kate and the ladder seemed to hover in the air before they both came crashing down. Straight onto Chet. And as they lay there in a heap, Kate was as grateful for Chet's bulk as she was for her small stature. Between the combination of the two, she didn't actually kill him.

"Chet didn't do it, you know," Matt said to Kate that night as they headed west through Detroit's endless string of suburbs.

She peeked into the backseat to check on Stella in her travel crate. "How can you be so sure?"

"Because he's a lot like your ex-husband. Lots of bluster and no action."

Kate looked out the window. "You don't know the half of it."

"All I'm saying is that Chet couldn't get out of his own way to pull off this stuff. And even if he did trash the booth—which he didn't—he doesn't have the right contacts in Keene's Harbor. Yeah, spare brewery kegs could have been floating around, but how would Chet have gotten his hands on one?"

Kate sighed. "Okay, good point, but we're right back to where we started. *More vandalism and too many sus-*

pects. We'll put Jerry on the back burner, since he wasn't around. That leaves us with the Mortensens, Junior, and Harley. Do we know where the Mortensens were last night?"

"In bed by nine, probably. They're a pretty low-key couple."

"We'll put them aside for now." She paused. "I did pick up Harley's lighter, though."

"He said he dropped it while straightening the booth. Did you find it someplace where that couldn't be possible?"

"No, it was on top of a box of coasters."

"Not exactly enough to convict the guy," Matt said. "Besides, Junior and Harley have each other for alibis. They were at a sports bar until the Pistons game ended, then back at the hotel bar until last call. Judging by the way they looked today, I'm sure they can prove it."

Kate sighed again. "I'm sure they can."

Stella whimpered from the backseat.

"Do you mind if I get her out?" Kate asked.

"No problem."

Matt kept his eyes on the road as Kate violated a couple of traffic laws while freeing her poodle.

"I can't believe how tired I am," Kate said once she and the dog were safely in front. "I think I'll just close my eyes and . . ." She yawned, and Matt filled in the rest of her words for himself.

Somewhere just east of Lansing, a slight whistling sound drew Matt's attention from the road. Kate was curled up with Stella. Both woman and dog were out cold. A louder whistling came his way. The dog was snoring.

FIFTEEN

ON THURSDAY MORNING KATE WOKE TO A POODLE NES-
tled next to her head. And, as had been true every morning since the workweek had started, her phone was
ringing. Kate's. Not Stella's. Kate had spoiled her baby
with long beach walks, but the dog would not be getting
a phone.

"Hello?" Kate said, feeling rested and ridiculously
content.

"Let me guess," Matt said. "You overslept."

Kate sat upright, and Stella grunted her disapproval
of the change in her sleeping arrangements.

"No way. Again? I set my alarm. Really."

She couldn't stop smiling, though. Several nights in a
row of more than eight consecutive hours of sleep. She
might not have any walls or a master bathroom or a living room floor, but at least the mold and most of the bees
were gone. She felt human again.

"If you could amble on in here before I take any more
guff about giving you special treatment, I just might
forgive you," Matt said.

He sounded amused, and Kate's smile grew into a grin.

"Let me take a shower and give Stella her morning
walk, and then I'll be right there."

Matt laughed. "So, like noon, right?"

"No later than ten, I promise."

"Hey, and find Bart when you get here, okay? Laila's ready to come back, so you're going to be assistant to the assistant brewers."

"Sounds filled with responsibility," Kate said. But really, she didn't care what Matt had her doing so long as she was earning and snooping . . . and getting to see him. She had fallen for him, and the ginger poodle had sealed the deal.

At precisely ten o'clock, Kate found Bart the brewmaster by a large wipe-off board where he was scribbling dates and other random things. Floyd, his assistant, stood to his right. The older man possessed a rather impressively sized beer belly. Kate had to appreciate a guy who showed that much love for his chosen career.

Next to Floyd was Nan O'Brien, assistant brewer number two. Nan was an Amazon of a woman, at least six feet tall, and fit. A hunter, triathlete, and seasoned sailor, Nan could whip any television survival show dude with one arm tied behind her back.

"Hey, Bart," Kate said. "Sorry I'm late."

"Let's talk before we get started," he said. He waved off his assistants, telling them they'd finish later.

Kate joined him at the whiteboard. "So tell me what you're going to be doing back here today."

"I'm going to be getting another batch of Dog Day ready to boil, which means that *you* are going to be cleaning the brewhouse for me."

She looked around. "The whole place?"

He laughed. "It looks like you're in need of a little more training, eh?"

Bart led her across the room and patted a big, almost bullet-shaped, tank that stood seven or so feet tall. "This is the brewhouse. A thirty-barrel brewhouse, to be exact. And those other tanks attached to it are the fermenters. After the boil, the wort is sent through the pipes to its left, and into those fermenters, where the yeast is added."

Really, the brewhouse was kind of pretty, all copper and stainless and shiny. And it looked very clean already, which she pointed out to Bart.

"It's not the same picture on the inside, and that's what you're going to be concerned with," he said.

"Hang on. You mean I have to get in there?"

"Yes. And believe me, it's a much easier fit for someone your size than it is for me or Nan or Floyd." He hitched his thumb toward the two assistant brewers who were now in conversation by the door to the large keg cooler room.

Great, Kate thought. She'd panicked in the walk-in a few weeks ago, and that room had nothing on this bomb-like capsule.

"I'm not a huge fan of dark, enclosed spaces," she told Bart.

"Who is, other than bats and mushrooms? You'll have a flashlight. And you won't be in there long. It's just a matter of doing a wipe-down to get rid of any leftover debris from the last batch before we quick-flush the system."

"Right, then," she said over the scared slamming of her heart.

"You'll be fine. I promise. I've got to get a couple of things lined up for a meeting with Matt, but Floyd and Nan will get you set up and keep a good eye on you."

He called them over, and Kate began to reconcile herself to this process. All the same, she was no longer impressed by the brewhouse's shiny rivets and copper accents. And its pressure gauges, valves, and pipes freaked her out.

"It's not as bad as it looks," Nan said. "We'll help you get in through that hatch at the top and then hand the supplies to you."

"How about I just watch you this time and I do it the next?" she asked Nan.

The other woman grinned. "Let me think about it. *No.*"

It had been worth a shot.

"I'll be right back with water, towels, and a flashlight," Nan said. "Floyd, why don't you grab the ladder?"

Floyd returned with the ladder, set it up, and climbed a couple of steps until he could reach the hatch at the top of the brewhouse. Once it was open, he scrambled back down.

"I've got it secured. Your turn now," he said.

"Okay . . ."

Nan returned and handed her the flashlight. Kate jammed it into the back of her jeans, for lack of another secure location that would also keep her hands free.

"You're a big, strong dog who can jump high," she said to herself.

"What?" Nan asked.

"It works on my dog when she's scared, so I thought I'd give it a try on me," Kate said as she climbed the ladder. But the affirmation hadn't helped. She peered into the darkness and then back at the assistant brewers. "So I just . . ."

"Climb in," Nan said.

Kate took a deep breath and tried to maneuver her body down the hole. Coordination and grace were not going to be part of the equation. She slid through the hatch in the top of the brewhouse, dropping herself into the darkness.

Once there, she sat and assessed the situation. Except for the lingering, evil smell of hops, it could have been worse. Light shone in through the open hatch like a big, fat ray of hope, and the confines weren't as tight as she'd thought they would be. She pulled the flashlight from the back of her jeans and switched it on. Nothing happened.

"Hey, the flashlight batteries are dead," she called to Nan.

Nan's face appeared in the hatchway. "I could look for more, but by the time I find them, you'll be done." She threw a roll of paper towels down to Kate, quickly followed by a spray bottle.

"Nan, Floyd, come on into my office. It's time to meet with Matt," Kate heard Bart saying.

Nan stuck her head in the hatch again. "Sounds like I have to take off."

"Couldn't you hang on a minute?" Kate asked. She liked knowing there was a lifeline outside her copper kettle.

"Don't worry about it. You're going to do great," Nan said. "Be sure to pay attention to all the seams and outlets. That's where the grunge sticks. Just throw the used paper towels out the top."

"Okay," Kate said. There was no answer. Nan had disappeared.

And the sooner Kate finished, the sooner she could stop being brave. She ripped a couple of paper towels off the roll and reached for the spray bottle. Taking a top-down approach, she began to wipe the tank's interior and hum a little vintage Eric Carmen, which she knew courtesy of her parents' ancient stereo. When she reached the chorus, she burst into full song.

"All by myyyyy-self . . ."

The tank's hatch fell shut with a clang.

"Hey, I wasn't even off-key," she said.

And then reality hit her. She was trapped. Sweat

popped out on her palms and, she was pretty sure, the soles of her feet.

"You're a big, strong dog who can jump high," she said.

Kate braced herself on the sides of the tank and pushed at the hatch. It didn't give. She might be a big, strong dog, but she couldn't sit alone in a metal coffin.

"Come on! Open the hatch!" she shouted.

The only answer was the rattle of the ladder being removed. And then water began flowing into the tank. It crept its way up her ankles and to her calves, and panic set in, big-time.

"Someone, *anyone*, come get me!"

Kate kicked at the side of the tank. She knew what was going to happen next. Wort was boiled. She was about to be boiled alive.

Matt paused in his discussions with his brewing staff.

"Did you hear something?" he asked Bart.

"Just you being too damn stubborn about the winter ale recipe," Bart said.

"No, from out there."

Nan shook her head. "I don't hear any—"

Matt raised his hand to silence her. A dull thud sounded again. "That!"

Matt shot from Bart's office and back into the brewery. The ladder to the brewhouse lay on its side, the hatch was closed, and Kate was nowhere to be seen. He caught the sound of running water and a muffled shout.

Matt grabbed the ladder and was at the top hatch in an instant. Someone had locked the unit, and the only ones who could do that had been with him. He flung open the metal door.

Kate stood down in the darkness.

"Are you okay?" Matt called to her.

"I think I need a raise."

Matt reached in an arm. "Can you make it up here?"

She grabbed his hand, scrambled out, and pinned herself against his body. She was soaked from the waist down.

Kate was gasping so much she could barely get her words out. "That sucked. That really, really sucked. I know you're supposed to face your fears, but seriously, never again."

Whoever did this to her would pay, Matt thought. He'd find them and then it would get ugly.

"Come on, let's get you dried off," he said.

By the time they'd reached the ground, Bart had dragged over a chair and Floyd had shut down the brewhouse.

Matt led Kate to the chair. "Bart, could you call the police?"

Bart looked shaken. "Sure thing."

Kate settled into Bart's chair, bent over, and untied her soggy sneakers. "Why would someone do that to me?"

Matt had his guesses, and they had to do with what—and who—he held of value.

"I don't know," he said. Now wasn't the time to point out the obvious.

She pulled off her shoes and socks. Matt noted that one sock was light blue and the other gray with little yellow ducks on it. Despite his tension, he smiled at the mismatch.

"Do you have any other clothes here?" he asked.

"No."

He did a mental inventory of his office, then said, "Hang on."

"Believe me, I'm not going anywhere."

And he didn't want her to, either. But for her own

safety, she would be. After today, Matt was going to make sure Kate was far from Depot Brewing Company.

Maybe boyfriend jeans were in style, but boss-or-whatever-more-he-was-to-her sweatpants weren't. Kate rolled the waist over as many times as possible and still she swam in the fabric. She paired the sweatpants with a T-shirt from the brewery store and did a small grimace. Okay, she thought, so she looked like a goofus, but at least she was a dry goofus.

Matt was waiting for her by the brewhouse with Chief Erikson.

"Do you feel up to answering some questions, Kate?" the police chief asked.

"Sure."

Matt glanced toward the latest in a stream of sympathetic Depot employees who'd been checking on Kate since her big swim. "How about in my office?" Matt suggested.

Clete closed the office door behind them. "Kate, did you see your attacker?"

"I was at the bottom of a tank, Chief Erikson. It was just me and a whole lot of dark."

The chief scribbled some notes, then turned to Matt, who'd taken a seat behind his desk. "You were close enough to be the first to Kate, Matt. Did you see anything unusual?"

"No. Bart, Floyd, Nan, and I were in Bart's office. We'd been having a pretty intense discussion, so I didn't hear or see anything at first." He picked up a pen and started jotting on a legal pad. When he was done, he tore off a piece and slid it across his desk to Clete. "These are the names of the people who were here this morning at ten. The taproom was still closed, so there were no customers in the house."

"Not paying, at least," Clete said. "But could an outsider have gotten into the brewery?"

"It's possible, I suppose," Matt said. "Except it's unlikely an outsider would have known that someone was in the tank."

"Not so true," Kate said. "I was singing 'All By Myself.' Kind of loudly, too."

Clete smiled. "Good song. Other than the brewers, does anyone else touch the brewing tank?"

"No," Matt replied. "The only exception would be if Bart has given any private tours. You'll have to ask him about that."

Clete nodded. "Matt, I don't know what you had planned for that unit today, but I need to call in my fingerprint team. We'll need to fingerprint your staff and you, Matt, though I suppose we already have your prints on file."

Matt showed a flash of a smile at that. "Yeah, I suppose you do from way back when. The file might be a little dusty."

The police chief rose from his chair. "Remember, no one near the brewhouse."

Clete left, and Matt's face grew somber.

"Kate, we have to talk," he said.

She knew what that meant. She'd last heard those words from Harley Bagger. Would she never hold a job in this town for longer than a month?

"You're kidding, right?" she asked. "You can't possibly be about to fire me."

Matt looked shocked. "I'm sorry."

"I don't want sorry. I just want my job."

"Kate, I have to do this," he said. "Yes, you survived this just wet and scared, but you said it earlier—this attack was aimed straight at you. I can't keep placing you in harm's way."

"I know all that, but you're forgetting one crucial thing. I can't eat, repair The Nutshell, or begin to plan for the future without money. And I need the bonus to stop the villain who plans to take my house if I can't get current on my mortgage by Thanksgiving."

"How about if I keep paying you? You can have the bonus money, the whole thing."

She shook her head. "I'm not going to let you pay me for doing nothing."

"Why not?" Matt asked. "Apparently, I do it for Jerry all the time."

"With you or without you, I need to find out who did this, or I'm never going to be able to put what happened in the brewhouse behind me. And what about you? You need this thing solved as much as I do. We must be getting closer if the creep's pushed it this far."

Matt started to speak a couple of times, but cut himself off. She waited.

"Okay. Work here," he finally said. "But understand that means you're going to be with me twenty-four/seven."

She smiled. "I think they have employment laws against those sorts of hours."

He gave her another frustrated look. "You know what I'm saying, and you know why. Someone is after you, and that person isn't messing around. So when we're here, you're with me, and when we're not, you're in my house."

She wanted to say he was exaggerating the situation, except that she'd just been treated like a beer additive.

"And at the risk of sounding even more like I'm trying to run your life, did you get the locks changed out at your place this week, Kate?"

"Actually, no." She'd been in a haze of poodle contentment and had forgotten Matt's suggestion.

"So anyone can walk in and hide until they're ready to come out. Does that sound about right?"

"Yes," Kate admitted.

"And do you have any walls or floors or a bathroom?"

"Jeesh. I have some walls and floors. And the bees are practically all gone."

"You like living with 'some' bees in a gutted house with no locks on an isolated stretch of the lake with a psycho after you?"

Kate kicked at the floor and looked at her shoe. "It's not gutted, it's decorator-ready. And, besides, every house has 'some' bees."

Matt rolled his eyes. "Then it's settled. I'll come with you while you pack. You and your poodle will stay with me until an arrest is made and your house is renovated and one hundred percent bee free."

"That could be a very long time."

Matt shrugged. "True."

He'd sounded almost happy, and secretly, Kate was, too.

"And you know that we'll probably end up wanting to kill each other," she said.

He smiled. "Old news."

"And that people are going to talk."

"They always do."

But what was gossip mere seconds ago now would be true. She, Matt Culhane, a fussy poodle, and a three-legged dog were going to be shacking up. The circus had just come to town.

SIXTEEN

MATT THOUGHT HIS HOUSE WAS PRETTY COOL. HE'D PUT a good couple of years into harvesting the timber from his property and then building the place. Because it had been designed to suit his needs, he'd never thought too much about how others might view it. Until now.

Kate climbed out of her Jeep, then scooped up Stella, who'd hopped into the driver's seat as soon as it had been vacated. That was close to their actual dog/woman relationship. To be totally accurate, Stella should have been driving the car.

Kate checked out his house. "I take it you had a thing for Lincoln Logs when you were a kid. This is one very impressive adult version thereof."

"You know what they say . . . The bigger the boys, the bigger—"

"We'll probably do better if we don't talk about the size of anything, especially your toys," she said, lingering by her vehicle. "This seemed a lot more sensible in the abstract than in reality. You . . . me . . . under one roof . . ."

He smiled. "I like it. A lot."

"That's what I'm worried about."

Okay, and she was worried that she'd like it a lot. She was worried she'd like it way too much.

"Come on in and have a look around," he said.

They climbed the cut flagstone steps to his front porch. He opened the door for Kate and the pooch.

She hesitated again. "Is Chuck in there?"

"Yes, but don't worry about him. I'll lock him in my bedroom until you and Stella get settled."

Kate stepped across the threshold. "Wow. This is gorgeous. There's a lot more light than I expected."

Matt had designed the house so that the back of the main living space had an expanse of windows overlooking the pond and woods beyond.

"It's a good-sized place, but there aren't that many actual rooms," he said. "I've put you in the only other fully enclosed bedroom, right next to mine, since I didn't think you'd want to deal with the loft." He pointed to the ladder that led to the house's half-floor. "The space up there is good, but the climbs up and down might be tough on the poodle."

She set her dog down. "A Stella-accessible room would be nice."

If this were Chuck, he'd be cruising and sniffing around. Not Stella. She checked out one floor tile and put her nose in the air. Matt guessed she wasn't much for the scent of hound. And she clearly wasn't into him.

After stowing Chuck away, Matt led Kate to the guest room. Stella stuck to her side.

"It's pretty basic." He gestured at the queen-sized log bed he'd built from wood they hadn't been able to use in the house. "You have your own bathroom through there."

"Works for me."

She sat on the edge of the bed, and Matt watched as she leaned back on her palms like she was testing the mattress for play. His favorite kind of play . . . Matt couldn't look away. In his mind, he'd already joined her.

They were both wearing a helluva lot less, and Stella was napping elsewhere.

"Nice," he said.

Kate flopped back, arms spread, luxuriating on the patchwork quilt he'd swiped from his mother. "It is. It's wonderful."

Matt hadn't been talking about the bed. He'd been thinking out loud, congratulating himself for maneuvering Kate into his house and his life. He moved closer to Kate and the wonderful bed, and a low growl sounded from somewhere very close to his left ankle. He looked down to see Kate's dog baring piranha-sharp teeth.

"Stella, stop that," Kate said. "You're going to have to get over it. We're guests here."

The dog's lip curled upward even more and Matt knew he had to make a tactical retreat until he stocked up on treats. He was going to lose this battle, but the war wasn't over.

Matt backed off. "What do you say we move on to the kitchen?"

The galley-style kitchen wasn't large, but Matt had built it to last, with granite countertops and quality appliances. Not that he used much of anything but the microwave.

"We haven't talked about cooking," he said.

"And we should probably keep it that way, too," she said. "My cooking would scare you. How about I'll fend for me and you fend for you?"

"Sure. But if I decide to actually cook a meal, I'm going to cook for you, too."

"Thank you," she said, smiling. She moved closer to the fridge, where he kept various niece—and now nephew—photos and scraps of kid art on the door.

Kate pointed to the hospital baby shot of Maura and Todd's latest. "There's TJ."

Matt nodded. "Yup, that's the bruiser. How did you know they were calling him TJ?"

"From the birth announcement."

"You got a birth announcement?"

"Of course," she said. "And I'm going to the pamper mom party that Lizzie is throwing next week."

"Party? I didn't know about a party."

"It's for women only. Lizzie probably wouldn't think of mentioning it to you."

Apparently, Kate was more looped into the Culhane clan than Matt had known. This was yet another sign that his sisters had a full underground social machine in place. A slightly ominous thought, but since it also meant Kate was both watched over and building friendships that might make her feel more at home in the town, he'd learn to deal.

"Anything else you'd like to share?" he asked.

"Not a thing."

After six days with Kate under his roof, Matt was having a hard time imagining her not being there. Unfortunately, the man-and-poodle relationship remained nothing to brag about.

"Are you sure you're okay with me being here on card night?" Kate called from the kitchen. "I could always meet up with Ella for a girls' night out."

"You're cool here," Matt said as he stowed beer by the poker table set up in his living room. "Chuck likes having you around."

Plus, Matt didn't want Kate too far out of sight. He remained spooked by last Thursday's near miss, and he flat-out enjoyed her company.

Kate came into the room with her dog trotting after her. She handed Matt a bowl of potato chips, and he stuck them on the table.

"I'm glad *Chuck's* fond of me," she said. "Probably best that I stay in tonight, anyway. After all the fries I chowed at work today, if I ate any more bar food, I'd never fit in these jeans again."

"Couldn't have that," Matt said, eyeing both the jeans and the hot curves that filled them. For two days, Matt had fought hard not to give in to temptation and touch her. He was done fighting.

Matt took a step toward her. Stella growled. He glared at the poodle.

Kate couldn't help a little smile. "I'll go grab that sandwich tray."

She cruised into the kitchen, but Stella kept eyeballing Matt.

Figuring it couldn't hurt, he tossed the dog a potato chip. The poodle crunched through it in three chomps. She wagged her tail at Matt, clearly seeking more. Just to see if the chip-eating had been a fluke, he gave her another. It disappeared immediately.

Matt smiled. "I think this is the beginning of a beautiful friendship."

A knock sounded at the front door, and Bart and Travis came in. After they dumped their jackets on the sofa, Bart handed out cigars.

Kate popped out of the kitchen with the sandwich tray. While she said hello to Travis and Bart, Matt put the tray up high enough that Chuck, who was faking a nap by the fireplace, couldn't grab it.

Kate spotted the cigars and wrinkled her nose. "Do you guys really smoke those things?"

"Sure," Matt said, though his usually just smoldered in the ashtray.

"Gross."

Travis cut his eyes to her. "Ever tried one? You should before dissing them."

Kate laughed. "Thanks, but I'm still recovering from the beer tasting. I'll just mosey on into the kitchen and think healthy thoughts while I eat my salad. Come on, Stella, let's go."

Stella stared at her owner, but didn't move from Matt's side.

Kate motioned to her. "Come on, girl." When Stella stayed put, she said to Matt, "It looks like you two are getting along better."

"We're working on it," Matt said. *One chip at a time.* "Don't worry about her. She can hang with us for a while."

Kate gave the poodle one last, speculative look and headed back into the kitchen alone. Five minutes later, Matt's brother-in-law Jack arrived with a bottle of Irish whiskey in hand.

"Let's get rolling," Matt said. "Todd called this afternoon. He can't make it. TJ has him too sleep-deprived to function."

"Which is why he should be here," Jack said. "We could use a donkey."

Bart poured everyone a shot. "We still have you." For a second, Jack looked as sharp-edged as his red brush cut, but then he joined in on the laughter. After that, the ceremonial opening whiskey was downed, some bull was shot, and stacks of quarters were lined up.

Matt slid the dealer button in front of himself on the table and shuffled the deck.

"Texas Hold 'Em," he announced to the players.

Kate wandered back into the room. "Is Stella still here?"

Matt grinned. "Right next to me. Jealous?"

"Possibly."

Matt chose to take that as a sign that she wanted his company, and not the poodle's.

"Have you ever played poker?"

She paused. "Once." Maybe no one else in the room could read her, but Matt knew she was messing with the truth. Kate's tell was a subtle widening of her eyes.

"So, Kate, want to join in?" Jack asked in a casual voice.

"I guess I could. I mean, if it wouldn't slow you guys down too much?"

"Never!" Jack said.

He clearly thought he'd landed his donkey, but Matt bet Jack was going to keep the tail and big ears.

"Sure, then," Kate said. "I'd love to."

Matt gave Kate his chair and half his quarters. After he'd brought another chair from the kitchen and settled in next to her, a low growl sounded from beneath the table. Matt grabbed a couple of chips. He popped one into his mouth and subtly let the other one drop to an overly possessive poodle.

"Since we have a new player, how about we go with a little straight poker, aces high, sevens wild? And I'll sit out on the first couple of hands and help Kate get started," Matt said.

The table agreed, and Matt dealt.

Once Kate had her hand, he moved his chair closer to coach her. Stella wasn't square with the new arrangement and let everyone know by barking.

Matt edged the potato chip bowl closer. He was going to need it.

A couple more chips and many hands later, everyone was played out. Jack, Travis, and Bart had rounded up their remaining change, razzed Kate about her big win, and headed home.

Kate now sat at the kitchen table as Matt worked his way through the last of the night's mess. Stella was flopped at her owner's feet, zoned out on carbs.

"So how many times have you really played poker?"

Matt asked, hoping to keep Kate's attention from the chip-enriched poodle.

"Lots," Kate said.

Matt smiled. "As I thought."

He finished packing away the guys' unsmoked cigars. While they'd played, he'd silently nixed any attempt to light one. Matt had wanted Kate next to him too much to risk her leaving the game over a stogie.

She rose and reached for the nearly empty potato chip bag. "I started playing a while back. Casino night fundraisers were a fad downstate a couple of years ago. Any time one of Richard's clients' pet charities had one, we'd go." Kate moved on to put glasses into the dishwasher, and Stella followed. "Anyway, after a couple of events, Richard stopped playing at my table," Kate said. "It irked him to see me kick butt. It was luck, mostly."

"Luck and being able to read others," Matt said.

He was done hiding what he wanted from Kate. It was time to be read, loud and clear. He tucked a couple of chips into his right hand while she was closing the dishwasher.

"I liked having you next to me tonight," he said. "And Stella didn't seem to mind us being close."

She held so still that Matt wondered for an instant whether she was going to bolt from the kitchen. But he knew she wanted him, too.

"In fact, I'll bet my winnings we could get even closer," Matt said.

As he moved in to kiss her, he dropped a chip for Stella. Then he wished like hell that dogs chewed with their mouths closed.

Kate glanced down. "Did you just give her a treat?"

Matt kept it short and sweet. "Yes."

"Now I know why you two are making friends. Smart move. But I didn't see you get anything from the treat jar.

The last thing I saw you near was that bag of potato chips. Did you give her a chip?"

"No."

She stepped back, looked him up and down, and smiled. "You are the worst bluffer, *ever.*"

Which was bull. Except when it came to Kate.

"Open your hand," she said.

Matt shifted his feet, stalling. "Which one?"

She wrapped her fingers around his right hand and squeezed. Matt's lone chip died an ugly death.

"Now open it," she said.

Matt did as directed. A few crumbs slipped from his hand, and Stella dove for them.

"Stella, no!" Kate said.

Too late. Stella snapped up the bits before they hit the floor.

Kate gave Matt a stern look. "You know I don't feed her from the table."

Matt dumped the remaining crumbs into the wastebasket. "We aren't at the table. We're in the kitchen."

Stella trotted up to Matt and braced her front feet on his shin as she begged for more.

Kate sighed. "You've created a monster. Down, Stella."

The dog grudgingly obeyed, but stayed close to Matt.

SEVENTEEN

FOR ABOUT THE TENTH TIME SINCE WEDNESDAY POKER night, Kate tripped over a pair of Matt's shoes . . . and it was only Friday. Why would a guy think it was smart to drop his shoes exactly where he'd taken them off? He had big feet, too. And many, many pairs of shoes.

Kate picked up the latest pair and chucked them just to the left of his closed bedroom door, where they joined a bunch of their kin.

"If you want to develop a shoe-eating habit, I promise I won't say a word," she told Stella. "It would be a good payback for Matt getting you hooked on potato chips."

The dog was now a serious chip junkie. Even though she'd gotten sick on them, she still sat longingly in front of the pantry cabinet, where Matt always kept his stash.

Kate's poodle had food issues on another front, too. Stella had been raised with an open supply of food. Kate would put kibble in her bowl in the morning and the poodle would graze at will. But now, the second Kate filled Stella's bowl, glutton Chuck appeared, excited as if Thanksgiving had come around yet again. The instant Kate looked away, the chow was gone in one gulp. Chuck did not believe in chewing.

As though he knew Kate was thinking about him, a bark rolled into the hallway from the living room. And then another. These weren't excited sounds, more expository statements.

"Woof."

Kate joined Chuck in front of the fireplace.

"Woof."

He had barely lifted his head from his napping position.

"What?" she asked him.

"Woof."

Kate looked at Stella, who had followed in her tracks. "You speak dog. Tell him to stop."

But Stella couldn't be persuaded to negotiate, and Chuck had no intention of stopping.

"Okay, Lassie. Did Timmy fall down the well again?"

"Woof."

"Am I the prettiest princess in the land?"

"Woof."

Kate could have played her game awhile longer, but Chuck's hound bark was beginning to make her teeth rattle. She walked through the kitchen and on to the basement door, which was by the house's back entry. Stella stood at the back door and stared expectantly at her.

"Okay, you first, then I'll deal with the big dog." She stuck Stella on the outdoor lead that had been brought over from The Nutshell, and headed back inside.

"Matt?" she called.

He was downstairs working out, a daily event. She heard the whine of a treadmill going at warp speed, but no word from Matt.

"Hey, Culhane!" she yelled, cupping her hands to either side of her mouth.

"What?"

"Your dog needs you."

The treadmill's hum lowered as he brought its speed down, then stopped entirely.

"Woof."

"See? Like that," she said as he climbed the steps.

When he made the top, Kate was transfixed. He used his right hand to wipe sweat from a six-pack of abs so hard she wanted to trace each ridge with her tongue. Twice.

His smile was slow and knowing. "You probably should let me by."

Or not, she thought.

"Woof."

"He's just lying there, barking," she said.

Matt moved past her, close enough that she could catch the heat rolling off his body . . . though it just might have been hers.

Kate followed him to Chuck.

"What's up, buddy?" he asked the dog.

"Woof."

"What's he barking at?" Kate asked.

"He's barking *at* nothing. That's his water bark. He has specific barks for specific things."

"You've got to be kidding."

"You think? Come with me to the kitchen."

Kate trailed after him. "Amazing," she said as she watched him claim the empty water bowl and refill it.

And really, she wasn't just talking about the dog. When it came to Matt, the view from the rear was almost as impressive as that from the front. She catalogued each of these moments to tide her over in her lonely, dog-guarded bed.

"So Stella the Wonderpoodle doesn't have different barks?" he asked.

"No, but she can now identify an unopened potato chip bag by sight."

Matt laughed. "A lot of dogs have different barks for different needs. Stella's pretty smart. Maybe you just don't know her signs anymore."

"Maybe, but for now, let's talk about shoes."

"Isn't that the kind of thing that would go over better with Ella and my sisters?"

"Doubtful, Imelda," she said. "I'm betting if I stacked all of my shoes against yours, you'd win."

He looked almost wounded. "I don't have that many."

"This way, please." She beckoned him away from the kitchen and to the bedroom hallway in tour guide fashion. "And here we have Mount Culhane, an active volcano, altitude six pairs and growing daily."

He regarded the pile suspiciously. "How did they all end up here?"

"I've been moving them every day."

"From where?"

"Exactly where you take them off, it appears. It was becoming a minefield out there."

He was still staring at the shoes. "I'd wondered where they all went."

"What? They're right by your door. Don't you look at the ground?"

"No need," he said. "I could walk this house blindfolded."

"Then next time, I'll trip you up and take them all the way into your bedroom."

A slow smile spread across his face. "Would you?"

Kate realized she had just committed a tactical error and morphed into his maid.

He leaned down and kissed her. "Thanks, sweetheart."

Okay, make that two tactical errors, because she didn't stop him. And now three, because she was kissing him back.

It had been tough work forgetting just what it felt like

to be kissed by Matt Culhane. And it had been tougher yet to block the thought that she was one wall away from him every night. She knew that he sometimes talked in his sleep. She knew that he woke and showered at six. And she knew that right now she'd be beyond blissed-out should they make love.

Telling herself she was ten kinds of crazy, Kate deepened the kiss and touched the wall of muscle on his chest. And while they kissed some more, she ran her fingers down to the waistband of his shorts.

She didn't know for sure what he'd look like totally naked, but she could give it a good guess based on the size of his shoes. He brought her tighter against his body. She drew in a surprised breath. She had underestimated.

"Aren't you going to do that magical thing where I'm suddenly on a bed?" she asked. Because she really, really wanted him to.

He made some space between the two of them. "I don't know. I haven't made my mind up yet."

"What could possibly involve our minds?"

She'd been joking, but he looked serious.

"One question," he said. "If we do this . . . if I make love to you . . . what happens next?"

"We go unconscious?"

"No, after that. Does it mean that you're going to move from your room and into mine?"

"Well, no. But it does mean we'll both be less tense."

He shook his head. "That's not good enough for me, Kate."

"But back at the hotel you would have . . ."

"You're right. But I've been thinking about this since we were out of town, and it turns out that I'm not a fling sort of guy. Actually, once I considered it, I realized I never have been."

Something wasn't computing. "What about your Keene's Harbor's reputation as the resident Don Juan?"

He shrugged. "I've dated my share of women, but none of those women have anything to do with you," Matt said. "You and I are in a different place. We're friends—the kind of friends I don't want to give up unless we become something more. So if you and I go there, it has to be with the full commitment to be my lover, because no way am I going to risk our friendship for less."

"You're scaring me a little."

"I probably should be scaring you a lot. Because I mean it, Kate. Once I'm in, I'm *all* in."

So unless she was ready for commitment, she had struck out?

"And what about The Nutshell?" she asked.

"It has nothing to do with us. It's all business."

Kate crossed her arms. "You wouldn't say that if it was your house or your brewery."

"Kate, I paid the bank $200,000 for that mortgage. I gave you until Thanksgiving to make a go of it. But I can't afford to wait any longer than that. I need the money, either from you or from the restaurant I plan to open next summer."

"I'm sorry," she said. "I'm just not ready for this."

And while it was tougher than any trek she'd ever taken, Kate retreated to reclaim her poodle. She might be ten kinds of stupid, but for now, she'd managed to avoid adding an eleventh.

The next morning, Matt walked into his office—or what had been his office before he'd made Kate his personal assistant. Now ownership was questionable.

"Ginger just called," Kate said.

"What did she want?" Until he had a signal from Kate otherwise, he planned to keep it all business.

"She'd like to know your Traverse City schedule. We're working on coordinating your calendar so that someone other than you has a clue where you'll be at any given time."

"Nobody but me really needs to know."

"Nice try, but untrue. We also talked about getting bids from subcontractors on the Tropicana, since you've decided to be the general contractor. I know you wanted to keep the bids local, but it's a motel, Matt. You need to take advantage of that. We think you should widen your net some, since you can offer up rooms in exchange for lower price quotes."

Matt smiled. "You look comfortable there."

She looked around. "Where?"

"Behind my desk. With your papers everywhere." There was a certain order to his pile filing system, and he hoped she hadn't messed with it.

"Where else would I work? I mean, I suppose I could go use the phone at the servers' stand, but I figure folks should have to work a little harder for their gossip than just lurking behind me."

"How about we switch off and at least I get the spot behind my desk for a while?" he asked. "I need to get to the computer."

She rose. "Do you want me out of here?"

And that was the thing of it. Even though they had a long way to go on a personal basis, and it made him a little crazy to have her close, he wanted her nearby.

"You can stick around," he said. "I'm just placing a yeast order. We're coming to the last generation we can use to brew."

Kate had just moved to the visitor's side of the desk when a knock sounded at the door and Lizzie poked her head into the office.

"So, business or pleasure?" Matt asked.

"Business, definitely." Lizzie sat down. "Chief Erikson asked me to stop by and give you an update on the incident with Kate in the brewhouse."

"I'm guessing that it's more of a no-news update, or Clete would be here himself," he said.

Lizzie nodded. "You've got his act down. The bottom line is that the brewhouse is as clean of evidence as the arson event. There were no prints that couldn't be accounted for. I can rule someone out, though."

"Really? Who?" Matt asked.

"Jerry. It seems that he took on a second job when his wife got laid off from the bank. He was there when Kate took her swim."

"Good to know. Sort of," Matt said.

"He thought he could pull off a second job without rocking the boat, but it's been a scheduling mess," Lizzie said. "He's going to come talk to you."

Matt nodded. He wished his manager had done that earlier, but he knew all about overconfidence sending a guy out to the end of a branch about to break. Matt had done it both literally and figuratively. He could forgive Jerry for doing the same.

"It's a start, but not much of one," Lizzie said. "For now, let's keep things status quo. I know you've got the guard service, but we'll continue with the extra drive-bys, too. And Kate, you keep staying at Matt's."

Matt looked down at his desk to hide his reaction to this mixed blessing. Then he started reading the papers Kate had left there. He picked one up.

"Kate, what's this about?"

"It's a booking contract."

"I see that. And I see that Depot Brewing Company is contracting with someone named Dr. Love."

"A blues band. I need you to sign the contract first, of course."

"Nice of you to recall that detail," he said.

"I know where I am on the org chart."

"I don't have an org chart."

Kate pointed at a file folder at the top edge of the desk. "You do, now. I was going to post it by the time clock."

"This is a microbrewery, not a multinational corporation," Matt said. "With the possible exception of you, everyone knows who's in charge here."

Lizzie stood. "I'm all done here. I'll just leave you to do . . . whatever it is you're doing."

"Witnessing a pretty impressive attempted coup, I think," Matt said.

"Okay, then." Lizzie gave Kate a wave. "Coup away!"

Matt turned to Kate as soon as Lizzie left the room. "What is the brewery going to do with a blues band?"

"Start a summer music series out on the terrace when the weather allows and in the taproom when it doesn't?"

At least she'd made her statement sound more like a question.

"Look, I'm not saying that the idea is bad, because actually it's great," he said. "I just don't have the time to deal with it. I've got too much going on up north."

"That's the best part. I can do all the grunt work," Kate said. "You don't give me enough to do, so if I have this on my plate, there's a good chance I won't be nosing into everything else."

"How good of a chance?" About all she had left to do was alphabetize the pantry and tick off the cooks.

"Very good. And I really think this could work, Matt. You have a lot of summer people who will drive all the way to Traverse City for live music. Keep them in town, and your business will jump."

Matt just shook his head. She was right. "Write me up a proposal."

Kate came around the desk and stood close to him. She riffled through some papers, then held up a neatly bound document. "Already done."

He opened the report and paged through a market study, cost analysis, and financial projections, complete with pie charts.

"You're good, Kate. *Very* good."

Kate smiled wickedly. "You don't know the half of it." But he wanted to.

EIGHTEEN

KATE DIDN'T WANT TO JINX THINGS, BUT SHE WAS ON A roll. Over a week had passed since Matt had given her permission to schedule music events, and she'd gotten next summer booked. And because she was in over-achiever mode, she'd also finished all the promo materials. Okay, maybe she wasn't so much in overachiever mode as fill-every-waking-hour-so-she-couldn't-think-of-Matt mode, but no matter. The results were the same. Kate rose and double-checked the events calendar she'd hung on the office wall.

Even better, her house was nearly repaired. The contractor had been very cooperative. He said he needed the work, so she could pay after the holidays. All it needed was some fresh paint, some new furniture, and a head-to-toe cleaning.

She stood hands on hip, pleased. "You're golden," she told herself.

Matt had scheduled a mandatory 10:30 staff meeting this morning. For no reason other than pride, she'd wanted to be done with these projects before then.

Kate's cell phone rang. She went back to the desk, picked it up, and did a double take at the name on the caller ID: Barb Appleton. She and her mom didn't talk frequently. It wasn't that her mom didn't love her, or that she didn't love her mom. They were just in different places in life. But today, Kate felt happy that her mom was calling.

"Hey, Mom."

"Hello, Kate. You're a tough one to reach."

"I answered on the third ring," she said.

"I didn't mean now, dear. I've been leaving messages on the phone at The Nutshell for days. Where have you been?"

Kate searched for an explanation. Her mom liked her kids in one piece.

"I . . . I've been having some work done out there and staying with friends until it's complete," Kate said.

"What sort of work?"

"I've been getting the exterior doors re-keyed," she replied. Which wasn't a total lie, because she still planned to. Eventually.

"Why would you do that? We've owned that cottage for decades and kept it unlocked for just as long. There's no place safer than Keene's Harbor."

Kate withheld comment.

"How is the house looking?"

"Just fine. Why?"

"Your father and I are feeling a little nostalgic. I know we usually stay in Naples October through May, but we were thinking that popping up to Keene's Harbor for a family Thanksgiving would be wonderful. Just like the old days."

"But we always had Thanksgiving at the country club," Kate said. "You know, the Thanksgiving Day Parade in Detroit, then turkey with your choice of stuffing and sides, overlooking the putting green."

"We must have had it at The Nutshell once," Mom said.

"No. Never."

"Then it's definitely time. Your father and I aren't getting any younger, you know, Kate."

Man, she hated it when her mother played the aging card.

"Neither am I, Mom."

"True. So this year, let's get you, Chip, Bunny, and all the family up to the cottage for an old-fashioned meal."

A couple weeks ago, Kate might have been horrified. The insecurity and jealousy that had infected her marriage to Richard had just sort of bled all over her other relationships, including the one with her family. But the truth was that, before Richard, holidays like Thanksgiving had always been a really big deal to her.

Suddenly, Kate realized that she missed her mom. She missed her dad. She missed her brother and sister. They were her family and they loved her and she loved them. She might as well get on the turkey train. "That sounds fun. Can't wait."

"Good, dear. Now see if you can find a chef to cook for us. I just want to relax with the family. If you can't, we might have to come up with another option. Perhaps a restaurant up that way?"

"I'll start looking."

"Keep me abreast of the plans."

"Sure thing. Give my love to Dad."

Kate hung up and went facedown on the desk. She'd forgotten about Matt. How was she going to explain that they were living together to her parents? Matt entered the room and settled into a guest chair. "What's up?"

Little wrinkle lines were forming on Kate's forehead. "My whole family is coming to The Nutshell for Thanksgiving."

"And?"

Kate bit her lower lip. "I've got two problems. One is of the big variety. The other could be huge."

"Lay it on me."

Kate sighed. "You know how Charlie Brown had a Thanksgiving party for Peppermint Patty, except that he could only make popcorn and toast?"

Matt laughed. "Yeah."

"Well, I can only make toast."

Matt got out of his chair and hugged her close. It was nice—friendly and loving. Like she had known him all her life. "No worries. I'll help. It'll be fun. Was that the big or huge problem?"

In Matt's arms, her problems seemed small. "My parents are a little . . ." She paused. "Conservative."

Matt smiled. "No problem. We can bond over our shared opposition to the hippie menace."

"If they find out I'm living with a guy, they'll be horrified. They won't understand that cosmic forces are to blame."

Matt shook his head. "Isn't this Barb the table dancer we're talking about?"

"Barb, the *married* table dancer," Kate pointed out. "It's like the 1960s in my family. It's all about the order of events. You don't skip past the entrée straight to dessert and you don't shack up. The only thing that could make it worse is announcing at Thanksgiving that you're my baby daddy."

Matt's eyebrows perked up. He held her tighter. "That can be arranged, too. And, on the plus side, no one will care about only having toast for Thanksgiving."

"I'm serious."

Matt brushed her hair away from her face. "So we have a minor inconvenience to deal with."

Kate looked at him for a long while. "And it's Thanksgiving. And if I can't find your saboteur by then, my house belongs to you. So it really isn't a 'we' problem. It's my problem."

"I see."

Kate felt bad. The truth was, she wanted it to be their problem. And, in her heart, she'd said something very different to Matt. But her hasty words had just sort of popped out and hung in the air like a bad smell. Kate decided to change the subject. She'd try to make it right with Matt later, after work.

"The first thing I need to do is get a locksmith, then move back and get The Nutshell ready for them," she said.

"Thanksgiving is still over a week off. What's the rush?"

"I just think it's time. It's been pretty quiet the past few weeks. Maybe the jerk has gotten bored with the whole thing and moved on. Anyway, I'm feeling safer now."

She hesitated and looked at Matt with wide, hopeful eyes. "And you can get your life back."

"For the record, I'm okay with my life the way it is. But all the same, even though I don't like it or fully understand it, I'm not going to stop you from moving back out there," Matt said.

"Thanks."

It was what she'd asked for, but it wasn't what she'd wanted. She wanted to add that she knew she was being weird. That this was what dealing with her parents did to her, and she just couldn't stop herself.

"Chuck has kind of grown to like having Stella around," Matt said.

She knew what he was saying, and it had nothing to do with dogs. But maybe she was more traditional than she wanted to believe.

"Maybe I can bring Stella over to visit every now and then?"

"Chuck would like that," Matt said. He hitched his thumb toward the door. "Do you think you could head out to the taproom? I need a couple of minutes to get my notes together."

She needed a couple of minutes to pull herself together, too. This had hurt way more than she'd thought it would.

After Kate left, Matt sat at his desk. He had no notes. All he had was a numb sensation he'd last felt when he'd fallen off his roof and nearly knocked himself out.

Matt couldn't nail the exact moment, but at some point reality and he had parted ways. Having Kate in his house and in his life had felt real to him, not just an arrangement. But even though they'd had breakfast together, gone to work together, and flipped a coin over whether to watch football or movies at night, it hadn't been real.

If he'd been rational, he'd have known it had been all the illusion and none of the substance of being a couple. But he wasn't rational. He was in love.

Still, no matter how crappy he might be feeling, he had a roomful of people waiting for him out there. So he'd move on and deal with his feelings for Kate later. Matt joined his crew in the taproom, and when he looked at his gang, he felt better, if not perfect.

"Thanks to those of you who weren't scheduled for coming in, and the rest of you for being here early," he said. "I don't have a lot of big-picture updates about what's going on here at Depot Brewing, except to officially announce the start of a music series next summer that Kate's been putting together, and I'm sure most of you have heard about it, anyway. I think we're going to see a big jump in business on formerly slow nights, and I want to put on more part-time staff. If you know of anyone good, send them my way."

Steve, the server, raised his hand. "I've heard that Bagger's is cutting staff down to one server a shift. You might pick up someone there."

"Thanks," Matt said.

He'd known that traffic had been down for Harley, but he hadn't known it was that bad. If it was time to give Harley a hand, Matt was glad to do it.

"And now on to other news," Matt said. "I know that a lot of you have had questions about where I go when I'm not around the brewery. To make a long answer short, I've been spending a lot of time in Traverse City, and that time investment is starting to pay off. By next summer, I'll be looking for staff for a microbrewery up there, plus for a new motel and restaurant. I'm also opening a new restaurant in Keene's Harbor. It's a couple miles out of town on the lake. If any of you are interested in making the move, you'll get first shot at the openings. Think it over and let me know. No rush, okay? And now I'm going to turn the meeting over to Jerry to update you on front of the house matters."

His manager had just started talking when Matt motioned Kate over. They walked into the hallway by his office.

"Why don't you take the rest of the day off? Get your locksmith and whatever else you need done lined up so that you can move back to The Nutshell," he said.

"And what's the point?" She felt anger rising in her voice. "New locks on a great old house you're just going to bulldoze. I never had a chance. I wouldn't be surprised if you put Junior up to the mess he caused me just to seal the deal."

She knew she'd gone too far, but he'd caught her by surprise with his announcement, and it had all come gushing out.

Four days later, Kate stood in The Nutshell's living room steeling herself for her parents' impending arrival. She was pretty sure she had her act together, since she'd prepared as she would for any natural disaster. Kate had stocked up on Manhattan mixings and maraschino cherries for her dad and champagne and crossword puzzles for her mom. She'd also hidden a handful of candy bars and three bags of potato chips in her bedroom in case she needed to take shelter for an extended period of time.

It was nearly six, and a pot of beef stew simmered in the kitchen. Kate had thrown in a jar of cocktail onions and some red wine, hoping she could fake her mom into thinking it was a classic *boeuf bourguignon*. Mom had always been all about dinner being a sit-down meal, even if the house had been falling down around them. When she was a kid, it sometimes seemed inconvenient. Now, she realized it was one of the best parts of her childhood—a constant in her adolescent life that made her feel safe and protected.

Kate smoothed her hands over the black pencil skirt, which she'd last worn when working at *Detroit Monthly*. Mom didn't believe in jeans, paper napkins, or ketchup at the dinner table. As a teen, Kate had tried to assure her mother that all those things were perfectly real and even kind of cool. Mom had never bought in.

Tonight, Kate didn't mind being dressed up. If nothing else, the change in wardrobe kept it front and center in her mind that she'd been right not to expose Matt to this. Somehow, she couldn't picture him wearing a button-down shirt just to eat beef stew.

Stella's ears perked at the sound of a car in the drive. She trotted toward the front door and gave a welcoming yip.

Kate gave the dog a gentle pat. "Sure, it's all happiness and sunshine, now. But let's see what tune you're singing by turkey day." The truth was, she was excited, too.

Kate pulled on her jacket and went outside to greet her parents. Stella, who wasn't a fan of the icy wind off the lake, lurked indoors.

Though Kate had visited with her parents just a handful of months ago, she felt a surprising sense of nostalgia seeing them here, at The Nutshell. The years had treated her father well. With his Florida tan, silver hair, and aristocratic features, he still reminded Kate of a diplomat in the foreign service.

Mom was no slacker, either. Her hair might have tipped the scales from blond to gray, but otherwise, she looked much as she had when Kate was a teen. And she still stood a good four inches taller than Kate, too.

After hugs and greetings, Kate looked into the back of the SUV her dad had rented.

"That sure is a lot of luggage, Mom," Kate said.

Kate's mom removed a suiter from the back. "It might seem excessive, but you never know what events might pop up and how the weather might be."

"In this case, not many events and freezing would be good bets." Kate glanced at her mom's pale pink and very thin cardigan sweater. "Do you have a coat in one of those suitcases?"

"I have another sweater or two, but I left my mink in cold storage."

Kate was no fan of furs, but if her mom had to wear one, now would be the time. "You can borrow one of my jackets while you're here."

"That's all right. I'll ring up Bunny and ask her to bring something appropriate," Mom said. "In the meantime, your father and I can pretend we're snowbound and stay indoors. It could be very romantic."

Kate put her muscles to work, helping her dad haul the luggage. In the time it took them to get everything inside, Stella had fallen asleep on her mom's lap.

Kate's mother sat on the flowery sofa, stroking Stella. "Your dog's a charmer, Kate. What do you think I should get her for Christmas?"

"Anything in cashmere would probably do."

Her mother laughed. "Well, naturally. She is an Appleton female. And how about you?"

"I . . . uh . . . Let me get back to you on that one." Kate couldn't think of the last time her mother had gotten her anything other than a gift card. Of course, she also couldn't recall when she'd gotten her mother anything other than a silk scarf. "Why don't you two get settled in, and I'll get dinner on the table?"

Half an hour later, after her parents had their cocktails in hand, the family sat down to Kate's fake *boeuf bourguignon*. The onions tasted weird even to Kate, but no one mentioned them. In fact, her dad said that stew made the perfect meal when snowed in. Never mind that they weren't really snowed in, and that Kate had started the stew hours before their arrival.

Toward the end of the meal, Kate's dad stuck an old Johnny Mathis album on the stereo. "Katie, the house looks just great. Better than I remember. I really think you could make your plan to turn this place into a B&B work."

He turned to Kate's mom. "Remember seeing Johnny perform that winter in Lake Tahoe?"

The two of them shared a smile and clasped hands on the tabletop. Kate pushed around the onions in her stew, not wanting to break into their moment.

"Kate, if you'll excuse us, your mother and I need to have this dance. And don't worry about clearing the table. We'll do that . . . later."

"Sure," Kate said. "I'll just go take care of some stuff in my room." She didn't feel like telling them right now about Matt and his plans to turn the house into a restaurant.

She listened to her parents laugh through the walls of her room. If this was to be a nightly event while playing snowed-in, Kate was going to need more chips and chocolate in her stash. For crying out loud. These people were her parents.

According to Kate's clock, it was now ten at night. It felt more like three in the morning. Kate was bored out of her mind. The music downstairs was still going strong, though her parents had moved on to Frank Sinatra.

For lack of anything else to do, Kate dumped her purse onto the dresser and began to sort through the bag's contents. A cleaning might make it weigh less than a ton. Kate pulled out her wallet, makeup bag, and the notepad she carried to write "to do" lists that she could then ignore. At the purse's bottom, in a nest of pennies and market receipts, lay the letter from her mom that she'd tucked away and never finished reading.

"Now's as good a time as any."

Kate settled on the bed. Because she'd already heard a fresh update on all nieces and nephews during dinner, she fast-forwarded past the opening chat and the bit where her mom wished that Kate would have gotten a business degree.

But there's no remaking the past. Your road won't be as easy as mine, her mother wrote. *Still, I know you're up to the challenge. Yes, you've been struggling, and it was obvious to both your father and me how much it upset you to ask us for help. But we were happy to give it, darling. And though it's not kind to say, neither your father nor I were especially fond of Richard. He tended to try to build himself up at your expense. You'll be a happier woman without him.*

"You've got that right," Kate said.

I think in many ways, I envy you, Kate. You have a spirit I didn't have at your age. Oh, I had my moments, but you have me beat. You also have the determination

to weather the tough times. I'm not so sure I would have
had your sort of grit. I am very proud of you. I need to
tell you that more often, and you need to begin believ-
ing it. Then we'll rule the world.

Kate smiled. Maybe she could imagine her mother
dancing on tabletops, after all. And maybe she had been
wrong about her parents all these years. It wasn't that
they thought she couldn't do anything, it was that they
thought she could do everything.

A while before midnight, Matt sat alone at his closed bar
nursing a tall glass of water. Since Kate had moved out,
his universe had been totally jacked up. He'd even been
feeling sorry for himself, which was a new and unpleasant sensation.

When the cuckoo clock over the bar struck twelve,
Matt planned to get the hell over this. Somehow. And in
the meantime, he'd watch the clock's minute hand move.

A sharp rapping sounded on the taproom window,
pulling Matt's attention from the clock. Lizzie stood at
the glass in her police officer's uniform, flashlight in
hand.

Matt pointed her toward the front entrance.

"What are you doing here?"

"My promised late-night rounds," she said. "The
bigger question is, what are you still doing here?"

"Waiting for midnight."

"Why? Are you going to turn into the guy version of
Cinderella or something?" She grinned. "Kate mentioned
your shoe fixation."

"More like I was hoping to turn back into myself."

"I didn't know you weren't yourself. I mean, you
skipped last Friday's fund-raiser and everything," Lizzie
said.

He rubbed the back of his neck. "Yeah, well, Kate

moved out, and I wanted to enjoy my new peace and quiet, but Chuck really misses her."

"He's really stuck on Kate, huh?"

"This isn't the kind of stuff we talk about," he said. "It feels wrong."

She gave him a crooked smile. "It's just that 'Chuck' doesn't generally have relationship problems, and I don't generally have relationships."

"Good point," he said.

Lizzie sat down on a barstool next to Matt. "So why did Kate move out?"

Matt was surprised by the question. Kate and Lizzie had grown pretty close.

"You mean she hasn't talked to you?"

"Not in the past few days."

"She found out her parents were coming in for Thanksgiving, and she kind of freaked out. Apparently, they don't believe in sleeping in a guy's guest bedroom before you're married."

"Interesting," Lizzie said. "And in more ways than one. Kate slept in the guest bedroom?"

"Don't let it get around. My false reputation is at stake."

"As if I would. And no one would believe me, anyway. But, really, so what if she moved home? Things have been calm here, and she'll be safe."

"Well, I'm also about to foreclose on her childhood home and destroy her dreams so I can expand my evil empire."

"I know."

"You do?"

"Yeah. I'm a police officer and I'm a woman. That makes me a big snoop. I also know you made arrangements with Kate's contractor to secretly pay him yourself and have him reimburse you once he gets the money from her. Does she really believe a contractor would ever wait for his money?"

Matt grinned sheepishly. He'd been caught. "Does anyone else know?"

"No. I don't think so. Why'd you do it? You have a lot of money invested in this project, don't you?"

Matt shrugged. "I love her."

Lizzie burst out laughing. "Look at you. You're a mess. Do you want my advice?"

"Give it your best shot, because I'm coming up blank."

"I love Kate. I think she's fabulous. I hope you two work it out and have a million kids, or whatever it is you're looking for. You're my big brother . . . heck, my *only* brother. I want to see you happy. My advice to you is—Suck it up."

Matt raised an eyebrow at his sister.

"Since when was Matt Culhane a quitter? You never gave up in football or hockey. You didn't give up in the eighth grade when Mary Lou Petty refused to go to junior prom with you. You certainly never gave up on Depot Brewing—even when a lot of people thought you should. If you love Kate that much, go get her!"

Lizzie was right. He'd go to Traverse City for a couple of days, giving Kate the space she needed and a chance to get reacquainted with her parents. When he returned, he was sure Kate would be ready to invite him to dinner, and if she wasn't, he'd invite himself. Desperate times called for desperate measures. After all, Chuck really missed her.

NINETEEN

IT WAS THE MONDAY EVENING BEFORE THANKSGIVING. Kate's mom and dad were still living out their snowbound fantasy, and Kate was beginning to lose her mind. Sinatra playing on the stereo twelve hours out of twenty-four was part of the issue. The rest was that her parents gave her little privacy.

In a house this size, how could they be everywhere at once? Kate was beginning to think cloning was involved. She was currently holed up in her bathroom for both prime cell phone reception and a little alone time.

The doorknob rattled. "Kate? Are you in there?"

"Yes, Mom," Kate said from her resting spot in the dry bathtub.

"You've been in there awhile."

"Yes, I have. I'm taking a bath."

"That's odd. I didn't hear the water run, and you know how the pipes in this place are."

Kate turned the page in her magazine and readjusted the pillow beneath her head. "Maybe Sinatra drowned it out."

"Maybe," her mother said. "Are you going to be out soon? I think Stella needs to go potty."

Kate felt a little guilty for having abandoned her poodle in the name of solitude, but Stella would get over it. Dad could feed the dog table scraps, since Kate wasn't out there to stop him.

"Her chain is at the kitchen door, Mom," Kate said. "Just put her on it, and she'll do the rest."

"You're sure you're okay in there?"

"Absolutely."

Her mother moved off, leaving Kate to her thoughts and a cell phone that didn't want to ring back. She knew from Ginger that Matt was going to be up in Traverse City on Tuesday and Wednesday. From Matt, she'd heard nothing directly. Not even so much as a hello since the staff meeting early last week. She missed him. She wanted to find a way back into his life. It was chilly here on the outside.

"Attempt number four," she announced, then pressed the speed dial number she'd assigned him. At this point, she didn't really expect an answer. It was more for the sport of hearing his voice mail message that she called. But this time, Matt answered.

"Hi, Kate."

Kate's hands started feeling a little sweaty. For the love of Mike! She hadn't felt this nervous since asking Scotty McDougall to the Sadie Hawkins dance in ninth grade. "I hear you're heading out of town for a couple of days."

"I'm on the road now."

"I was wondering if you'd like me to help take care of Chuck? I can check on him as many times a day as you think he'd need, and he knows who I am, so that would be nice for him." She was babbling and couldn't stop. "And, honestly, it's no big deal. You'd be doing me a favor by giving me an excuse to get away from here in the evening for a while, and—oh hell, I really miss you."

"I miss you, too."

Kate smiled with her entire body. She felt like the Grinch when his heart grew three sizes that day.

"How are you doing with your parents?" he asked.

"I'm hiding in the bathtub to make this call. No place is private anymore. If I go into my bedroom, my mother wants to have a girl-to-girl. She wants to know if I'm recovering from my divorce. She wants to tell me how to find a new man. I mean, I'm glad we're talking a whole lot more than we used to, but sometimes I just need a break from her advice."

He laughed. "That good, eh?"

"That 1960s outlook. I don't get it, but I guess I don't have to. Bottom line is that I love her and Dad."

"I think I'd like your parents," he said.

Kate smiled. "You probably would. And they'd like you, too."

They were silent, but it wasn't in the least uncomfortable.

"So I'd really be doing you a favor if I had you check on Chuck?"

Kate's smile had taken up permanent residence. "Definitely."

"Actually, that would be great," he said. "Lizzie has promised to stop by, but she has the next couple of days off. Before I enlisted her, she'd been talking about visiting a college friend downstate."

"I'd be happy to cover for her. Really."

"Well, thank you. I'm going to try to hustle it along, but I need to meet with my attorney and get things wrapped up with Chet before we get any closer to Thursday and family time."

"Thanksgiving . . . That's kind of a tough time of the year to be doing something like that. I never thought I'd say it, but I almost feel sorry for poor Chet."

She paused before continuing. "I want to tell you

something, though. . . . I know Chet has been thinking about things. He's probably sitting in his bathtub right now, feeling a little selfish and hoping that he hasn't messed up a great friendship."

The bathroom door rattled again.

"Kate, is there someone in there with you?"

"No, Mom, I'm just talking to myself."

"I worry about you, Kate."

"I'm fine. Promise. Could you check on Stella? I think I hear her barking." Another lie, but she wanted to finish this call.

"Goodness!" her mother said. "That dog is worse than a toddler."

"I think she's gone, but I know she's going to be back," Kate said to Matt after listening to the sound of her mother's footsteps fade. "How often should I check on Chuck?"

"Lizzie's going to be there tonight, but if you could stop out tomorrow morning, then again in the evening, that should work. And Wednesday morning should be good. I'll be back in the afternoon. And I know he doesn't like it, but put him on his leash when you let him out. It's deer season."

"And you haven't painted him orange," she said, and smiled at the sound of his laughter.

"Chuck has enough dignity issues as it is," he said.

"So true."

Kate sat upright at the sound of her mother back at the door.

"I have to go. And thank you for letting me watch Chuck."

Her mother was back, rapping on the door. "Kate? It's almost dinnertime, and I can't find a single thing to light the candles."

* * *

After waiting an appropriate amount of time to theoretically dry off and get dressed, Kate cruised downstairs. As she'd expected, Dad was slipping Stella some of whatever Mom had served as an appetizer. At least he was keeping his double Manhattan, extra cherries, to himself.

He looked over at Kate. "Who'd have thought a dog would like kippered herring?"

She chose to take the question as rhetorical, since she couldn't say she knew many humans who liked the stuff. "Just do me a favor and don't feed her too much."

He raised his Manhattan and gave her a wink. "All things in moderation, Katie-bug."

Her mom popped into the room. She was a festival of color this evening. Her dress competed with the sofa for which held the most flowers. But her mom's dress was more in Monet watercolor shades than the sofa's warring hues.

"Are you positive you don't want to join us for dinner, Kate? We'd love more time with you before the rest of the family arrives tomorrow."

"Thanks, but I'm not all that hungry."

Which wasn't quite accurate. She'd turned down dinner before she'd talked to Matt. Now that they'd talked, the knot in her stomach had disappeared and she was starved. But no way was she interrupting what looked to be another major romantic event. She'd just grab something from the kitchen and go read a book.

Kate's mom looped a lock of her silver-blond hair behind one ear. "Sorry to be a bother, but I still don't have the candles on the dining table lit. And they set the mood for love, after all."

Kate managed not to wince. "Let me go look in the kitchen." She was totally okay with the senior set having an active love life. It was just growing to be TMI as it pertained to her parents.

"Now that I think of it, that might not be necessary." Kate's mom gave her husband a teasing smile. "Larry, you must have a lighter with that box of cigars you think you're hiding from me."

Her father laughed. "It could be. Let me go check."

He rose and stopped long enough to kiss her mom's cheek. Kate smiled. Her parents made love and intimacy look easy. She could learn a thing or two from them.

Sunrise was approaching. Still, Kate couldn't sleep. Even her furry Stella comforter, who snored from the next pillow over, hadn't been enough. Kate reached for the nightstand lamp and switched it on. Her parents' talk of lighters and love had dug its way into her mind. Until she figured out why, she was back in insomnia land.

"Lighters and love," she said aloud, not that Stella woke to listen.

Kate opened the nightstand drawer. Maybe if she wrote down everything she'd been dwelling on, she could sleep. Before she could even reach for paper, though, an image of Laila lighting jack-o'-lanterns outside Depot Brewing popped into her head.

But why?

Kate flopped back against her pillow and focused on the details of that moment. It had been cold and windy, and Kate had been crushing on Matt. Nothing new there. . . .

Laila had used the same kind of lighter Harley carried. That would be no biggie, except it had been fancy, complete with crystals. Like a gift from a sweetheart. Maybe one who had a lighter collection, like Harley Bagger. Kate considered the concept of a Harley-Laila hookup. Both were single, so why not? The idea was kind of cute.

Or maybe not so cute, after all.

She'd finally made the connection. Between the two of them, they had every event of vandalism covered.

Kate bolted from bed and went to her dresser. She pulled out the stuff she'd found on the floor at Depot Brewing before she'd taken her beer Slip 'n Slide ride.

The white cocktail napkin meant nothing. It could be found in a hundred bars within a hundred miles of Keene's Harbor. But the string, that was another story. She twisted it, noting the slender red thread laced through it. This was no ordinary utility twine, and now she was pretty sure she knew what it was.

Taking care not to disturb her parents, Kate padded downstairs to the computer set up in the corner of the living room. She fed a couple of words into the images section of her favorite search engine.

"Bingo!" she said as she looked at the pictures on the screen.

The string in question was a replacement wick for a vintage windproof lighter. Laila had been laid up and couldn't have turned on the taps. But her lover could have. Kate had pegged at least one saboteur. His name was Harley Bagger.

Tuesday morning was still fresh with frost, and already Matt was running out of reasons to stay in Traverse City. A two-day trip had made sense when it had seemed easier to be far away from Kate than close enough to rush things and do something stupid. Now that they were talking, he was all for soon and stupid.

He'd met with his attorney over coffee at seven, and a suit would be filed to collect from Chet unless the brewer was willing to settle out of court. For both their sakes, he hoped Chet would.

A quick stop out to see Travis last night had been positive and productive. The guy had come up with a business plan and some ideas for a citrus summer beer to celebrate the opening of the Tropicana. All was well with the world.

Almost.

At just past nine, Matt walked out of his office and into Ginger's reception area. She looked up from the crossword puzzle she was doing.

"What's a four-letter word for idiot?" she asked.

"Matt."

"Really. Throw me a word."

"Dolt."

She frowned down at the puzzle, then smiled up at him. "That fits."

And it fit him, too. Since when had he not grabbed for what he wanted?

"Can you call and reschedule tomorrow's meetings until next week?" he asked.

"Sure. What's the matter?"

"Unfinished business back home."

Ginger snorted. "Right. Business. Blond unfinished business, maybe?"

"Yeah, another four-letter word, and it means happiness," Matt said.

He'd let Ginger guess on her own, because he wanted to get home and grab love.

Kate glared at her cell phone as she parked in front of Matt's place. It wasn't quite ten, and already she'd struck out on three separate calls.

First, she'd called Matt, but the call went straight to voice mail. Then she'd called the police station and come up empty. She'd sort of expected that, since she'd noticed the office was unattended a lot this time of year. Clete's voice on the answering machine had instructed her to hang up and call 911 if this was an emergency. Having a suspicion of who'd been sabotaging Matt didn't seem to fit the bill, so she'd left Clete a message, asking him to call her as soon as possible.

Because she was trying to be thorough, she'd done the same on Lizzie's voice mail, even though she knew Matt's sister was probably on her way downstate. She'd try all three again, once Chuck had been fed and loved.

Kate exited her Jeep. The air was crisp enough so that it felt sharp in her lungs. By the time evening fell, it was going to be nose-numbingly cold out here in the country. She'd be back at The Nutshell by then, and Chip and Bunny and their respective crews would be, too. All the more reason to cherish the quiet out here.

But as Kate walked toward the front door, a *"Buh-woof"* sounded from the back of the house.

She halted. Only one dog she'd ever met had a voice that could carry with such conviction.

"Chuck?"

"Buh-woof."

Kate rounded the side of the house, her shoes sweeping through the blanket of leaves underfoot. Chuck stood on the back deck, tail wagging.

"Dude, when did you become an escape artist?"

"Buh-woof."

He butted the back door with one broad shoulder, begging to get in. She supposed that Lizzie might have accidentally left him out when she'd departed last night. Kate pulled out her keys, opened the back door, and ushered Chuck in. He gazed up at her with worried hound eyes and let roll another round of *"Buh-woof."*

"I don't speak dog as fluently as your owner, so we're going to have to play a game of twenty questions. I know you don't need to go out, so what's the deal?"

"Buh-woof."

"Water? Do you need water?"

He wagged his tail. *"Buh-woof."*

Kate checked out Chuck's water bowl. Over half remained, but, hey, she appreciated the concept of not drinking one's own slobber. If he wanted fresh, fresh he'd get. She bent over to pick up the bowl and caught a faint whiff of something. Thought number one was that Chuck had passed gas, but the scent was more wood smoke than unpleasant.

"You're off the hook, buddy."

"Buh-woof."

"You're welcome." She rinsed his bowl at the kitchen sink, and the same scent grew strong enough to make her eyes burn. *Just like fire.*

Chuck's metal bowl clattered against the bottom of the aluminum sink as the thought sunk in. Kate turned off the water and followed the scent to the main living area. Flames flickered through a haze of suffocatingly thick smoke.

Okay, so *buh-woof* meant *The place is burning, you idiot human!*

Kate turned back to the kitchen, grabbed Chuck by his collar, and hauled him toward the back door. She needed him safe before she did anything else. He dug in his heels once they'd reached the back deck.

"Come on, buddy."

It seemed unsporting to shove a three-legged dog along, but it was for his own safety. Once they were on solid ground, Kate pulled her cell phone from her jeans pocket, dialed 911, and waited. When the operator came on the line, Kate said "fire" and gave Matt's address. Then she caught a glimpse of Chuck going back inside.

"Are you out of the house?" the operator asked. "Can you tell me what's going on, ma'am?"

"Chuck, no!"

But Chuck didn't seem to speak human any better than

she spoke dog, because he kept going. It was her fault for leaving the door open, and she'd never be able to live with herself if she didn't make an effort to snag the hound. And she never, ever wanted to have to tell Matt how she'd screwed up.

"Just please get the trucks here," she said to the operator, then hung up and jammed the phone back into her pocket.

Kate climbed the deck's steps. "Chuck, come on out!" She could risk this. The fire had been limited to the front room, and while Chuck was crafty, speed wasn't part of his repertoire.

Kate stepped inside, and the smell of smoke assailed her. It now drifted in a thick haze at ceiling height.

Stupid dog.

"Chuck, treat! Side of beef! Whole turkey!"

Kate started coughing. She should have asked Matt what magic words brought his dog running. But all she could do now was go inside. Of all the fire advice she'd ever learned, she discarded *get out* and focused on *stay low*.

Three more steps in and she heard a familiar voice behind her saying, "You never learn."

Kate turned and opened her mouth to ask what was going on. A sharp pain shot through her head. Then Kate could say nothing at all.

TWENTY

KATE AWAKENED SLOWLY. SHE WAS LYING ON A FREEZ-
ing cold, rotted plywood floor that was gritty with dirt.
She touched her fingertips to the side of her head and they
came away sticky with blood. Kate fought a wave of
nausea.

Harley Bagger stood over her. "You're heavier than
you look," he said.

She scoped out her surroundings. "And you're meaner
than you look."

The shack smelled decayed, and its narrow doorway
and window slits didn't let in much air. She'd bet she was
in an old deer blind that had fallen to the ground. Not a
helpful clue, since deer blinds dotted the woods for miles
around.

"You made me do this," Harley said.

"Made you? How do you figure that?"

"You shouldn't have come back for the stupid dog. I
coulda gotten away, except for you. I could have been in
and out that window I jimmied." He glared at her. "You
messed up my work."

Kate's heart turned over at the thought of poor, sweet
Chuck. The dog had gone back in to fetch Harley and had
probably paid with his life. But she couldn't think about

that now, or she'd break down. She braced her hands against the floor and sat up.

Harley pointed a gun at her. "You stay right there."

"What are you doing, Harley? Do you really think that's going to help matters?"

He wiped the sweat off his forehead. "Not for you, maybe."

"What have I ever done to you?" She inched her hand toward her front right pocket and her cell phone.

"Don't bother. I threw the phone into the pond in back of his house. Do you think I'm stupid?"

Honesty wasn't always the best policy. Kate kept her mouth closed.

"It's Culhane. All Culhane. He's ruining me," Harley said.

She closed her eyes for a second, trying to push back the pain. "How?"

"He's got all the business in town."

"When you fired me, you'd let that keg of his beer go flat, hadn't you?"

Harley paced back and forth. "It wasn't about you. It was about messing with his reputation a little."

"And after that you started messing with Matt, too."

"Prove it," he said.

"Not that it matters at this point, but I can. The morning you left all the taps open at Matt's place, I found a replacement wick to one of your lighters on the floor. And I even know who gave you the keys to get in . . . Laila."

"Wh—what do you mean, Laila?"

"I know you two are an item. She was using one of your vintage lighters before Shay VanAntwerp's party. From what I've learned cruising around on my computer, that crystal number is far too valuable to toss to a buddy."

"Well, it's none of your business. But just so you

know, she had nothing to do with this. I copied her keys without her knowing."

"Do you love her?" If she softened him up, maybe he'd let her go.

Harley nodded. "We've been keepin' it quiet-like, since she's still collecting a pension from her last husband that'll go away if we get married. All we want are winters in Florida and good food, but I spent my savings when business dropped."

"That's not Matt's fault."

The gun shook in his hand. "The hell it's not. I'm the victim here, not him! All I wanted was Depot Brewing down for a while so people would come back to my place. But that boy is like that battery rabbit on television. No matter what I do, he just keeps on going and going and going. And then he's got the nerve to ask *me* if I need a loan. I made him—not the other way around!"

Kate kept calm, figuring it was all she had left. "I'm sorry all of this has happened. But maybe it should all just stop now. Maybe we should just walk out of here."

"I can't. And don't you see? I had no choice in any of this. I'm getting too far along in years. Laila and I shoulda stayed away from the casinos. All we were looking for was some money for retirement."

She'd been nearly boiled and now kidnapped so Bonnie and Clyde could go to dog races and jai alai and eat grouper?

Hell, no!

Harley's hand had stopped shaking. He had made a decision. "I'm not gonna go to jail. No way!"

Kate didn't like the calm that had replaced his anger. "Serving even more time for murder doesn't make much sense. Think you could put that thing away?"

"At my age, murder and arson are both life sentences.

Why should I go to jail for either when if I finish you off, there's no witness left?"

She wouldn't have thought until today that Harley had a murder in him, but then again, she also would have said that arson was out of his range, and he had already tried to drown her in the brewhouse. "Don't get carried away, Harley," she said. "Relax and let's decide what to do next. Why don't you sit down?"

"No! Shut up and let me think!"

Kate realized Harley had crossed the line into crazy land. She was going to have to find a way to run.

Matt had ten miles of tight road before he reached Keene's Harbor. That was ten miles too many with a slow-moving rusty red tractor in front of him. He needed to talk to Kate while he had all this love stuff straight in his head. It had taken him damn long enough to get it that way. He spotted a break, passed the farmer, and put his foot to the floor.

Another mile down the road, Matt's cell phone rang.

"Matt, it's Ella."

He smiled. He liked Ella. Hell, he loved her for being Kate's first friend in Keene's Harbor.

"Hey, how are you doing?"

"Are you in town?"

Something about her usually cheerful tone was off, he thought. "No, I'm just outside it, on my way back from T.C. Why?"

She paused. "I want you to pull to the side of the road, okay?"

This wasn't going to be good.

He put the truck in park and threw on his flashers. "What's up?"

"I've got some bad news. There was a fire in the main room at your house. Kate called it in, and we got it under control with as little damage as you could expect, all things considered."

Which was the least of his worries. "But what about Kate? Did she and Chuck get out okay?"

"That's why I asked Captain Norm if I could be the one to call you. Kate's car is out front, but there's no sign of her or your dog in the house."

"Did you check the outbuildings?"

"All we found was Harley Bagger's car parked behind your pole barn. The police, including your sister, are on the way, but I was kind of hoping you'd heard from Kate?"

"No."

"Okay," Ella said. "Well, let's not worry before we have to. It could be that everything's just fine."

Matt's gut was telling him otherwise.

Sunday, when he'd dropped in on Harley to offer him a loan, it had been a mess. Harley had been angry and insulted, and Matt had ended up feeling like a jerk. If Harley had come out to Matt's place just to talk to him, he wouldn't have parked behind the pole barn. And if he'd come to do something more, Kate might be in danger.

Again.

"Ella, I have to hang up now. I need you to find Clete and tell him I said that Harley is his man."

"I'll do that," she said.

The wind was pushing through the woods. And Harley had taken to muttering to himself. Kate was trying to be a big, strong dog who could jump high, but she was scared. Very scared.

She needed to focus on the positive. Someone had to be looking for her by now. Her car had been right in front of Matt's house. And she couldn't be all that far away, either. She would be no easy drag for a man in Harley's shape. Plus, with all her scrapes and aches, and all the grunge clinging to her, she had to have left a trail.

Harley sprang to attention, his voice shrill. "Did you hear that?"

She'd definitely liked it better when he'd been ignoring her. "Hear what?"

"That!"

Kate picked up the distant sound of underbrush crackling.

"It was a deer, maybe," she said, though she was hoping for something better armed than Bambi. Say, like the police.

Harley moved to the blind's doorway. He gripped his gun in two shaking hands and aimed. At what, she wasn't sure.

"He has a gun," Kate shouted.

Harley jumped, and a shot went off. Whatever was heading their way rolled on through the leaves.

"Woof!"

Kate laughed with relief. "It's Chuck!"

Harley didn't seem to have the same level of happiness. He lowered the gun and started muttering to himself again.

"Woof!"

Chuck clambered past Harley and went to Kate.

Kate wrapped her arms around the dog. "I'm so glad you're alive."

"Woof!"

Kate flinched. "I'm having sort of a headache issue. Could you keep it down?"

"Woof!"

Harley waved his gun at her. "Make that dog shut up!"

"If I could, I would," she said.

"Woof!"

"Do it, now!"

"*Woof! Woof!*"

Harley swung his arm violently, waving the gun. "Get out of here, mutt!"

"Hey! Do *not* threaten the dog." Kate got up on her knees and urged Chuck toward the doorway. "Just go on out there, dude. I'm right here, and pretty soon Matt will be here to take us to Stella."

"*Woof! Woof!*"

Harley gave him a boot to the rear, and Chuck yelped.

Something inside Kate snapped, the same way it had when her ex admitted he'd dumped Stella.

"Nice, Harley. Kicking a three-legged dog. This is your day for proving just how low you can go, isn't it?"

Chuck advanced on Harley. The dog's cheerful bark had been replaced by a vicious growl. His hair stood up along his spine, and he eyed Harley as though he were a Porterhouse steak.

"Back off!" Harley screamed at the dog. He aimed the gun at Chuck.

As a former sensible city girl, Kate had taken a self-defense course. "Use your strongest weapons against his weakest targets," her instructor had said. Kate's strongest weapon was surprise. Or anger. It didn't matter which, because Harley was about to get hammered by both.

Kate scrambled to her feet and went in low.

Cut him off at the knees, then go for the throat.

Together, they hit the cold earth outside the crumbling shack with a hard jolt. She heard the *swoosh!* of the wind being knocked from Harley. Out of the corner of her eye, she saw the gun go skittering. No way was he getting near it again. Still on top of him, she took the flats of her palms and slammed them hard onto his ears.

Harley howled.

"I was just warming up," she said. "Because you're going down."

* * *

Until Matt had to cover sixty acres of dense woods at a dead run, the privacy of a big property had always seemed like a good thing. If nothing else, it gave him a buffer from the semi-militia types living on the other side of the trees. He'd heard his share of strange sounds out here, but never anything quite like this. And he knew it wasn't coming from his arms-bearing neighbors. The howls he heard were Chuck exercising his right to free speech . . . plus something more. Matt picked up his pace.

"The deer blind's just ahead," he yelled to Clete and Lizzie, who were a stretch behind him.

He cleared a cluster of trees and high brush and stopped just short of Kate and Harley. Harley was thrashing around on the ground, and Kate was whacking the bejeezus out of him.

Matt hauled Kate off Harley and hugged her to him. Harley started to rise and Chuck chomped into Harley's pants leg. A beat later, Lizzie and Clete burst onto the scene.

Matt held Kate at arm's length and looked at her. "Are you okay?"

"Yes. Except for my head."

Matt took in the blood-caked blond hair and wondered if he could persuade Clete to let him take a shot at Harley.

Lizzie flipped Harley over and cuffed him. "Good dog," she said to Chuck, scratching him behind his ear.

Matt cuddled Kate back against him and gave her a gentle kiss. "What happened here?"

"He was going to kill Chuck. And I love Chuck."

"Chuck, huh?"

She nodded.

"Any chance you might love me, too?"

She nodded again.

"That's good," Matt said, "because I love you."

Kate looked up at him. "You do?"

"I told you, sweetheart. When I'm in, I'm *all* in."

And Matt was in. Forever.

Kate sat on the edge of the emergency room's triage cot. She could sum up her state as hurting and happy. She was going to have one heck of a headache, but she could handle it because she was in love. She'd tried to hold her heart safe from Matt, but it had opened anyway. Everything seemed brighter and better, though she supposed that could be from the pain meds, too.

"Are you ready to leave?" Matt asked her.

"Absolutely."

He took her elbow while she stood. She smiled up at him. It wasn't so bad, having a handsome guy's occasional help.

Matt motioned to an envelope that had been left near her purse. "Don't forget that."

Kate opened the envelope. It contained a cashier's check for twenty thousand dollars.

"You caught my stalker. You earned every penny," he said. "I suppose I'm going to have to look for another place to build my restaurant."

Kate felt herself starting to cry. "Maybe you'd rather be the part owner of a struggling B&B. I need a partner to help me, since I have a second job at this awesome brewery working with a guy I absolutely love."

"I love you, too."

"We should get me back to The Nutshell," Kate said. "I know my mom and dad must be wondering where I am."

Kate had called them from Matt's cell phone on the

way to the hospital and said she'd been a little delayed, but would be home soon. She figured this sort of story was better delivered in person. That way, everyone could see she was still in one piece.

Matt looked toward a set of double doors. "I should warn you that a whole lot of people are out there waiting for you."

"Really? Why?"

He smiled. "It's Keene's Harbor. Word got out among the locals about what happened, and they want to be sure you're okay."

So this was what it felt like to belong. Kate never wanted to lose the feeling, even if she did have a couple of tears threatening to roll.

Everyone was there. Ella and Lizzie, the whole Culhane clan, Marcie Landon, Junior Greinwold, a horde from the Depot, Mayor and Missy Mortensen.

Kate waved Miss America style. "I'm fine," she said.

Marcie made a clucking sound. "Not yet, you're not." She held out a brown paper bag. "No Keene's Harbor local comes out of the hospital without getting some of my chicken noodle soup."

Kate accepted the gift. "Thank you. That's really sweet of you, Marcie, but you didn't need to fuss."

"You're family, now. It's no fuss."

Kate sniffled. "Okay, now I'm going to cry. How uncool is that?" But, really, she thought this whole scene was cool, possibly the coolest thing ever.

Kate moved through her friends, accepting hugs and words of reassurance until she finally found herself face-to-face with Junior Greinwold.

Junior held out the blue cooler to Kate. "I feel really bad about the mess I made, what with all the bees and dooky. This is for you."

Kate opened up the cooler. It was filled with Snickers

bars and wadded-up hundred dollar bills. Enough to cover the cost of Kate's repairs.

Junior leaned close to Kate so he could whisper in her ear. "Don't tell anyone. I won the lottery a bunch of years ago, but I like being a handyman."

Matt finally pulled her away from the crowd. "We'd better get you home." Which was exactly how Keene's Harbor now felt to her.

Twenty minutes later, Kate and Matt sat in his truck, the last in line behind three luxury cars in The Nutshell's driveway.

"So," Matt said, "are you going to be okay in there?"

"About that . . ."

"Yes?"

Kate had thought this was going to be hard, but everything felt so right. "I was wondering if you'd like to come in and meet my family?"

"You're not asking me just because you don't feel like explaining what happened, are you?"

She laughed. "And if I were?"

He smiled. "You know I'd do it."

"I'd love the help, but that's not why I asked. I want them to meet you. I want them to see why I've fallen in love." She unbuckled her seat belt and slid closer to Matt. "If I'm going to stay in Keene's Harbor and put down some roots, this is where I want to start." She leaned in until her lips met Matt's. "Right here."

And this time the kiss was perfect.